Robert Barr (16 September 1849 – 21 October 1912) was a Scottish-Canadian short story writer and novelist. Robert Barr was born in Barony, Lanark, Scotland to Robert Barr and Jane Watson. In 1854, he emigrated with his parents to Upper Canada at the age of four years old. His family settled on a farm near the village of Muirkirk. Barr assisted his father with his job as a carpenter, and developed a sound work ethic. Robert Barr then worked as a steel smelter for a number of years before he was educated at Toronto Normal School in 1873 to train as a teacher. After graduating Toronto Normal School, Barr became a teacher, and eventually headmaster/principal of the Central School of Windsor, Ontario in 1874. While Barr worked as head master of the Central School of Windsor, Ontario, he began to contribute short stories—often based on personal experiences, and recorded his work. On August 1876, when he was 27, Robert Barr married Ontario-born Eva Bennett, who was 21. (Source: Wikipedia)

Literary works:
"The Face And The Mask" (1894)
In the Midst of Alarms (1894, 1900, 1912)
From Whose Bourne (1896)
One Day's Courtship (1896)
Revenge!
The Strong Arm
A Woman Intervenes (1896)
Tekla: A Romance of Love and War (1898)
Jennie Baxter, Journalist (1899)
The Unchanging East (1900)
The Victors (1901)
A Prince of Good Fellows (1902)
Over The Border: A Romance (1903)
The O'Ruddy, A Romance, with Stephen Crane

THORNE CLASSICS

ONE DAY'S COURTSHIP
AND THE HERALDS OF FAME
&
IN A STEAMER CHAIR
AND OTHER STORIES
ROBERT BARR

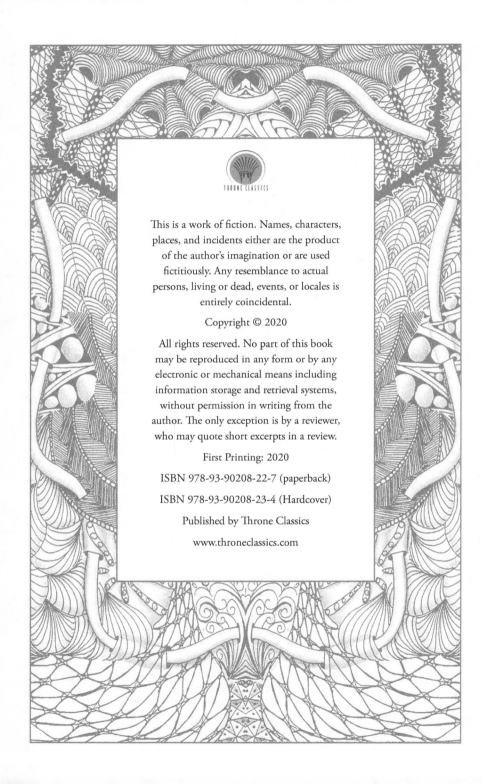

THRONE CLASSICS

Copyright © 2020

First Printing: 2020

ISBN 978-93-90208-22-7 (paperback)

ISBN 978-93-90208-23-4 (Hardcover)

Published by Throne Classics

www.throneclassics.com

Contents

ONE DAY'S COURTSHIP
AND THE HERALDS OF FAME
&
IN A STEAMER CHAIR
AND OTHER STORIES

ONE DAY'S COURTSHIP, AND THE HERALDS OF FAME

One Day's Courtship

Chapter I

John Trenton, artist, put the finishing touches to the letter he was writing, and then read it over to himself. It ran as follows:—

"My Dear Ed.,

"I sail for England on the 27th. But before I leave I want to have another look at the Shawenegan Falls. Their roar has been in my ears ever since I left there. That tremendous hillside of foam is before my eyes night and day. The sketches I took are not at all satisfactory, so this time I will bring my camera with me, and try to get some snapshots at the falls.

"Now, what I ask is this. I want you to hold that canoe for me against all comers for Tuesday. Also, those two expert half-breeds. Tell them I am coming, and that there is money in it if they take me up and back as safely as they did before. I don't suppose there will be much demand for the canoe on that day; in fact, it astonishes me that Americans, who appreciate the good things of our country better than we do ourselves, practically know nothing of this superb cataract right at their own doors. I suppose your new canoe is not finished yet, and as the others are up in the woods I write so that you will keep this particular craft for me. I do not wish to take any risks, as I leave so soon. Please drop me a note to this hotel at Quebec, and I will meet you in Le Gres on Tuesday morning at daybreak.

"Your friend,

"John Trenton."

Mason was a millionaire and a lumber king, but every one called him Ed. He owned baronial estates in the pine woods, and saw-mills without number. Trenton had brought a letter of introduction to him from a mutual friend in Quebec, who had urged the artist to visit the Shawenegan Falls. He heard the Englishman inquire about the cataract, and told him that he knew the man who would give him every facility for reaching the falls. Trenton's acquaintance with Mason was about a fortnight old, but already they were the firmest of friends. Any one who appreciated the Shawenegan Falls found a ready path to the heart of the big lumberman. It was almost impossible to reach the falls without the assistance of Mr. Mason. However, he was no monopolist. Any person wishing to visit the cataract got a canoe from the lumber king free of all cost, except a tip to the two boatmen who acted as guides and watermen. The artist had not long to wait for his answer. It was—

"My **Dear John,**

"The canoe is yours; the boatmen are yours: and the Shawenegan is yours for Tuesday. Also,

"I am yours,

"E. Mason."

On Monday evening John Trenton stepped off the C. P. R. train at Three Rivers. With a roughing-it suit on, and his camera slung over his shoulders, no one would have taken him for the successful landscape artist who on Piccadilly was somewhat particular about his attire.

John Trenton was not yet R. A., nor even A. R. A., but all his friends would tell you that, if the Royal Academy was not governed by a clique, he would have been admitted long ago, and that anyhow it was only a question of time. In fact, John admitted this to himself, but to no one else.

He entered the ramshackle 'bus, and was driven a long distance through very sandy streets to the hotel on the St. Lawrence, and, securing a room, made arrangements to be called before daybreak. He engaged the same driver who had taken him out to "The Greys," as it was locally called, on the occasion of his former visit.

The morning was cold and dark. Trenton found the buckboard at the door, and he put his camera under the one seat—a kind of a box for the holding of bits of harness and other odds and ends. As he buttoned up his overcoat he noticed that a great white steamer had come in the night, and was tied up in front of the hotel.

"The Montreal boat," explained the driver.

As they drove along the silent streets of Three Rivers, Trenton called to mind how, on the former occasion, he thought the Lower Canada buckboard by all odds, the most uncomfortable vehicle he had ever ridden in, and he felt that his present experience was going to corroborate this first impression. The seat was set in the centre, between the front and back wheels, on springy boards, and every time the conveyance jolted over a log—a not unfrequent occurrence—the seat went down and the back bent forward, as if to throw him over on the heels of the patient horse.

The road at first was long and straight and sandy, but during the latter part of the ride there were plenty of hills, up many of which a plank roadway ran; so that loads which it would be impossible to take through the deep sand, might be hauled up the steep incline.

At first the houses they passed had a dark and deserted look; then a light twinkled here and there. The early habitant was making his fire. As daylight began gradually to bring out the landscape, the sharp sound of the distant axe was heard. The early habitant was laying in his day's supply of firewood.

"Do you notice how the dawn slowly materialises the landscape?" said the artist to the boy beside him.

The boy saw nothing wonderful about that. Daylight always did it.

"Then it is not unusual in these parts? You see, I am very seldom up at this hour."

The boy wished that was his case.

"Does it not remind you of a photographer in a dark room carefully developing a landscape plate? Not one of those rapid plates, you know, but a slow, deliberate plate."

15

No, it didn't remind him of anything of the kind. He had never seen either a slow or a rapid plate developed.

"Then you have no prejudices as to which is the best developer, pyrogallic acid or ferrous oxalate, not to mention such recent decoctions as eikonogen, quinol, and others?"

No, the boy had none.

"Well, that's what I like. I like a young man whose mind is open to conviction."

The boy was not a conversational success. He evidently did not enter into the spirit of the artist's remarks. He said most people got off at that point and walked to warm up, and asked Trenton if he would not like to follow their example.

"No, my boy," said the Englishman, "I don't think I shall. You see, I have paid for this ride, and I want to get all I can out of it. I shall shiver here and try to get the worth of my money. But with you it is different. If you want to get down, do so. I will drive."

The boy willingly handed over the reins, and sprang out on the road. Trenton, who was a boy himself that morning, at once whipped up the horse and dashed down the hill to get away from the driver. When a good half-mile had been worried out of the astonished animal, Trenton looked back to see the driver come panting after. The young man was calmly sitting on the back part of the buckboard, and when the horse began to walk again, the boy slid off, and, without a smile on his face, trotted along at the side.

"That fellow has evidently a quiet sense of humour, although he is so careful not to show it," said Trenton to himself.

On reaching the hilltop, they caught a glimpse of the rim of the sun rising gloriously over the treetops on the other side of the St. Maurice River. Trenton stopped the horse, and the boy looked up to see what was wrong. He could not imagine any one stopping merely to look at the sun.

"Isn't that splendid?" cried Trenton, with a deep breath, as he watched the great globe slowly ascend into the sky. The distant branches of the trees were delicately etched against its glowing surface, and seemed to cling to it like tendrils, slipping further and further down as the sun leisurely disentangled itself, and at last stood in its incomparable grandeur full above the forest.

The woods all around had on their marvellous autumn tints, and now the sun added a living lustre to them that made the landscape more brilliant than anything the artist had ever seen before.

"Ye gods!" he cried enthusiastically, "that scene is worth coming from England to have one glimpse of."

"See here," said the driver, "if you want to catch Ed. Mason before he's gone to the woods you'll have to hurry up. It's getting late."

"True, O driver. You have brought me from the sun to the earth. Have you ever heard of the person who fell from the sun to the earth?"

No, he hadn't.

"Well, that was before your time. You will never take such a tumble. I—I suppose they don't worship the sun in these parts?"

No, they didn't.

"When you come to think of it, that is very strange. Have you ever reflected that it is always in warm countries they worship the sun? Now, I should think it ought to be just the other way about. Do you know that when I got on with you this morning I was eighty years old, every day of it. What do you think my age is now?"

"Eighty years, sir."

"Not a bit of it. I'm eighteen. The sun did it. And yet they claim there is no fountain of youth. What fools people are, my boy!"

The young man looked at his fare slyly, and cordially agreed with him.

"You certainly have a concealed sense of humour," said the artist.

They wound down a deep cut in the hill, and got a view of the lumber village—their destination. The roar of the waters tumbling over the granite rocks—the rocks from which the village takes its name—came up the ravine. The broad river swept in a great semicircle to their right, and its dark waters were flecked with the foam of the small falls near the village, and the great cataract miles up the river. It promised to be a perfect autumn day. The sky, which had seemed to Trenton overcast when they started, was now one deep dome of blue without even the suggestion of a cloud.

The buckboard drew up at the gate of the house in which Mr. Mason lived when he was in the lumber village, although his home was at Three Rivers. The old Frenchwoman, Mason's housekeeper, opened the door for Trenton, and he remembered as he went in how the exquisite cleanliness of everything had impressed him during his former visit. She smiled as she recognised the genial Englishman. She had not forgotten his compliments in her own language on her housekeeping some months before, and perhaps she also remembered his liberality. Mr. Mason, she said, had gone to the river to see after the canoe, leaving word that he would return in a few minutes. Trenton, who knew the house, opened the door at his right, to enter the sitting-room and leave there his morning wraps, which the increasing warmth rendered no longer necessary. As he burst into the room in his impetuous way, he was taken aback to see standing at the window, looking out towards the river, a tall young woman. Without changing her position, she looked slowly around at the intruder. Trenton's first thought was a hasty wish that he were better dressed. His roughing-it costume, which up to that time had seemed so comfortable, now appeared uncouth and out of place. He felt as if he had suddenly found himself in a London drawing-room with a shooting-jacket on. But this sensation was quickly effaced by the look which the beauty gave him over her shoulder. Trenton, in all his experience, had never encountered such a glance of indignant scorn. It was a look of resentment and contempt, with just a dash of feminine reproach in it.

"What have I done?" thought the unhappy man; then he stammered aloud, "I—I—really—I beg your pardon. I thought the—ah—room was empty."

The imperious young woman made no reply. She turned to the window again, and Trenton backed out of the room as best he could.

"Well!" he said to himself, as he breathed with relief the outside air again, "that was the rudest thing I ever knew a lady to do. She is a lady, there is no doubt of that. There is nothing of the backwoods about her. But she might at least have answered me. What have I done, I wonder? It must be something terrible and utterly unforgivable, whatever it is. Great heavens!" he murmured, aghast at the thought, "I hope that girl isn't going up to the Shawenegan Falls."

Trenton was no ladies' man. The presence of women always disconcerted him, and made him feel awkward and boorish. He had been too much of a student in higher art to acquire the smaller art of the drawing-room. He felt ill at ease in society, and seemed to have a fatal predilection for saying the wrong thing, and suffered the torture afterwards of remembering what the right thing would have been.

Trenton stood at the gate for a moment, hoping Mason would come. Suddenly he remembered with confusion that he was directly in range of those disdainful eyes in the parlour, and he beat a hasty retreat toward the old mill that stood by the falls. The roar of the turbulent water over the granite rocks had a soothing effect on the soul of the man who knew he was a criminal, yet could not for the life of him tell what his crime had been. Then he wandered up the river-bank toward where he saw the two half-breeds placing the canoe in the still water at the further end of the village. Half-way there he was relieved to meet the genial Ed. Mason, who greeted him, as Trenton thought, with a somewhat overwrought effusion. There evidently was something on the genial Ed.'s mind.

"Hello, old man," he cried, shaking Trenton warmly by the hand. "Been here long? Well, I declare, I'm glad to see you. Going to have a splendid day for it, aren't you? Yes, sir, I am glad to see you."

"When a man says that twice in one breath, a fellow begins to doubt him. Now, you good-natured humbug, what's the matter? What have I done? How did you find me out? Who turned Queen's evidence? Look here, Edward Mason, why are you not glad to see me?"

19

"Nonsense; you know I am. No one could be more welcome. By the way, my wife's here. You never met her, I think?"

"I saw a young lady remarkably—"

"No, no; that is Miss —. By the way, Trenton, I want you to do me a favour, now that I think of it. Of course the canoe is yours for to-day, but that young woman wants to go up to the Shawenegan. You wouldn't mind her going up with you, would you? You see, I have no other canoe to-day, and she can't stay till to-morrow."

"I shall be delighted, I'm sure," answered Trenton. But he didn't look it.

Chapter II

Eva Sommerton, of Boston, knew that she lived in the right portion of that justly celebrated city, and this knowledge was evident in the poise of her queenly head, and in every movement of her graceful form. Blundering foreigners—foreigners as far as Boston is concerned, although they may be citizens of the United States—considered Boston to be a large city, with commerce and railroads and busy streets and enterprising newspapers, but the true Bostonian knows that this view is very incorrect. The real Boston is penetrated by no railroads. Even the jingle of the street-car bell does not disturb the silence of the streets of this select city. It is to the ordinary Boston what the empty, out-of-season London is to the rest of the busy metropolis. The stranger, jostled by the throng, may not notice that London is empty, but his lordship, if he happens during the deserted period to pass through, knows there is not a soul in town.

Miss Sommerton had many delusions, but fortunately for her peace of mind she had never yet met a candid friend with courage enough to tell her so. It would have required more bravery than the ordinary society person possesses to tell Miss Sommerton about any of her faults. The young gentlemen of her acquaintance claimed that she had no faults, and if her lady friends thought otherwise, they reserved the expression of such opinions for social gatherings not graced by the presence of Miss Sommerton.

Eva Sommerton thought she was not proud, or if there was any tinge of pride in her character, it was pride of the necessary and proper sort.

She also possessed the vain belief that true merit was the one essential, but if true merit had had the misfortune to be presented to Miss Sommerton without an introduction of a strictly unimpeachable nature, there is every reason to fear true merit would not have had the exquisite privilege of basking in the smiles of that young Bostonian. But perhaps her chief delusion was the belief that she was an artist. She had learned all that Boston could teach of drawing, and this thin veneer had received a beautiful foreign polish abroad. Her friends pronounced her sketches really wonderful. Perhaps if Miss Sommerton's entire capital had been something less than her half-yearly income, she might have made a name for herself; but the rich man gets a foretaste of the scriptural difficulty awaiting him at the gates of heaven, when he endeavours to achieve an earthly success, the price of which is hard labour, and not hard cash.

We are told that pride must have a fall, and there came an episode in Miss Sommerton's career as an artist which was a rude shock to her self-complacency. Having purchased a landscape by a celebrated artist whose work she had long admired, she at last ventured to write to him and enclose some of her own sketches, with a request for a candid judgment of them— that is, she said she wanted a candid judgment of them.

The reply seemed to her so ungentlemanly, and so harsh, that, in her vexation and anger, she tore the letter to shreds and stamped her pretty foot with a vehemence which would have shocked those who knew her only as the dignified and self-possessed Miss Eva Sommerton.

Then she looked at her libelled sketches, and somehow they did not appear to be quite so faultless as she had supposed them to be.

This inspection was followed by a thoughtful and tearful period of meditation; and finally, with contriteness, the young woman picked up from her studio floor the shreds of the letter and pasted them carefully together on a white sheet of paper, in which form she still preserved the first honest opinion she had ever received.

In the seclusion of her aesthetic studio Miss Sommerton made a heroic resolve to work hard. Her life was to be consecrated to art. She would win reluctant recognition from the masters. Under all this wave of heroic resolution was an under-current of determination to get even with the artist who had treated her work so contemptuously.

Few of us quite live up to our best intentions, and Miss Sommerton was no exception to the rule. She did not work as devotedly as she had hoped to do, nor did she become a recluse from society. A year after she sent to the artist some sketches which she had taken in Quebec—some unknown waterfalls, some wild river scenery—and received from him a warmer letter of commendation than she had hoped for. He remembered her former sketches, and now saw a great improvement. If the waterfall sketches were not exaggerations, he would like to see the originals. Where were they? The lady was proud of her discoveries in the almost unknown land of Northern Quebec, and she wrote a long letter telling all about them, and a polite note of thanks for the information ended the correspondence.

Miss Sommerton's favourite discovery was that tremendous downward plunge of the St. Maurice, the Falls of Shawenegan. She had sketched it from a dozen different standpoints, and raved about it to her friends, if such a dignified young person as Miss Sommerton could be said to rave over anything. Some Boston people, on her recommendation, had visited the falls, but their account of the journey made so much of the difficulties and discomforts, and so little of the magnificence of the cataract, that our amateur artist resolved to keep the falls, as it were, to herself. She made yearly pilgrimages to the St. Maurice, and came to have a kind of idea of possession which always amused Mr. Mason. She seemed to resent the fact that others went to look at the falls, and, worse than all, took picnic baskets there, actually lunching on its sacred shores, leaving empty champagne bottles and boxes of sardines that had evidently broken some one's favourite knife in the opening. This particular summer she had driven out to "The Greys," but finding that a party was going up in canoes every day that week, she promptly ordered her driver to take her back to Three Rivers, saying to Mr. Mason she would return when she could have the falls to herself.

"You remind me of Miss Porter," said the lumber king.

"Miss Porter! Who is she?"

"When Miss Porter visited England and saw Mr. Gladstone, he asked her if she had ever seen the Niagara Falls. 'Seen them?' she answered. 'Why, I own them!'"

"What did she mean by that? I confess I don't see the point, or perhaps it isn't a joke."

"Oh yes, it is. You mustn't slight my good stories in that way. She meant just what she said. I believe the Porter family own, or did own, Goat Island, and, I suppose, the other bank, and, therefore, the American Fall. The joke—I do dislike to have to explain jokes, especially to you cool, unsympathising Bostonians—is the ridiculousness of any mere human person claiming to own such a thing as the Niagara Falls. I believe, though, that you are quite equal to it—I do indeed."

"Thank you, Mr. Mason."

"I knew you would be grateful when I made myself clearly understood. Now, what I was going to propose is this. You should apply to the Canadian Government for possession of the Shawenegan. I think they would let it go at a reasonable figure. They look on it merely as an annoying impediment to the navigation of the river, and an obstruction which has caused them to spend some thousands of dollars in building a slide by the side of it, so that the logs may come down safely."

"If I owned it, the slide is the first thing I would destroy."

"What? And ruin the lumber industry of the Upper St. Maurice? Oh, you wouldn't do such a thing! If that is your idea, I give you fair warning that I will oppose your claims with all the arts of the lobbyist. If you want to become the private owner of the falls, you should tell the Government that you have some thoughts of encouraging the industries of the province by building a mill—"

"A mill?"

"Yes; why not? Indeed, I have half a notion to put a saw-mill there myself. It always grieves me to see so much magnificent power going to waste."

"Oh, seriously, Mr. Mason, you would never think of committing such an act of sacrilege?"

"Sacrilege, indeed! I like that. Why, the man who makes one saw-mill hum where no mill ever hummed before is a benefactor to his species. Don't they teach political economy at Boston? I thought you liked saw-mills. You drew a very pretty picture of the one down the stream."

"I admire a ruined saw-mill, as that one was; but not one in a state of activity, or of eruption, as a person might say."

"Well, won't you go up to the falls to-day, Miss Sommerton? I assure you we have a most unexceptionable party. Why, one of them is a Government official. Think of that!"

"I refuse to think of it; or, if I do think of it, I refuse to be dazzled by his magnificence. I want to see the Shawenegan, not a picnic party drinking.

"You wrong them, really you do, Miss Sommerton, believe me. You have got your dates mixed. It is the champagne party that goes to-day. The beer crowd is not due until to-morrow."

"The principle is the same."

"The price of the refreshment is not. I speak as a man of bitter experience. Let's see. If recollection holds her throne, I think there was a young lady from New England—I forget the name of the town at the moment—who took a lunch with her the last time she went to the Shawenegan. I merely give this as my impression, you know. I am open to contradiction."

"Certainly, I took a lunch. I always do. I would to-day if I were going up there, and Mrs. Mason would give me some sandwiches. You would give me a lunch, wouldn't you, dear?"

"I'll tell them to get it ready now, if you will only stay," replied that lady, on being appealed to.

"No, it isn't the lunch I object to. I object to people going there merely for the lunch. I go for the scenery; the lunch is incidental."

"When you get the deed of the falls, I'll tell you what we'll do," put in Mason. "We will have a band of trained Indians stationed at the landing, and they will allow no one to disembark who does not express himself in sufficiently ecstatic terms about the great cataract. You will draw up a set of adjectives, which I will give to the Indians, instructing them to allow no one to land who does not use at least three out of five of them in referring to the falls. People whose eloquent appreciation does not reach the required altitude will have to stay there till it does, that's all. We will treat them as we do our juries—starve them into a verdict, and the right verdict at that."

"Don't mind him, Eva. He is just trying to exasperate you. Think of what I have to put up with. He goes on like that all the time," said Mrs. Mason.

"Really, my dear, your flattery confuses me. You can't persuade any one that I keep up this brilliancy in the privacy of my own house. It is only turned on for company."

"Why, Mr. Mason, I didn't think you looked on me as company. I thought I enjoyed the friendship of the Mason family."

"Oh, you do, you do indeed! The company I referred to was the official party which has just gone to the falls. This is some of the brilliancy left over. But, really, you had better stay after coming all this distance."

"Yes, do, Eva. Let me go back with you to the Three Rivers, and then you stay with me till next week, when you can visit the falls all alone. It is very pleasant at Three Rivers just now. And besides, we can go for a day's shopping at Montreal."

"I wish I could."

"Why, of course you can," said Mason. "Imagine the delight of smuggling your purchases back to Boston. Confess that this is a pleasure you hadn't thought of."

"I admit the fascination of it all, but you see I am with a party that has gone on to Quebec, and I just got away for a day. I am to meet them there to-night or to-morrow morning. But I will return in the autumn, Mrs. Mason, when it is too late for the picnics. Then, Mr. Mason, take warning. I mean to have a canoe to myself, or—well, you know the way we Bostonians treated you Britishers once upon a time."

"Distinctly. But we will return good for evil, and give you warm tea instead of the cold mixture you so foolishly brewed in the harbour."

As the buckboard disappeared around the corner, and Mr. and Mrs. Mason walked back to the house, the lady said—

"What a strange girl Eva is."

"Very. Don't she strike you as being a trifle selfish?"

"Selfish? Eva Sommerton? Why, what could make you think such a thing? What an absurd idea! You cannot imagine how kind she was to me when I visited Boston."

"Who could help it, my dear? I would have been so myself if I had happened to meet you there."

"Now, Ed., don't be absurd."

"There is something absurd in being kind to a person's wife, isn't there? Well, it struck me her objection to any one else being at the falls, when her ladyship was there, might seem—not to me, of course, but to an outsider—a trifle selfish."

"Oh, you don't understand her at all. She has an artistic temperament, and she is quite right in wishing to be alone. Now, Ed., when she does come again I want you to keep anyone else from going up there. Don't forget it, as you do most of the things I tell you. Say to anybody who wants to go up that the canoes are out of repair."

"Oh, I can't say that, you know. Anything this side of a crime I am willing to commit; but to perjure myself, no, not for Venice. Can you think of any other method that will combine duplicity with a clear conscience? I'll tell you what I'll do. I will have the canoe drawn up, and gently, but firmly, slit it with my knife. One of the men can mend it in ten minutes. Then I can look even the official from Quebec in the face, and tell him truly that the canoe will not hold water. I suppose as long as my story will hold water you and Miss Sommerton will not mind?"

"If the canoe is ready for her when she comes, I shall be satisfied. Please to remember I am going to spend a week or two in Boston next winter."

"Oh ho, that's it, is it? Then it was not pure philanthropy—"

"Pure nonsense, Ed. I want the canoe to be ready, that's all."

When Mrs. Mason received the letter from Miss Sommerton, stating the time the young woman intended to pay her visit to the Shawenegan, she gave the letter to her husband, and reminded him of the necessity of keeping the canoe for that particular date. As the particular date was some weeks off, and as Ed. Mason was a man who never crossed a stream until he came to it, he said, "All right," put the letter in his inside pocket, and the next time he thought of it was on the fine autumn afternoon—Monday afternoon—when he saw Mrs. Mason drive up to the door of his lumber-woods residence with Miss Eva Sommerton in the buggy beside her. The young lady wondered, as Mr. Mason helped her out, if that genial gentleman, whom she regarded as the most fortunate of men, had in reality some secret, gnawing sorrow the world knew not of.

"Why, Ed., you look ill," exclaimed Mrs. Mason; "is there anything the matter?"

"Oh, it is nothing—at least, not of much consequence. A little business worry, that's all."

"Has there been any trouble?"

"Oh no—at the least, not yet."

"Trouble about the men, is it?"

"No, not about the men," said the unfortunate gentleman, with a somewhat unnecessary emphasis on the last word.

"Oh, Mr. Mason, I am afraid I have come at a wrong time. If so, don't hesitate to tell me. If I can do anything to help you, I hope I may be allowed."

"You have come just at the right time," said the lumberman, "and you are very welcome, I assure you. If I find I need help, as perhaps I may, you will be reminded of your promise."

To put off as long as possible the evil time of meeting his wife, Mason went with the man to see the horse put away, and he lingered an unnecessarily long time in ascertaining that everything was right in the stable. The man was astonished to find his master so particular that afternoon. A crisis may be postponed, but it can rarely be avoided altogether, and knowing he had to face the inevitable sooner or later, the unhappy man, with a sigh, betook himself to the house, where he found his wife impatiently waiting for him. She closed the door and confronted him.

"Now, Ed., what's the matter?"

"Where's Miss Sommerton?" was the somewhat irrelevant reply.

"She has gone to her room. Ed., don't keep me in suspense. What is wrong?"

"You remember John Trenton, who was here in the summer?"

"I remember hearing you speak of him. I didn't meet him, you know."

"Oh, that's so. Neither you did. You see, he's an awful good fellow, Trenton is—that is, for an Englishman."

"Well, what has Trenton to do with the trouble?"

"Everything, my dear—everything."

"I see how it is. Trenton visited the Shawenegan?"

"He did."

"And he wants to go there again?"

"He does."

"And you have gone and promised him the canoe for to-morrow?"

"The intuition of woman, my dear, is the most wonderful thing on earth."

"It is not half so wonderful as the negligence of man—I won't say the stupidity."

"Thank you, Jennie, for not saying it, but I really think I would feel better if you did."

"Now, what are you going to do about it?"

"Well, my dear, strange as it may appear, that very question has been racking my brain for the last ten minutes. Now, what would you do in my position?"

"Oh, I couldn't be in your position."

"No, that's so, Jennie. Excuse me for suggesting the possibility. I really think this trouble has affected my mind a little. But if you had a husband—if a sensible woman like you could have a husband who got himself into such a position—what would you advise him to do?"

"Now, Ed., don't joke. It's too serious."

"My dear, no one on earth can have such a realisation of its seriousness as I have at this moment. I feel as Mark Twain did with that novel he never finished. I have brought things to a point where I can't go any further. The game seems blocked. I wonder if Miss Sommerton would accept ten thousand feet of lumber f.o.b. and call it square."

"Really, Ed., if you can't talk sensibly, I have nothing further to say."

"Well, as I said, the strain is getting too much for me. Now, don't go away, Jennie. Here is what I am thinking of doing. I'll speak to Trenton. He won't mind Miss Sommerton's going in the canoe with him. In fact, I should think he would rather like it."

"Dear me, Ed., is that all the progress you've made? I am not troubling myself about Mr. Trenton. The difficulty will be with Eva. Do you think for a moment she will go if she imagined herself under obligations to a stranger for the canoe? Can't you get Mr. Trenton to put off his visit until the day after tomorrow? It isn't long to wait."

"No, that is impossible. You see, he has just time to catch his steamer as it is. No, he has the promise in writing, while Miss Sommerton has no legal evidence if this thing ever gets into the courts. Trenton has my written promise. You see, I did not remember the two dates were the same. When I wrote to Trenton—"

"Ed., don't try to excuse yourself. You had her letter in your pocket, you know you had. This is a matter for which there is no excuse, and it cannot be explained away."

"That's so, Jennie. I am down in the depths once more. I shall not try to crawl out again—at least, not while my wife is looking."

"No, your plan will not work. I don't know that any will. There is only one thing to try, and it is this—Miss Sommerton must think that the canoe is hers. You must appeal to her generosity to let Mr. Trenton go with her."

"Won't you make the appeal, Jen?"

"No, I will not. In the first place she'll be sorry for you, because you will make such a bungle of it. Trial is your only hope."

"Oh, if success lies in bungling, I will succeed."

"Don't be too sure. I suppose that man will be here by daybreak to-morrow?"

"Not so bad as that, Jennie. You always try to put the worst face on things. He won't be here till sunrise at the earliest."

"I will ask Eva to come down."

"You needn't hurry just because of me. Besides, I would like a few moments to prepare myself for my fate. Even a murderer is given a little time."

"Not a moment, Ed. We had better get this thing settled as soon as possible."

"Perhaps you are right," he murmured, with a deep sigh. "Well, if we Britishers, as Miss S. calls us, ever faced the Americans with as faint a heart as I do now, I don't wonder we got licked."

"Don't say 'licked,' Ed."

"I believe it's historical. Oh, I see. You object to the word, not to the allegation. Well, I won't cavil about that. All my sympathy just now is concentrated on one unfortunate Britisher. My dear, let the sacrifice begin."

Mrs. Mason went to the stairway and called—

"Eva, dear, can you come down for a moment? We want you to help us out of a difficulty."

Miss Sommerton appeared smilingly, smoothing down the front of the dress that had taken the place of the one she travelled in. She advanced towards Mason with sweet compassion in her eyes, and that ill-fated man thought he had never seen any one look so altogether charming—excepting, of course, his own wife in her youthful days. She seemed to have smoothed away all the Boston stiffness as she smoothed her dress.

"Oh, Mr. Mason," she said, sympathetically, as she approached, "I am so sorry anything has happened to trouble you, and I do hope I am not intruding."

"Indeed, you are not, Miss Eva. In fact, your sympathy has taken away half the trouble already, and I want to beg of you to help me off with the other half."

A glance at his wife's face showed him that he had not made a bad beginning.

"Miss Sommerton, you said you would like to kelp me. Now I am going to appeal to you. I throw myself on your mercy."

There was a slight frown on Mrs. Mason's face, and her husband felt that he was perhaps appealing too much.

"In fact, the truth is, my wife gave me—"

Here a cough interrupted him, and he paused and ran his hand through his hair. "Pray don't mind me, Mr. Mason," said Miss Sommerton, "if you would rather not tell—"

"Oh, but I must; that is, I want you to know."

He glanced at his wife, but there was no help there, so he plunged in headlong.

"To tell the truth, there is a friend of mine who wants to go to the falls tomorrow. He sails for Europe immediately, and has no other day."

The Boston rigidity perceptibly returned.

"Oh, if that is all, you needn't have had a moment's trouble. I can just as well put off my visit."

"Oh, can you?" cried Mason, joyously.

His wife sat down in the rocking-chair with a sigh of despair. Her infatuated husband thought he was getting along famously.

"Then your friends are not waiting for you at Quebec this time, and you can stay a day or two with us."

"Eva's friends are at Montreal, Edward, and she cannot stay."

"Oh, then—why, then, to-morrow's your only day, too?"

"It doesn't matter in the least, Mr. Mason. I shall be most glad to put off my visit to oblige your friend—no, I didn't mean that," she cried, seeing the look of anguish on Mason's face, "it is to oblige you. Now, am I not good?"

"No, you are cruel," replied Mason. "You are going up to the falls. I insist on that. Let's take that as settled. The canoe is yours." He caught an encouraging look from his wife. "If you want to torture me you will say you will not go. If you want to do me the greatest of favours, you will let my friend go in the canoe with you to the landing."

"What! go alone with a stranger?" cried Miss Sommerton, freezingly.

"No, the Indians will be there, you know."

"Oh, I didn't expect to paddle the canoe myself."

"I don't know about that. You strike me as a girl who would paddle her own canoe pretty well."

"Now, Edward," said his wife. "He wants to take some photographs of the falls, and—"

"Photographs? Why, Ed., I thought you said he was an artist."

"Isn't a photographer an artist?"

"You know he isn't."

"Well, my dear, you know they put on their signs, 'artist—photographer, pictures taken in cloudy weather.' But he's an amateur photographer; an amateur is not so bad as a professional, is he, Miss Sommerton?"

"I think he's worse, if there is any choice. A professional at least takes good pictures, such as they are."

"He is an elderly gentleman, and I am sure—"

"Oh, is he?" cried Miss Sommerton; "then the matter is settled. He shall go. I thought it was some young fop of an amateur photographer."

"Oh, quite elderly. His hair is grey, or badly tinged at least."

The frown on Miss Sommerton's brow cleared away, and she smiled in a manner that was cheering to the heart of her suppliant. He thought it reminded him of the sun breaking through the clouds over the hills beyond the St. Maurice.

"Why, Mr. Mason, how selfishly I've been acting, haven't I? You really must forgive me. It is so funny, too, making you beg for a seat in your own canoe."

"Oh no, it's your canoe—that is, after twelve o'clock to-night. That's when your contract begins."

"The arrangement does not seem to me quite regular; but, then, this is the Canadian woods, and not Boston. But, I want to make my little proviso. I do not wish to be introduced to this man; he must have no excuse for beginning a conversation with me. I don't want to talk to-morrow."

"Heroic resolution," murmured Mason.

"So, I do not wish to see the gentleman until I go into the canoe. You can be conveniently absent. Mrs. Perrault will take me down there; she speaks no English, and it is not likely he can speak French."

"We can arrange that."

"Then it is settled, and all I hope for is a good day to-morrow."

Mrs. Mason sprang up and kissed the fair Bostonian, and Mason felt a sensation of joyous freedom that recalled his youthful days when a half-holiday was announced.

"Oh, it is too good of you," said the elder lady.

"Not a bit of it," whispered Miss Sommerton; "I hate the man before I have seen him."

Chapter III

When John Trenton came in to breakfast, he found his friend Mason waiting for him. That genial gentleman was evidently ill at ease, but he said in an offhand way—

"The ladies have already breakfasted. They are busily engaged in the preparations for the trip, and so you and I can have a snack together, and then we will go and see to the canoe."

After breakfast they went together to the river, and found the canoe and the two half-breeds waiting for them. A couple of rugs were spread on the bottom of the canoe rising over the two slanting boards which served as backs to the lowly seats.

"Now," said Mason with a blush, for he always told a necessary lie with some compunction, "I shall have to go and see to one of my men who was injured in the mill this morning. You had better take your place in the canoe, and wait for your passenger, who, as is usual with ladies, will probably be a little late. I think you should sit in the back seat, as you are the heavier of the two. I presume you remember what I told you about sitting in a canoe? Get in with caution while these two men hold the side of it; sit down carefully, and keep steady, no matter what happens. Perhaps you may as well put your camera here at the back, or in the prow."

"No," said Trenton, "I shall keep it slung over my shoulder. It isn't heavy, and I am always afraid of forgetting it if I leave it anywhere."

Trenton got cautiously into the canoe, while Mason bustled off with a very guilty feeling at his heart. He never thought of blaming Miss Sommerton for the course she had taken, and the dilemma into which she placed him, for he felt that the fault was entirely his own.

John Trenton pulled out his pipe, and, absent-mindedly, stuffed it full of tobacco. Just as he was about to light it, he remembered there was to be a lady in the party, and so with a grimace of disappointment he put the loaded pipe into his pocket again.

It was the most lovely time of the year. The sun was still warm, but the dreaded black fly and other insect pests of the region had disappeared before the sharp frosts that occurred every night. The hilly banks of the St. Maurice were covered with unbroken forest, and "the woods of autumn all around, the vale had put their glory on." Presently Trenton saw Miss Sommerton, accompanied by old Mrs. Perrault, coming over the brow of the hill. He attempted to rise, in order to assist the lady to a seat in the canoe, when the half-breed-said in French—:

"Better sit still. It is safer. We will help the lady."

Miss Sommerton was talking rapidly in French—with rather overdone eagerness—to Mrs. Perrault. She took no notice of her fellow-voyager as she lightly stepped exactly in the centre of the canoe, and sank down on the rug in front of him, with the ease of one thoroughly accustomed to that somewhat treacherous craft. The two stalwart boatmen—one at the prow, the other at the stern of the canoe—with swift and dexterous strokes, shot it out into the stream. Trenton could not but admire the knowledge of these two men and their dexterous use of it. Here they were on a swiftly flowing river, with a small fall behind them and a tremendous cataract several miles in front, yet these two men, by their knowledge of the currents, managed to work their way up stream with the least possible amount of physical exertion. The St. Maurice at this point is about half a mile wide, with an island here and there, and now and then a touch of rapids. Sometimes the men would dash right across the river to the opposite bank, and there fall in with a miniature Gulf Stream that would carry them onward without exertion. Sometimes they were near the densely wooded shore, sometimes in the center of the river. The half-breed who stood behind Trenton, leant over to him, and whispered—

"You can now smoke if you like, the wind is down stream."

Naturally, Mr. Trenton wished to smoke. The requesting of permission to do so, it struck him, might open the way to conversation. He was not an ardent conversationalist, but it seemed to him rather ridiculous that two persons should thus travel together in a canoe without saying a word to each other.

"I beg your pardon, madam," he began; "but would you have any objection to my smoking? I am ashamed to confess that I am a slave to the pernicious habit."

There was a moment or two of silence, broken only by the regular dip of the paddle, then Miss Sommerton said, "If you wish to desecrate this lovely spot by smoking, I presume anything I can say will not prevent you."

Trenton was amazed at the rudeness of this reply, and his face flushed with anger. Finally he said, "You must have a very poor opinion of me!"

Miss Sommerton answered tartly, "I have no opinion whatever of you." Then, with womanly inconsistency, she proceeded to deliver her opinion, saying, "A man who would smoke here would smoke in a cathedral."

"I think you are wrong there," said Mr. Trenton, calmly. "I would smoke here, but I would not think of smoking in a cathedral. Neither would I smoke in the humblest log-cabin chapel."

"Sir," said Miss Sommerton, turning partly round, "I came to the St. Maurice for the purpose of viewing its scenery. I hoped to see it alone. I have been disappointed in that, but I must insist on seeing it in silence. I do not wish to carry on a conversation, nor do I wish to enter into a discussion on any subject whatever. I am sorry to have to say this, but it seems to be necessary."

Her remarks so astonished Trenton that he found it impossible to get angrier than he had been when she first spoke. In fact, he found his anger receding rather than augmenting. It was something so entirely new to meet a lady who had such an utter disregard for the rules of politeness that obtain in any civilized society that Mr. Trenton felt he was having a unique and valuable experience.

"Will you pardon me," he said, with apparent submissiveness—"will you pardon me if I disregard your request sufficiently to humbly beg forgiveness for having spoken to you in the first place?"

To this Miss Sommerton made no reply, and the canoe glided along.

After going up the river for a few miles the boatmen came to a difficult part of the voyage. Here the river was divided by an island. The dark waters moved with great swiftness, and with the smoothness of oil, over the concealed rocks, breaking into foam at the foot of the rapids. Now for the first time the Indians had hard work. For quite half an hour they paddled as if in despair, and the canoe moved upward inch by inch. It was not only hard work, but it was work that did not allow of a moment's rest until it was finished. Should the paddles pause but an instant, the canoe would be swept to the bottom of the rapids. When at last the craft floated into the still water above the rapids, the boatmen rested and mopped the perspiration from their brows. Then, without a word, they resumed their steady, easy swing of the paddle. In a short time the canoe drew up at a landing, from which a path ascended the steep hill among the trees. The silence was broken only by the deep, distant, low roar of the Shawenegan Falls. Mr. Trenton sat in his place, while the half-breeds held the canoe steady. Miss Sommerton rose and stepped with firm, self-reliant tread on the landing. Without looking backward she proceeded up the steep hill, and disappeared among the dense foliage. Then Trenton leisurely got out of the canoe.

"You had a hard time of it up that rapid," said the artist in French to the boatmen. "Here is a five-dollar bill to divide when you get down; and, if you bring us safely back, I shall have another ready for you."

The men were profusely grateful, as indeed they had a right to be, for the most they expected was a dollar each as a fee.

"Ah," said the elder, "if we had gentlemen like you to take up every day," and he gave an expressive shrug.

"You shouldn't take such a sordid view of the matter," said the artist. "I should think you would find great pleasure in taking up parties of handsome ladies such as I understand now and then visit the falls."

"Ah," said the boatman, "it is very nice, of course; but, except from Miss Sommerton, we don't get much."

"Really," said the artist; "and who is Miss Sommerton, pray?"

The half-breed nodded up the path.

"Oh, indeed, that is her name. I did not know."

"Yes," said the man, "she is very generous, and she always brings us tobacco in her pocket—good tobacco."

"Tobacco!" cried the artist. "The arrant hypocrite. She gives you tobacco, does she? Did you understand what we were talking about coming up here?"

The younger half-breed was about to say "Yes," and a gleam of intelligence came into his face; but a frown on the other's brow checked him, and the elder gravely shook his head.

"We do not understand English," he said.

As Trenton walked slowly up the steep hillside, he said to himself, "That young woman does not seem to have the slightest spark of gratitude in her composition. Here I have been good-natured enough to share my canoe with her, yet she treats me as if I were some low ruffian instead of a gentleman."

As Miss Sommerton was approaching the Shawenegan Falls, she said to herself, "What an insufferable cad that man is? Mr. Mason doubtless told him that he was indebted to me for being allowed to come in the canoe, and yet, although he must see I do not wish to talk with him, he tried to force conversation on me."

Miss Sommerton walked rapidly along the very imperfect woodland path, which was completely shaded by the overhanging trees. After a walk of nearly a mile, the path suddenly ended at the top of a tremendous precipice of granite, and opposite this point the great hillside of tumbling white foam plunged for ever downward. At the foot of the falls the waters flung themselves against the massive granite barrier, and then, turning at a right angle, plunged downward in a series of wild rapids that completely eclipsed in picturesqueness and grandeur and force even the famous rapids at Niagara. Contemplating this incomparable scene, Miss Sommerton forgot all about her objectionable travelling companion. She sat down on a fallen log, placing her sketch-book on her lap, but it lay there idly as, unconscious of the passing time, she gazed dreamily at the great falls and listened to their vibrating deafening roar. Suddenly the consciousness of some one near startled her from her reverie. She sprang to her feet, and had so completely forgotten her companion that she stared at him for a moment in dumb amazement. He stood back some distance from her, and beside him on its slender tripod was placed a natty little camera. Connected with the instantaneous shutter was a long black rubber tube almost as thin as a string. The bulb of this instantaneous attachment Mr. Trenton held in his hand, and the instant Miss Sommerton turned around, the little shutter, as if in defiance of her, gave a snap, and she knew her picture had been taken, and also that she was the principal object in the foreground.

"You have photographed me, sir!" cried the young woman, with her eyes blazing.

"I have photographed the falls, or, at least, I hope I have," replied Trenton.

"But my picture is in the foreground. You must destroy that plate."

"You will excuse me, Miss Sommerton, if I tell you I shall do nothing of the kind. It is very unusual with me to deny the request of a lady, but in this case I must do so. This is the last plate I have, and it may be the one successful picture of the lot. I shall, therefore, not destroy the plate."

"Then, sir, you are not a gentleman!" cried the impetuous young lady, her face aflame with anger.

"I never claimed to be one," answered Trenton, calmly.

"I shall appeal to Mr. Mason; perhaps he has some means of making you understand that you are not allowed to take a lady's photograph without her permission, and in defiance of her wishes."

"Will you allow me to explain why it is unnecessary to destroy the plate? If you understand anything about photography, you must be aware of the fact—"

"I am happy to say I know nothing of photography, and I desire to know nothing of it. I will not hear any explanation from you, sir. You have refused to destroy the plate. That is enough for me. Your conduct to-day has been entirely contemptible. In the first place you have forced yourself, through Mr. Mason, into my company. The canoe was mine for to-day, and you knew it. I granted you permission to come, but I made it a proviso that there should be no conversation. Now, I shall return in the canoe alone, and I shall pay the boatmen to come back for you this evening." With this she swept indignantly past Mr. Trenton, leaving the unfortunate man for the second or third time that day too much dumbfounded to reply. She marched down the path toward the landing. Arriving at the canoe, she told the boatmen they would have to return for Mr. Trenton; that she was going back alone, and she would pay them handsomely for their extra trip. Even the additional pay offered did not seem to quite satisfy the two half-breeds.

"It will be nearly dark before we can get back," grumbled the elder boatman.

"That does not matter," replied Miss Sommerton, shortly.

"But it is dangerous going down the river at night."

"That does not matter," was again the reply.

"But he has nothing—"

"The longer you stand talking here the longer it will be before you get back. If you are afraid for the safety of the gentleman, pray stay here with him and give me the paddle—I will take the boat down alone."

The boatman said nothing more, but shot the canoe out from the landing and proceeded rapidly down the stream.

Miss Sommerton meditated bitterly on the disappointments and annoyances of the day. Once fairly away, conscience began to trouble her, and she remembered that the gentleman so unceremoniously left in the woods without any possibility of getting away was a man whom Mr. Mason, her friend, evidently desired very much to please. Little had been said by the

42

boatmen, merely a brief word of command now and then from the elder who stood in the stern, until they passed down the rapids. Then Miss Sommerton caught a grumbling word in French which made her heart stand still.

"What is that you said?" she cried to the elder boatman.

He did not answer, but solemnly paddled onward.

"Answer me," demanded Miss Sommerton. "What is that you said about the gentleman who went up with us this morning?"

"I said," replied the half-breed, with a grim severity that even the remembrance of gifts of tobacco could not mitigate, "that the canoe belonged to him today."

"How dare you say such a thing! The canoe was mine. Mr. Mason gave it to me. It was mine for to-day."

"I know nothing about that," returned the boatman doggedly; "but I do know that three days ago Mr. Mason came to me with this gentleman's letter in his hand and said, 'Pierre, Mr. Trenton is to have the canoe for Tuesday. See it is in good order, and no one else is to have it for that day.' That is what Mr. Mason said, and when they were down at the canoe this morning, Mr. Mason asked Mr. Trenton if he would let you go up to the falls in his canoe, and he said 'Yes.'"

Miss Sommerton sat there too horrified to speak. A wild resentment against the duplicity of Ed. Mason arose for a moment in her heart, but it speedily sank as she viewed her own conduct in the light of this astounding revelation. She had abused an unknown gentleman like a pickpocket, and had finally gone off with his canoe, leaving him marooned, as it were, to whose courtesy she was indebted for being there at all. Overcome by the thoughts that crowded so quickly upon her, she buried her face in her hands and wept. But this was only for an instant. Raising her head again, with the imperious air characteristic of her, she said to the boatman—

"Turn back at once, please."

"We are almost there now," he answered, amazed at the feminine inconsistency of the command.

"Turn back at once, I say. You are not too tired to paddle up the river again, are you?"

"No, madame," he answered, "but it is so useless; we are almost there. We shall land you, and then the canoe will go up lighter."

"I wish to go with you. Do what I tell you, and I will pay you."

The stolid boatman gave the command; the man at the bow paddled one way, while the man at the stern paddled another, and the canoe swung round upstream again.

Chapter IV

The sun had gone down when Miss Sommerton put her foot once more on the landing.

"We will go and search for him," said the boatman.

"Stay where you are," she commanded, and disappeared swiftly up the path. Expecting to find him still at the falls, she faced the prospect of a good mile of rough walking in the gathering darkness without flinching. But at the brow of the hill, within hearing distance of the landing, she found the man of whom she was in search. In her agony of mind Miss Sommerton had expected to come upon him pacing moodily up and down before the falls, meditating on the ingratitude of womankind. She discovered him in a much less romantic attitude. He was lying at full length below a white birch-tree, with his camera-box under his head for a pillow. It was evident he had seen enough of the Shawenegan Falls for one day, and doubtless, because of the morning's early rising, and the day's long journey, had fallen soundly asleep. His soft felt hat lay on the ground beside him. Miss Sommerton looked at him for a moment, and thought bitterly of Mason's additional perjury in swearing that he was an elderly man. True, his hair was tinged with grey at the temples, but there was nothing elderly about his appearance. Miss Sommerton saw that he was a handsome man, and wondered this had escaped her notice before, forgetting that she had scarcely deigned to look at him. She thought he had spoken to her with inexcusable bluntness at the falls, in refusing to destroy his plate; but she now remembered with compunction that he had made no allusion to his ownership of the boat for that day, while she had boasted that it was hers. She determined to return and send one of the boatmen up to awaken him, but at that moment Trenton suddenly opened his eyes, as a person often does when some one looks at him in his sleep. He sprang quickly to his feet, and put up his hand in bewilderment to remove his hat, but found it wasn't there. Then he laughed uncomfortably, stooping to pick it up again.

"I—I—I wasn't expecting visitors," he stammered—

"Why did you not tell me," she said, "that Mr. Mason had promised you the boat for the day?"

"Good gracious!" cried Trenton, "has Ed. Mason told you that?"

"I have not seen Mr. Mason," she replied; "I found it out by catching an accidental remark made by one of the boatmen. I desire very humbly to apologise to you for my conduct."

"Oh, that doesn't matter at all, I assure you."

"What! My conduct doesn't?"

"No, I didn't mean quite that; but I—Of course, you did treat me rather abruptly; but then, you know, I saw how it was. You looked on me as an interloper, as it were, and I think you were quite justified, you know, in speaking as you did. I am a very poor hand at conversing with ladies, even at my best, and I am not at my best to-day. I had to get up too early, so there is no doubt what I said was said very awkwardly indeed. But it really doesn't matter, you know—that is, it doesn't matter about anything you said."

"I think it matters very much—at least, it matters very much to me. I shall always regret having treated you as I did, and I hope you will forgive me for having done so."

"Oh, that's all right," said Mr. Trenton, swinging his camera over his shoulder. "It is getting dark, Miss Sommerton; I think we should hurry down to the canoe."

As they walked down the hill together, he continued—

"I wish you would let me give you a little lesson in photography, if you don't mind."

"I have very little interest in photography, especially amateur photography," replied Miss Sommerton, with a partial return of her old reserve.

"Oh, I don't wish to make an amateur photographer of you. You sketch very nicely, and—"

"How do you know that?" asked Miss Sommerton, turning quickly towards him: "you have never seen any of my sketches."

"Ah, well," stammered Trenton, "no—that is—you know—are not those water-colours in Mason's house yours?"

"Mr. Mason has some of my sketches. I didn't know you had seen them."

"Well, as I was saying," continued Trenton, "I have no desire to convert you to the beauties of amateur photography. I admit the results in many cases are very bad. I am afraid if you saw the pictures I take myself you would not be much in love with the art. But what I wish to say is in mitigation of my refusal to destroy the plate when you asked me to."

"Oh, I beg you will not mention that, or refer to anything at all I have said to you. I assure you it pains me very much, and you know I have apologised once or twice already."

"Oh, it isn't that. The apology should come from me; but I thought I would like to explain why it is that I did not take your picture, as you thought I did."

"Not take my picture? Why I saw you take it. You admitted yourself you took it."

"Well, you see, that is what I want to explain. I took your picture, and then again I didn't take it. This is how it is with amateur photography. Your picture on the plate will be a mere shadow, a dim outline, nothing more. No one can tell who it is. You see, it is utterly impossible to take a dark object and one in pure white at the instantaneous snap. If the picture of the falls is at all correct, as I expect it will be, then your picture will be nothing but a shadow unrecognisable by any one."

"But they do take pictures with the cataract as a background, do they not? I am sure I have seen photos of groups taken at Niagara Falls; in fact, I have seen groups being posed in public for that purpose, and very silly they looked, I must say. I presume that is one of the things that has prejudiced me so much against the camera."

"Those pictures, Miss Sommerton, are not genuine; they are not at all what they pretend to be. The prints that you have seen are the results of the manipulation of two separate plates, one of the plates containing the group or the person photographed, and the other an instantaneous picture of the falls. If you look closely at one of those pictures you will see a little halo of light or dark around the person photographed. That, to an experienced photographer, shows the double printing. In fact, it is double dealing all round. The deluded victim of the camera imagines that the pictures he gets of the falls, with himself in the foreground, is really a picture of the falls taken at the time he is being photographed. Whereas, in the picture actually taken of him, the falls themselves are hopelessly over-exposed, and do not appear at all on the plate. So with the instantaneous picture I took; there will really be nothing of you on that plate that you would recognise as yourself. That was why I refused to destroy it."

"I am afraid," said Miss Sommerton, sadly, "you are trying to make my punishment harder and harder. I believe in reality you are very cruel. You know how badly I feel about the whole matter, and now even the one little point that apparently gave me any excuse is taken away by your scientific explanation."

"Candidly, Miss Sommerton, I am more of a culprit than you imagine, and I suppose it is the tortures of a guilty conscience that caused me to make this explanation. I shall now confess without reserve. As you sat there with your head in your hand looking at the falls, I deliberately and with malice aforethought took a timed picture, which, if developed, will reveal you exactly as you sat, and which will not show the falls at all."

Miss Sommerton walked in silence beside him, and he could not tell just how angry she might be. Finally he said, "I shall destroy that plate, if you order me to."

Miss Sommerton made no reply, until they were nearly at the canoe. Then she looked up at him with a smile, and said, "I think it a pity to destroy any pictures you have had such trouble to obtain."

"Thank you, Miss Sommerton," said the artist. He helped her into the canoe in the gathering dusk, and then sat down himself. But neither of them saw the look of anxiety on the face of the elder boatman. He knew the River St. Maurice.

Chapter V

From the words the elder boatman rapidly addressed to the younger, it was evident to Mr. Trenton that the half-breed was anxious to pass the rapids before it became very much darker.

The landing is at the edge of comparatively still water. At the bottom of the falls the river turns an acute angle and flows to the west. At the landing it turns with equal abruptness, and flows south.

The short westward section of the river from the falls to the point where they landed is a wild, turbulent rapid, in which no boat can live for a moment. From the Point downwards, although the water is covered with foam, only one dangerous place has to be passed. Toward that spot the stalwart half-breeds bent all their energy in forcing the canoe down with the current. The canoe shot over the darkening rapid with the speed of an arrow. If but one or two persons had been in it, the chances are the passage would have been made in safety. As it was one wrong turn of the paddle by the younger half-breed did the mischief. The bottom barely touched a sharp-pointed hidden rock, and in an instant the canoe was slit open as with a knife.

As he sat there Trenton felt the cold water rise around him with a quickness that prevented his doing anything, even if he had known what to do.

"Sit still!" cried the elder boatman; and then to the younger he shouted sharply, "The shore!"

They were almost under the hanging trees when the four found themselves in the water. Trenton grasped an overhanging branch with one hand, and with the other caught Miss Sommerton by the arm. For a moment it was doubtful whether the branch would hold. The current was very swift, and it threw each of them against the rock bank, and bent the branch down into the water.

"Catch hold of me!" cried Trenton. "Catch hold of my coat; I need both hands."

Miss Sommerton, who had acted with commendable bravery throughout, did as she was directed. Trenton, with his released hand, worked himself slowly up the branch, hand over hand, and finally catching a sapling that grew close to the water's edge, with a firm hold, reached down and helped Miss Sommerton on the bank. Then he slowly drew himself up to a safe position and looked around for any signs of the boatmen. He shouted loudly, but there was no answer.

"Are they drowned, do you think?" asked Miss Sommerton, anxiously.

"No, I don't suppose they are; I don't think you could drown a half-breed. They have done their best to drown us, and as we have escaped I see no reason why they should drown."

"Oh, it's all my fault! all my fault!" wailed Miss Sommerton.

"It is, indeed," answered Trenton, briefly.

She tried to straighten herself up, but, too wet and chilled and limp to be heroic, she sank on a rock and began to cry.

"Please don't do that," said the artist, softly. "Of course I shouldn't have agreed with you. I beg pardon for having done so, but now that we are here, you are not to shirk your share of the duties. I want you to search around and get materials for a fire."

"Search around?" cried Miss Sommerton dolefully.

"Yes, search around. Hunt, as you Americans say. You have got us into this scrape, so I don't propose you shall sit calmly by and not take any of the consequences."

"Do you mean to insult me, Mr. Trenton, now that I am helpless?"

"If it is an insult to ask you to get up and gather some wood and bring it here, then I do mean to insult you most emphatically. I shall gather some, too, for we shall need a quantity of it."

Miss Sommerton rose indignantly, and was on the point of threatening to leave the place, when a moment's reflection showed her that she didn't know where to go, and remembering she was not as brave in the darkness and in the woods as in Boston, she meekly set about the search for dry twigs and sticks. Flinging down the bundle near the heap Trenton had already collected, the young woman burst into a laugh.

"Do you see anything particularly funny in the situation?" asked Trenton, with chattering teeth. "I confess I do not."

"The funniness of the situation is that we should gather wood, when, if there is a match in your pocket, it must be so wet as to be useless."

"Oh, not at all. You must remember I come from a very damp climate, and we take care of our matches there. I have been in the water before now on a tramp, and my matches are in a silver case warranted to keep out the wet." As he said this Trenton struck a light, and applied it to the small twigs and dry autumn leaves. The flames flashed up through the larger sticks, and in a very few moments a cheering fire was blazing, over which Trenton threw armful after armful of the wood he had collected.

"Now," said the artist, "if you will take off what outer wraps you have on, we can spread them here, and dry them. Then if you sit, first facing the fire and next with your back to it, and maintain a sort of rotatory motion, it will not be long before you are reasonably dry and warm."

Miss Sommerton laughed, but there was not much merriment in her laughter.

"Was there ever anything so supremely ridiculous?" she said. "A gentleman from England gathering sticks, and a lady from Boston gyrating before the fire. I am glad you are not a newspaper man, for you might be tempted to write about the situation for some sensational paper."

"How do you know I am not a journalist?"

"Well, I hope you are not. I thought you were a photographer."

"Oh, not a professional photographer, you know."

"I am sorry; I prefer the professional to the amateur."

"I like to hear you say that."

"Why? It is not very complimentary, I am sure."

"The very reason I like to hear you say it. If you were complimentary I would be afraid you were going to take a chill and be ill after this disaster; but now that you are yourself again, I have no such fear."

"Myself again!" blazed the young woman. "What do you know about me? How do you know whether I am myself or somebody else? I am sure our acquaintance has been very short."

"Counted by time, yes. But an incident like this, in the wilderness, does more to form a friendship, or the reverse, than years of ordinary acquaintance in Boston or London. You ask how I know that you are yourself. Shall I tell you?"

"If you please."

"Well, I imagine you are a young lady who has been spoilt. I think probably you are rich, and have had a good deal of your own way in this world. In fact, I take it for granted that you have never met any one who frankly told you your faults. Even if such good fortune had been yours, I doubt if you would have profited by it. A snub would have been the reward of the courageous person who told Miss Sommerton her failings."

"I presume you have courage enough to tell me my faults without the fear of a snub before your eyes."

"I have the courage, yes. You see I have already received the snub three or four times, and it has lost its terrors for me."

"In that case, will you be kind enough to tell me what you consider my faults?"

"If you wish me to."

"I do wish it."

"Well, then, one of them is inordinate pride."

"Do you think pride a fault?"

"It is not usually reckoned one of the virtues."

"In this country, Mr. Trenton, we consider that every person should have a certain amount of pride."

"A certain amount may be all right. It depends entirely on how much the certain amount is."

"Well, now for fault No. 2."

"Fault No. 2 is a disregard on your part for the feelings of others. This arises, I imagine, partly from fault No. 1. You are in the habit of classing the great mass of the public very much beneath you in intellect and other qualities, and you forget that persons whom you may perhaps dislike, have feelings which you have no right to ignore."

"I presume you refer to this morning," said Miss Sommerton, seriously. "I apologised for that two or three times, I think. I have always understood that a gentleman regards an apology from another gentleman as blotting out the original offence. Why should he not regard it in the same light when it comes from a woman?"

"Oh, now you are making a personal matter of it. I am talking in an entirely impersonal sense. I am merely giving you, with brutal rudeness, opinions formed on a very short acquaintance. Remember, I have done so at your own request."

"I am very much obliged to you, I am sure. I think you are more than half right. I hope the list is not much longer."

"No, the list ends there. I suppose you imagine that I am one of the rudest men you ever met?"

"No, we generally expect rudeness from Englishmen."

"Oh, do you really? Then I am only keeping up the reputation my countrymen have already acquired in America. Have you had the pleasure of meeting a rude Englishman before?"

54

"No, I can't say that I have. Most Englishmen I have met have been what we call very gentlemanly indeed. But the rudest letter I ever received was from an Englishman; not only rude, but ungrateful, for I had bought at a very high price one of his landscapes. He was John Trenton, the artist, of London. Do you know him?"

"Yes," hesitated Trenton, "I know him. I may say I know him very well. In fact, he is a namesake of mine."

"Why, how curious it is I had never thought of that. Is your first name J—, the same as his?"

"Yes."

"Not a relative, is he?"

"Well, no. I don't think I can call him a relative. I don't know that I can even go so far as to call him my friend, but he is an acquaintance."

"Oh, tell me about him," cried Miss Sommerton, enthusiastically. "He is one of the Englishmen I have longed very much to meet."

"Then you forgave him his rude letter?"

"Oh, I forgave that long ago. I don't know that it was rude, after all. It was truthful. I presume the truth offended me."

"Well," said Trenton, "truth has to be handled very delicately, or it is apt to give offence. You bought a landscape of his, did you? Which one, do you remember?"

"It was a picture of the Thames valley."

"Ah, I don't recall it at the moment. A rather hackneyed subject, too. Probably he sent it to America because he couldn't sell it in England."

"Oh, I suppose you think we buy anything here that the English refuse, I beg to inform you this picture had a place in the Royal Academy, and was very highly spoken of by the critics. I bought it in England."

"Oh yes, I remember it now, 'The Thames at Sonning.' Still, it was a hackneyed subject, although reasonably well treated."

"Reasonably well! I think it one of the finest landscape pictures of the century."

"Well, in that at least Trenton would agree with you."

"He is very conceited, you mean?"

"Even his enemies admit that."

"I don't believe it. I don't believe a man of such talent could be so conceited."

"Then, Miss Sommerton, allow me to say you have very little knowledge of human nature. It is only reasonable that a great man should know he is a great man. Most of our great men are conceited. I would like to see Trenton's letter to you. I could then have a good deal of amusement at his expense when I get back."

"Well, in that case I can assure you that you will never see the letter."

"Ah, you destroyed it, did you?"

"Not for that reason."

"Then you did destroy it?"

"I tore it up, but on second thoughts I pasted it together again, and have it still."

"In that case, why should you object to showing me the letter?"

"Well, because I think it rather unusual for a lady to be asked by a gentleman show him a letter that has been written to her by another gentleman."

"In matters of the heart that is true; but in matters of art it is not."

"Is that intended for a pun?"

"It is as near to one as I ever allow myself to come, I should like very much to see Mr. Trenton's letter. It was probably brutally rude. I know the man, you see."

"It was nothing of the sort," replied Miss Sommerton, hotly. "It was a truthful, well-meant letter."

"And yet you tore it up?"

"But that was the first impulse. The pasting it together was the apology."

"And you will not show it to me?"

"No, I will not."

"Did you answer it?"

"I will tell you nothing more about it. I am sorry I spoke of the letter at all. You don't appreciate Mr. Trenton's work."

"Oh, I beg your pardon, I do. He has no greater admirer in England than I am—except himself, of course."

"I suppose it makes no difference to you to know that I don't like a remark like that."

"Oh, I thought it would please you. You see, with the exception of myself, Mr. Trenton is about the rudest man in England. In fact, I begin to suspect it was Mr. Trenton's letter that led you to a wholesale condemning of the English race, for you admit the Englishmen you have met were not rude."

"You forget I have met you since then."

"Well bowled, as we say in cricket."

"Has Mr. Trenton many friends in London?"

"Not a great number. He is a man who sticks rather closely to his work, and, as I said before, he prides himself on telling the truth. That doesn't do in London any more than it does in Boston."

"Well, I honour him for it."

"Oh, certainly; everybody does in the abstract. But it is not a quality that tends to the making or the keeping of friends, you know."

"If you see Mr. Trenton when you return, I wish you would tell him there is a lady in America who is a friend of his; and if he has any pictures the people over there do not appreciate, ask him to send them to Boston, and his friend will buy them."

"Then you must be rich, for his pictures bring very good prices, even in England."

"Yes," said Miss Sommerton, "I am rich."

"Well, I suppose it's very jolly to be rich," replied the artist, with a sigh.

"You are not rich, then, I imagine?"

"No, I am not. That is, not compared with your American fortunes. I have enough of money to let me roam around the world if I wish to, and get half drowned in the St. Maurice River."

"Oh, is it not strange that we have heard nothing from those boatmen? You surely don't imagine they could have been drowned?"

"I hardly think so. Still, it is quite possible."

"Oh, don't say that; it makes me feel like a murderer."

"Well, I think it was a good deal your fault, don't you know." Miss Sommerton looked at him.

"Have I not been punished enough already?" she said.

"For the death of two men—if they are dead? Bless me! no. Do you imagine for a moment there is any relation between the punishment and the fault?"

Miss Sommerton buried her face in her hands.

"Oh, I take that back," said Trenton. "I didn't mean to say such a thing."

"It is the truth—it is the truth!" wailed the young woman. "Do you honestly think they did not reach the shore?"

"Of course they did. If you want to know what has happened, I'll tell you exactly, and back my opinion by a bet if you like. An Englishman is always ready to back his opinion, you know. Those two men swam with the current until they came to some landing-place. They evidently think we are drowned. Nevertheless, they are now making their way through the woods to the settlement. Then comes the hubbub. Mason will stir up the neighbourhood, and the men who are back from the woods with the other canoes will be roused and pressed into service, and some time to-night we will be rescued."

"Oh, I hope that is the case," cried Miss Sommerton, looking brightly at him.

"It is the case. Will you bet about it?"

"I never bet," said Miss Sommerton.

"Ah, well, you miss a good deal of fun then. You see I am a bit of a mind reader. I can tell just about where the men are now."

"I don't believe much in mind reading."

"Don't you? Shall I give you a specimen of it? Take that letter we have spoken so much about. If you think it over in your mind I will read you the letter—not word for word, perhaps, but I shall give you gist of it, at least."

"Oh, impossible!"

"Do you remember it?"

"I have it with me."

"Oh, have you? Then, if you wish to preserve it, you should spread it out upon the ground to dry before the fire."

"There is no need of my producing the letter," replied Miss Sommerton; "I remember every word it."

"Very well, just think it over in your mind, and see if I cannot repeat it. Are you thinking about it?"

"Yes, I am thinking about it."

"Here goes, then. 'Miss Edith Sommerton—'"

"Wrong," said that young lady.

"The Sommerton is right, is it not?"

"Yes, but the first name is not."

"What is it, then?"

"I shall not tell you."

"Oh, very well. Miss Sommerton,—'I have some hesitation in answering your letter.' Oh, by the way, I forgot the address. That is the first sentence of the letter, but the address is some number which I cannot quite see, 'Beacon Street, Boston.' Is there any such street in that city?"

"There is," said Miss Sommerton. "What a question to ask."

"Ah, then Beacon Street is one of the principal streets, is it?"

"One of them? It is the street. It is Boston."

"Very good. I will now proceed with the letter. 'I have some hesitation in answering your letter, because the sketches you send are so bad, that it seems to me no one could seriously forward them to an artist for criticism. However, if you really desire criticism, and if the pictures are sent in good faith, I may say I see in them no merit whatever, not even good drawing; while the colours are put on in a way that would seem to indicate you have not yet learned the fundamental principle of mixing the paints. If you are thinking of earning a livelihood with your pencil, I strongly advise you to abandon the idea. But if you are a lady of leisure and wealth, I suppose there is no harm in your continuing as long as you see fit.—Yours truly, JOHN TRENTON.'"

Miss Sommerton, whose eyes had opened wider and wider as this reading went on, said sharply—

"He has shown you the letter. You have seen it before it was sent."

"I admit that," said the artist.

"Well—I will believe all you like to say about Mr. John Trenton."

"Now, stop a moment; do not be too sweeping in your denunciation of him. I know that Mr. Trenton showed the letter to no one."

"Why, I thought you said a moment ago that he showed it to you."

"He did. Yet no one but himself saw the letter."

The young lady sprang to her feet.

"Are you, then, John Trenton, the artist?"

"Miss Sommerton, I have to plead guilty."

Chapter VI

Miss Eva Sommerton and Mr. John Trenton stood on opposite sides of the blazing fire and looked at each other. A faint smile hovered around the lips of the artist, but Miss Sommerton's face was very serious. She was the first to speak.

"It seems to me," she said, "that there is something about all this that smacks of false pretences."

"On my part, Miss Sommerton?"

"Certainly on your part. You must have known all along that I was the person who had written the letter to you. I think, when you found that out, you should have spoken of it."

"Then you do not give me credit for the honesty of speaking now. You ought to know that I need not have spoken at all, unless I wished to be very honest about the matter."

"Yes, there is that to be said in your favour, of course."

"Well, Miss Sommerton, I hope you will consider anything that happens to be in my favour. You see, we are really old friends, after all."

"Old enemies, you mean."

"Oh, I don't know about that. I would rather look on myself as your friend than your enemy."

"The letter you wrote me was not a very friendly one."

"I am not so sure. We differ on that point, you know."

"I am afraid we differ on almost every point."

"No, I differ with you there again. Still, I must admit I would prefer being your enemy—"

"To being my friend?" said Miss Sommerton, quickly.

"No, to being entirely indifferent to you."

"Really, Mr. Trenton, we are getting along very rapidly, are we not?" said the young lady, without looking up at him.

"Now, I am pleased to be able to agree with you there, Miss Sommerton. As I said before, an incident like this does more to ripen acquaintance or friendship, or—" The young man hesitated, and did not complete his sentence.

"Well," said the artist, after a pause, "which is it to be, friends or enemies?"

"It shall be exactly as you say," she replied.

"If you leave the choice to me, I shall say friends. Let us shake hands on that."

She held out her hand frankly to him as he crossed over to her side, and as he took it in his own, a strange thrill passed through him, and acting on the impulse of the moment, he drew her toward him and kissed her.

"How dare you!" she cried, drawing herself indignantly from him. "Do you think I am some backwoods girl who is flattered by your preference after a day's acquaintance?"

"Not a day's acquaintance, Miss Sommerton—a year, two years, ten years. In fact, I feel as though I had known you all my life."

"You certainly act as if you had. I did think for some time past that you were a gentleman. But you take advantage now of my unprotected position."

"Miss Sommerton, let me humbly apologise!"

"I shall not accept your apology. It cannot be apologised for. I must ask you not to speak to me again until Mr. Mason comes. You may consider yourself very fortunate when I tell you I shall say nothing of what has passed to Mr. Mason when he arrives."

John Trenton made no reply, but gathered another armful of wood and flung it on the fire.

Miss Sommerton sat very dejectedly looking at the embers.

For half an hour neither of them said anything.

Suddenly Trenton jumped up and listened intently.

"What is it?" cried Miss Sommerton, startled by his action.

"Now," said Trenton, "that is unfair. If I am not to be allowed to speak to you, you must not ask me any questions."

"I beg your pardon," said Miss Sommerton, curtly.

"But really I wanted to say something, and I wanted you to be the first to break the contract imposed. May I say what I wish to? I have just thought about something."

"If you have thought of anything that will help us out of our difficulty, I shall be very glad to hear it indeed."

"I don't know that it will help us out of our difficulties, but I think it will help us now that we're in them. You know, I presume, that my camera, like John Brown's knapsack, was strapped on my back, and that it is one of the few things rescued from the late disaster?"

He paused for a reply, but she said nothing. She evidently was not interested in his camera.

"Now, that camera-box is water-tight. It is really a very natty arrangement, although you regard it so scornfully."

He paused a second time, but there was no reply.

"Very well; packed in that box is, first the camera, then the dry plates, but most important of all, there are at least two or three very nice Three Rivers sandwiches. What do you say to our having supper?"

Miss Sommerton smiled in spite of herself, and Trenton busily unstrapped the camera-box, pulled out the little instrument, and fished up from the bottom a neatly-folded white table-napkin, in which were wrapped several sandwiches.

"Now," he continued, "I have a folding drinking-cup and a flask of sherry. It shows how absent-minded I am, for I ought to have thought of the wine long ago. You should have had a glass of sherry the moment we landed here. By the way, I wanted to say, and I say it now in case I shall forget it, that when I ordered you so unceremoniously to go around picking up sticks for the fire, it was not because I needed assistance, but to keep you, if possible, from getting a chill."

"Very kind of you," remarked Miss Sommerton.

But the Englishman could not tell whether she meant just what she said or not.

"I wish you would admit that you are hungry. Have you had anything to eat to-day?"

"I had, I am ashamed to confess," she answered. "I took lunch with me and I ate it coming down in the canoe. That was what troubled me about you. I was afraid you had eaten nothing all day, and I wished to offer you some lunch when we were in the canoe, but scarcely liked to. I thought we would soon reach the settlement. I am very glad you have sandwiches with you."

"How little you Americans really know of the great British nation, after all. Now, if there is one thing more than another that an Englishman looks after, it is the commissariat."

After a moment's silence he said—

"Don't you think, Miss Sommerton, that notwithstanding any accident or disaster, or misadventure that may have happened, we might get back at least on the old enemy footing again? I would like to apologise"—he paused for a moment, and added, "for the letter I wrote you ever so many years ago."

"There seem to be too many apologies between us," she replied. "I shall neither give nor take any more."

"Well," he answered, "I think after all that is the best way. You ought to treat me rather kindly though, because you are the cause of my being here."

"That is one of the many things I have apologised for. You surely do not wish to taunt me with it again?"

"Oh, I don't mean the recent accident. I mean being here in America. Your sketches of the Shawenegan Falls, and your description of the Quebec district, brought me out to America; and, added to that—I expected to meet you."

"To meet me?"

"Certainly. Perhaps you don't know that I called at Beacon Street, and found you were from home—with friends in Canada, they said—and I want to say, in self-defence, that I came very well introduced. I brought letters to people in Boston of the most undoubted respectability, and to people in New York, who are as near the social equals of the Boston people as it is possible for mere New York persons to be. Among other letters of introduction I had two to you. I saw the house in Beacon Street. So, you see, I have no delusions about your being a backwoods girl, as you charged me with having a short time since."

"I would rather not refer to that again, if you please."

"Very well. Now, I have one question to ask you—one request to make. Have I your permission to make it?"

"It depends entirely on what your request is."

"Of course, in that case you cannot tell until I make it. So I shall now make my request, and I want you to remember, before you refuse it, that you are indebted to me for supper. Miss Sommerton, give me a plug of tobacco."

Miss Sommerton stood up in dumb amazement.

"You see," continued the artist, paying no heed to her evident resentment, "I have lost my tobacco in the marine disaster, but luckily I have my pipe. I admit the scenery is beautiful here, if we could only see it; but darkness is all around, although the moon is rising. It can therefore be no desecration for me to smoke a pipeful of tobacco, and I am sure the tobacco you keep will be the very best that can be bought. Won't you grant my request, Miss Sommerton?"

At first Miss Sommerton seemed to resent the audacity of this request. Then a conscious light came into her face, and instinctively her hand pressed the side of her dress where her pocket was supposed to be.

"Now," said the artist, "don't deny that you have the tobacco. I told you I was a bit of a mind reader, and besides, I have been informed that young ladies in America are rarely without the weed, and that they only keep the best."

The situation was too ridiculous for Miss Sommerton to remain very long indignant about it. So she put her hand in her pocket and drew out a plug of tobacco, and with a bow handed it to the artist.

"Thanks," he replied; "I shall borrow a pipeful and give you back the remainder. Have you ever tried the English birdseye? I assure you it is a very nice smoking tobacco."

"I presume," said Miss Sommerton, "the boatmen told you I always gave them some tobacco when I came up to see the falls?"

"Ah, you will doubt my mind-reading gift. Well, honestly, they did tell me, and I thought perhaps you might by good luck have it with you now. Besides, you know, wasn't there the least bit of humbug about your objection to smoking as we came up the river? If you really object to smoking, of course I shall not smoke now."

"Oh, I haven't the least objection to it. I am sorry I have not a good cigar to offer you."

"Thank you. But this is quite as acceptable. We rarely use plug tobacco in England, but I find some of it in this country is very good indeed."

"I must confess," said Miss Sommerton, "that I have very little interest in the subject of tobacco. But I cannot see why we should not have good tobacco in this country. We grow it here."

"That's so, when you come to think of it," answered the artist.

Trenton sat with his back against the tree, smoking in a meditative manner, and watching the flicker of the firelight on the face of his companion, whose thoughts seemed to be concentrated on the embers.

"Miss Sommerton," he said at last, "I would like permission to ask you a second question.

"You have it," replied that lady, without looking up. "But to prevent disappointment, I may say this is all the tobacco I have. The rest I left in the canoe when I went up to the falls."

"I shall try to bear the disappointment as well as I may. But in this case the question is of a very different nature. I don't know just exactly how to put it. You may have noticed that I am rather awkward when it comes to saying the right thing at the right time. I have not been much accustomed to society, and I am rather a blunt man."

"Many persons," said Miss Sommerton with some severity, "pride themselves on their bluntness. They seem to think it an excuse for saying rude things. There is a sort of superstition that bluntness and honesty go together."

"Well, that is not very encouraging, However, I do not pride myself on my bluntness, but rather regret it. I was merely stating a condition of things, not making a boast. In this instance I imagine I can show that honesty is the accompaniment. The question I wished to ask was something like this: Suppose I had had the chance to present to you my letters of introduction, and suppose that we had known each other for some time, and suppose that everything had been very conventional, instead of somewhat unconventional; supposing all this, would you have deemed a recent action of mine so unpardonable as you did a while ago?"

"You said you were not referring to smoking."

"Neither am I. I am referring to my having kissed you. There's bluntness for you."

"My dear sir," replied Miss Sommerton, shading her face with her hand, "you know nothing whatever of me."

"That is rather evading the question."

"Well, then, I know nothing whatever of you."

"That is the second evasion. I am taking it for granted that we each know something of the other."

"I should think it would depend entirely on how the knowledge influenced each party in the case. It is such a purely supposititious state of things that I cannot see how I can answer your question. I suppose you have heard the adage about not crossing a bridge until you come to it."

"I thought it was a stream."

"Well, a stream then. The principle is the same.'"

"I was afraid I would not be able to put the question in a way to make you understand it. I shall now fall back on my bluntness again, and with this question, are you betrothed?"

"We generally call it engaged in this country."

"Then I shall translate my question into the language of the country, and ask if—"

"Oh, don't ask it, please. I shall answer before you do ask it by saying, No. I do not know why I should countenance your bluntness, as you call it, by giving you an answer to such a question; but I do so on condition that the question is the last."

"But the second question cannot be the last. There is always the third reading of a bill. The auctioneer usually cries, 'Third and last time,' not 'Second and last time,' and the banns of approaching marriage are called out three times. So, you see, I have the right to ask you one more question."

"Very well. A person may sometimes have the right to do a thing, and yet be very foolish in exercising that right."

"I accept your warning," said the artist, "and reserve my right."

"What time is it, do you think?" she asked him.

"I haven't the least idea," he replied; "my watch has stopped. That case was warranted to resist water, but I doubt if it has done so."

"Don't you think that if the men managed to save themselves they would have been here by this time?"

"I am sure I don't know. I have no idea of the distance. Perhaps they may have taken it for granted we are drowned, and so there is one chance in a thousand that they may not come back at all."

"Oh, I do not think such a thing is possible. The moment Mr. Mason heard of the disaster he would come without delay, no matter what he might believe the result of the accident to be."

"Yes, I think you are right. I shall try to get out on this point and see if I can discover anything of them. The moon now lights up the river, and if they are within a reasonable distance I think I can see them from this point of rock."

The artist climbed up on the point, which projected over the river. The footing was not of the safest, and Miss Sommerton watched him with some anxiety as he slipped and stumbled and kept his place by holding on to the branches of the overhanging trees.

"Pray be careful, Mr. Trenton," she said; "remember you are over the water there, and it is very swift."

"The rocks seem rather slippery with the dew," answered the artist; "but I am reasonably surefooted."

"Well, please don't take any chances; for, disagreeable as you are, I don't wish to be left here alone."

"Thank you, Miss Sommerton."

The artist stood on the point of rock, and, holding by a branch of a tree, peered out over the river.

"Oh, Mr. Trenton, don't do that!" cried the young lady, with alarm.

"Please come back."

"Say 'John,' then," replied the gentleman.

"Oh, Mr. Trenton, don't!" she cried as he leaned still further over the water, straining the branch to its utmost.

"Say 'John.'"

"Mr. Trenton."

"'John.'"

The branch cracked ominously as Trenton leaned yet a little further.

"John!" cried the young lady, sharply, "cease your fooling and come down from that rock."

The artist instantly recovered his position, and, coming back, sprang down to the ground again.

Miss Sommerton drew back in alarm; but Trenton merely put his hands in his pockets, and said—

"Well, Eva, I came back because you called me."

"It was a case of coercion," she said. "You English are too fond of coercion. We Americans are against it."

"Oh, I am a Home Ruler, if you are," replied the artist. "Miss Eva, I am going to risk my third and last question, and I shall await the answer with more anxiety than I ever felt before in my life. The question is this: Will—"

"Hello! there you are. Thank Heaven! I was never so glad to see anybody in my life," cried the cheery voice of Ed. Mason, as he broke through the bushes towards them.

Trenton looked around with anything but a welcome on his brow. If Mason had never been so glad in his life to see anybody, it was quite evident his feeling was not entirely reciprocated by the artist.

"How the deuce did you get here?" asked Trenton. "I was just looking for you down the river."

"Well, you see, we kept pretty close to the shore. I doubt if you could have seen us. Didn't you hear us shout?"

"No, we didn't hear anything. We didn't hear them shout, did we, Miss Sommerton?"

"No," replied that young woman, looking at the dying fire, whose glowing embers seemed to redden her face.

"Why, do you know," said Mason, "it looks as if you had been quarrelling. I guess I came just in the nick of time."

"You are always just in time, Mr. Mason," said Miss Sommerton. "For we were quarrelling, as you say. The subject of the quarrel is which of us was rightful owner of that canoe."

Mason laughed heartily, while Miss Sommerton frowned at him with marked disapprobation.

"Then you found me out, did you? Well, I expected you would before the day was over. You see, it isn't often that I have to deal with two such particular people in the same day. Still, I guess the ownership of the canoe doesn't amount to much now. I'll give it to the one who finds it."

"Oh, Mr. Mason," cried Miss Sommerton, "did the two men escape all right?"

"Why, certainly, I have just been giving them 'Hail Columbia,' because they didn't come back to you; but you see, a little distance down, the bank gets very steep—so much so that it is impossible to climb it, and then the woods here are thick and hard to work a person's way through. So they thought it best to come down and tell me, and we have brought two canoes up with us."

"Does Mrs. Mason know of the accident?"

"No, she doesn't; but she is just as anxious as if she did. She can't think what in the world keeps you."

"She doesn't realise," said the artist, "what strong attractions the

72

Shawenegan Falls have for people alive to the beauties of nature."

"Well," said Mason, "we mustn't stand here talking. You must be about frozen to death." Here he shouted to one of the men to come up and put out the fire.

"Oh, don't bother," said the artist; "it will soon burn out."

"Oh yes," put in Ed. Mason; "and if a wind should happen to rise in the night, where would my pine forest be? I don't propose to have a whole section of the country burnt up to commemorate the quarrel between you two."

The half-breed flung the biggest brand into the river, and speedily trampled out the rest, carrying up some water in his hat to pour on the centre of the fire. This done, they stepped into the canoe and were soon on their way down the river. Reaching the landing, the artist gave his hand to Miss Sommerton and aided her out on the bank.

"Miss Sommerton," he whispered to her, "I intended to sail to-morrow. I shall leave it for you to say whether I shall go or not."

"You will not sail," said Miss Sommerton promptly.

"Oh, thank you," cried the artist; "you do not know how happy that makes me."

"Why should it?"

"Well, you know what I infer from your answer."

"My dear sir, I said that you would not sail, and you will not, for this reason: To sail you require to catch to-night's train for Montreal, and take the train from there to New York to get your boat. You cannot catch to-night's train, and, therefore, cannot get to your steamer. I never before saw a man so glad to miss his train or his boat. Good-night, Mr. Trenton. Good-night, Mr. Mason," she cried aloud to that gentleman, as she disappeared toward the house.

"You two appear to be quite friendly," said Mr. Mason to the artist.

"Do we? Appearances are deceitful. I really cannot tell at this moment whether we are friends or enemies."

"Well, not enemies, I am sure. Miss Eva is a very nice girl when you understand her."

"Do you understand her?" asked the artist.

"I can't say that I do. Come to think of it, I don't think anybody does."

"In that case, then, for all practical purposes, she might just as well not be a nice girl."

"Ah, well, you may change your opinion some day—when you get better acquainted with her," said Mason, shaking hands with his friend. "And now that you have missed your train, anyhow, I don't suppose you care for a very early start to-morrow. Good-night."

Chapter VII

After Trenton awoke next morning he thought the situation over very calmly, and resolved to have question number three answered that day if possible.

When called to breakfast he found Ed. Mason at the head of the table.

"Shan't we wait for the ladies?" asked the artist.

"I don't think we'd better. You see we might have to wait quite a long time. I don't know when Miss Sommerton will be here again, and it will be a week at least before Mrs. Mason comes back. They are more than half-way to Three Rivers by this time."

"Good gracious!" cried Trenton, abashed; "why didn't you call me? I should have liked very much to have accompanied them."

"Oh, they wouldn't hear of your being disturbed; and besides, Mr. Trenton, our American ladies are quite in the habit of looking after themselves. I found that out long ago."

"I suppose there is nothing for it but get out my buckboard and get back to Three Rivers."

"Oh, I dismissed your driver long ago," said the lumberman. "I'll take you there in my buggy. I am going out to Three Rivers to-day anyhow."

"No chance of overtaking the ladies?" asked Trenton.

"I don't think so. We may overtake Mrs. Mason but I imagine Miss Sommerton will be either at Quebec or Montreal before we reach Three Rivers. I don't know in which direction she is going. You seem to be somewhat interested in that young lady. Purely artistic admiration, I presume. She is rather a striking girl. Well, you certainly have made the most of your opportunities. Let's see, you have known her now for quite a long while. Must be nearly twenty-four hours."

"Oh, don't underestimate it, Mason; quite thirty-six hours at least."

"So long as that? Ah, well, I don't wish to discourage you; but I wouldn't be too sure of her if I were you."

"Sure of her! Why, I am not sure of anything."

"Well, that is the proper spirit. You Englishmen are rather apt to take things for granted. I think you would make a mistake in this case if you were too sure. You are not the only man who has tried to awaken the interest of Miss Sommerton of Boston."

"I didn't suppose that I was. Nevertheless, I am going to Boston."

"Well, it's a nice town," said Mason, with a noncommittal air. "It hasn't the advantages of Three Rivers, of course; but still it is a very attractive place in some respects."

"In some respects, yes," said the artist.

* * * * *

Two days later Mr. John Trenton called at the house on Beacon Street.

"Miss Sommerton is not at home," said the servant. "She is in Canada somewhere."

And so Mr. Trenton went back to his hotel.

The artist resolved to live quietly in Boston until Miss Sommerton returned. Then the fateful number three could be answered. He determined not to present any of his letters of introduction. When he came to Boston first, he thought he would like to see something of society, of the art world in that city, if there was an art world, and of the people; but he had come and gone without being invited anywhere, and now he anticipated no trouble in living a quiet life, and thinking occasionally over the situation. But during his absence it appeared Boston had awakened to the fact that in its midst had resided a real live artist of prominence from the other side, and nothing had been done to overcome his prejudices, and show him that, after all, the real intellectual centre of the world was not London, but the capital of

Massachusetts.

The first day he spent in his hotel he was called upon by a young gentleman whose card proclaimed him a reporter on one of the large daily papers.

"You are Mr. Trenton, the celebrated English artist, are you not?"

"My name is Trenton, and by profession I am an artist. But I do not claim the adjective, 'celebrated.'"

"All right. You are the man I am after. Now, I should like to know what you think of the art movement in America?"

"Well, really, I have been in America but a very short time, and during that time I have had no opportunity of seeing the work of your artists or of visiting any collections, so you see I cannot give an opinion."

"Met any of our American artists?"

"I have in Europe, yes. Quite a number of them, and very talented gentlemen some of them are, too."

"I suppose Europe lays over this country in the matter of art, don't it?"

"I beg your pardon."

"Knocks the spots out of us in pictures?"

"I don't know that I quite follow you. Do you mean that we produce pictures more rapidly than you do here?"

"No, I just mean the whole tout ensemble of the thing. They are 'way ahead of us, are they not, in art?"

"Well, you see, as I said before—really, I am not in a position to make any comparison, because I am entirely ignorant of American painting. It seems to me that certain branches of art ought to flourish here. There is no country in the world with grander scenery than America."

"Been out to the Rockies?"

"Where is that?"

"To the Rocky Mountains?"

"Oh no, no. You see I have been only a few weeks in this country. I have confined my attention to Canada mainly, the Quebec region and around there, although I have been among the White Mountains, and the Catskills, and the Adirondacks."

"What school of art do you belong to?"

"School? Well, I don't know that I belong to any. May I ask if you are a connoisseur in art matters. Are you the art critic of your journal?"

"Me? No—oh no. I don't know the first darn thing about it. That's why they sent me."

"Well, I should have thought, if he wished to get anything worth publishing, your editor would have sent somebody who was at least familiar with the subject he has to write about."

"I dare say; but, that ain't the way to get snappy articles written. You take an art man, now, for instance; he's prejudiced. He thinks one school is all right, and another school isn't; and he is apt to work in his own fads. Now, if our man liked the French school, and despised the English school, or the German school, if there is one, or the Italian school, whatever it happened to be, and you went against that; why, don't you see, he would think you didn't know anything, and write you up that way. Now, I am perfectly unprejudiced. I want to write a good readable article, and I don't care a hang which school is the best or the worst, or anything else about it."

"Ah! I see. Well, in that case, you certainly approach your work without bias."

"You bet I do. Now, who do you think is the best painter in England?"

"In what line?"

"Well, in any line. Who stands ahead? Who's the leader? Who tops them all? Who's the Raphael?"

"I don't know that we have any Raphael? We have good painters each in his own branch."

"Isn't there one, in your opinion, that is 'way ahead of all the rest?"

"Well, you see, to make an intelligent comparison, you have to take into consideration the specialty of the painter. You could hardly compare Alma Tadema, for instance, with Sir John Millais, or Sir Frederic Leighton with Hubert Herkomer, or any of them with some of your own painters. Each has his specialty, and each stands at the head of it."

"Then there is no one man in England like Old Man Rubens, or Van Dyke, or those other fellows, I forget their names, who are head and shoulders above everybody else? Sort of Jay Gould in art, you know."

"No, I wouldn't like to say there is. In fact, all of your questions require some consideration. Now, if you will write them down for me, and give me time to think them over, I will write out such answers as occur to me. It would be impossible for me to do justice to myself, or to art, or to your paper, by attempting to answer questions off-hand in this way."

"Oh, that's too slow for our time here. You know this thing comes out to-morrow morning, and I have got to do a column and a half of it. Sometimes, you know, it is very difficult; but you are different from most Englishmen I have talked with. You speak right out, and you talk to a fellow. I can make a column and a half out of what you have said now."

"Dear me! Can you really? Well, now, I should be careful, if I were you. I am afraid that, if you don't understand anything about art, you may give the public some very erroneous impressions."

"Oh, the public don't care a hang. All they want is to read something snappy and bright. That's what the public want. No, sir, we have catered too long for the public not to know what its size is. You might print the most learned article you could get hold of, it might be written by What's-his-name De Vinci, and be full of art slang, and all that sort of thing, but it wouldn't touch the general public at all."

"I don't suppose it would."

"What do you think of our Sunday papers here? You don't have any Sunday papers over in London."

"Oh yes, we do. But none of the big dailies have Sunday editions."

"They are not as big, or as enterprising as ours, are they? One Sunday paper, you know, prints about as much as two or three thirty-five cent magazines."

"What, the Sunday paper does?"

"Yes, the Sunday paper prints it, but doesn't sell for that. We give 'em more for the money than any magazine you ever saw."

"You certainly print some very large papers."

With this the reporter took his leave, and next morning Mr. Trenton saw the most astonishing account of his ideas on art matters imaginable. What struck him most forcibly was, that an article written by a person who admittedly knew nothing at all about art should be in general so free from error. The interview had a great number of head lines, and it was evident the paper desired to treat the artist with the utmost respect, and that it felt he showed his sense in preferring Boston to New York as a place of temporary residence; but what appalled him was the free and easy criticisms he was credited with having made on his own contemporaries in England. The principal points of each were summed up with a great deal of terseness and force, and in many cases were laughably true to life. It was evident that whoever touched up that interview possessed a very clear opinion and very accurate knowledge of the art movement in England.

Mr. Trenton thought he would sit down and write to the editor of the paper, correcting some of the more glaring inaccuracies; but a friend said—

"Oh, it is no use. Never mind. Nobody pays any attention to that. It's all right anyhow."

"Yes, but suppose the article should be copied in England, or suppose some of the papers should get over there?"

"Oh, that'll be all right," said his friend, with easy optimism. "Don't bother about it. They all know what a newspaper interview is; if they don't, why, you can tell them when you get back."

It was not long before Mr. Trenton found himself put down at all the principal clubs, both artistic and literary; and he also became, with a suddenness that bewildered him, quite the social lion for the time being. He was astonished to find that the receptions to which he was invited, and where he was, in a way, on exhibition, were really very grand occasions, and compared favourably with the finest gatherings he had had experience of in London.

His hostess at one of these receptions said to him, "Mr. Trenton, I want to introduce you to some of our art lovers in this city, whom I am sure you will be pleased to meet. I know that as a general thing the real artists are apt to despise the amateurs; but in this instance I hope you will be kind enough not to despise them, for my sake. We think they are really very clever indeed, and we like to be flattered by foreign preference."

"Am I the foreign preference in this instance?"

"You are, Mr. Trenton."

"Now, I think it is too bad of you to say that, just when I have begun to feel as much at home in Boston as I do in London. I assure you I do not feel in the least foreign here. Neither do I maintain, like Mrs. Brown, that you are the foreigners."

"How very nice of you to say so, Mr. Trenton. Now I hope you will say something like that to the young lady I want you to meet. She is really very charming, and I am sure you will like her; and I may say, in parenthesis, that she, like the rest of us, is perfectly infatuated with your pictures."

As the lady said this, she brought Mr. Trenton in her wake, as it were, and said, "Miss Sommerton, allow me to present to you Mr. Trenton."

Miss Sommerton rose with graceful indolence, and held out her hand frankly to the artist. "Mr. Trenton," she said, "I am very pleased indeed to meet you. Have you been long in Boston?"

"Only a few days," replied Trenton. "I came up to Boston from Canada a short time since."

"Up? You mean down. We don't say up from Canada."

"Oh, don't you? Well, in England, you know, we say up to London, no matter from what part of the country we approach it. I think you are wrong in saying down, I think it really ought to be up to Boston from wherever you come."

His hostess appeared to be delighted with this bit of conversation, and she said, "I shall leave you two together for a few moments to get acquainted. Mr. Trenton, you know you are in demand this evening."

"Do you think that is true?" said Trenton to Miss Sommerton.

"What?"

"Well, that I am in demand."

"I suppose it is true, if Mrs. Lennox says it is. You surely don't intend to cast any doubt on the word of your hostess, do you?"

"Oh, not at all. I didn't mean in a general way, you know, I meant in particular."

"I don't think I understand you, Mr. Trenton. By the way, you said you had been in Canada. Do you not think it is a very charming country?"

"Charming, Miss Sommerton, isn't the word for it. It is the most delightful country in the world."

"Ah, you say that because it belongs to England. I admit it is very delightful; but then there are other places on the Continent quite as beautiful as any part of Canada. You seem to have a prejudice in favour of monarchical institutions."

"Oh, is Canada monarchical? I didn't know that. I thought Canada was quite republican in its form of government."

"Well, it is a dependency; that's what I despise about Canada. Think of a glorious country like that, with hundreds of thousands of square miles, in fact, millions, I think, being dependent on a little island, away there among the fogs and rains, between the North Sea and the Atlantic Ocean. To be a dependency of some splendid tyrannical power like Russia wouldn't be so bad; but to be dependent on that little island—I lose all my respect for Canada when I think of it."

"Well, you know, the United States were colonies once."

"Ah, that is a very unfortunate comparison, Mr. Trenton. The moment the colonies, as you call them, came to years of discretion, they soon shook off their dependency. You must remember you are at Boston, and that the harbour is only a short distance from here."

"Does that mean that I should take advantage of its proximity and leave?"

"Oh, not at all. I could not say anything so rude, Mr. Trenton. Perhaps you are not familiar with the history of our trouble with England? Don't you remember it commenced in Boston Harbour practically?"

"Oh yes, I recollect now. I had forgotten it. Something about tea, was it not?"

"Yes, something about tea."

"Well, talking of tea, Miss Sommerton, may I take you to the conservatory and bring you a cup of it?"

"May I have an ice instead of the tea, if I prefer it, Mr. Trenton?"

"Why, certainly. You see how I am already dropping into the American phraseology."

"Oh, I think you are improving wonderfully, Mr. Trenton."

When they reached the conservatory, Miss Sommerton said—

"This is really a very great breach of good manners on both your part and mine. I have taken away the lion of the evening, and the lion has forgotten his duty to his hostess and to the other guests."

"Well, you see, I wanted to learn more of your ideas in the matter of dependencies. I don't at all agree with you on that. Now, I think if a country is conquered, it ought to be a dependency of the conquering people. It is the right of conquest. I—I am a thorough believer in the right of conquest."

"You seem to have very settled opinions on the matter, Mr. Trenton."

"I have indeed, Miss Sommerton. It is said that an Englishman never knows when he is conquered. Now I think that is a great mistake. There is no one so quick as an Englishman to admit that he has met his match."

"Why, have you met your match already, Mr. Trenton? Let me congratulate you."

"Well, don't congratulate me just yet. I am not at all certain whether I shall need any congratulations or not."

"I am sure I hope you will be very successful."

"Do you mean that?"

Miss Sommerton looked at him quietly for a moment.

"Do you think," she said, "I am in the habit of saying things I do not mean?"

"I think you are."

"Well, you are not a bit more complimentary than—than—you used to be."

"You were going to say than I was on the banks of the St. Maurice?"

"Oh, you visited the St. Maurice, did you? How far away from Boston that seems, doesn't it?"

"It is indeed a great distance, Miss Sommerton. But apparently not half as long as the round-about way we are traveling just now. Miss Sommerton, I waited and waited in Boston for you to return. I want to be a dependence. I admit the conquest. I wish to swear fealty to Miss Eva Sommerton of Boston, and now I ask my third question, will you accept the allegiance?"

Miss Sommerton was a little slow in replying, and before she had spoken Mrs. Lennox bustled in, and said—

"Oh, Mr. Trenton, I have been looking everywhere for you. There are a hundred people here who wish to be introduced, and all at once. May I have him, Miss Sommerton?"

"Well, Mrs. Lennox, you know, if I said 'Yes,' that would imply a certain ownership in him."

"I brought Miss Sommerton here to get her to accept an ice from me, which as yet I have not had the privilege of bringing. Will you accept—the ice, Miss Sommerton?"

The young lady blushed, as she looked at the artist.

"Yes," she said with a sigh; the tone was almost inaudible.

The artist hurried away to bring the refreshment.

"Why, Eva Sommerton," cried Mrs. Lennox, "you accept a plate of ice cream as tragically as if you were giving the answer to a proposal."

Mrs. Lennox said afterward that she thought there was something very peculiar about Miss Sommerton's smile in reply to her remark.

The Heralds of Fame

Chapter I

Now, when each man's place in literature is so clearly defined, it seems ridiculous to state that there was a time when Kenan Buel thought J. Lawless Hodden a great novelist. One would have imagined that Buel's keen insight into human nature would have made such a mistake impossible, but it must be remembered that Buel was always more or less of a hero-worshipper. It seems strange in the light of our after-knowledge that there ever was a day when Hodden's books were selling by the thousand, and Buel was tramping the streets of London fruitlessly searching for a publisher. Not less strange is the fact that Buel thought Hodden's success well deserved. He would have felt honoured by the touch of Hodden's hand.

No convict ever climbed a treadmill with more hopeless despair than Buel worked in his little room under the lofty roof. He knew no one; there were none to speak to him a cheering or comforting word; he was ignorant even of the names of the men who accepted the articles from his pen, which appeared unsigned in the daily papers and in some of the weeklies. He got cheques—small ones—with illegible and impersonal signatures that told him nothing. But the bits of paper were honoured at the bank, and this lucky fact enabled him to live and write books which publishers would not look at.

Nevertheless, showing how all things are possible to a desperate and resolute man, two of his books had already seen the light, if it could be called light. The first he was still paying for, on the instalment plan. The publishers were to pay half, and he was to pay half. This seemed to him only a fair division of the risk at the time. Not a single paper had paid the slightest attention to the book. The universal ignoring of it disheartened him. He had been prepared for abuse, but not for impenetrable silence.

He succeeded in getting another and more respectable publisher to take up his next book on a royalty arrangement. This was a surprise to him, and a gratification. His satisfaction did not last long after the book came out. It was mercilessly slated. One paper advised him to read "Hodden;" another said he had plagiarized from that popular writer. The criticisms cut him like a whip. He wondered why he had rebelled at the previous silence. He felt like a man who had heedlessly hurled a stone at a snow mountain and had been buried by the resulting avalanche.

He got his third publisher a year after that. He thought he would never succeed in getting the same firm twice, and wondered what would happen when he exhausted the London list. It is not right that a man should go on for ever without a word of encouragement. Fate recognised that there would come a breaking-point, and relented in time. The word came from an unexpected source. Buel was labouring, heavy-eyed, at the last proof-sheets of his third book, and was wondering whether he would have the courage not to look at the newspapers when the volume was published. He wished he could afford to go to some wilderness until the worst was over. He knew he could not miss the first notice, for experience had taught him that Snippit & Co., a clipping agency, would send it to him, with a nice type-written letter, saying—

"Dear Sir,

"As your book is certain to attract a great deal of attention from the Press, we shall be pleased to send you clippings similar to the enclosed at the following rates."

It struck him as rather funny that any company should expect a sane man to pay so much good money for Press notices, mostly abusive. He never subscribed.

The word of encouragement gave notice of its approach in a letter, signed by a man of whom he had never heard. It was forwarded to him by his publishers. The letter ran:—

"Dear Sir,

"Can you make it convenient to lunch with me on Friday at the

Métropole? If you have an engagement for that day can you further oblige me by writing and putting it off? Tell the other fellow you are ill or have broken your leg, or anything, and charge up the fiction to me. I deal in fiction, anyhow. I leave on Saturday for the Continent, not wishing to spend another Sunday in London if I can avoid it. I have arranged to get out your book in America, having read the proof-sheets at your publisher's. All the business part of the transaction is settled, but I would like to see you personally if you don't mind, to have a talk over the future—always an interesting subject. "Yours very truly, "L. F. BRANT, "Of Rainham Bros., Publishers, New York."

Buel read this letter over and over again. He had never seen anything exactly like it. There was a genial flippancy about it that was new to him, and he wondered what sort of a man the New Yorker was. Mr. Brant wrote to a stranger with the familiarity of an old friend, yet the letter warmed Buel's heart. He smiled at the idea the American evidently had about a previous engagement. Invitations to lunch become frequent when a man does not need them. No broken leg story would have to be told. He wrote and accepted Mr. Brant's invitation.

"You're Mr. Buel, I think?"

The stranger's hand rested lightly on the young author's shoulder. Buel had just entered the unfamiliar precincts of the Métropole Hotel. The tall man with the gold lace on his hat had hesitated a moment before he swung open the big door, Buel was so evidently not a guest of the hotel.

"My name is Buel."

"Then you're my victim. I've been waiting impatiently for you. I am L. F. Brant."

"I thought I was in time. I am sorry to have kept you waiting."

"Don't mention it. I have been waiting but thirty seconds. Come up in the elevator. They call it a lift here, not knowing any better, but it gets there ultimately. I have the title-deeds to a little parlour while I am staying in this tavern, and I thought we could talk better if we had lunch there. Lunch costs more on that basis, but I guess we can stand it."

A cold shudder passed over the thin frame of Kenan Buel. He did not know but it was the custom in America to ask a man to lunch and expect him to pay half. Brant's use of the plural lent colour to this view, and Buel knew he could not pay his share. He regretted they were not in a vegetarian restaurant.

The table in the centre of the room was already set for two, and the array of wine-glasses around each plate looked tempting. Brant pushed the electric button, drew up his chair, and said—

"Sit down, Buel, sit down. What's your favourite brand of wine? Let's settle on it now, so as to have no unseemly wrangle when the waiter comes. I'm rather in awe of the waiter. It doesn't seem natural that any mere human man should be so obviously superior to the rest of us mortals as this waiter is. I'm going to give you only the choice of the first wines. I have taken the champagne for granted, and it's cooling now in a tub somewhere. We always drink champagne in the States, not because we like it, but because it's expensive. I calculate that I pay the expenses of my trip over here merely by ordering unlimited champagne. I save more than a dollar a bottle on New York prices, and these saved dollars count up in a month. Personally I prefer cider or lager beer, but in New York we dare not own to liking a thing unless it is expensive."

"It can hardly be a pleasant place for a poor man to live in, if that is the case."

"My dear Buel, no city is a pleasant place for a poor man to live in. I don't suppose New York is worse than London in that respect. The poor have a hard time of it anywhere. A man owes it to himself and family not to be poor. Now, that's one thing I like about your book; you touch on poverty in a sympathetic way, by George, like a man who had come through it himself. I've been there, and I know how it is. When I first struck New York I hadn't even a ragged dollar bill to my back. Of course every successful man will tell you the same of himself, but it is mostly brag, and in half the instances it isn't true at all; but in my case—well, I wasn't subscribing to the heathen in those days. I made up my mind that poverty didn't pay, and I have succeeded in remedying the state of affairs. But I haven't forgotten how it felt to be hard up, and I sympathise with those who are. Nothing would afford me greater pleasure than to give a helping hand to a fellow—that is, to a clever fellow who was worth saving—who is down at bed rock. Don't you feel that way too?"

"Yes," said Buel, with some hesitation, "it would be a pleasure."

"I knew when I read your book you felt that way—I was sure of it. Well, I've helped a few in my time; but I regret to say most of them turned out to be no good. That is where the trouble is. Those who are really deserving are just the persons who die of starvation in a garret, and never let the outside world know their trouble."

"I do not doubt such is often the case."

"Of course it is. It's always the case. But here's the soup. I hope you have brought a good appetite. You can't expect such a meal here as you would get in New York; but they do fairly well. I, for one, don't grumble about the food in London, as most Americans do. Londoners manage to keep alive, and that, after all, is the main thing."

Buel was perfectly satisfied with the meal, and thought if they produced a better one in New York, or anywhere else, the art of cookery had reached wonderful perfection. Brant, however, kept apologising for the spread as he went along. The talk drifted on in an apparently aimless fashion, but the publisher was a shrewd man, and he was gradually leading it up to the point he had in view from the beginning, and all the while he was taking the measure of his guest. He was not a man to waste either his time or his dinners without an object. When he had once "sized up" his man, as he termed it, he was either exceedingly frank and open with him, or the exact opposite, as suited his purpose. He told Buel that he came to England once a year, if possible, rapidly scanned the works of fiction about to be published by the various houses in London, and made arrangements for the producing of those in America that he thought would go down with the American people.

"I suppose," said Buel, "that you have met many of the noted authors of this country?"

"All of them, I think; all of them, at one time or another. The publishing business has its drawbacks like every other trade," replied Brant, jauntily.

"Have you met Hodden?"

"Several times. Conceited ass!"

"You astonish me. I have never had the good fortune to become acquainted with any of our celebrated writers. I would think it a privilege to know Hodden and some of the others."

"You're lucky, and you evidently don't know it. I would rather meet a duke any day than a famous author. The duke puts on less side and patronises you less."

"I would rather be a celebrated author than a duke if I had my choice."

"Well, being a free and independent citizen of the Democratic United States, I wouldn't. No, sir! I would rather be Duke Brant any day in the week than Mr. Brant, the talented author of, etc., etc. The moment an author receives a little praise and becomes talked about, he gets what we call in the States 'the swelled head.' I've seen some of the nicest fellows in the world become utterly spoiled by a little success. And then think of the absurdity of it all. There aren't more than two or three at the most of the present-day writers who will be heard of a century hence. Read the history of literature, and you will find that never more than four men in any one generation are heard of after. Four is a liberal allowance. What has any writer to be conceited about anyhow? Let him read his Shakespeare and be modest."

Buel said with a sigh, "I wish there was success in store for me. I would risk the malady you call the 'swelled head.'"

"Success will come all right enough, my boy. 'All things come to him who waits,' and while he is waiting puts in some good, strong days of work. It's the working that tells, not the waiting. And now, if you will light one of these cigars, we will talk of you for a while, if your modesty will stand it. What kind of Chartreuse will you have? Yellow or green?"

"Either."

"Take the green, then. Where the price is the same I always take the green. It is the stronger, and you get more for your money. Now then, I will be perfectly frank with you. I read your book in the proof-sheets, and I ran it down in great style to your publisher."

"I am sorry you did not like it."

"I don't say I didn't like it. I ran it down because it was business. I made up my mind when I read that book to give a hundred pounds for the American rights. I got it for twenty."

Brant laughed, and Buel felt uncomfortable. He feared that after all he did not like this frank American.

"Having settled about the book, I wanted to see you, and here you are. Of course, I am utterly selfish in wanting to see you, for I wish you to promise me that we will have the right of publishing your books in America as long as we pay as much as any other publisher. There is nothing unfair in that, is there?"

"No. I may warn you, however, that there has been no great competition, so far, for the privilege of doing any publishing, either here or in America."

"That's all right. Unless I'm a Dutchman there will be, after your new book is published. Of course, that is one of the things no fellow can find out. If he could, publishing would be less of a lottery than it is. A book is sometimes a success by the merest fluke; at other times, in spite of everything, a good book is a deplorable failure. I think yours will go; anyhow, I am willing to bet on it up to a certain amount, and if it does go, I want to have the first look-in at your future books. What do you say?"

"Do you wish me to sign a contract?"

"No, I merely want your word. You may write me a letter if you like, that I could show to my partners, saying that we would have the first refusal of your future books."

"I am quite willing to do that."

"Very good. That's settled. Now, you look fagged out. I wish you would take a trip over to New York. I'll look after you when you get there. It would do you a world of good, and would show in the pages of your next book. What do you say to that? Have you any engagements that would prevent you making the trip?"

Buel laughed, "I am perfectly free as far as engagements are concerned."

"That's all right, then. I wish I were in that position. Now, as I said, I considered your book cheap at £100. I got it for £20. I propose to hand over the £80 to you. I'll write out the cheque as soon as the waiters clear away the débris. Then your letter to the firm would form the receipt for this money, and—well, it need not be a contract, you know, or anything formal, but just your ideas on any future business that may crop up."

"I must say I think your offer is very generous."

"Oh, not at all. It is merely business. The £80 is on account of royalties. If the book goes, as I think it will, I hope to pay you much more than that. Now I hope you will come over and see me as soon as you can."

"Yes. As you say, the trip will do me good. I have been rather hard at it for some time."

"Then I'll look out for you. I sail on the French line Saturday week. When will you come?"

"As soon as my book is out here, and before any of the reviews appear."

"Sensible man. What's your cable address?"

"I haven't one."

"Well, I suppose a telegram to your publishers will find you. I'll cable if anything turns up unexpectedly. You send me over a despatch saying what steamer you sail on. My address is 'Rushing, New York.' Just cable the name of the steamer, and I will be on the look-out for you."

It was doubtless the effect of the champagne, for Buel went back to his squalid room with his mind in the clouds. He wondered if this condition was the first indication of the swelled head Brant had talked about. Buel worked harder than ever at his proofs, and there was some growling at head-quarters because of the numerous corrections he made. These changes were regarded as impudence on the part of so unknown a man. He sent off to America a set of the corrected proofs, and received a cablegram, "Proofs received. Too late. Book published today."

This was a disappointment. Still he had the consolation of knowing that the English edition would be as perfect as he could make it. He secured a berth on the Geranium, sailing from Liverpool, and cabled Brant to that effect. The day before he sailed he got a cablegram that bewildered him. It was simply, "She's a-booming." He regretted that he had never learned the American language.

Chapter II

Kenan Buel received from his London publisher a brown paper parcel, and on opening it found the contents to be six exceedingly new copies of his book. Whatever the publisher thought of the inside of the work, he had not spared pains to make the outside as attractive as it could be made at the price. Buel turned it over and over, and could almost imagine himself buying a book that looked so tastefully got up as this one. The sight of the volume gave him a thrill, for he remembered that the Press doubtless received its quota at about the same time his parcel came, and he feared he would not be out of the country before the first extract from the clipping agency arrived. However, luck was with the young man, and he found himself on the platform of Euston Station, waiting for the Liverpool express, without having seen anything about his book in the papers, except a brief line giving its title, the price, and his own name, in the "Books Received" column.

As he lingered around the well-kept bookstall before the train left, he saw a long row of Hodden's new novel, and then his heart gave a jump as he caught sight of two copies of his own work in the row labelled "New Books." He wanted to ask the clerk whether any of them had been sold yet, but in the first place he lacked the courage, and in the second place the clerk was very busy. As he stood there, a comely young woman, equipped for traveling, approached the stall, and ran her eye hurriedly up and down the tempting array of literature. She bought several of the illustrated papers, and then scanned the new books. The clerk, following her eye, picked out Buel's book.

"Just out, miss. Three and sixpence."

"Who is the author?" asked the girl.

"Kenan Buel, a new man," answered the clerk, without a moment's hesitation, and without looking at the title-page. "Very clever work."

Buel was astonished at the knowledge shown by the clerk. He knew that W.H. Smith & Son never had a book of his before, and he wondered how the clerk apparently knew so much of the volume and its author, forgetting that it was the clerk's business. The girl listlessly ran the leaves of the book past the edge of her thumb. It seemed to Buel that the fate of the whole edition was in her hands, and he watched her breathlessly, even forgetting how charming she looked. There stood the merchant eager to sell, and there, in the form of a young woman, was the great public. If she did not buy, why should any one else; and if nobody bought, what chance had an unknown author?

She put the book down, and looked up as she heard some one sigh deeply near her.

"Have you Hodden's new book?" she asked.

"Yes, miss. Six shillings."

The clerk quickly put Buel's book beside its lone companion, and took down Hodden's.

"Thank you," said the girl, giving him a half sovereign; and, taking the change, she departed with her bundle of literature to the train.

Buel said afterwards that what hurt him most in this painful incident was the fact that if it were repeated often the bookstall clerk would lose faith in the book. He had done so well for a man who could not possibly have read a word of the volume, that Buel felt sorry on the clerk's account rather than his own that the copy had not been sold. He walked to the end of the platform, and then back to the bookstall.

"Has that new book of Buel's come out yet?" he asked the clerk in an unconcerned tone.

"Yes, sir. Here it is; three and sixpence, sir."

"Thank you," said Buel, putting his hand in his pocket for the money. "How is it selling?"

"Well, sir, there won't be much call for it, not likely, till the reviews begin to come out."

There, Mr. Buel, you had a lesson, if you had only taken it to heart, or pondered on its meaning. Since then you have often been very scornful of newspaper reviews, yet you saw yourself how the great public treats a man who is not even abused. How were you to know that the column of grossly unfair rancour which The Daily Argus poured out on your book two days later, when you were sailing serenely over the Atlantic, would make that same clerk send in four separate orders to the "House" during the week? Medicine may have a bad taste, and yet have beneficial results. So Mr. Kenan Buel, after buying a book of which he had six copies in his portmanteau, with no one to give them to, took his place in the train, and in due time found himself at Liverpool and on board the Geranium.

The stewards being busy, Buel placed his portmanteau on the deck, and, with his newly bought volume in his hand, the string and brown paper still around it, he walked up and down on the empty side of the deck, noticing how scrupulously clean the ship was. It was the first time he had ever been on board a steamship, and he could not trust himself unguided to explore the depths below, and see what kind of a state-room and what sort of a companion chance had allotted to him. They had told him when he bought his ticket that the steamer would be very crowded that trip, so many Americans were returning; but his state-room had berths for only two, and he had a faint hope the other fellow would not turn up. As he paced the deck his thoughts wandered to the pretty girl who did not buy his book. He had seen her again on the tender in company with a serene and placid older woman, who sat unconcernedly, surrounded by bundles, shawls, straps, valises, and hand-bags, which the girl nervously counted every now and then, fruitlessly trying to convince the elderly lady that something must have been left behind in the train, or lost in transit from the station to the steamer. The worry of travel, which the elderly woman absolutely refused to share, seemed to rest with double weight on the shoulders of the girl.

As Buel thought of all this, he saw the girl approach him along the deck with a smile of apparent recognition on her face. "She evidently mistakes me for some one else," he said to himself. "Oh, thank you," she cried, coming near, and holding out her hand. "I see you have found my book."

He helplessly held out the package to her, which she took.

"Is it yours?" he asked.

"Yes, I recognised it by the string. I bought it at Euston Station. I am forever losing things," she added. "Thank you, ever so much."

Buel laughed to himself as she disappeared. "Fate evidently intends her to read my book," he said to himself. "She will think the clerk has made a mistake. I must get her unbiased opinion of it before the voyage ends."

The voyage at that moment was just beginning, and the thud, thud of the screw brought that fact to his knowledge. He sought a steward, and asked him to carry the portmanteau to berth 159.

"You don't happen to know whether there is any one else in that room or not, do you?" he asked.

"It's likely there is, sir. The ship's very full this voyage."

Buel followed him into the saloon, and along the seemingly interminable passage; then down a narrow side alley, into which a door opened marked 159-160. The steward rapped at the door, and, as there was no response, opened it. All hopes of a room to himself vanished as Buel looked into the small state-room. There was a steamer trunk on the floor, a portmanteau on the seat, while the two bunks were covered with a miscellaneous assortment of hand-bags, shawl-strap bundles, and packages.

The steward smiled. "I think he wants a room to himself," he said.

On the trunk Buel noticed the name in white letters "Hodden," and instantly there arose within him a hope that his companion was to be the celebrated novelist. This hope was strengthened when he saw on the portmanteau the letters "J. L. H.," which were the novelist's initials. He pictured to himself interesting conversations on the way over, and hoped he would receive some particulars from the novelist's own lips of his early struggles for fame. Still, he did not allow himself to build too much on his supposition, for there are a great many people in this world, and the chances were that the traveller would be some commonplace individual of the same name.

98

The steward placed Buel's portmanteau beside the other, and backed out of the overflowing cabin. All doubt as to the identity of the other occupant was put at rest by the appearance down the passage of a man whom Buel instantly recognised by the portraits he had seen of him in the illustrated papers. He was older than the pictures made him appear, and there was a certain querulous expression on his face which was also absent in the portraits. He glanced into the state-room, looked for a moment through Buel, and then turned to the steward.

"What do you mean by putting that portmanteau into my room?"

"This gentleman has the upper berth, sir."

"Nonsense. The entire room is mine. Take the portmanteau out."

The steward hesitated, looking from one to the other.

"The ticket is for 159, sir," he said at last.

"Then there is some mistake. The room is mine. Don't have me ask you again to remove the portmanteau."

"Perhaps you would like to see the purser, sir."

"I have nothing to do with the purser. Do as I tell you."

All this time he had utterly ignored Buel, whose colour was rising. The young man said quietly to the steward, "Take out the portmanteau, please."

When it was placed in the passage, Hodden entered the room, shut and bolted the door.

"Will you see the purser, sir?" said the steward in an awed whisper.

"I think so. There is doubtless some mistake, as he says."

The purser was busy allotting seats at the tables, and Buel waited patiently. He had no friends on board, and did not care where he was placed.

When the purser was at liberty, the steward explained to him the difficulty which had arisen. The official looked at his list.

"159—Buel. Is that your name, sir? Very good; 160—Hodden. That is the gentleman now in the room. Well, what is the trouble?"

"Mr. Hodden says, sir, that the room belongs to him."

"Have you seen his ticket?"

"No, sir."

"Then bring it to me."

"Mistakes sometimes happen, Mr. Buel," said the purser, when the steward vanished. "But as a general thing I find that people simply claim what they have no right to claim. Often the agents promise that if possible a passenger shall have a room to himself, and when we can do so we let him have it. I try to please everybody; but all the steamers crossing to America are full at this season of the year, and it is not practicable to give every one the whole ship to himself. As the Americans say, some people want the earth for £12 or £15, and we can't always give it to them. Ah, here is the ticket. It is just as I thought. Mr. Hodden is entitled merely to berth 160."

The arrival of the ticket was quickly followed by the advent of Mr. Hodden himself. He still ignored Buel.

"Your people in London," he said to the purser, "guaranteed me a room to myself. Otherwise I would not have come on this line. Now it seems that another person has been put in with me. I must protest against this kind of usage."

"Have you any letter from them guaranteeing the room?" asked the purser blandly.

"No. I supposed until now that their word was sufficient."

"Well, you see, I am helpless in this case. These two tickets are exactly the same with the exception of the numbers. Mr. Buel has just as much right to insist on being alone in the room as far as the tickets go, and I have had no instructions in the matter."

"But it is an outrage that they should promise me one thing in London,

100

and then refuse to perform it, when I am helpless on the ocean."

"If they have done so—"

"If they have done so? Do you doubt my word, sir?"

"Oh, not at all, sir, not at all," answered the purser in his most conciliatory tone. "But in that case your ticket should have been marked 159-160."

"I am not to suffer for their blunders."

"I see by this list that you paid £12 for your ticket. Am I right?"

"That was the amount, I believe. I paid what I was asked to pay."

"Quite so, sir. Well, you see, that is the price of one berth only. Mr. Buel, here, paid the same amount."

"Come to the point. Do I understand you to refuse to remedy the mistake (to put the matter in its mildest form) of your London people?"

"I do not refuse. I would be only too glad to give you the room to yourself, if it were possible. Unfortunately, it is not possible. I assure you there is not an unoccupied state-room on the ship."

"Then I will see the captain. Where shall I find him?"

"Very good, sir. Steward, take Mr. Hodden to the captain's room."

When they were alone again Buel very contritely expressed his sorrow at having been the innocent cause of so much trouble to the purser.

"Bless you, sir, I don't mind it in the least. This is a very simple case. Where both occupants of a room claim it all to themselves, and where both are angry and abuse me at the same time, then it gets a bit lively. I don't envy him his talk with the captain. If the old man happens to be feeling a little grumpy today, and he most generally does at the beginning of the voyage, Mr. Hodden will have a bad ten minutes. Don't you bother a bit about it, sir, but go down to your room and make yourself at home. It will be all right."

Mr. Hodden quickly found that the appeal to Cæsar was not well timed.

The captain had not the suave politeness of the purser. There may be greater and more powerful men on earth than the captain of an ocean liner, but you can't get any seafaring man to believe it, and the captains themselves are rarely without a due sense of their own dignity. The man who tries to bluff the captain of a steamship like the Geranium has a hard row to hoe. Mr. Hodden descended to his state-room in a more subdued frame of mind than when he went on the upper deck. However, he still felt able to crush his unfortunate room-mate.

"You insist, then," he said, speaking to Buel for the first time, "on occupying this room?"

"I have no choice in the matter."

"I thought perhaps you might feel some hesitation in forcing yourself in where you were so evidently not wanted?"

The hero-worshipper in Buel withered, and the natural Englishman asserted itself.

"I have exactly the same right in this room that you have. I claim no privilege which I have not paid for."

"Do you wish to suggest that I have made such a claim?"

"I suggest nothing; I state it. You have made such a claim, and in a most offensive manner."

"Do you understand the meaning of the language you are using, sir? You are calling me a liar."

"You put it very tersely, Mr. Hodden. Thank you. Now, if you venture to address me again during this voyage, I shall be obliged if you keep a civil tongue in your head."

"Good heavens! You talk of civility?" cried the astonished man, aghast.

His room-mate went to the upper deck. In the next state-room pretty Miss Carrie Jessop clapped her small hands silently together. The construction of staterooms is such that every word uttered in one above the breath is audible in the next room; Miss Jessop could not help hearing the whole controversy, from the time the steward was ordered so curtly to remove the portmanteau, until the culmination of the discussion and the evident defeat of Mr. Hodden. Her sympathy was all with the other fellow, at that moment unknown, but a sly peep past the edge of the scarcely opened door told her that the unnamed party in the quarrel was the awkward young man who had found her book. She wondered if the Hodden mentioned could possibly be the author, and, with a woman's inconsistency, felt sure that she would detest the story, as if the personality of the writer had anything whatever to do with his work. She took down the parcel from the shelf and undid the string. Her eyes opened wide as she looked at the title.

"Well I never!" she gasped. "If I haven't robbed that poor, innocent young man of a book he bought for himself! Attempted eviction by his room-mate, and bold highway robbery by an unknown woman! No, it's worse than that; it's piracy, for it happened on the high seas." And the girl laughed softly to herself.

Chapter III

Kenan Buel walked the deck alone in the evening light, and felt that he ought to be enjoying the calmness and serenity of the ocean expanse around him after the noise and squalor of London; but now that the excitement of the recent quarrel was over, he felt the reaction, and his natural diffidence led him to blame himself. Most of the passengers were below, preparing for dinner, and he had the deck to himself. As he turned on one of his rounds, he saw approaching him the girl of Euston Station, as he mentally termed her. She had his book in her hand.

"I have come to beg your pardon," she said. "I see it was your own book I took from you to-day."

"My own book!" cried Buel, fearing she had somehow discovered his guilty secret.

"Yes. Didn't you buy this for yourself?" She held up the volume.

"Oh, certainly. But you are quite welcome to it, I am sure."

"I couldn't think of taking it away from you before you have read it."

"But I have read it," replied Buel, eagerly: "and I shall be very pleased to lend it to you."

"Indeed? And how did you manage to read it without undoing the parcel?"

"That is to say I—I skimmed over it before it was done up," he said in confusion. The clear eyes of the girl disconcerted him, and, whatever his place in fiction is now, he was at that time a most unskilful liar.

"You see, I bought it because it is written by a namesake of mine. My name is Buel, and I happened to notice that was the name on the book; in fact, if you remember, when you were looking over it at the stall, the clerk mentioned the author's name, and that naturally caught my attention."

The girl glanced with renewed interest at the volume.

"Was this the book I was looking at? The story I bought was Hodden's latest. I found it a moment ago down in my state-room, so it was not lost after all."

They were now walking together as if they were old acquaintances, the girl still holding the volume in her hand.

"By the way," she said innocently, "I see on the passenger list that there is a Mr. Hodden on board. Do you think he can be the novelist?"

"I believe he is," answered Buel, stiffly.

"Oh, that will be too jolly for anything. I would so like to meet him. I am sure he must be a most charming man. His books show such insight into human nature, such sympathy and noble purpose. There could be nothing petty or mean about such a man."

"I—I—suppose not."

"Why, of course there couldn't. You have read his books, have you not?"

"All of them except his latest."

"Well, I'll lend you that, as you have been so kind as to offer me the reading of this one."

"Thank you. After you have read it yourself."

"And when you have become acquainted with Mr. Hodden, I want you to introduce him to me."

"With pleasure. And—and when I do so, who shall I tell him the young lady is?"

The audacious girl laughed lightly, and, stepping back, made him a saucy bow.

"You will introduce me as Miss Caroline Jessop, of New York. Be sure that you say 'New York,' for that will account to Mr. Hodden for any eccentricities of conduct or conversation he may be good enough to notice. I suppose you think American girls are very forward? All Englishmen do."

"On the contrary, I have always understood that they are very charming."

"Indeed? And so you are going over to see?"

Buel laughed. All the depression he felt a short time before had vanished.

"I had no such intention when I began the voyage, but even if I should quit the steamer at Queenstown, I could bear personal testimony to the truth of the statement."

"Oh, Mr. Buel, that is very nicely put. I don't think you can improve on it, so I shall run down and dress for dinner. There is the first gong. Thanks for the book."

The young man said to himself, "Buel, my boy, you're getting on;" and he smiled as he leaned over the bulwark and looked at the rushing water. He sobered instantly as he remembered that he would have to go to his state-room and perhaps meet Hodden. It is an awkward thing to quarrel with your room-mate at the beginning of a long voyage. He hoped Hodden had taken his departure to the saloon, and he lingered until the second gong rang. Entering the stateroom, he found Hodden still there. Buel gave him no greeting. The other cleared his throat several times and then said—

"I have not the pleasure of knowing your name."

"My name is Buel."

"Well, Mr. Buel, I am sorry that I spoke to you in the manner I did, and I hope you will allow me to apologise for doing so. Various little matters had combined to irritate me, and—Of course, that is no excuse. But—"

"Don't say anything more. I unreservedly retract what I was heated enough to say, and so we may consider the episode ended. I may add that if the purser has a vacant berth anywhere, I shall be very glad to take it, if the occupants of the room make no objection."

"You are very kind," said Hodden, but he did not make any show of declining the offer.

"Very well, then, let us settle the matter while we are at it." And Buel pressed the electric button.

The steward looked in, saying,—

"Dinner is ready, gentlemen."

"Yes, I know. Just ask the purser if he can step here for a moment."

The purser came promptly, and if he was disturbed at being called at such a moment he did not show it. Pursers are very diplomatic persons.

"Have you a vacant berth anywhere, purser?"

An expression faintly suggestive of annoyance passed over the purser's serene brow. He thought the matter had been settled. "We have several berths vacant, but they are each in rooms that already contain three persons."

"One of those will do for me; that is, if the occupants have no objection."

"It will be rather crowded, sir."

"That doesn't matter, if the others are willing."

"Very good, sir. I will see to it immediately after dinner."

The purser was as good as his word, and introduced Buel and his portmanteau to a room that contained three wild American collegians who had been doing Europe "on the cheap" and on foot. They received the new-comer with a hilariousness that disconcerted him.

"Hello, purser!" cried one, "this is an Englishman. You didn't tell us you were going to run in an Englishman on us."

"Never, mind, we'll convert him on the way over."

"I say, purser, if you sling a hammock from the ceiling and put up a cot on the floor you can put two more men in here. Why didn't you think of that?"

"It's not too late yet. Why did you suggest it?"

"Gentlemen," said Buel, "I have no desire to intrude, if it is against your wish."

"Oh, that's all right. Never mind them. They have to talk or die. The truth is, we were lonesome without a fourth man."

"What's his name, purser?"

"My name is Buel."

One of them shouted out the inquiry, "What's the matter with Buel?" and all answered in concert with a yell that made the steamer ring, "He's all right."

"You'll have to sing 'Hail Columbia' night and morning if you stay in this cabin."

"Very good," said Buel, entering into the spirit of the occasion. "Singing is not my strong point, and after you hear me at it once, you will be glad to pay a heavy premium to have it stopped."

"Say, Buel, can you play poker?"

"No, but I can learn."

"That's business. America's just yearning for men who can learn. We have had so many Englishmen who know it all, that we'll welcome a change. But poker's an expensive game to acquire."

"Don't be bluffed, Mr. Buel. Not one of the crowd has enough money left to buy the drinks all round. We would never have got home if we hadn't return tickets."

"Say, boys, let's lock the purser out, and make Buel an American citizen before he can call for help. You solemnly swear that you hereby and hereon renounce all emperors, kings, princes, and potentates, and more especially—how does the rest of it go!"

"He must give up his titles, honours, knighthoods, and things of that sort."

108

"Say, Buel, you're not a lord or a duke by any chance? Because, if you are, we'll call back the purser and have you put out yet."

"No, I haven't even the title esquire, which, I understand, all American citizens possess."

"Oh, you'll do. Now, I propose that Mr. Buel take his choice of the four bunks, and that we raffle for the rest."

When Buel reached the deck out of this pandemonium, he looked around for another citizen of the United States, but she was not there. He wondered if she were reading his book, and how she liked it.

Chapter IV

Next morning Mr. Buel again searched the deck for the fair American, and this time he found her reading his book, seated very comfortably in her deck chair. The fact that she was so engaged put out of Buel's mind the greeting he had carefully prepared beforehand, and he stood there awkwardly, not knowing what to say. He inwardly cursed his unreadiness, and felt, to his further embarrassment, that his colour was rising. He was not put more at his ease when Miss Jessop looked up at him coldly, with a distinct frown on her pretty face.

"Mr. Buel, I believe?" she said pertly.

"I—I think so," he stammered.

She went on with her reading, ignoring him, and he stood there not knowing how to get away. When he pulled himself together, after a few moments' silence, and was about to depart, wondering at the caprice of womankind, she looked up again, and said icily—

"Why don't you ask me to walk with you? Do you think you have no duties, merely because you are on shipboard?"

"It isn't a duty, it is a pleasure, if you will come with me. I was afraid I had offended you in some way."

"You have. That is why I want to walk with you. I wish to give you a piece of my mind, and it won't be pleasant to listen to, I can assure you. So there must be no listener but yourself."

"Is it so serious as that?"

"Quite. Assist me, please. Why do you have to be asked to do such a thing? I don't suppose there is another man on the ship who would see a lady struggling with her rugs, and never put out his hand."

Before the astonished young man could offer assistance the girl sprang to her feet and stood beside him. Although she tried to retain her severe look of displeasure, there was a merry twinkle in the corner of her eye, as if she enjoyed shocking him.

"I fear I am very unready."

"You are."

"Will you take my arm as we walk?"

"Certainly not," she answered, putting the tips of her fingers into the shallow pockets of her pilot jacket. "Don't you know the United States are long since independent of England?"

"I had forgotten for the moment. My knowledge of history is rather limited, even when I try to remember. Still, independence and all, the two countries may be friends, may they not?"

"I doubt it. It seems to be natural that an American should hate an Englishman."

"Dear me, is it so bad as that? Why, may I ask? Is it on account of the little trouble in 1770, or whenever it was?"

"1776, when we conquered you."

"Were we conquered? That is another historical fact which has been concealed from me. I am afraid England doesn't quite realise her unfortunate position. She has a good deal of go about her for a conquered nation. But I thought the conquering, which we all admit, was of much more recent date, when the pretty American girls began to come over. Then Englishmen at once capitulated."

"Yes," she cried scornfully. "And I don't know which to despise most, the American girls who marry Englishmen, or the Englishmen they marry. They are married for their money."

"Who? The Englishmen?"

The girl stamped her foot on the deck as they turned around.

"You know very well what I mean. An Englishman thinks of nothing but money."

"Really? I wonder where you got all your cut-and-dried notions about Englishmen? You seem to have a great capacity for contempt. I don't think it is good. My experience is rather limited, of course, but, as far as it goes, I find good and bad in all nations. There are Englishmen whom I find it impossible to like, and there are Americans whom I find I admire in spite of myself. There are also, doubtless, good Englishmen and bad Americans, if we only knew where to find them. You cannot sum up a nation and condemn it in a phrase, you know."

"Can't you? Well, literary Englishmen have tried to do so in the case of America. No English writer has ever dealt even fairly with the United States."

"Don't you think the States are a little too sensitive about the matter?"

"Sensitive? Bless you, we don't mind it a bit."

"Then where's the harm? Besides, America has its revenge in you. Your scathing contempt more than balances the account."

"I only wish I could write. Then I would let you know what I think of you."

"Oh, don't publish a book about us. I wouldn't like to see war between the two countries."

Miss Jessop laughed merrily for so belligerent a person.

"War?" she cried. "I hope yet to see an American army camped in London."

"If that is your desire, you can see it any day in summer. You will find them tenting out at the Métropole and all the expensive hotels. I bivouacked with an invader there some weeks ago, and he was enduring the rigours of camp life with great fortitude, mitigating his trials with unlimited champagne."

"Why, Mr. Buel," cried the girl admiringly, "you're beginning to talk just like an American yourself."

"Oh, now, you are trying to make me conceited."

Miss Jessop sighed, and shook her head.

"I had nearly forgotten," she said, "that I despised you. I remember now why I began to walk with you. It was not to talk frivolously, but to show you the depth of my contempt! Since yesterday you have gone down in my estimation from 190 to 56."

"Fahrenheit?"

"No, that was a Wall Street quotation. Your stock has 'slumped,' as we say on the Street."

"Now you are talking Latin, or worse, for I can understand a little Latin."

"'Slumped' sounds slangy, doesn't it? It isn't a pretty word, but it is expressive. It means going down with a run, or rather, all in a heap."

"What have I done?"

"Nothing you can say will undo it, so there is no use in speaking any more about it. Second thoughts are best. My second thought is to say no more."

"I must know my crime. Give me a chance to, at least, reach par again, even if I can't hope to attain the 90 above."

"I thought an Englishman had some grit. I thought he did not allow any one to walk over him. I thought he stood by his guns when he knew he was in the right. I thought he was a manly man, and a fighter against injustice!"

"Dear me! Judging by your conversation of a few minutes ago, one would imagine that you attributed exactly the opposite qualities to him."

"I say I thought all this—yesterday. I don't think so to-day."

"Oh, I see! And all on account of me?"

"All on account of you."

"Once more, what have I done?"

"What have you done? You have allowed that detestably selfish specimen of your race, Hodden, to evict you from your room."

The young man stopped abruptly in his walk, and looked at the girl with astonishment. She, her hands still coquettishly thrust in her jacket-pockets, returned his gaze with unruffled serenity.

"What do you know about it?" he demanded at last.

"Everything. From the time you meekly told the steward to take out your valise until the time you meekly apologised to Hodden for having told him the truth, and then meekly followed the purser to a room containing three others."

"But Hodden meekly, as you express it, apologised first. I suppose you know that too, otherwise I would not have mentioned it."

"Certainly he did. That was because he found his overbearing tactics did not work. He apologised merely to get rid of you, and did. That's what put me out of patience with you. To think you couldn't see through his scheme!"

"Oh! I thought it was the lack of manly qualities you despised in me. Now you are accusing me of not being crafty."

"How severely you say that! You quite frighten me! You will be making me apologise by-and-by, and I don't want to do that."

Buel laughed, and resumed his walk.

"It's all right," he said; "Hodden's loss is my gain. I've got in with a jolly lot, who took the trouble last night to teach me the great American game at cards—and counters."

Miss Jessop sighed.

"Having escaped with my life," she said, "I think I shall not run any more risks, but shall continue with your book. I had no idea you could look so fierce. I have scarcely gotten over it yet. Besides, I am very much interested in that book of yours."

"Why do you say so persistently 'that book of mine'?"

"Isn't it yours? You bought it, didn't you? Then it was written by your relative, you know."

"I said my namesake."

"So you did. And now I'm going to ask you an impudent question. You will not look wicked again, will you?"

"I won't promise. That depends entirely on the question."

"It is easily answered."

"I'm waiting."

"What is your Christian name, Mr. Buel?"

"My Christian name?" he repeated, uncomfortably.

"Yes, what is it?"

"Why do you wish to know?"

"A woman's reason—because."

They walked the length of the deck in silence.

"Come, now," she said, "confess. What is it?"

"John."

Miss Jessop laughed heartily, but quietly.

"You think John commonplace, I suppose?"

"Oh, it suits you, Mr. Buel. Goodbye."

As the young woman found her place in the book, she mused, "How blind men are, after all—with his name in full on the passage list." Then she said to herself, with a sigh, "I do wish I had bought this book instead of Hodden's."

Chapter V

At first Mr. Hodden held somewhat aloof from his fellow-passengers; but, finding perhaps that there was no general desire to intrude upon him, he condescended to become genial to a select few. He walked the deck alone, picturesquely attired. He was a man who paid considerable attention to his personal appearance. As day followed day, Mr. Hodden unbent so far as to talk frequently with Miss Jessop on what might almost be called equal terms. The somewhat startling opinions and unexpected remarks of the American girl appeared to interest him, and doubtless tended to confirm his previous unfavourable impressions of the inhabitants of the Western world. Mr. Buel was usually present during these conferences, and his conduct under the circumstances was not admirable. He was silent and moody, and almost gruff on some occasions. Perhaps Hodden's persistent ignoring of him, and the elder man's air of conscious superiority, irritated Buel; but if he had had the advantage of mixing much in the society of his native land he would have become accustomed to that. People thrive on the condescension of the great; they like it, and boast about it. Yet Buel did not seem to be pleased. But the most astounding thing was that the young man should actually have taken it upon himself to lecture Miss Jessop once, when they were alone, for some remarks she had made to Hodden as she sat in her deck-chair, with Hodden loquacious on her right and Buel taciturn on her left. What right had Buel to find fault with a free and independent citizen of another country? Evidently none. It might have been expected that Miss Jessop, rising to the occasion, would have taught the young man his place, and would perhaps have made some scathing remark about the tendency of Englishmen to interfere in matters that did not concern them. But she did nothing of the kind. She looked down demurely on the deck, with the faint flicker of a smile hovering about her pretty lips, and now and then flashed a quick glance at the serious face of the young man. The attitude was very sweet and appealing, but it was not what we have a right to expect from one whose ruler is her servant towards one whose ruler is his sovereign. In fact, the conduct of those two young people at this time was utterly inexplicable.

"Why did you pretend to Hodden that you had never heard of him, and make him state that he was a writer of books?" Buel had said.

"I did it for his own good. Do you want me to minister to his insufferable vanity? Hasn't he egotism enough already? I saw in a paper a while ago that his most popular book had sold to the extent of over 100,000 copies in America. I suppose that is something wonderful; but what does it amount to after all? It leaves over fifty millions of people who doubtless have never heard of him. For the time being I merely went with the majority. We always do that in the States."

"Then I suppose you will not tell him you bought his latest book in London, and so you will not have the privilege of bringing it up on deck and reading it?"

"No. The pleasure of reading that book must be postponed until I reach New York. But my punishment does not end there. Would you believe that authors are so vain that they actually carry with them the books they have written?"

"You astonish me."

"I thought I should. And added to that, would you credit the statement that they offer to lend their works to inoffensive people who may not be interested in them and who have not the courage to refuse? Why do you look so confused, Mr. Buel? I am speaking of Mr. Hodden. He kindly offered me his books to read on the way over. He has a prettily bound set with him. He gave me the first to-day, which I read ever so many years ago."

"I thought you liked his books?"

"For the first time, yes; but I don't care to read them twice."

The conversation was here interrupted by Mr. Hodden himself, who sank into the vacant chair beside Miss Jessop. Buel made as though he would rise and leave them together, but with an almost imperceptible motion of the hand nearest him, Miss Jessop indicated her wish that he should remain, and then thanked him with a rapid glance for understanding. The young man felt a glow of satisfaction at this, and gazed at the blue sea with less discontent than usual in his eyes.

"I have brought you," said the novelist, "another volume."

"Oh, thank you," cried Miss Duplicity, with unnecessary emphasis on the middle word.

"It has been considered," continued Mr. Hodden, "by those whose opinions are thought highly of in London, to be perhaps my most successful work. It is, of course, not for me to pass judgment on such an estimate; but for my own part I prefer the story I gave you this morning. An author's choice is rarely that of the public."

"And was this book published in America?"

"I can hardly say it was published. They did me the honour to pirate it in your most charming country. Some friend—or perhaps I should say enemy—sent me a copy. It was a most atrocious production, in a paper cover, filled with mistakes, and adorned with the kind of spelling, which is, alas! prevalent there."

"I believe," said Buel, speaking for the first time, but with his eyes still on the sea, "there is good English authority for much that we term American spelling."

"English authority, indeed!" cried Miss Jessop; "as if we needed English authority for anything. If we can't spell better than your great English authority, Chaucer—well!" Language seemed to fail the young woman.

"Have you read Chaucer?" asked Mr. Hodden, in surprise.

"Certainly not; but I have looked at his poems, and they always remind me of one of those dialect stories in the magazines."

Miss Jessop turned over the pages of the book which had been given her, and as she did so a name caught her attention. She remembered a problem that had troubled her when she read the book before. She cried impulsively—

"Oh, Mr. Hodden, there is a question I want to ask you about this book. Was—" Here she checked herself in some confusion.

Buel, who seemed to realise the situation, smiled grimly.

"The way of the transgressor is hard," he whispered in a tone too low for Hodden to hear.

"Isn't it?" cordially agreed the unblushing young woman.

"What did you wish to ask me?" inquired the novelist.

"Was it the American spelling or the American piracy that made you dislike the United States?"

Mr. Hodden raised his eyebrows.

"Oh, I do not dislike the United States. I have many friends there, and see much to admire in the country. But there are some things that do not commend themselves to me, and those I ventured to touch upon lightly on one or two occasions, much to the displeasure of a section of the inhabitants—a small section, I hope."

"Don't you think," ventured Buel, "that a writer should rather touch on what pleases him than on what displeases him, in writing of a foreign country?"

"Possibly. Nations are like individuals; they prefer flattery to honest criticism."

"But a writer should remember that there is no law of libel to protect a nation."

To this remark Mr. Hodden did not reply.

"And what did you object to most, Mr. Hodden?" asked the girl.

"That is a hard question to answer. I think, however, that one of the most deplorable features of American life is the unbridled license of the Press. The reporters make existence a burden; they print the most unjustifiable things in their so-called interviews, and a man has no redress. There is no

119

escaping them. If a man is at all well known, they attack him before he has a chance to leave the ship. If you refuse to say anything, they will write a purely imaginative interview. The last time I visited America, five of them came out to interview me—they came out in the Custom House steamer, I believe."

"Why, I should feel flattered if they took all that trouble over me, Mr. Hodden."

"All I ask of them is to leave me alone."

"I'll protect you, Mr. Hodden. When they come, you stand near me, and I'll beat them off with my sunshade. I know two newspaper men—real nice young men they are too—and they always do what I tell them."

"I can quite believe it, Miss Jessop."

"Well, then, have no fear while I'm on board."

Mr. Hodden shook his head. He knew how it would be, he said.

"Let us leave the reporters. What else do you object to? I want to learn, and so reform my country when I get back."

"The mad passion of the people after wealth, and the unscrupulousness of their methods of obtaining it, seem to me unpleasant phases of life over there."

"So they are. And what you say makes me sigh for dear old London. How honest they are, and how little they care for money there! They don't put up the price 50 per cent. merely because a girl has an American accent. Oh no. They think she likes to buy at New York prices. And they are so honourable down in the city that nobody ever gets cheated. Why, you could put a purse up on a pole in London, just as—as—was it Henry the Eighth—?"

"Alfred, I think!" suggested Buel.

"Thanks! As Alfred the Great used to do."

Mr. Hodden looked askance at the young woman.

"Remember," he said, "that you asked me for my opinion. If what I have said is offensive to one who is wealthy, as doubtless you are, Miss Jessop, I most sincerely—"

"Me? Well, I never know whether I'm wealthy or not. I expect that before long I shall have to take to typewriting. Perhaps, in that case, you will give me some of your novels to do, Mr. Hodden. You see, my father is on the Street."

"Dear me!" said Mr. Hodden, "I am sorry to hear that."

"Why? They are not all rogues on Wall Street, in spite of what the papers say. Remember your own opinion of the papers. They are not to be trusted when they speak of Wall Street men. When my father got very rich once I made him give me 100,000 dollars, so that, should things go wrong—they generally go wrong for somebody on Wall Street—we would have something to live on, but, unfortunately, he always borrows it again. Some day, I'm afraid, it will go, and then will come the typewriter. That's why I took my aunt with me and saw Europe before it was too late. I gave him a power of attorney before I left, so I've had an anxious time on the Continent. My money was all right when we left Liverpool, but goodness knows where it will be when I reach New York."

"How very interesting. I never heard of a situation just like it before."

Chapter VI

The big vessel lay at rest in New York Bay waiting for the boat of the health officers and the steamer with the customs men on board. The passengers were in a state of excitement at the thought of being so near home. The captain, who was now in excellent humour, walked the deck and chatted affably with every one. A successful voyage had been completed. Miss Jessop feared the coming of the customs boat as much as Hodden feared the reporters. If anything, he was the more resigned of the two. What American woman ever lands on her native shore without trembling before the revenue laws of her country? Kenan Buel, his arms resting on the bulwarks, gazed absently at the green hills he was seeing for the first time, but his thoughts were not upon them. The young man was in a quandary. Should he venture, or should he not, that was the question. Admitting, for the sake of argument, that she cared for him, what had he to offer? Merely himself, and the debt still unpaid on his first book. The situation was the more embarrassing because of a remark she had made about Englishmen marrying for money. He had resented that on general principles when he heard it, but now it had a personal application that seemed to confront him whichever way he turned. Besides, wasn't it all rather sudden, from an insular point of view? Of course they did things with great rapidity in America, so perhaps she would not object to the suddenness. He had no one to consult, and he felt the lack of advice. He did not want to make a mistake, neither did he wish to be laughed at. Still, the laughing would not matter if everything turned out right. Anyhow, Miss Jessop's laugh was very kindly. He remembered that if he were in any other difficulty he would turn quite naturally to her for advice, although he had known her so short a time, and he regretted that in his present predicament he was debarred from putting the case before her. And yet, why not? He might put the supposititious case of a friend, and ask what the friend ought to do. He dismissed this a moment later. It was too much like what people did in a novel, and besides, he could not carry it through. She would see through the sham at once. At this point he realised that he was just where he began.

"Dear me, Mr. Buel, how serious you look. I am afraid you don't approve of America. Are you sorry the voyage is ended?"

"Yes, I am," answered Buel, earnestly. "I feel as if I had to begin life over again."

"And are you afraid?"

"A little."

"I am disappointed in you. I thought you were not afraid of anything."

"You were disappointed in me the first day, you remember."

"So I was. I had forgotten."

"Will your father come on board to meet you?"

"It depends altogether on the state of the market. If things are dull, he will very likely meet me out here. If the Street is brisk, I won't see him till he arrives home to-night. If medium, he will be on the wharf when we get in."

"And when you meet him I suppose you will know whether you are rich or poor?"

"Oh, certainly. It will be the second thing I ask him."

"When you know, I want you to tell me. Will you?"

"Are you interested in knowing?"

"Very much so."

"Then I hope I shall be rich."

Mr. Buel did not answer. He stared gloomily down at the water lapping the iron side of the motionless steamer. The frown on his brow was deep. Miss Jessop looked at him for a moment out of the corners of her eyes. Then she said, impulsively—

"I know that was mean. I apologise. I told you I did not like to apologise, so you may know how sorry I am. And, now that I have begun, I also apologise

123

for all the flippant things I have said during the voyage, and for my frightful mendacity to poor Mr. Hodden, who sits there so patiently and picturesquely waiting for the terrible reporters. Won't you forgive me?"

Buel was not a ready man, and he hesitated just the smallest fraction of a second too long.

"I won't ask you twice, you know," said Miss Jessop, drawing herself up with dignity.

"Don't—don't go!" cried the young man, with sudden energy, catching her hand. "I'm an unmannerly boor. But I'll risk everything and tell you the trouble. I don't care a—I don't care whether you are rich or poor. I—"

Miss Jessop drew away her hand.

"Oh, there's the boat, Mr. Buel, and there's my papa on the upper deck."

She waved her handkerchief in the air in answer to one that was fluttering on the little steamer. Buel saw the boat cutting a rapid semicircle in the bay as she rounded to, leaving in her wake a long, curving track of foam. She looked ridiculously small compared with the great ship she was approaching, and her deck seemed crowded.

"And there are the reporters!" she cried; "ever so many of them. I guess Mr. Hodden will be sorry he did not accept my offer of protection. I know that young man who is waving his hand. He was on the Herald when I left; but no one can say what paper he's writing for now."

As the boat came nearer a voice shouted—

"All well, Carrie?"

The girl nodded. Her eyes and her heart were too full for speech. Buel frowned at the approaching boat, and cursed its inopportune arrival. He was astonished to hear some one shout from her deck—

"Hello, Buel!"

"Why, there's some one who knows you!" said the girl, looking at him.

Buel saw a man wave his hand, and automatically he waved in return. After a moment he realised that it was Brant the publisher. The customs officers were first on board, for it is ordained by the law that no foot is to tread the deck before theirs; but the reporters made a good second.

Miss Jessop rushed to the gangway, leaving Buel alone. "Hello, Cap!" cried one of the young men of the Press, with that lack of respect for the dignitaries of this earth which is characteristic of them. "Had a good voyage?"

"Splendid," answered the captain, with a smile.

"Where's your celebrity? Trot him out."

"I believe Mr. Hodden is aft somewhere."

"Oh,—Hodden!" cried the young man, profanely; "he's a chestnut. Where's Kenan Buel?"

The reporter did not wait for a reply, for he saw by the crowd around a very flushed young man that the victim had been found and cornered.

"Really, gentlemen," said the embarrassed Englishman, "you have made a mistake. It is Mr. Hodden you want to see. I will take you to him."

"Hodden's played," said one of the young men in an explanatory way, although Buel did not understand the meaning of the phrase. "He's petered out;" which addition did not make it any plainer. "You're the man for our money every time."

"Break away there, break away!" cried the belated Brant, forcing his way through them and taking Buel by the hand. "There's no rush, you know, boys. Just let me have a minute's talk with Mr. Buel. It will be all right. I have just set up the champagne down in the saloon. It's my treat, you know. There's tables down there, and we can do things comfortably. I'll guarantee to produce Buel inside of five minutes."

Brant linked arms with the young man, and they walked together down the deck.

"Do you know what this means, Buel?" he said, waving his hand towards the retreating newspaper men.

"I suppose it means that you have got them to interview me for business purposes. I can think of no other reason."

"I've had nothing to do with it. That shows just how little you know about the American Press. Why, all the money I've got wouldn't bring those men out here to interview anybody who wasn't worth interviewing. It means fame; it means wealth; it means that you have turned the corner; it means you have the world before you; it means everything. Those young men are not reporters to you; they are the heralds of fame, my boy. A few of them may get there themselves some day, but it means that you have got there now. Do you realise that?"

"Hardly. I suppose, then, the book has been a success?"

"A success? It's been a cyclone. I've been fighting pirates ever since it came out. You see, I took the precaution to write some things in the book myself."

Buel looked alarmed.

"And then I copyrighted the whole thing, and they can't tell which is mine and which is yours until they get a hold of the English edition. That's why I did not wait for your corrections."

"We are collaborators, then?"

"You bet. I suppose some of the English copies are on this steamer? I'm going to try to have them seized by the customs if I can. I think I'll make a charge of indecency against the book."

"Good heavens!" cried Buel, aghast. "There is nothing of that in it."

"I am afraid not," said Brant, regretfully. "But it will give us a week more at least before it is decided. Anyhow, I'm ready for the pirates, even if they do come out. I've printed a cheap paper edition, 100,000 copies, and they are now in the hands of all the news companies—sealed up, of course—from New York to San Francisco. The moment a pirate shows his head, I'll telegraph the word 'rip' all over the United States, and they will rip open the packages and flood the market with authorised cheap editions before the pirates leave New York. Oh, L. F. Brant was not born the day before yesterday."

"I see he wasn't," said Buel, smiling.

"Now you come down and be introduced to the newspaper boys. You'll find them jolly nice fellows."

"In a moment. You go down and open the champagne. I'll follow you. I—I want to say a few words to a friend on board."

"No tricks now, Buel. You're not going to try to dodge them?"

"I'm a man of my word, Mr. Brant. Don't be afraid."

"And now," said the other, putting his hands on the young man's shoulders, "you'll be kind to them. Don't put on too much side, you know. You'll forgive me for mentioning this, but sometimes your countrymen do the high and mighty act a little too much. It doesn't pay."

"I'll do my best. But I haven't the slightest idea what to say. In fact, I've nothing to say."

"Oh, that's all right. Don't you worry. Just have a talk with them, that's all they want. You'll be paralysed when the interviews come out to-morrow; but you'll get over that."

"You're sure the book is a success in its own merits, and not through any newspaper puffing or that sort of thing, you know?"

"Why, certainly. Of course our firm pushed it. We're not the people to go to sleep over a thing. It might not have done quite so well with any other house; but I told you in London I thought it was bound to go. The pushing was quite legitimate."

"In that case I shall be down to see the reporters in a very few minutes." Although Buel kept up his end of the conversation with Brant, his mind was not on it. Miss Jessop and her father were walking near them; snatches of their talk came to him, and his attention wandered in spite of himself. The

127

Wall Street man seemed to be trying to reassure his daughter, and impart to her some of the enthusiasm he himself felt. He patted her affectionately on the shoulder now and then, and she walked with springy step very close to his side.

"It's all right, Carrie," he said, "and as safe as the bank."

"Which bank, papa?"

Mr. Jessop laughed.

"The Chemical Bank, if you like; or, as you are just over from the other side, perhaps I should say the Bank of England."

"And did you take out every cent?"

"Yes; and I wished there was double the amount to take. It's a sure thing. There's no speculation about it. There isn't a bushel of wheat in the country that isn't in the combination. It would have been sinful not to have put every cent I could scrape together into it. Why, Carrie, I'll give you a quarter of a million when the deal comes off."

Carrie shook her head.

"I've been afraid of wheat corners," she said, "ever since I was a baby. Still, I've no right to say anything. It's all your money, anyway, and I've just been playing that it was mine. But I do wish you had left a hundred dollars for a typewriter."

Mr. Jessop laughed again in a very hearty and confident way.

"Don't you fret about that, Carrie. I've got four type machines down at the office. I'll let you have your choice before the crash comes. Now I'll go down and see those customs men. There won't be any trouble. I know them."

It was when Mr. Jessop departed that Buel suddenly became anxious to get rid of Brant. When he had succeeded, he walked over to where the girl leaned on the bulwark.

"Well?" he said, taking his place beside her.

"Well!" she answered, without looking up at him.

"Which is it? Rich or poor?"

"Rich, I should say, by the way the reporters flocked about you. That means, I suppose, that your book has been a great success, and that you are going to make your fortune out of it. Let me congratulate you, Mr. Buel."

"Wait a minute. I don't know yet whether I am to be congratulated or not; that will depend on you. Of course you know I was not speaking of myself when I asked the question."

"Oh, you meant me, did you? Well, I can't tell for some time to come, but I have my fears. I hear the click of the typewriter in the near future."

"Caroline, I am very serious about this. I don't believe you think, or could think, that I care much about riches. I have been on too intimate terms with poverty to be afraid of it. Of course my present apparent success has given me courage, and I intend to use that courage while it lasts. I have been rather afraid of your ridicule, but I think, whether you were rich or poor, or whether my book was a success or a failure, I would have risked it, and told you I loved you."

The girl did not look up at him, and did not answer for a moment. Then she said, in a voice that he had to bend very close to hear—

"I—I would have been sorry all my life if you hadn't—risked it."

IN A STEAMER CHAIR, AND
OTHER STORIES

As the incidents related herein took place during voyages between England and America, I dedicate this book to the Vagabond Club of London, and the Witenagemote Club of Detroit, in the hope that, if any one charges me with telling a previously told tale, the fifty members of each club will rise as one man and testify that they were called upon to endure the story in question from my own lips prior to the alleged original appearance of the same.

R. B.

In a Steamer Chair

The First Day

Mr. George Morris stood with his arms folded on the bulwarks of the steamship City of Buffalo, and gazed down into the water. All around him was the bustle and hurry of passengers embarking, with friends bidding good-bye. Among the throng, here and there, the hardworking men of the steamer were getting things in order for the coming voyage. Trunks were piled up in great heaps ready to be lowered into the hold; portmanteaux, satchels, and hand-bags, with tags tied to them, were placed in a row waiting to be claimed by the passengers, or taken down into the state-rooms. To all this bustle and confusion George Morris paid no heed. He was thinking deeply, and his thoughts did not seem to be very pleasant. There was nobody to see him off, and he had evidently very little interest in either those who were going or those who were staying behind. Other passengers who had no friends to bid them farewell appeared to take a lively interest in watching the hurry and scurry, and in picking out the voyagers from those who came merely to say good-bye.

At last the rapid ringing of a bell warned all lingerers that the time for the final parting had come. There were final hand-shakings, many embraces, and not a few tears, while men in uniform with stentorian voices cried, "All ashore." The second clanging of the bell, and the preparations for pulling up the gang-planks hurried the laggards to the pier. After the third ringing the gang-plank was hauled away, the inevitable last man sprang to the wharf, the equally inevitable last passenger, who had just dashed up in a cab, flung his valises to the steward, was helped on board the ship, and then began the low pulsating stroke, like the beating of a heart, that would not cease until the vessel had sighted land on the other side. George Morris's eyes were fixed on the water, yet apparently he was not looking at it, for when it began to spin away from the sides of the ship he took no notice, but still gazed at the mass of seething foam that the steamer threw off from her as she moved through the bay. It was evident that the sights of New York harbour were very familiar to the young man, for he paid no attention to them, and the vessel was beyond Sandy Hook before he changed his position. It is doubtful if he would have changed it then, had not a steward touched him on the elbow, and said— had not a steward touched him on the elbow, and said—

"Any letters, sir?"

"Any what?" cried Morris, suddenly waking up from his reverie.

"Any letters, sir, to go ashore with the pilot?"

"Oh, letters. No, no, I haven't any. You have a regular post-office on

board, have you? Mail leaves every day?"

"No, sir," replied the steward with a smile, "not every day, sir. We

send letters ashore for passengers when the pilot leaves the ship. The next mail, sir, will leave at Queenstown."

The steward seemed uncertain as to whether the passenger was trying to joke with him or was really ignorant of the ways of steamships. However, his tone was very deferential and explanatory, not knowing but that this particular passenger might come to his lot at the table, and stewards take very good care to offend nobody. Future fees must not be jeopardized.

Being aroused, Mr. Morris now took a look around him. It seemed wonderful how soon order had been restored from the chaos of the starting. The trunks had disappeared down the hold; the portmanteaux were nowhere to be seen. Most of the passengers apparently were in their state-rooms exploring their new quarters, getting out their wraps, Tam-o-Shanters, fore-and-aft caps, steamer chairs, rugs, and copies of paper-covered novels. The deck was almost deserted, yet here and there a steamer chair had already been placed, and one or two were occupied. The voyage had commenced. The engine had settled down to its regular low thud, thud; the vessel's head rose gracefully with the long swell of the ocean, and, to make everything complete, several passengers already felt that inward qualm—the accompaniment of so many ocean voyages. George Morris yawned, and seemed the very picture of ennui. He put his hands deeply into his coat pockets, and sauntered across the deck. Then he took a stroll up the one side and down the other. As he lounged along it was very evident that he was tired of the voyage, even before it began. Judging from his listless manner nothing on earth could arouse the interest of the young man. The gong sounded faintly in the inner depths of the ship somewhere announcing dinner. Then, as the steward appeared up the companion way, the sonorous whang, whang became louder, and the hatless official, with the gong in hand, beat that instrument several final strokes, after which he disappeared into the regions below.

"I may as well go down," said Morris to himself, "and see where they have placed me at table. But I haven't much interest in dinner."

As he walked to the companion-way an elderly gentleman and a young lady appeared at the opposite door, ready to descend the stairs. Neither of them saw the young man. But if they had, one of them at least would have doubted the young man's sanity. He stared at the couple for a moment with a look of grotesque horror on his face that was absolutely comical. Then he turned, and ran the length of the deck, with a speed unconscious of all obstacles.

"Say," he cried to the captain, "I want to go ashore. I must go ashore. I want to go ashore with the pilot."

The captain smiled, and said, "I shall be very happy to put you ashore, sir, but it will have to be at Queenstown. The pilot has gone."

"Why, it was only a moment ago that the steward asked me if I had any letters to post. Surely he cannot have gone yet?"

"It is longer than that, I am afraid," said the captain. "The pilot left the ship half an hour ago."

"Is there no way I can get ashore? I don't mind what I pay for it."

"Unless we break a shaft and have to turn back there is no way that I know of. I am afraid you will have to make the best of it until we reach Queenstown."

"Can't you signal a boat and let me get off on her?"

"Well, I suppose we could. It is a very unusual thing to do. But that would delay us for some time, and unless the business is of the utmost necessity, I would not feel justified in delaying the steamer, or in other words delaying several hundred passengers for the convenience of one. If you tell me what the trouble is I shall tell you at once whether I can promise to signal a boat if I get the opportunity of doing so."

Morris thought for a moment. It would sound very absurd to the captain for him to say that there was a passenger on the ship whom he desired very much not to meet, and yet, after all, that was what made the thought of the voyage so distasteful to him.

He merely said, "Thank you," and turned away, muttering to himself something in condemnation of his luck in general. As he walked slowly down the deck up which he had rushed with such headlong speed a few moments before, he noticed a lady trying to set together her steamer chair, which had seemingly given way—a habit of steamer chairs. She looked up appealing at Mr. Morris, but that gentleman was too preoccupied with his own situation to be gallant. As he passed her, the lady said—

"Would you be kind enough to see if you can put my steamer chair together?"

Mr. Morris looked astonished at this very simple request. He had resolved to make this particular voyage without becoming acquainted with anybody, more especially a lady.

"Madam," he said, "I shall be pleased to call to your assistance the deck steward if you wish."

"If I had wished that," replied the lady, with some asperity, "I would have asked you to do so. As it is, I asked you to fix it yourself."

"I do not understand you," said Mr. Morris, with some haughtiness. "I do not see that it matters who mends the steamer chair so long as the steamer chair is mended. I am not a deck steward." Then, thinking he had spoken rather harshly, he added, "I am not a deck steward, and don't understand the construction of steamer chairs as well as they do, you see."

The lady rose. There was a certain amount of indignation in her voice as she said—

"Then pray allow me to present you with this steamer chair."

"I—I—really, madam, I do not understand you," stammered the young man, astonished at the turn the unsought conversation had taken.

"I think," replied the lady, "that what I said was plain enough. I beg you to accept this steamer chair as your own. It is of no further use to me."

Saying this, the young woman, with some dignity, turned her back upon him, and disappeared down the companion-way, leaving Morris in a state of utter bewilderment as he looked down at the broken steamer chair, wondering if the lady was insane. All at once he noticed a rent in his trousers, between the knee and the instep.

"Good heavens, how have I done this? My best pair of trousers, too. Gracious!" he cried, as a bewildered look stole over his face, "it isn't possible that in racing up this deck I ran against this steamer chair and knocked it to flinders, and possibly upset the lady at the same time? By George! that's just what the trouble is."

Looking at the back of the flimsy chair he noticed a tag tied to it, and on the tag he saw the name, "Miss Katherine Earle, New York." Passing to the other side he called the deck steward.

"Steward," he said, "there is a chair somewhere among your pile with the name 'Geo. Morris' on it. Will you get it for me?"

"Certainly, sir," answered the steward, and very shortly the other steamer chair, which, by the way, was a much more elegant, expensive, and stable affair than the one that belonged to Miss Katherine Earle, was brought to him. Then he untied the tag from his own chair and tied it to the flimsy structure that had just been offered to him; next he untied the tag from the lady's chair and put it on his own.

"Now, steward," he said, "do you know the lady who sat in this chair?"

"No, sir," said the steward, "I do not. You see, we are only a few hours out, sir."

"Very well, you will have no trouble finding her. When she comes on deck again, please tell her that this chair is hers, with the apologies of the gentleman who broke her own, and see if you can mend this other chair for me."

"Oh yes," said the steward, "there will be no trouble about that. They are rather rickety things at best, sir."

"Very well, if you do this for me nicely you will not be a financial sufferer."

"Thank you, sir. The dinner gong rang some time ago, sir."

"Yes, I heard it," answered Morris.

Placing his hands behind him he walked up and down the deck, keeping an anxious eye now and then on the companion way. Finally, the young lady whom he had seen going down with the elderly gentleman appeared alone on deck. Then Morris acted very strangely. With the stealthy demeanour of an Indian avoiding his deadly enemy, he slunk behind the different structures on the deck until he reached the other door of the companion-way, and then, with a sigh of relief, ran down the steps. There were still quite a number of people in the saloon, and seated at the side of one of the smaller tables he noticed the lady whose name he imagined was Miss Katherine Earle.

"My name is Morris," said that gentleman to the head steward. "Where have you placed me?"

The steward took him down the long table, looking at the cards beside the row of plates.

"Here you are, sir," said the steward. "We are rather crowded this voyage, sir."

Morris did not answer him, for opposite he noticed the old gentleman, who had been the companion of the young lady, lingering over his wine.

"Isn't there any other place vacant? At one of the smaller tables, for instance? I don't like to sit at the long table," said Morris, placing his finger and thumb significantly in his waistcoat pocket.

"I think that can be arranged, sir," answered the steward, with a smile.

"Is there a place vacant at the table where that young lady is sitting alone?" said Morris, nodding in the direction.

"Well, sir, all the places are taken there; but the gentleman who has been placed at the head of the table has not come down, sir, and if you like I will change his card for yours at the long table."

"I wish you would."

So with that he took his place at the head of the small table, and had the indignant young lady at his right hand.

"There ought to be a master of ceremonies," began Morris with some hesitation, "to introduce people to each other on board a steamship. As it is, however, people have to get acquainted as best they may. My name is Morris, and, unless I am mistaken, you are Miss Katherine Earle. Am I right?"

"You are right about my name," answered the young lady, "I presume you ought to be about your own."

"Oh, I can prove that," said Morris, with a smile. "I have letters to show, and cards and things like that."

Then he seemed to catch his breath as he remembered there was also a young woman on board who could vouch that his name was George Morris This took him aback for a moment, and he was silent. Miss Earle made no reply to his offer of identification.

"Miss Earle," he said hesitatingly at last, "I wish you would permit me to apologise to you if I am as culpable as I imagine. Did I run against your chair and break it?"

"Do you mean to say," replied the young lady, looking at him steadily, "that you do not know whether you did or not?"

"Well, it's a pretty hard thing to ask a person to believe, and yet I assure you that is the fact. I have only the dimmest remembrance of the disaster, as of something I might have done in a dream. To tell you the truth, I did not even suspect I had done so until I noticed I had torn a portion of my clothing by the collision. After you left, it just dawned upon me that I was the one who smashed the chair. I therefore desire to apologise very humbly, and hope you will permit me to do so."

"For what do you intend to apologise, Mr. Morris? For breaking the chair, or refusing to mend it when I asked you?"

"For both. I was really in a good deal of trouble just the moment before I ran against your chair, Miss Earle, and I hope you will excuse me on the ground of temporary insanity. Why, you know, they even let off murderers on that plea, so I hope to be forgiven for being careless in the first place, and boorish in the second."

"You are freely forgiven, Mr. Morris. In fact, now that I think more calmly about the incident, it was really a very trivial affair to get angry over, and I must confess I was angry."

"You were perfectly justified."

"In getting angry, perhaps; but in showing my anger, no—as some one says in a play. Meanwhile, we'll forget all about it," and with that the young lady rose, bidding her new acquaintance good night.

George Morris found he had more appetite for dinner than he expected to have.

Second Day

Mr. George Morris did not sleep well his first night on the City of Buffalo. He dreamt that he was being chased around the deck by a couple of young ladies, one a very pronounced blonde, and the other an equally pronounced brunette, and he suffered a great deal because of the uncertainty as to which of the two pursuers he desired the most to avoid. It seemed to him that at last he was cornered, and the fiendish young ladies began literally, as the slang phrase is, to mop the deck with him. He felt himself being slowly pushed back and forward across the deck, and he wondered how long he would last if this treatment were kept up. By and by he found himself lying still in his bunk, and the swish, swish above him of the men scrubbing the deck in the early morning showed him his dream had merged into reality. He remembered then that it was the custom of the smoking-room steward to bring a large silver pot of fragrant coffee early every morning and place it on the table of the smoking-room. Morris also recollected that on former voyages that early morning coffee had always tasted particularly good. It was grateful and comforting, as the advertisement has it. Shortly after, Mr. Morris was on the wet deck, which the men were still scrubbing with the slow, measured swish, swish of the brush he had heard earlier in the morning. No rain was falling, but everything had a rainy look. At first he could see only a short distance from the ship. The clouds appeared to have come down on the water, where they hung, lowering. There was no evidence that such a thing as a sun existed. The waves rolled out of this watery mist with an oily look, and the air was so damp and chilly that it made Morris shiver as he looked out on the dreary prospect. He thrust his hands deep into his coat pockets, which seemed to be an indolent habit of his, and walked along the slippery deck to search for the smoking-room. He was thinking of his curious and troublesome dream, when around the corner came the brunette, wrapped in a long cloak that covered her from head to foot. The cloak had a couple of side pockets set angleways in front, after the manner of the pockets in ulsters. In these pockets Miss Earle's hands were placed, and she walked the deck with a certain independent manner which Mr. Morris remembered that he disliked. She seemed to be about to pass him without recognition, when the young man took off his cap and said pleasantly, "Good morning, Miss Earle. You are a very early riser."

"The habit of years," answered that young lady, "is not broken by merely coming on board ship."

Mr. Morris changed step and walked beside her.

"The habit of years?" he said. "Why, you speak as if you were an old woman."

"I am an old woman," replied the girl, "in everything but one particular."

143

"And that particular," said her companion, "is the very important one, I imagine, of years."

"I don't know why that is so very important."

"Oh, you will think so in after life, I assure you. I speak as a veteran myself."

The young lady gave him a quick side glance with her black eyes from under the hood that almost concealed her face.

"You say you are a veteran," she answered, "but you don't think so. It would offend you very deeply to be called old."

"Oh, I don't know about that. I think such a remark is offensive only when there is truth in it. A young fellow slaps his companion on the shoulder and calls him 'old man.' The grey-haired veteran always addresses his elderly friend as 'my boy.'"

"Under which category do you think you come, then?"

"Well, I don't come under either exactly. I am sort of on the middle ground. I sometimes feel very old. In fact, to confess to you, I never felt older in my life than I did yesterday. Today I am a great deal younger."

"Dear me," replied the young lady, "I am sorry to hear that."

"Sorry!" echoed her companion; "I don't see why you should be sorry. It is said that every one rejoices in the misfortunes of others, but it is rather unusual to hear them admit it."

"It is because of my sympathy for others that I am sorry to hear you are younger today than you were yesterday. If you take to running along the deck today then the results will be disastrous and I think you owe it to your fellow passengers to send the steward with his gong ahead of you so as to give people in steamer chairs warning."

"Miss Earle," said the young man, "I thought you had forgiven me for yesterday. I am sure I apologised very humbly, and am willing to apologise again to-day."

"Did I forgive you? I had forgotten?"

"But you remembered the fault. I am afraid that is misplaced forgetfulness. The truth is, I imagine, you are very unforgiving."

"My friends do not think so."

"Then I suppose you rank me among your enemies?"

"You forget that I have known you for a day only."

"That is true, chronologically speaking. But you must remember a day on shipboard is very much longer than a day on shore. In fact, I look on you now as an old acquaintance, and I should be sorry to think you looked on me as an enemy."

"You are mistaken. I do not. I look on you now as you do on your own age—sort of between the two."

"And which way do you think I shall drift? Towards the enemy line, or towards the line of friendship?"

"I am sure I cannot tell."

"Well, Miss Earle, I am going to use my best endeavours to reach the friendship line, which I shall make unless the current is too strong for me. I hope you are not so prejudiced against me that the pleasant effort will be fruitless."

"Oh, I am strictly neutral," said the young lady. "Besides, it really amounts to nothing. Steamer friendships are the most evanescent things on earth."

"Not on earth, surely, Miss Earle. You must mean on sea."

"Well, the earth includes the sea, you know."

"Have you had experience with steamer friendships? I thought, somehow, this was your first voyage."

"What made you think so?"

"Well, I don't know. I thought it was, that's all."

"I hope there is nothing in my manner that would induce a stranger to think I am a verdant traveller."

"Oh, not at all. You know, a person somehow classifies a person's fellow-passengers. Some appear to have been crossing the ocean all their lives, whereas, in fact, they are probably on shipboard for the first time. Have you crossed the ocean before?"

"Yes."

"Now, tell me whether you think I ever crossed before?"

"Why, of course you have. I should say that you cross probably once a year. Maybe oftener."

"Really? For business or pleasure?"

"Oh, business, entirely. You did not look yesterday as if you ever had any pleasure in your life."

"Oh, yesterday! Don't let us talk about yesterday. It's to-day now, you know. You seem to be a mind-reader. Perhaps you could tell my occupation?"

"Certainly. Your occupation is doubtless that of a junior partner in a prosperous New York house. You go over to Europe every year—perhaps twice a year, to look after the interests of your business."

"You think I am a sort of commercial traveller, then?"

"Well, practically, yes. The older members of the firm, I should imagine, are too comfortably situated, and care too little for the pleasures of foreign travel, to devote much of their time to it. So what foreign travel there is to be done falls on the shoulders of the younger partner. Am I correct?"

"Well, I don't quite class myself as a commercial traveller, you know, but in the main you are—in fact, you are remarkably near right. I think you must be something of a mind-reader, as I said before, Miss Earle, or is it possible that I carry my business so plainly in my demeanour as all that?"

146

Miss Earle laughed. It was a very bright, pleasant, cheerful laugh.

"Still, I must correct you where you are wrong, for fear you become too conceited altogether about your powers of observation. I have not crossed the ocean as often as you seem to think. In the future I shall perhaps do so frequently. I am the junior partner, as you say, but have not been a partner long. In fact I am now on my first voyage in connection with the new partnership. Now, Miss Earle, let me try a guess at your occupation."

"You are quite at liberty to guess at it."

"But will you tell me if I guess correctly?"

"Yes. I have no desire to conceal it."

"Then, I should say off-hand that you are a teacher, and are now taking a vacation in Europe. Am I right?"

"Tell me first why you think so?"

"I am afraid to tell you. I do not want to drift towards the line of enmity."

"You need have no fear. I have every respect for a man who tells the truth when he has to."

"Well, I think a school teacher is very apt to get into a certain dictatorial habit of speech. School teachers are something like military men. They are accustomed to implicit obedience without question, and this, I think, affects their manner with other people."

"You think I am dictatorial, then?"

"Well, I shouldn't say that you were dictatorial exactly. But there is a certain confidence—I don't know just how to express it, but it seems to me, you know—well, I am going deeper and deeper into trouble by what I am saying, so really I shall not say any more. I do not know just how to express it."

"I think you express it very nicely. Go on, please."

"Oh, you are laughing at me now."

"Not at all, I assure you. You were trying to say that I was very dictatorial."

"No, I was trying to say nothing of the kind. I was merely trying to say that you have a certain confidence in yourself and a certain belief that everything you say is perfectly correct, and is not to be questioned. Now, do as you promised, and tell me how near right I am."

"You are entirely wrong. I never taught school."

"Well, Miss Earle, I confessed to my occupation without citing any mitigating circumstances. So now, would you think me impertinent if I asked you to be equally frank?"

"Oh, not at all! But I may say at once that I wouldn't answer you."

"But you will tell me if I guess?"

"Yes, I promise that."

"Well, I am certainly right in saying that you are crossing the ocean for pleasure."

"No, you are entirely wrong. I am crossing for business."

"Then, perhaps you cross very often, too?"

"No; I crossed only once before, and that was coming the other way."

"Really, this is very mysterious. When are you coming back?"

"I am not coming back."

"Oh, well," said Morris, "I give it up. I think I have scored the unusual triumph of managing to be wrong in everything that I have said. Have I not?"

"I think you have."

"And you refuse to put me right?"

"Certainly."

"I don't think you are quite fair, Miss Earle."

"I don't think I ever claimed to be, Mr. Morris. But I am tired of walking now. You see, I have been walking the deck for considerably longer than you have. I think I shall sit down for a while."

"Let me take you to your chair."

Miss Earle smiled. "It would be very little use," she said.

The deck steward was not to be seen, and Morris, diving into a dark and cluttered-up apartment, in which the chairs were piled, speedily picked out his own, brought it to where the young lady was standing, spread it out in its proper position, and said—

"Now let me get you a rug or two."

"You have made a mistake. That is not my chair."

"Oh yes, it is. I looked at the tag. This is your name, is it not?"

"Yes, that is my name; but this is not my chair."

"Well, I beg that you will use it until the owner calls for it."

"But who is the owner? Is this your chair?"

"It was mine until after I smashed up yours."

"Oh, but I cannot accept your chair, Mr. Morris."

"You surely wouldn't refuse to do what you desired, in fact, commanded, another to do. You know you practically ordered me to take your chair. Well, I have accepted it. It is going to be put right to-day. So, you see, you cannot refuse mine."

Miss Earle looked at him for a moment.

"This is hardly what I would call a fair exchange," she said. "My chair was really a very cheap and flimsy one. This chair is much more expensive. You see, I know the price of them. I think you are trying to arrange your revenge, Mr. Morris. I think you want to bring things about so that I shall have to apologise to you in relation to that chair-breaking incident. However, I see that this chair is very comfortable, so I will take it. Wait a moment till I get my rugs."

"No, no," cried Morris, "tell me where you left them. I will get them for you."

"Thank you. I left them on the seat at the head of the companion-way. One is red, the other is more variegated; I cannot describe it, but they are the only two rugs there, I think."

A moment afterwards the young man appeared with the rugs on his arm, and arranged them around the young lady after the manner of deck stewards and gallant young men who are in the habit of crossing the ocean.

"Would you like to have a cup of coffee?"

"I would, if it can be had."

"Well, I will let you into a shipboard secret. Every morning on this vessel the smoking-room steward brings up a pot of very delicious coffee, which he leaves on the table of the smoking-room. He also brings a few biscuits—not the biscuit of American fame, but the biscuit of English manufacture, the cracker, as we call it—and those who frequent the smoking-room are in the habit sometimes of rising early, and, after a walk on deck, pouring out a cup of coffee for themselves."

"But I do not expert to be a habitué of the smoking-room," said Miss Earle.

"Nevertheless, you have a friend who will be, and so in that way, you see, you will enjoy the advantages of belonging to the smoking club."

A few moments afterwards, Morris appeared with a camp-stool under his arm, and two cups of coffee in his hands. Miss Earle noticed the smile suddenly fade from his face, and a look of annoyance, even of terror, succeed it. His hands trembled, so that the coffee spilled from the cup into the saucer.

"Excuse my awkwardness," he said huskily; then, handing her the cup, he added, "I shall have to go now. I will see you at breakfast-time. Good morning." With the other cup still in his hand, he made his way to the stair.

Miss Earle looked around and saw, coming up the deck, a very handsome young lady with blonde hair.

Third Day

On the morning of the third day, Mr. George Morris woke up after a sound and dreamless sleep. He woke up feeling very dissatisfied with himself, indeed. He said he was a fool, which was probably true enough, but even the calling himself so did not seem to make matters any better. He reviewed in his mind the events of the day before. He remembered his very pleasant walk and talk with Miss Earle. He knew the talk had been rather purposeless, being merely that sort of preliminary conversation which two people who do not yet know each other indulge in, as a forerunner to future friendship. Then, he thought of his awkward leave-taking of Miss Earle when he presented her with the cup of coffee, and for the first time he remembered with a pang that he had under his arm a camp-stool. It must have been evident to Miss Earle that he had intended to sit down and have a cup of coffee with her, and continue the acquaintance begun so auspiciously that morning. He wondered if she had noticed that his precipitate retreat had taken place the moment there appeared on the deck a very handsome and stylishly dressed young lady. He began to fear that Miss Earle must have thought him suddenly taken with insanity, or, worse still, sea-sickness. The more Morris thought about the matter the more dissatisfied he was with himself and his actions. At breakfast—he had arrived very late, almost as Miss Earle was leaving—he felt he had preserved a glum, reticent demeanour, and that he had the general manner of a fugitive anxious to escape justice. He wondered what Miss Earle must have thought of him after his eager conversation of the morning. The rest of the day he had spent gloomily in the smoking-room, and had not seen the young lady again. The more he thought of the day the worse he felt about it. However, he was philosopher enough to know that all the thinking he could do would not change a single item in the sum of the day's doing. So he slipped back the curtain on its brass rod and looked out into his state-room. The valise which he had left carelessly on the floor the night before was now making an excursion backwards and forwards from the bunk to the sofa, and the books that had been piled up on the sofa were scattered all over the room. It was evident that dressing was going to be an acrobatic performance.

The deck, when he reached it, was wet, but not with the moisture of the scrubbing. The outlook was clear enough, but a strong head-wind was blowing that whistled through the cordage of the vessel, and caused the black smoke of the funnels to float back like huge sombre streamers. The prow of the big ship rose now into the sky and then sank down into the bosom of the sea, and every time it descended a white cloud of spray drenched everything forward and sent a drizzly salt rain along the whole length of the steamer.

"There will be no ladies on deck this morning," said Morris to himself, as he held his cap on with both hands and looked around at the threatening sky. At this moment one wave struck the steamer with more than usual force and raised its crest amidship over the decks. Morris had just time to escape into the companion-way when it fell with a crash on the deck, flooding the promenade, and then rushing out through the scuppers into the sea.

"By George!" said Morris. "I guess there won't be many at breakfast either, if this sort of thing keeps up. I think the other side of the ship is the best."

Coming out on the other side of the deck, he was astonished to see, sitting in her steamer chair, snugly wrapped up in her rugs, Miss Katherine Earle, balancing a cup of steaming coffee in her hand. The steamer chair had been tightly tied to the brass stanchion, or hand-rail, that ran along the side of the housed-in portion of the companion-way, and although the steamer swayed to and fro, as well as up and down, the chair was immovable. An awning had been put up over the place where the chair was fastened, and every now and then on that dripping piece of canvas the salt rain fell, the result of the waves that dashed in on the other side of the steamer.

"Good morning, Mr. Morris!" said the young lady, brightly. "I am very glad you have come. I will let you into a shipboard secret. The steward of the smoking-room brings up every morning a pot of very fragrant coffee. Now, if you will speak to him, I am sure he will be very glad to give you a cup."

"You do like to make fun of me, don't you?" answered the young man.

"Oh, dear no," said Miss Earle, "I shouldn't think of making fun of anything so serious. Is it making fun of a person who looks half frozen to

152

offer him a cup of warm coffee? I think there is more philanthropy than fun about that."

"Well, I don't know but you are right. At any rate, I prefer to take it as philanthropy rather than fun. I shall go and get a cup of coffee for myself, if you will permit me to place a chair beside yours?"

"Oh, I beg you not to go for the coffee yourself. You certainly will never reach here with it. You see the remains of that cup down by the side of the vessel. The steward himself slipped and fell with that piece of crockery in his hands. I am sure he hurt himself, although he said he didn't."

"Did you give him an extra fee on that account?" asked Morris, cynically.

"Of course I did. I am like the Government in that respect. I take care of those who are injured in my service."

"Perhaps, that's why he went down. They are a sly set, those stewards. He knew that a man would simply laugh at him, or perhaps utter some maledictions if he were not feeling in very good humour. In all my ocean voyages I have never had the good fortune to see a steward fall. He knew, also, the rascal, that a lady would sympathise with him, and that he wouldn't lose anything by it, except the cup, which is not his loss."

"Oh yes, it is," replied the young lady, "he tells me they charge all breakages against him."

"He didn't tell you what method they had of keeping track of the breakages, did he? Suppose he told the chief steward that you broke the cup, which is likely he did. What then?"

"Oh, you are too cynical this morning, and it would serve you just right if you go and get some coffee for yourself, and meet with the same disaster that overtook the unfortunate steward. Only you are forewarned that you shall have neither sympathy nor fee."

"Well, in that case," said the young man, "I shall not take the risk. I shall sacrifice the steward rather. Oh, here he is. I say, steward, will you bring me a cup of coffee, please?"

"Yes, sir. Any biscuit, sir?"

"No, no biscuit. Just a cup of coffee and a couple of lumps of sugar, please; and if you can first get me a chair, and strap it to this rod in the manner you do so well, I shall be very much obliged."

"Yes, sir. I shall call the deck steward, sir."

"Now, notice that. You see the rascals never interfere with each other. The deck steward wants a fee, and the smoking-room steward wants a fee, and each one attends strictly to his own business, and doesn't interfere with the possible fees of anybody else."

"Well," said Miss Earle, "is not that the correct way? If things are to be well done, that is how they should be done. Now, just notice how much more artistically the deck steward arranged these rugs than you did yesterday morning. I think it is worth a good fee to be wrapped up so comfortably as that."

"I guess I'll take lessons from the deck steward then, and even if I do not get a fee, I may perhaps get some gratitude at least."

"Gratitude? Why, you should think it a privilege."

"Well, Miss Earle, to tell the truth, I do. It is a privilege that—I hope you will not think I am trying to flatter you when I say—any man might be proud of."

"Oh, dear," replied the young lady, laughing, "I did not mean it in that way at all. I meant that it was a privilege to be allowed to practise on those particular rugs. Now, a man should remember that he undertakes a very great responsibility when he volunteers to place the rugs around a lady on a steamer chair. He may make her look very neat and even pretty by a nice disposal of the rugs, or he may make her look like a horrible bundle."

"Well, then, I think I was not such a failure after all yesterday morning, for you certainly looked very neat and pretty."

"Then, if I did, Mr. Morris, do not flatter yourself it was at all on account

154

of your disposal of the rugs, for the moment you had left a very handsome young lady came along, and, looking at me, said, with such a pleasant smile, 'Why, what a pretty rug you have there; but how the steward has bungled it about you! Let me fix it,' and with that she gave it a touch here and a smooth down there, and the result was really so nice that I hated to go down to breakfast. It is a pity you went away so quickly yesterday morning. You might have had an opportunity of becoming acquainted with the lady, who is, I think, the prettiest girl on board this ship."

"Do you?" said Mr. Morris, shortly.

"Yes, I do. Have you noticed her? She sits over there at the long table near the centre. You must have seen her; she is so very, very pretty, that you cannot help noticing her."

"I am not looking after pretty women this voyage," said Morris, savagely.

"Oh, are you not? Well, I must thank you for that. That is evidently a very sincere compliment. No, I can't call it a compliment, but a sincere remark, I think the first sincere one you have made to-day."

"Why, what do you mean?" said Morris, looking at her in a bewildered sort of way.

"You have been looking after me this morning, have you not, and yesterday morning? And taking ever so much pains to be helpful and entertaining, and now, all at once you say—Well, you know what you said just now."

"Oh yes. Well, you see—"

"Oh, you can't get out of it, Mr. Morris. It was said, and with evident sincerity."

"Then you really think you are pretty?" said Mr. Morris, looking at his companion, who flushed under the remark.

"Ah, now," she said, "you imagine you are carrying the war into the enemy's country. But I don't at all appreciate a remark like that. I don't know but I dislike it even more than I do your compliments, which is saying a good deal."

"I assure you," said Morris, stiffly, "that I have not intended to pay any compliments. I am not a man who pays compliments."

"Not even left-handed ones?"

"Not even any kind, that I know of. I try as a general thing to speak the truth."

"Ah, and shame your hearers?"

"Well, I don't care who I shame as long as I succeed in speaking the truth."

"Very well, then; tell me the truth. Have you noticed this handsome young lady I speak of?"

"Yes, I have seen her."

"Don't you think she is very pretty?"

"Yes, I think she is."

"Don't you think she is the prettiest woman on the ship?"

"Yes, I think she is."

"Are you afraid of pretty women?"

"No, I don't think I am."

"Then, tell me why, the moment she appeared on the deck yesterday morning, you were so much agitated that you spilled most of my coffee in the saucer?"

"Did I appear agitated?" asked Morris, with some hesitation.

"Now, I consider that sort of thing worse than a direct prevarication."

"What sort of thing?"

"Why, a disingenuous answer. You know you appeared agitated. You know you were agitated. You know you had a camp-stool, and that you intended to sit down here and drink your coffee. All at once you changed your mind, and that change was coincident with the appearance on deck of the handsome young lady I speak of. I merely ask why?"

"Now, look here, Miss Earle, even the worst malefactor is not expected to incriminate himself. I can refuse to answer, can I not?"

"Certainly you may. You may refuse to answer anything, if you like. It was only because you were boasting about speaking the truth that I thought I should test your truth-telling qualities. I have been expecting every moment that you would say to me I was very impertinent, and that it was no business of mine, which would have been quite true. There, you see, you had a beautiful chance of speaking the truth which you let slip entirely unnoticed. But there is the breakfast gong. Now, I must confess to being very hungry indeed. I think I shall go down into the saloon."

"Please take my arm, Miss Earle," said the young man.

"Oh, not at all," replied that young lady; "I want something infinitely more stable. I shall work my way along this brass rod until I can make a bolt for the door. If you want to make yourself real useful, go and stand on the stairway, or the companion-way I think you call it, and if I come through the door with too great force you'll prevent me from going down the stairs."

"'Who ran to help me when I fell,'" quoted Mr. Morris, as he walked along ahead of her, having some difficulty in maintaining his equilibrium.

"I wouldn't mind the falling," replied the young lady, "if you only would some pretty story tell; but you are very prosaic, Mr. Morris. Do you ever read anything at all?"

"I never read when I have somebody more interesting than a book to talk to."

"Oh, thank you. Now, if you will get into position on the stairway, I shall make my attempts at getting to the door."

"I feel like a base-ball catcher," said Morris, taking up a position somewhat similar to that of the useful man behind the bat.

Miss Earle, however, waited until the ship was on an even keel, then walked to the top of the companion-way, and, deftly catching up the train of her dress with as much composure as if she were in a ballroom, stepped lightly down the stairway. Looking smilingly over her shoulder at the astonished baseball catcher, she said—

"I wish you would not stand in that ridiculous attitude, but come and accompany me to the breakfast table. As I told you, I am very hungry."

The steamer gave a lurch that nearly precipitated Morris down the stairway, and the next moment he was by her side.

"Are you fond of base-ball?" she said to him.

"You should see me in the park when our side makes a home run. Do you like the game?"

"I never saw a game in my life."

"What! you an American girl, and never saw a game of base-ball? Why, I am astonished."

"I did not say that I was an American girl."

"Oh, that's a fact. I took you for one, however."

They were both of them so intent on their conversation in walking up the narrow way between the long table and the short ones, that neither of them noticed the handsome blonde young lady standing beside her chair looking at them. It was only when that young lady said, "Why, Mr. Morris, is this you?" and when that gentleman jumped as if a cannon had been fired beside him, that either of them noticed their fair fellow-traveller.

"Y—es," stammered Morris, "it is!"

The young lady smiled sweetly and held out her hand, which Morris took in an awkward way.

"I was just going to ask you," she said, "when you came aboard. How ridiculous that would have been. Of course, you have been here all the time. Isn't it curious that we have not met each other?—we of all persons in the world."

Morris, who had somewhat recovered his breath, looked steadily at her as she said this, and her eyes, after encountering his gaze for a moment, sank to the floor.

Miss Earle, who had waited for a moment expecting that Morris would introduce her, but seeing that he had for the time being apparently forgotten everything on earth, quietly left them, and took her place at the breakfast table. The blonde young lady looked up again at Mr. Morris, and said—

"I am afraid I am keeping you from breakfast."

"Oh, that doesn't matter."

"I am afraid, then," she continued sweetly, "that I am keeping you from your very interesting table companion."

"Yes, that does matter," said Morris, looking at her. "I wish you good morning, madam." And with that he left her and took his place at the head of the small table.

There was a vindictive look in the blonde young lady's pretty eyes as she sank into her own seat at the breakfast table.

Miss Earle had noticed the depressing effect which even the sight of the blonde lady exercised on Morris the day before, and she looked forward, therefore, to rather an uncompanionable breakfast. She was surprised, however, to see that Morris had an air of jaunty joviality, which she could not help thinking was rather forced.

"Now," he said, as he sat down on the sofa at the head of the table, "I think it's about time for us to begin our chutney fight."

"Our what?" asked the young lady, looking up at him with open eyes.

"Is it possible," he said, "that you have crossed the ocean and never engaged in the chutney fight? I always have it on this line."

"I am sorry to appear so ignorant," said Miss Earle, "but I have to confess I do not know what chutney is."

"I am glad of that," returned the young man. "It delights me to find in your nature certain desert spots—certain irreclaimable lands, I might say—of ignorance."

"I do not see why a person should rejoice in the misfortunes of another person," replied the young lady.

"Oh, don't you? Why, it is the most natural thing in the world. There is nothing that we so thoroughly dislike as a person, either lady or gentleman, who is perfect. I suspect you rather have the advantage of me in the reading of books, but I certainly have the advantage of you on chutney, and I intend to make the most of it."

"I am sure I shall be very glad to be enlightened, and to confess my ignorance whenever it is necessary, and that, I fear, will be rather often. So, if our acquaintance continues until the end of the voyage, you will be in a state of perpetual delight."

"Well, that's encouraging. You will be pleased to learn that chutney is a sauce, an Indian sauce, and on this line somehow or other they never have more than one or two bottles. I do not know whether it is very expensive. I presume it is. Perhaps it is because there is very little demand for it, a great number of people not knowing what chutney is."

"Thank you," said the young lady, "I am glad to find that I am in the majority, at least, even in the matter of ignorance."

"Well, as I was saying, chutney is rather a seductive sauce. You may not like it at first, but it grows on you. You acquire, as it were, the chutney habit. An old Indian traveller, whom I had the pleasure of crossing with once, and who sat at the same table with me, demanded chutney. He initiated me into the mysteries of chutney, and he had a chutney fight all the way across."

"I still have to confess that I do not see what there is to fight about in the matter of chutney."

"Don't you? Well, you shall soon have a practical illustration of the terrors of a chutney fight. Steward," called Morris, "just bring me a bottle of chutney, will you?"

"Chutney, air?" asked the steward, as if he had never heard the word before.

"Yes, chutney. Chutney sauce."

"I am afraid, sir," said the steward, "that we haven't any chutney sauce."

"Oh yes, you have. I see a bottle there on the captain's table. I think there is a second bottle at the smaller table. Just two doors up the street. Have the kindness to bring it to me."

The steward left for the chutney, and Morris looking after him, saw that there was some discussion between him and the steward of the other table. Finally, Morris's steward came back and said, "I am very sorry, sir, but they are using the chutney at that table."

"Now look here, steward," said Morris, "you know that you are here to take care of us, and that at the end of the voyage I will take care of you. Don't make any mistake about that. You understand me?"

"Yes, sir, I do," said the steward. "Thank you, sir."

"All right," replied Morris. "Now you understand that I want chutney, and chutney I am going to have."

Steward number one waited until steward number two had disappeared after another order, and then he deftly reached over, took the chutney sauce, and placed it before Mr. Morris.

"Now, Miss Earle, I hope that you will like this chutney sauce. You see there is some difficulty in getting it, and that of itself ought to be a strong recommendation for it."

"It is a little too hot to suit me," answered the young lady, trying the Indian sauce, "still, there is a pleasant flavour about it that I like."

"Oh, you are all right," said Morris, jauntily; "you will be a victim of the

161

chutney habit before two days. People who dislike it at first are its warmest advocates afterwards. I use the word warmest without any allusion to the sauce itself, you know. I shall now try some myself."

As he looked round the table for the large bottle, he saw that it had been whisked away by steward number two, and now stood on the other table. Miss Earle laughed.

"Oh, I shall have it in a moment," said the young man.

"Do you think it is worth while?"

"Worth while? Why, that is the excitement of a chutney fight. It is not that we care for chutney at all, but that we simply are bound to have it. If there were a bottle of chutney at every table, the delights of chutney would be gone. Steward," said Morris, as that functionary appeared, "the chutney, please."

The steward cast a rapid glance at the other table, and waited until steward number two had disappeared. Then Morris had his chutney. Steward number two, seeing his precious bottle gone, tried a second time to stealthily obtain possession of it, but Morris said to him in a pleasant voice, "That's all right, steward, we are through with the chutney. Take it along, please. So that," continued Mr. Morris, as Miss Earle rose from the table, "that is your first experience of a chutney fight—one of the delights of ocean travel."

Fourth Day

Mr. George Morris began to find his "early coffees," as he called them, very delightful. It was charming to meet a pretty and entertaining young lady every morning early when they had the deck practically to themselves. The fourth day was bright and clear, and the sea was reasonably calm. For the first time he was up earlier than Miss Earle, and he paced the deck with great impatience, waiting for her appearance. He wondered who and what she was. He had a dim, hazy idea that some time before in his life, he had met her, and probably had been acquainted with her. What an embarrassing thing it would be, he thought, if he had really known her years before, and had forgotten her, while she knew who he was, and had remembered him.

He thought of how accurately she had guessed his position in life—if it was a guess. He remembered that often, when he looked at her, he felt certain he had known her and spoken to her before. He placed the two steamer chairs in position, so that Miss Earle's chair would be ready for her when she did appear, and then, as he walked up and down the deck waiting for her, he began to wonder at himself. If any one had told him when he left New York that, within three or four days he could feel such an interest in a person who previous to that time had been an utter stranger to him, he would have laughed scornfully and bitterly at the idea. As it was, when he thought of all the peculiar circumstances of the case, he laughed aloud, but neither scornfully nor bitterly.

"You must be having very pleasant thoughts, Mr. Morris," said Miss Earle, as she appeared with a bright shawl thrown over her shoulders, instead of the long cloak that had encased her before, and with a Tam o' Shanter set jauntily on her black, curly hair.

"You are right," said Morris, taking off his cap, "I was thinking of you."

"Oh, indeed," replied the young lady, "that's why you laughed, was it? I may say that I do not relish being laughed at in my absence, or in my presence either, for that matter."

"Oh, I assure you I wasn't laughing at you. I laughed with pleasure to see you come on deck. I have been waiting for you."

"Now, Mr. Morris, that from a man who boasts of his truthfulness is a little too much. You did not see me at all until I spoke; and if, as you say, you were thinking of me, you will have to explain that laugh."

"I will explain it before the voyage is over, Miss Earle. I can't explain it just now."

"Ah, then you admit you were untruthful when you said you laughed because you saw me?"

"I may as well admit it. You seem to know things intuitively. I am not nearly as truthful a person as I thought I was until I met you. You seem the very embodiment of truth. If I had not met you, I imagine I should have gone through life thinking myself one of the most truthful men in New York."

"Perhaps that would not be saying very much for yourself," replied the young lady, as she took her place in the steamer chair.

"I am sorry you have such a poor opinion of us New Yorkers," said the young man. "Why are you so late this morning?"

"I am not late; it is you who are early. This is my usual time. I have been a very punctual person all my life."

"There you go again, speaking as if you were ever so old."

"I am."

"Well, I don't believe it. I wish, however, that you had confidence enough in me to tell me something about yourself. Do you know, I was thinking this morning that I had met you before somewhere? I feel almost certain I have."

"Well, that is quite possible, you know. You are a New Yorker, and I have lived in New York for a great number of years, much as you seem to dislike that phrase."

"New York! Oh, that is like saying you have lived in America and I have lived in America. We might live for hundreds of years in New York and never meet one another!"

"That is very true, except that the time is a little long."

"Then won't you tell me something about yourself?"

"No, I will not."

"Why?"

"Why? Well, if you will tell me why you have the right to ask such a question, I shall answer why."

"Oh, if you talk of rights, I suppose I haven't the right. But I am willing to tell you anything about myself. Now, a fair exchange, you know—"

"But I don't wish to know anything about you."

"Oh, thank you."

George Morris's face clouded, and he sat silent for a few moments.

"I presume," he said again, "that you think me very impertinent?"

"Well, frankly, I do."

Morris gazed out at the sea, and Miss Earle opened the book which she had brought with her, and began to read. After a while her companion said—

"I think that you are a little too harsh with me, Miss Earle."

The young lady placed her finger between the leaves of the book and closed it, looking up at him with a frank, calm expression in her dark eyes, but said nothing.

"You see, it's like this. I said to you a little while since that I seem to have known you before. Now, I'll tell you what I was thinking of when you met me this morning. I was thinking what a curious thing it would be if I had been acquainted with you some time during my past life, and had forgotten you, while you had remembered me."

"That was very flattering to me," said the young lady; "I don't wonder you laughed."

"That is why I did not wish to tell you what I had been thinking of—just for fear that you would put a wrong construction on it—as you have done. But now you can't say anything much harsher to me than you have said, and so I tell you frankly just what I thought, and why I asked you those questions which you seem to think are so impertinent. Besides this, you know, a sea acquaintance is different from any other acquaintance. As I said, the first time I spoke to you—or the second—there is no one here to introduce us. On land, when a person is introduced to another person, he does not say, 'Miss Earle, this is Mr. Morris, who is a younger partner in the house of So-and-so.' He merely says, 'Miss Earle, Mr. Morris,' and there it is. If you want to find anything out about him you can ask your introducer or ask your friends, and you can find out. Now, on shipboard it is entirely different. Suppose, for instance, that I did not tell you who I am, and—if you will pardon me for suggesting such an absurd supposition——imagine that you wanted to find out, how could you do it?"

Miss Earle looked at him for a moment, and then she answered—

"I would ask that blonde young lady."

This reply was so utterly unexpected by Morris that he looked at her with wide eyes, the picture of a man dumbfounded. At that moment the smoking-room steward came up to them and said—

"Will you have your coffee now, sir?"

"Coffee!" cried Morris, as if he had never heard the word before. "Coffee!"

"Yes," answered Miss Earle, sweetly, "we will have the coffee now, if you please. You will have a cup with me, will you not, Mr. Morris?"

"Yes, I will, if it is not too much trouble."

"Oh, it is no trouble to me," said, the young lady; "some trouble to the steward, but I believe even for him that it is not a trouble that cannot be recompensed."

Morris sipped his coffee in silence. Every now and then Miss Earle stole a quiet look at him, and apparently was waiting for him to again resume the conversation. This he did not seem in a hurry to do. At last she said—

"Mr. Morris, suppose we were on shipboard and that we had become acquainted without the friendly intervention of an introducer, and suppose, if such a supposition is at all within the bounds of probability, that you wanted to find out something about me, how would you go about it?"

"How would I go about it?"

"Yes. How?"

"I would go about it in what would be the worst possible way. I would frankly ask you, and you would as frankly snub me.

"

"Suppose, then, while declining to tell you anything about myself I were to refer you to somebody who would give you the information you desire, would you take the opportunity of learning?"

"I would prefer to hear from yourself anything I desired to learn."

"Now, that is very nicely said, Mr. Morris, and you make me feel almost sorry, for having spoken to you as I did. Still, if you really want to find out something about me, I shall tell you some one whom you can ask, and who will doubtless answer you."

"Who is that? The captain?"

"No. It is the same person to whom I should go if I wished to have information of you—the blonde young lady."

"Do you mean to say you know her?" asked the astonished young man.

"I said nothing of the sort."

"Well, do you know her?"

"No, I do not."

"Do you know her name?"

"No, I do not even know her name."

"Have you ever met her before you came on board this ship?"

"Yes, I have."

"Well, if that isn't the most astonishing thing I ever heard!"

"I don't see why it is. You say you thought you had met me before. As you are a man no doubt you have forgotten it. I say I think I have met that young lady before. As she is a woman I don't think she will have forgotten. If you have any interest in the matter at all you might inquire."

"I shall do nothing of the sort."

"Well, of course, I said I thought you hadn't very much interest. I only supposed the case."

"It is not that I have not the interest, but it is that I prefer to go to the person who can best answer my question if she chooses to do so. If she doesn't choose to answer me, then I don't choose to learn."

"Now, I like that ever so much," said the young lady; "if you will get me another cup of coffee I shall be exceedingly obliged to you. My excuse is that these cups are very small, and the coffee is very good."

"I am sure you don't need any excuse," replied Morris, springing to his feet, "and I am only too happy to be your steward without the hope of the fee at the end of the voyage."

When he returned she said, "I think we had better stop the personal conversation into which we have drifted. It isn't at all pleasant to me, and I don't think it is very agreeable to you. Now, I intended this morning to give you a lesson on American literature. I feel that you need enlightening on the subject, and that you have neglected your opportunities, as most New York men do, and so I thought you would be glad of a lesson or two."

"I shall be very glad of it indeed. I don't know what our opportunities are, but if most New York men are like me I imagine a great many of them are in the same fix. We have very little time for the study of the literature of any country."

"And perhaps very little inclination."

"Well, you know, Miss Earle, there is some excuse for a busy man. Don't you think there is?"

"I don't think there is very much. Who in America is a busier man than Mr. Gladstone? Yet he reads nearly everything, and is familiar with almost any subject you can mention."

"Oh, Gladstone! Well, he is a man of a million. But you take the average

New York man. He is worried in business, and kept on the keen jump all the year round. Then he has a vacation, say for a couple of weeks or a month, in summer, and he goes off into the woods with his fishing kit, or canoeing outfit, or his amateur photographic set, or whatever the tools of his particular fad may be. He goes to a book-store and buys up a lot of paper-covered novels. There is no use of buying an expensive book, because he would spoil it before he gets back, and he would be sure to leave it in some shanty. So he takes those paper-covered abominations, and you will find torn copies of them scattered all through the Adirondacks, and down the St. Lawrence, and everywhere else that tourists congregate. I always tell the book-store man to give me the worst lot of trash he has got, and he does. Now, what is that book you have with you?"

"This is one of Mr. Howells' novels. You will admit, at least, that you have heard of Howells, I suppose?"

"Heard of him? Oh yes; I have read some of Howells' books. I am not as ignorant as you seem to think."

"What have you read of Mr. Howells'?"

"Well, I read The American, I don't remember the others."

"The American! That is by Henry James."

"Is it? Well, I knew that it was by either Howells or James, I forgot which. They didn't write a book together, did they?"

"Well, not that I know of. Why, the depth of your ignorance about American literature is something appalling. You talk of it so jauntily that you evidently have no idea of it yourself."

"I wish you would take me in hand, Miss Earle. Isn't there any sort of condensed version that a person could get hold of? Couldn't you give me a synopsis of what is written, so that I might post myself up in literature without going to the trouble of reading the books?"

"The trouble! Oh, if that is the way you speak, then your case is hopeless! I suspected it for some time, but now I am certain. The trouble! The delight

169

of reading a new novel by Howells is something that you evidently have not the remotest idea of. Why, I don't know what I would give to have with me a novel of Howells' that I had not read."

"Goodness gracious! You don't mean to say that you have read everything he has written?"

"Certainly I have, and I am reading one now that is coming out in the magazine; and I don't know what I shall do if I am not able to get the magazine when I go to Europe."

"Oh, you can get them over there right enough, and cheaper than you can in America. They publish them over there."

"Do they? Well, I am glad to hear it."

"You see, there is something about American literature that you are not acquainted with, the publication of our magazines in England, for instance. Ah, there is the breakfast gong. Well, we will have to postpone our lesson in literature until afterwards. Will you be up here after breakfast?"

"Yes, I think so."

"Well, we will leave our chairs and rugs just where they are. I will take your book down for you. Books have the habit of disappearing if they are left around on shipboard."

After breakfast Mr. Morris went to the smoking-room to enjoy his cigar, and there was challenged to a game of cards. He played one game; but his mind was evidently not on his amusement, so he excused himself from any further dissipation in that line, and walked out on deck. The promise of the morning had been more than fulfilled in the day, and the warm sunlight and mild air had brought on deck many who had not been visible up to that time. There was a long row of muffled up figures on steamer chairs, and the deck steward was kept busy hurrying here and there attending to the wants of the passengers. Nearly every one had a book, but many of the books were turned face downwards on the steamer rugs, while the owners either talked to those next them, or gazed idly out at the blue ocean. In the long and narrow open space between the chairs and the bulwarks of the ship, the energetic pedestrians were walking up and down.

At this stage of the voyage most of the passengers had found congenial companions, and nearly everybody was acquainted with everybody else. Morris walked along in front of the reclining passengers, scanning each one eagerly to find the person he wanted, but she was not there. Remembering then that the chairs had been on the other side of the ship, he continued his walk around the wheel-house, and there he saw Miss Earle, and sitting beside her was the blonde young lady talking vivaciously, while Miss Earle listened.

Morris hesitated for a moment, but before he could turn back the young lady sprang to her feet, and said—"Oh, Mr. Morris, am I sitting in your chair?"

"What makes you think it is my chair?" asked that gentleman, not in the most genial tone of voice.

"I thought so," replied the young lady, with a laugh, "because it was near Miss Earle."

Miss Earle did not look at all pleased at this remark. She coloured slightly, and, taking the open book from her lap, began to read.

"You are quite welcome to the chair," replied Morris, and the moment the words were spoken he felt that somehow it was one of those things he would rather have left unsaid, as far as Miss Earle was concerned. "I beg that you will not disturb yourself," he continued; and, raising his hat to the lady, he continued his walk.

A chance acquaintance joined him, changing his step to suit that of Morris, and talked with him on the prospects of the next year being a good business season in the United States. Morris answered rather absent-mindedly, and it was nearly lunch-time before he had an opportunity of going back to see whether or not Miss Earle's companion had left. When he reached the spot where they had been sitting he found things the very reverse of what he had hoped. Miss Earle's chair was vacant, but her companion sat there, idly turning over the leaves of the book that Miss Earle had been reading. "Won't you sit down, Mr. Morris?" said the young woman, looking up at him with a winning smile. "Miss Earle has gone to dress for lunch. I should do the same thing, but, alas! I am too indolent."

Morris hesitated for a moment, and then sat down beside her.

"Why do you act so perfectly horrid to me?" asked the young lady, closing the book sharply.

"I was not aware that I acted horridly to anybody," answered Morris.

"You know well enough that you have been trying your very best to avoid me."

"I think you are mistaken. I seldom try to avoid any one, and I see no reason why I should try to avoid you. Do you know of any reason?"

The young lady blushed and looked down at her book, whose leaves she again began to turn.

"I thought," she said at last, "that you might have some feeling against me, and I have no doubt you judge me very harshly. You never did make any allowances."

Morris gave a little laugh that was half a sneer.

"Allowances?" he said.

"Yes, allowances. You know you always were harsh with me, George, always." And as she looked up at him her blue eyes were filled with tears, and there was a quiver at the corner of her mouth. "What a splendid actress you would make, Blanche," said the young man, calling her by her name for the first time.

She gave him a quick look as he did so. "Actress!" she cried. "No one was ever less an actress than I am, and you know that."

"Oh, well, what's the use of us talking? It's all right. We made a little mistake, that's all, and people often make mistakes in this life, don't they, Blanche?"

172

"Yes," sobbed that young lady, putting her dainty silk handkerchief to her eyes.

"Now, for goodness sake," said the young man, "don't do that. People will think I am scolding you, and certainly there is no one in this world who has less right to scold you than I have."

"I thought," murmured the young lady, from behind her handkerchief, "that we might at least be friends. I didn't think you could ever act so harshly towards me as you have done for the past few days."

"Act?" cried the young man. "Bless me, I haven't acted one way or the other. I simply haven't had the pleasure of meeting you till the other evening, or morning, which ever it was. I have said nothing, and done nothing. I don't see how I could be accused of acting, or of anything else."

"I think," sobbed the young lady, "that you might at least have spoken kindly to me."

"Good gracious!" cried Morris, starting up, "here comes Miss Earle. For heaven's sake put up that handkerchief."

But Blanche merely sank her face lower in it, while silent sobs shook her somewhat slender form.

Miss Earle stood for a moment amazed as she looked at Morris's flushed face, and at the bowed head of the young lady beside him; then, without a word, she turned and walked away.

"I wish to goodness," said Morris, harshly, "that if you are going to have a fit of crying you would not have it on deck, and where people can see you."

The young woman at once straightened up and flashed a look at him in which there were no traces of her former emotion.

"People!" she said, scornfully. "Much you care about people. It is because Miss Katherine Earle saw me that you are annoyed. You are afraid that it will interfere with your flirtation with her."

"Flirtation?"

"Yes, flirtation. Surely it can't be anything more serious?"

"Why should it not be something more serious?" asked Morris, very coldly. The blue eyes opened wide in apparent astonishment.

"Would you marry her?" she said, with telling emphasis upon the word.

"Why not?" he answered. "Any man might be proud to marry a lady like Miss Earle."

"A lady! Much of a lady she is! Why, she is one of your own shop-girls. You know it."

"Shop-girls?" cried Morris, in astonishment.

"Yes, shop-girls. You don't mean to say that she has concealed that fact from you, or that you didn't know it by seeing her in the store?"

"A shop-girl in my store?" he murmured, bewildered. "I knew I had seen her somewhere."

Blanche laughed a little irritating laugh.

"What a splendid item it would make for the society papers," she said. "The junior partner marries one of his own shop-girls, or, worse still, the junior partner and one of his shop-girls leave New York on the City of Buffalo, and are married in England. I hope that the reporters will not get the particulars of the affair." Then, rising, she left the amazed young man to his thoughts.

George Morris saw nothing more of Miss Katherine Earle that day.

"I wonder what that vixen has said to her," he thought, as he turned in for the night.

Fifth Day

In the early morning of the fifth day out, George Morris paced the deck alone.

"Shop-girl or not," he had said to himself, "Miss Katherine Earle is much more of a lady than the other ever was." But as he paced the deck, and as Miss Earle did not appear, he began to wonder more and more what had been said to her in the long talk of yesterday forenoon. Meanwhile Miss Earle sat in her own state-room thinking over the same subject. Blanche had sweetly asked her for permission to sit down beside her.

"I know no ladies on board," she said, "and I think I have met you before."

"Yes," answered Miss Earle, "I think we have met before."

"How good of you to have remembered me," said Blanche, kindly.

"I think," replied Miss Earle, "that it is more remarkable that you should remember me than that I should remember you. Ladies very rarely notice the shop-girls who wait upon them."

"You seemed so superior to your station," said Blanche, "that I could not help remembering you, and could not help thinking what a pity it was you had to be there."

"I do not think that there is anything either superior or inferior about the station. It is quite as honourable, or dishonourable, which ever it may be, as any other branch of business. I cannot see, for instance, why my station, selling ribbons at retail, should be any more dishonourable than the station of the head of the firm, who merely does on a very large scale what I was trying to do for him on a very limited scale."

"Still," said Blanche, with a yawn, "people do not all look upon it in exactly that light."

"Hardly any two persons look on any one thing in the same light. I hope you have enjoyed your voyage so far?"

"I have not enjoyed it very much," replied the young lady with a sigh.

"I am sorry to hear that. I presume your father has been ill most of the way?"

"My father?" cried the other, looking at her questioner.

"Yes, I did not see him at the table since the first day."

"Oh, he has had to keep his room almost since we left. He is a very poor sailor."

"Then that must make your voyage rather unpleasant?"

The blonde young lady made no reply, but, taking up the book which Miss Earle was reading, said, "You don't find Mr. Morris much of a reader, I presume? He used not to be."

"I know very little about Mr. Morris," said Miss Earle, freezingly.

"Why, you knew him before you came on board, did you not?" questioned the other, raising her eyebrows.

"No, I did not."

"You certainly know he is junior partner in the establishment where you work?"

"I know that, yes, but I had never spoken to him before I met him on board this steamer."

"Is that possible? Might I ask you if there is any probability of your becoming interested in Mr. Morris?"

"Interested! What do you mean?"

"Oh, you know well enough what I mean. We girls do not need to be humbugs with each other, whatever we may be before the men. When a young woman meets a young man in the early morning, and has coffee with him, and when she reads to him, and tries to cultivate his literary tastes, whatever they may be, she certainly shows some interest in the young man, don't you think so?"

Miss Earle looked for a moment indignantly at her questioner. "I do not recognise your right," she said, "to ask me such a question."

"No? Then let me tell you that I have every right to ask it. I assure you that I have thought over the matter deeply before I spoke. It seemed to me there was one chance in a thousand—only one chance in a thousand, remember—that you were acting honestly, and on that one chance I took the liberty of speaking to you. The right I have to ask such a question is this—Mr. George Morris has been engaged to me for several years."

"Engaged to you?"

"Yes. If you don't believe it, ask him."

"It is the very last question in the world I would ask anybody."

"Well, then, you will have to take my word for it. I hope you are not very shocked, Miss Earle, to hear what I have had to tell you."

"Shocked? Oh dear, no. Why should I be? It is really a matter of no interest to me, I assure you."

"Well, I am very glad to hear you say so. I did not know but you might have become more interested in Mr. Morris than you would care to own. I think myself that he is quite a fascinating young gentleman; but I thought it only just to you that you should know exactly how matters stood."

"I am sure I am very much obliged to you."

This much of the conversation Miss Earle had thought over in her own room that morning. "Did it make a difference to her or not?" that was the question she was asking herself. The information had certainly affected her opinion of Mr. Morris, and she smiled to herself rather bitterly as she thought of his claiming to be so exceedingly truthful. Miss Earle did not, however, go up on deck until the breakfast gong had rung.

"Good morning," said Morris, as he took his place at the little table. "I was like the boy on the burning deck this morning, when all but he had fled. I was very much disappointed that you did not come up, and have your usual cup of coffee."

"I am sorry to hear that," said Miss Earle; "if I had known I was disappointing anybody I should have been here."

"Miss Katherine," he said, "you are a humbug. You knew very well that I would be disappointed if you did not come."

The young lady looked up at him, and for a moment she thought of telling him that her name was Miss Earle, but for some reason she did not do so.

"I want you to promise now," he continued, "that to-morrow morning you will be on deck as usual."

"Has it become a usual thing, then?"

"Well, that's what I am trying to make it," he answered. "Will you promise?"

"Yes, I promise."

"Very well, then, I look on that as settled. Now, about to-day. What are you going to do with yourself after breakfast?"

"Oh, the usual thing, I suppose. I shall sit in my steamer chair and read an interesting book."

"And what is the interesting book for to-day?"

"It is a little volume by Henry James, entitled The Siege of London."

"Why, I never knew that London had been besieged. When did that happen?"

"Well, I haven't got very far in the book yet, but it seems to have happened quite recently, within a year or two, I think. It is one of the latest of Mr. James's short stories. I have not read it yet."

"Ah, then the siege is not historical?"

"Not historical further than Mr. James is the historian."

"Now, Miss Earle, are you good at reading out loud?"

"No, I am not."

"Why, how decisively you say that. I couldn't answer like that, because I don't know whether I am or not. I have never tried any of it. But if you will allow me, I will read that book out to you. I should like to have the good points indicated to me, and also the defects."

"There are not likely to be many defects," said the young lady. "Mr. James is a very correct writer. But I do not care either to read aloud or have a book read to me. Besides, we disturb the conversation or the reading of any one else who happens to sit near us. I prefer to enjoy a book by reading it myself."

"Ah, I see you are resolved cruelly to shut me out of all participation in your enjoyment."

"Oh, not at all. I shall be very happy to discuss the book with you afterwards. You should read it for yourself. Then, when you have done so, we might have a talk on its merits or demerits, if you think, after you have read it, that it has any."

"Any what? merits or demerits?"

"Well, any either."

"No; I will tell you a better plan than that. I am not going to waste my time reading it."

"Waste, indeed!"

"Certainly waste. Not when I have a much better plan of finding out what is in the book. I am going to get you to tell me the story after you have read it."

"Oh, indeed, and suppose I refuse?"

"Will you?"

"Well, I don't know. I only said suppose."

"Then I shall spend the rest of the voyage trying to persuade you."

"I am not very easily persuaded, Mr. Morris."

"I believe that," said the young man. "I presume I may sit beside you while you are reading your book?"

"You certainly may, if you wish to. The deck is not mine, only that portion of it, I suppose, which I occupy with the steamer chair. I have no authority over any of the rest."

"Now, is that a refusal or an acceptance?"

"It is which ever you choose to think."

"Well, if it is a refusal, it is probably softening down the No, but if it is an acceptance it is rather an ungracious one, it seems to me."

"Well, then, I shall be frank with you. I am very much interested in this book. I should a great deal rather read it than talk to you."

"Oh, thank you, Miss Earle. There can be no possible doubt about your meaning now."

"Well, I am glad of that, Mr. Morris. I am always pleased to think that I can speak in such a way as not to be misunderstood."

"I don't see any possible way of misunderstanding that. I wish I did."

"And then, after lunch," said the young lady, "I think I shall finish the book before that time;—if you care to sit beside me or to walk the deck with me, I shall be very glad to tell you the story."

"Now, that is perfectly delightful," cried the young man. "You throw a person down into the depths, so that he will appreciate all the more being brought up into the light again."

"Oh, not at all. I have no such dramatic ideas in speaking frankly with you. I merely mean that this forenoon I wish to have to myself, because I am interested in my book. At the end of the forenoon I shall probably be tired of my book and will prefer a talk with you. I don't see why you should think it odd that a person should say exactly what a person means."

"And then I suppose in the evening you will be tired of talking with me, and will want to take up your book again."

"Possibly."

"And if you are, you won't hesitate a moment about saying so?"

"Certainly not."

"Well, you are a decidedly frank young lady, Miss Earle; and, after all, I don't know but what I like that sort of thing best. I think if all the world were honest we would all have a better time of it here."

"Do you really think so?"

"Yes, I do."

"You believe in honesty, then?"

"Why, certainly. Have you seen anything in my conduct or bearing that would induce you to think that I did not believe in honesty?"

"No, I can't say I have. Still, honesty is such a rare quality that a person naturally is surprised when one comes unexpectedly upon it."

George Morris found the forenoon rather tedious and lonesome. He sat in the smoking room, and once or twice he ventured near where Miss Earle sat engrossed in her book, in the hope that the volume might have been put aside for the time, and that he would have some excuse for sitting down and talking with her. Once as he passed she looked up with a bright smile and nodded to him.

"Nearly through?" he asked dolefully.

"Of The Siege of London?" she asked.

"Yes."

"Oh, I am through that long ago, and have begun another story."

"Now, that is not according to contract," claimed Morris. "The contract was that when you got through with The Siege of London you were to let me talk with you, and that you were to tell me the story."

"That was not my interpretation of it. Our bargain, as I understood it, was that I was to have this forenoon to myself, and that I was to use the forenoon for reading. I believe my engagement with you began in the afternoon."

"I wish it did," said the young man, with a wistful look.

"You wish what?" she said, glancing up at him sharply.

He blushed as he bent over towards her and whispered, "That our engagement, Miss Katherine, began in the afternoon."

The colour mounted rapidly into her cheeks, and for a moment George Morris thought he had gone too far. It seemed as if a sharp reply was ready on her lips; but, as on another occasion, she checked it and said nothing. Then she opened her book and began to read. He waited for a moment and said—

"Miss Earle, have I offended you?"

"Did you mean to give offence?" she asked.

"No, certainly, I did not."

"Then why should you think you had offended me?"

"Well, I don't know, I—" he stammered.

Miss Earle looked at him with such clear, innocent, and unwavering eyes that the young man felt that he could neither apologise nor make an explanation.

"I'm afraid," he said, "that I am encroaching on your time."

"Yes, I think you are: that is, if you intend to live up to your contract, and let me live up to mine. You have no idea how much more interesting this book is than you are."

"Why, you are not a bit flattering, Miss Earle, are you?"

"No, I don't think I am. Do you try to be?"

"I'm afraid that in my lifetime I have tried to be, but I assure you, Miss Earle, that I don't try to be flattering, or try to be anything but what I really am when I am in your company. To tell the truth, I am too much afraid of

182

you."

Miss Earle smiled and went on with her reading, while Morris went once more back into the smoking-room.

"Now then," said George Morris, when lunch was over, "which is it to be? The luxurious languor of the steamer chair or the energetic exercise of the deck? Take your choice."

"Well," answered the young lady, "as I have been enjoying the luxurious languor all the forenoon, I prefer the energetic exercise, if it is agreeable to you, for a while, at least."

"It is very agreeable to me. I am all energy this afternoon. In fact, now that you have consented to allow me to talk with you, I feel as if I were imbued with a new life."

"Dear me," said she, "and all because of the privilege of talking to me?"

"All."

"How nice that is. You are sure that it is not the effect of the sea air?"

"Quite certain. I had the sea air this forenoon, you know."

"Oh, yes, I had forgotten that."

"Well, which side of the deck then?"

"Oh, which ever is the least popular side. I dislike a crowd."

"I think, Miss Earle, that we will have this side pretty much to ourselves. The madd'ing crowd seems to have a preference for the sunny part of the ship. Now, then, for the siege of London. Who besieged it?"

"A lady."

"Did she succeed?"

"She did."

"Well, I am very glad to hear it, indeed. What was she besieging it for?"

"For social position, I presume.

"Then, as we say out West, I suppose she had a pretty hard row to hoe?"

"Yes, she had."

"Well, I never can get at the story by cross-questioning. Now, supposing that you tell it to me."

"I think that you had better take the book and read it. I am not a good story-teller."

"Why, I thought we Americans were considered excellent story-tellers.'

"We Americans?"

"Oh, I remember now, you do not lay claim to being an American. You are English, I think you said?"

"I said nothing of the kind. I merely said I lay no claims to being an American."

"Yes, that was it."

"Well, you will be pleased to know that this lady in the siege of London was an American. You seem so anxious to establish a person's nationality that I am glad to be able to tell you at the very first that she was an American, and, what is more, seemed to be a Western American."

"Seemed? Oh, there we get into uncertainties again. If I like to know whether persons are Americans or not, it naturally follows that I am anxious to know whether they were Western or Eastern Americans. Aren't you sure she was a Westerner?"

"The story, unfortunately, leaves that a little vague, so if it displeases you I shall be glad to stop the telling of it."

"Oh no, don't do that. I am quite satisfied to take her as an American citizen; whether she is East or West, or North or South, does not make the slightest difference to me. Please go on with the story."

"Well, the other characters, I am happy to be able to say, are not at all indefinite in the matter of nationality. One is an Englishman; he is even more than that, he is an English nobleman. The other is an American. Then there is the English nobleman's mother, who, of course, is an English woman; and the American's sister, married to an Englishman, and she, of course, is English-American. Does that satisfy you?"

"Perfectly. Go on."

"It seems that the besieger, the heroine of the story if you may call her so, had a past."

"Has not everybody had a past?"

"Oh no. This past is known to the American and is unknown to the English nobleman."

"Ah, I see; and the American is in love with her in spite of her past?"

"Not in Mr. James's story."

"Oh, I beg pardon. Well, go on; I shall not interrupt again."

"It is the English nobleman who is in love with her in spite of his absence of knowledge about her past. The English nobleman's mother is very much against the match. She tries to get the American to tell what the past of this woman is. The American refuses to do so. In fact, in Paris he has half promised the besieger not to say anything about her past. She is besieging London, and she wishes the American to remain neutral. But the nobleman's mother at last gets the American to promise that he will tell her son what he knows of this woman's past. The American informs the woman what he has promised the nobleman's mother to do, and at this moment the nobleman enters the room. The besieger of London, feeling that her game is up, leaves them together. The American says to the nobleman, who stands rather stiffly before him, 'If you wish to ask me any questions regarding the lady who has gone out I shall be happy to tell you.' Those are not the words of the book, but they are in substance what he said. The nobleman looked at him for a moment with that hauteur which, we presume, belongs to noblemen, and said quietly, 'I wish to know nothing.' Now, that strikes me as a very dramatic point in the story."

"But didn't he wish to know anything of the woman whom he was going to marry?"

"I presume that, naturally, he did."

"And yet he did not take the opportunity of finding out when he had the chance?"

"No, he did not."

"Well, what do you think of that?"

"What do I think of it? I think it's a very dramatic point in the story."

"Yes, but what do you think of his wisdom in refusing to find out what sort of a woman he was going to marry? Was he a fool or was he a very noble man?"

"Why, I thought I said at the first that he was a nobleman, an Englishman."

"Miss Katherine, you are dodging the question. I asked your opinion of that man's wisdom. Was he wise, or was he a fool?"

"What do you think about it? Do you think he was a fool, or a wise man?"

"Well, I asked you for your opinion first. However, I have very little hesitation in saying, that a man who marries a woman of whom he knows nothing, is a fool."

"Oh, but he was well acquainted with this woman. It was only her past that he knew nothing about."

"Well, I think you must admit that a woman's past and a man's past are very important parts of their lives. Don't you agree with me?"

"I agree with you so seldom that I should hesitate to say I did on this occasion. But I have told the story very badly. You will have to read it for

186

yourself to thoroughly appreciate the different situations, and then we can discuss the matter intelligently."

"You evidently think the man was very noble in refusing to hear anything about the past of the lady he was interested in."

"I confess I do. He was noble, at least, in refusing to let a third party tell him. If he wished any information he should have asked the lady himself."

"Yes, but supposing she refused to answer him?"

"Then, I think he should either have declined to have anything more to do with her, or, if he kept up his acquaintance, he should have taken her just as she was, without any reference to her past."

"I suppose you are right. Still, it is a very serious thing for two people to marry without knowing something of each other's lives."

"I am tired of walking," said Miss Earle, "I am now going to seek comfort in the luxuriousness, as you call it, of my steamer chair."

"And may I go with you?" asked the young man.

"If you also are tired of walking."

"You know," he said, "you promised the whole afternoon. You took the forenoon with The Siege, and now I don't wish to be cheated out of my half of the day."

"Very well, I am rather interested in another story, and if you will take The Siege of London, and read it, you'll find how much better the book is than my telling of the story."

George Morris had, of course, to content himself with this proposition, and they walked together to the steamer chairs, over which the gaily coloured rugs were spread.

"Shall I get your book for you?" asked the young man, as he picked up the rugs.

"Thank you," answered Miss Earle, with a laugh, "you have already done so," for, as he shook out the rugs, the two books, which were small handy volumes, fell out on the deck.

"I see you won't accept my hint about not leaving the books around. You will lose some precious volume one of these days."

"Oh, I fold them in the rugs, and they are all right. Now, here is your volume. Sit down there and read it." "That means also, 'and keep quiet,' I suppose?"

"I don't imagine you are versatile enough to read and talk at the same time. Are you?"

"I should be very tempted to try it this afternoon."

Miss Earle went on with her reading, and Morris pretended to go on with his. He soon found, however, that he could not concentrate his attention on the little volume in his hand, and so quickly abandoned the attempt, and spent his time in meditation and in casting furtive glances at his fair companion over the top of his book. He thought the steamer chair a perfectly delightful invention. It was an easy, comfortable, and adjustable apparatus, that allowed a person to sit up or to recline at almost any angle. He pushed his chair back a little, so that he could watch the profile of Miss Katherine Earle, and the dark tresses that formed a frame for it, without risking the chance of having his espionage discovered.

"Aren't you comfortable?" asked the young lady, as he shoved back his chair.

"I am very, very comfortable," replied the young man.

"I am glad of that," she said, as she resumed her reading.

George Morris watched her turn leaf after leaf as he reclined lazily in his chair, with half-closed eyes, and said to himself, "Shop-girl or not, past or not, I'm going to propose to that young lady the first good opportunity I get. I wonder what she will say?"

"How do you like it?" cried the young lady he was thinking of, with a suddenness that made Morris jump in his chair.

"Like it?" he cried; "oh, I like it immensely."

"How far have you got?" she continued.

"How far? Oh, a great distance. Very much further than I would have thought it possible when I began this voyage."

Miss Earle turned and looked at him with wide-open eyes, as he made this strange reply.

"What are you speaking of?" she said.

"Oh, of everything—of the book, of the voyage, of the day."'

"I was speaking of the book," she replied quietly. "Are you sure you have not fallen asleep and been dreaming?"

"Fallen asleep? No. Dreaming? Yes."

"Well, I hope your dreams have been pleasant ones."

"They have."

Miss Earle, who seemed to think it best not to follow her investigations any further, turned once more to her own book, and read it until it was time to dress for dinner. When that important meal was over, Morris said to Miss Earle: "Do you know you still owe me part of the day?"

"I thought you said you had a very pleasant afternoon."

"So I had. So pleasant, you see, that I want to have the pleasure prolonged. I want you to come out and have a walk on the deck now in the starlight. It is a lovely night, and, besides, you are now halfway across the ocean, and yet I don't think you have been out once to see the phosphorescence. That is one of the standard sights of an ocean voyage. Will you come?"

Although the words were commonplace enough, there was a tremor in his voice which gave a meaning to them that could not be misunderstood. Miss Earle looked at him with serene composure, and yet with a touch of reproachfulness in her glance. "He talks like this to me," she said to herself, "while he is engaged to another woman."

"Yes," she answered aloud, with more firmness in her voice than might have seemed necessary, "I will be happy to walk on the deck with you to see the phosphorescence."

He helped to hinder her for a moment in adjusting her wraps, and they went out in the starlit night together.

"Now," he said, "if we are fortunate enough to find the place behind the after-wheel house vacant we can have a splendid view of the phosphorescence."

"Is it so much in demand that the place is generally crowded?" she asked.

"I may tell you in confidence," replied Mr. Morris, "that this particular portion of the boat is always very popular. Soon as the evening shades prevail the place is apt to be pre-empted by couples that are very fond of—"

"Phosphorescence," interjected the young lady.

"Yes," he said, with a smile that she could not see in the darkness, "of phosphorescence."

"I should think," said she, as they walked towards the stern of the boat, "that in scientific researches of that sort, the more people who were there, the more interesting the discussion would be, and the more chance a person would have to improve his mind on the subject of phosphorescence, or other matters pertaining to the sea."

"Yes," replied Morris. "A person naturally would think that, and yet, strange as it may appear, if there ever was a time when two is company and three is a crowd, it is when looking at the phosphorescence that follows the wake of an ocean steamer."

"Really?" observed the young lady, archly. "I remember you told me that you had crossed the ocean several times."

The young man laughed joyously at this repartee, and his companion joined him with a laugh that was low and musical.

190

"He seems very sure of his ground," she said to herself. "Well, we shall see."

As they came to the end of the boat and passed behind the temporary wheel-house erected there, filled with debris of various sorts, blocks and tackle and old steamer chairs, Morris noticed that two others were there before them standing close together with arms upon the bulwarks. They were standing very close together, so close in fact, that in the darkness, it seemed like one person. But as Morris stumbled over some chains, the dark, united shadow dissolved itself quickly into two distinct separate shadows. A flagpole stood at the extreme end of the ship, inclining backwards from the centre of the bulwarks, and leaning over the troubled, luminous sea beneath. The two who had taken their position first were on one side of the flag-pole and Morris and Miss Earle on the other. Their coming had evidently broken the spell for the others. After waiting for a few moments, the lady took the arm of the gentleman and walked forward. "Now," said Morris, with a sigh, "we have the phosphorescence to ourselves."

"It is very, very strange," remarked the lady in a low voice. "It seems as if a person could see weird shapes arising in the air, as if in torment."

The young man said nothing for a few moments. He cleared his throat several times as if to speak, but still remained silent. Miss Earle gazed down at the restless, luminous water. The throb, throb of the great ship made the bulwarks on which their arms rested tremble and quiver.

Finally Morris seemed to muster up courage enough to begin, and he said one word—

"Katherine." As he said this he placed his hand on hers as it lay white before him in the darkness upon the trembling bulwark. It seemed to him that she made a motion to withdraw her hand, and then allowed it to remain where it was.

"Katherine," he continued, in a voice that he hardly recognised as his own, "we have known each other only a very short time comparatively; but, as I think I said to you once before, a day on shipboard may be as long as a month on shore. Katherine, I want to ask you a question, and yet I do not know—I cannot find—I—I don't know what words to use."

The young lady turned her face towards him, and he saw her clear-cut profile sharply outlined against the glowing water as he looked down at her. Although the young man struggled against the emotion, which is usually experienced by any man in his position, yet he felt reasonably sure of the answer to his question. She had come with him out into the night. She had allowed her hand to remain in his. He was, therefore, stricken dumb with amazement when she replied, in a soft and musical voice—

"You do not know what to say? What do you usually say on such an occasion?"

"Usually say?" he gasped in dismay. "I do not understand you. What do you mean?"

"Isn't my meaning plain enough? Am I the first young lady to whom you have not known exactly what to say?"

Mr. Morris straightened up, and folded his arms across his breast; then, ridiculously enough, this struck him as a heroic attitude, and altogether unsuitable for an American, so he thrust his hands deep in his coat pockets.

"Miss Earle," he said, "I knew that you could be cruel, but I did not think it possible that you could be so cruel as this."

"Is the cruelty all on my side, Mr. Morris?" she answered. "Have you been perfectly honest and frank with me? You know you have not. Now, I shall be perfectly honest and frank with you. I like you very much indeed. I have not the slightest hesitation in saying this, because it is true, and I don't care whether you know it, or whether anybody else knows it or not."

As she said this the hope which Morris had felt at first, and which had been dashed so rudely to the ground, now returned, and he attempted to put his arm about her and draw her to him; but the young lady quickly eluded his grasp, stepping to the other side of the flag-pole, and putting her hand upon it.

"Mr. Morris," she said, "there is no use of your saying anything further. There is a barrier between us; you know it as well as I. I would like us to be friends as usual; but, if we are to be, you will have to remember the barrier, and keep to your own side of it."

"I know of no barrier," cried Morris, vehemently, attempting to come over to her side.

"There is the barrier," she said, placing her hand on the flag-pole. "My place is on this side of that barrier; your place is on the other. If you come on this side of that flag-pole, I shall leave you. If you remain on your own side, I shall be very glad to talk with you."

Morris sullenly took his place on the other side of the flag-pole. "Has there been anything in my actions," said the young lady, "during the time we have been acquainted that would lead you to expect a different answer?"

"Yes. You have treated me outrageously at times, and that gave me some hope."

Miss Earle laughed her low, musical laugh at this remark.

"Oh, you may laugh," said Morris, savagely; "but it is no laughing matter to me, I assure you."

"Oh, it will be, Mr. Morris, when you come to think of this episode after you get on shore. It will seem to you very, very funny indeed; and when you speak to the next young lady on the same subject, perhaps you will think of how outrageously I have treated your remarks to-night, and be glad that there are so few young women in the world who would act as I have done."

"Where did you get the notion," inquired George Morris, "that I am in the habit of proposing to young ladies? It is a most ridiculous idea. I have been engaged once, I confess it. I made a mistake, and I am sorry for it. There is surely nothing criminal in that."

"It depends."

"Depends on what?"

"It depends on how the other party feels about it. It takes two to make an engagement, and it should take two to break it."

"Well, it didn't in my case," said the young man.

"So I understand," replied Miss Earle. "Mr. Morris, I wish you a very good evening." And before he could say a word she had disappeared in the darkness, leaving him to ponder bitterly over the events of the evening.

Sixth Day

In the vague hope of meeting Miss Earle, Morris rose early, and for a while paced the deck alone; but she did not appear. Neither did he have the pleasure of her company at breakfast. The more the young man thought of their interview of the previous evening, the more puzzled he was.

Miss Earle had frankly confessed that she thought a great deal of him, and yet she had treated him with an unfeelingness which left him sore and bitter. She might have refused him; that was her right, of course. But she need not have done it so sarcastically. He walked the deck after breakfast, but saw nothing of Miss Earle. As he paced up and down, he met the very person of all others whom he did not wish to meet. "Good morning, Mr. Morris," she said lightly, holding out her hand.

"Good morning," he answered, taking it without much warmth.

"You are walking the deck all alone, I see. May I accompany you?"

"Certainly," said the young man, and with that she put her hand on his arm and they walked together the first two rounds without saying anything to each other. Then she looked up at him, with a bright smile, and said, "So she refused you?"

"How do you know?" answered the young man, reddening and turning a quick look at her.

"How do I know?" laughed the other. "How should I know?"

For a moment it flashed across his mind that Miss Katherine Earle had spoken of their interview of last night; but a moment later he dismissed the

194

suspicion as unworthy.

"How do you know?" he repeated.

"Because I was told so on very good authority."

"I don't believe it."

"Ha, ha! now you are very rude. It is very rude to say to a lady that she doesn't speak the truth."

"Well, rude or not, you are not speaking the truth. Nobody told you such a thing."

"My dear George, how impolite you are. What a perfect bear you have grown to be. Do you want to know who told me?"

"I don't care to know anything about it."

"Well, nevertheless, I shall tell you. You told me."

"I did? Nonsense, I never said anything about it."

"Yes, you did. Your walk showed it. The dejected look showed it, and when I spoke to you, your actions, your tone, and your words told it to me plainer than if you had said, 'I proposed to Miss Earle last night and I was rejected.' You poor, dear innocent, if you don't brighten up you will tell it to the whole ship."

"I am sure, Blanche, that I am very much obliged to you for the interest you take in me. Very much obliged, indeed."

"Oh no, you are not; and now, don't try to be sarcastic, it really doesn't suit your manner at all. I was very anxious to know how your little flirtation had turned out. I really was. You know I have an interest in you, George, and always will have, and I wouldn't like that spiteful little black-haired minx to have got you, and I am very glad she refused you, although why she did so I cannot for the life of me imagine."

"It must be hard for you to comprehend why she refused me, now that I am a partner in the firm." Blanche looked down upon the deck, and did not answer.

"I am glad," she said finally, looking up brightly at him with her innocent blue eyes, "that you did not put off your proposal until to-night. We expect to be at Queenstown to-night some time, and we leave there and go on through by the Lakes of Killarney. So, you see, if you hadn't proposed last night I should have known nothing at all about how the matter turned out, and I should have died of curiosity and anxiety to know."

"Oh, I would have written to you," said Morris. "Leave me your address now, and I'll write and let you know how it turns out."

"Oh," she cried quickly, "then it isn't ended yet? I didn't think you were a man who would need to be refused twice or thrice."

"I should be glad to be refused by Miss Earle five hundred times."

"Indeed?"

"Yes, five hundred times, if on the five hundredth and first time she accepted."

"Is it really so serious as that?"

"It is just exactly that serious."

"Then your talk to me after all was only pretence?"

"No, only a mistake."

"What an escape I have had!"

"You have, indeed."

"Ah, here comes Miss Earle. Really, for a lady who has rejected a gentleman, she does not look as supremely happy as she might. I must go and have a talk with her."

"Look here, Blanche," cried the young man, angrily, "if you say a word to her about what we have been speaking of, I'll—"

"What will you do?" said the young lady, sweetly.

Morris stood looking at her. He didn't himself know what he would do; and Blanche, bowing to him, walked along the deck, and sat down in the steamer chair beside Miss Earle, who gave her a very scant recognition.

"Now, you needn't be so cool and dignified," said the lady. "George and I have been talking over the matter, and I told him he wasn't to feel discouraged at a first refusal, if he is resolved to have a shop-girl for his wife."

"What! Mr. Morris and you have been discussing me, have you?"

"Is there anything forbidden in that, Miss Earle? You must remember that George and I are very, very old friends, old and dear friends. Did you refuse him on my account? I know you like him."

"Like him?" said Miss Earle, with a fierce light in her eyes, as she looked at her tormentor. "Yes, I like him, and I'll tell you more than that;" she bent over and added in an intense whisper, "I love him, and if you say another word to me about him, or if you dare to discuss me with him, I shall go up to him where he stands now and accept him. I shall say to him, 'George Morris, I love you.' Now if you doubt I shall do that, just continue in your present style of conversation."

Blanche leaned back in the steamer chair and turned a trifle pale. Then she laughed, that irritating little laugh of hers, and said, "Really I did not think it had gone so far as that. I'll bid you good morning."

The moment the chair was vacated, George Morris strolled up and sat down on it.

"What has that vixen been saying to you?" he asked.

"That vixen," said Miss Earle, quietly, "has been telling me that you and she were discussing me this morning, and discussing the conversation that took place last night."

"It is a lie," said Morris.

"What is? What I say, or what she said, or what she says you said?"

"That we were discussing you, or discussing our conversation, is not true. Forgive me for using the coarser word. This was how it was; she came up to me—"

"My dear Mr. Morris, don't say a word. I know well enough that you would not discuss the matter with anybody. I, perhaps, may go so far as to say, least of all with her. Still, Mr. Morris, you must remember this, that even if you do not like her now—"

"Like her?" cried Morris; "I hate her."

"As I was going to say, and it is very hard for me to say it, Mr. Morris, you have a duty towards her as you—we all have our duties to perform," said Miss Earle, with a broken voice. "You must do yours, and I must do mine. It may be hard, but it is settled. I cannot talk this morning. Excuse me." And she rose and left him sitting there.

"What in the world does the girl mean? I am glad that witch gets off at Queenstown. I believe it is she who has mixed everything up. I wish I knew what she has been saying."

Miss Earle kept very closely to her room that day, and in the evening, as they approached the Fastnet Light, George Morris was not able to find her to tell her of the fact that they had sighted land. He took the liberty, however, of scribbling a little note to her, which the stewardess promised to deliver. He waited around the foot of the companion-way for an answer. The answer came in the person of Miss Katherine herself.

If refusing a man was any satisfaction, it seemed as if Miss Katherine Earle had obtained very little gratification from it. She looked weary and sad as she took the young man's arm, and her smile as she looked up at him had something very pathetic in it, as if a word might bring the tears. They sat in the chairs and watched the Irish coast. Morris pointed out objects here and there, and told her what they were. At last, when they went down to supper together, he said—

"We will be at Queenstown some time to-night. It will be quite a curious sight in the moonlight. Wouldn't you like to stay up and see it?"

"I think I would," she answered. "I take so few ocean voyages that I wish to get all the nautical experiences possible."

The young man looked at her sharply, then he said—

"Well, the stop at Queenstown is one of the experiences. May I send the steward to rap at your door when the engine stops?"

"Oh, I shall stay up in the saloon until that time?"

"It may be a little late. It may be as late as one or two o'clock in the morning. We can't tell. I should think the best thing for you to do would be to take a rest until the time comes. I think, Miss Earle, you need it."

It was a little after twelve o'clock when the engine stopped. The saloon was dimly lighted, and porters were hurrying to and fro, getting up the baggage which belonged to those who were going to get off at Queenstown. The night was very still, and rather cold. The lights of Queenstown could be seen here and there along the semi-circular range of hills on which the town stood. Passengers who were to land stood around the deck well muffled up, and others who had come to bid them good-bye were talking sleepily with them. Morris was about to send the steward to Miss Earle's room, when that young lady herself appeared. There was something spirit-like about her, wrapped in her long cloak, as she walked through the half-darkness to meet George Morris.

"I was just going to send for you," he said.

"I did not sleep any," was the answer, "and the moment the engine stopped I knew we were there. Shall we go on deck?"

"Yes," he said, "but come away from the crowd," and with that he led her towards the stern of the boat. For a moment Miss Earle seemed to hold back, but finally she walked along by his side firmly to where they had stood the night before. With seeming intention Morris tried to take his place beside her, but Miss Earle, quietly folding her cloak around her, stood on the opposite side of the flagpole, and, as if there should be no forgetfulness on his part, she reached up her hand and laid it against the staff.

"She evidently meant what she said," thought Morris to himself, with a sigh, as he watched the low, dim outlines of the hills around Queenstown Harbour, and the twinkling lights here and there.

"That is the tender coming now," he said, pointing to the red and green lights of the approaching boat. "How small it looks beside our monster steamship."

Miss Earle shivered.

"I pity the poor folks who have to get up at this hour of the night and go ashore. I should a great deal rather go back to my state-room."

"Well, there is one passenger I am not sorry for," said Morris, "and that is the young woman who has, I am afraid, been saying something to you which has made you deal more harshly with me than perhaps you might otherwise have done. I wish you would tell me what she said?"

"She has said nothing," murmured Miss Earle, with a sigh, "but what you yourself have confirmed. I do not pay much attention to what she says."

"Well, you don't pay much attention to what I say either," he replied. "However, as I say, there is one person I am not sorry for; I even wish it were raining. I am very revengeful, you see."

"I do not know that I am very sorry for her myself," replied Miss Earle, frankly; "but I am sorry for her poor old father, who hasn't appeared in the saloon a single day except the first. He has been sick the entire voyage."

"Her father?" cried Morris, with a rising inflection in his voice.

"Certainly."

"Why, bless my soul! Her father has been dead for ages and ages."

"Then who is the old man she is with?"

"Old man! It would do me good to have her hear you call him the old man. Why, that is her husband."

"Her husband!" echoed Miss Earle, with wide open eyes, "I thought he was her father."

200

"Oh, not at all. It is true, as you know, that I was engaged to the young lady, and I presume if I had become a partner in our firm sooner we would have been married. But that was a longer time coming than suited my young lady's convenience, and so she threw me over with as little ceremony as you would toss a penny to a beggar, and she married this old man for his wealth, I presume. I don't see exactly why she should take a fancy to him otherwise. I felt very cut up about it, of course, and I thought if I took this voyage I would at least be rid for a while of the thought of her. They are now on their wedding trip. That is the reason your steamer chair was broken, Miss Earle. Here I came on board an ocean steamer to get rid of the sight or thought of a certain woman, and to find that I was penned up with that woman, even if her aged husband was with her, for eight or nine days, was too much for me. So I raced up the deck and tried to get ashore. I didn't succeed in that, but I did succeed in breaking your chair."

Miss Earle was evidently very much astonished at this revelation, but she said nothing. After waiting in vain for her to speak, Morris gazed off at the dim shore. When he looked around he noticed that Miss Earle was standing on his side of the flagstaff. There was no longer a barrier between them.

Seventh Day

If George Morris were asked to say which day of all his life had been the most thoroughly enjoyable, he would probably have answered that the seventh of his voyage from New York to Liverpool was the red-letter day of his life. The sea was as calm as it was possible for a sea to be. The sun shone bright and warm. Towards the latter part of the day they saw the mountains of Wales, which, from the steamer's deck, seemed but a low range of hills. It did not detract from Morris's enjoyment to know that Mrs. Blanche was now on the troubleless island of Ireland, and that he was sailing over this summer sea with the lady who, the night before, had promised to be his wife.

During the day Morris and Katherine sat together on the sunny side of the ship looking at the Welsh coast. Their books lay unread on the rug, and there were long periods of silences between them.

"I don't believe," said Morris, "that anything could be more perfectly

201

delightful than this. I wish the shaft would break."

"I hope it won't," answered the young lady; "the chances are you would be as cross as a bear before two days had gone past, and would want to go off in a small boat."

"Oh, I should be quite willing to go off in a small boat if you would come with me. I would do that now."

"I am very comfortable where I am," answered Miss Katherine. "I know when to let well enough alone."

"And I don't, I suppose you mean?"

"Well, if you wanted to change this perfectly delightful day for any other day, or this perfectly luxurious and comfortable mode of travel for any other method, I should suspect you of not letting well enough alone."

"I have to admit," said George, "that I am completely and serenely happy. The only thing that bothers me is that to-night we shall be in Liverpool. I wish this hazy and dreamy weather could last for ever, and I am sure I could stand two extra days of it going just as we are now. I think with regret of how much of this voyage we have wasted."

"Oh, you think it was wasted, do you?"

"Well, wasted as compared with this sort of life. This seems to me like a rest after a long chase."

"Up the deck?" asked the young lady, smiling at him.

"Now, see here," said Morris, "we may as well understand this first as last, that unfortunate up-the-deck chase has to be left out of our future life. I am not going to be twitted about that race every time a certain young lady takes a notion to have a sort of joke upon me."

"That was no joke, George. It was the most serious race you ever ran in your life. You were running away from one woman, and, poor blind young man, you ran right in the arms of another. The danger you have run into is ever so much greater than the one you were running away from."

"Oh, I realise that," said the young man, lightly; "that's what makes me so solemn to-day, you know." His hand stole under the steamer rugs and imprisoned her own.

"I am afraid people will notice that," she said quietly.

"Well, let them; I don't care. I don't know anybody on board this ship, anyhow, except you, and if you realised how very little I care for their opinions you would not try to withdraw your hand."

"I am not trying very hard," answered the young woman; and then there was another long silence. Finally she continued—

"I am going to take the steamer chair and do it up in ribbons when I get ashore."

"I am afraid it will not be a very substantial chair, no matter what you do with it. It will be a trap for those who sit in it."

"Are you speaking of your own experience?"

"No, of yours."

"George," she said, after a long pause, "did you like her very much?"

"Her?" exclaimed the young man, surprised. "Who?"

"Why, the young lady you ran away from. You know very well whom I mean."

"Like her? Why, I hate her."

"Yes, perhaps you do now. But I am asking of former years. How long were you engaged to her?"

"Engaged? Let me see, I have been engaged just about—well, not twenty-four hours yet. I was never engaged before. I thought I was, but I wasn't really."

Miss Earle shook her head. "You must have liked her very much," she said, "or you never would have proposed marriage to her. You would never have been engaged to her. You never would have felt so badly when she—"

"Oh, say it out," said George, "jilted me, that is the word."

"No, that is not the phrase I wanted to use. She didn't really jilt you, you know. It was because you didn't have, or thought you didn't have, money enough. She would like to be married to you to-day."

George shuddered.

"I wish," he said, "that you wouldn't mar a perfect day by a horrible suggestion."

"The suggestion would not have been so horrible a month ago."

"My dear girl," said Morris, rousing himself up, "it's a subject that I do not care much to talk about, but all young men, or reasonably young men, make mistakes in their lives. That was my mistake. My great luck was that it was discovered in time. As a general thing, affairs in this world are admirably planned, but it does seem to me a great mistake that young people have to choose companions for life at an age when they really haven't the judgment to choose a house and lot. Now, confess yourself, I am not your first lover, am I?"

Miss Earle looked at him for a moment before replying.

"You remember," she said, "that once you spoke of not having to incriminate yourself. You refused to answer a question I asked you on that ground. Now, I think this is a case in which I would be quite justified in refusing to answer. If I told you that you were my first lover, you would perhaps be manlike enough to think that after all you had only taken what nobody else had expressed a desire for. A man does not seem to value anything unless some one else is struggling for it."

"Why, what sage and valuable ideas you have about men, haven't you, my dear?"

"Well, you can't deny but what there is truth in them."

"I not only can, but I do. On behalf of my fellow men, and on behalf of myself, I deny it."

"Then, on the other hand," she continued, "if I confessed to you that

I did have half a score or half a dozen of lovers, you would perhaps think I had been jilting somebody or had been jilted. So you see, taking it all in, and thinking the matter over, I shall refuse to answer your question."

"Then you will not confess?"

"Yes, I shall confess. I have been wanting to confess to you for some little time, and have felt guilty because I did not do so."

"I am prepared to receive the confession," replied the young man, lazily, "and to grant absolution."

"Well, you talk a great deal about America and about Americans, and talk as if you were proud of the country, and of its ways, and of its people."

"Why, I am," answered the young man.

"Very well, then; according to your creed one person is just as good as another."

"Oh, I don't say that, I don't hold that for a moment. I don't think I am as good as you, for instance."

"But what I mean is this, that one's occupation does not necessarily give one a lower station than another. If that is not your belief then you are not a true American, that is all."

"Well, yes, that is my belief. I will admit I believe all that. What of it?"

"What of it? There is this of it. You are the junior partner of a large establishment in New York?"

"Nothing criminal in that, is there?"

"Oh, I don't put it as an accusation, I am merely stating the fact. You admit the fact, of course?"

"Yes. The fact is admitted, and marked Exhibit A, and placed in evidence. Now, what next?"

"In the same establishment there was a young woman who sold ribbons to all comers?"

"Yes, I admit that also, and the young lady's name was Miss Katherine Earle."

"Oh, you knew it, then?"

"Why, certainly I did."

"You knew it before you proposed to me."

"Oh, I seem to have known that fact for years and years."

"She told it to you."

"She? What she?"

"You know very well who I mean, George. She told it to you, didn't she?"

"Why, don't you think I remembered you—remembered seeing you there?"

"I know very well you did not. You may have seen me there, but you did not remember me. The moment I spoke to you on the deck that day in the broken chair, I saw at once you did not remember me, and there is very little use of your trying to pretend you thought of it afterwards. She told it to you, didn't she?"

"Now, look here, Katherine, it isn't I who am making a confession, it is you. It is not customary for a penitent to cross-examine the father confessor in that style."

"It does not make any difference whether you confess or not, George; I shall always know she told you that. After all, I wish she had left it for me to tell. I believe I dislike that woman very much."

"Shake hands, Kate, over that. So do I. Now, my dear, tell me what she told you."

"Then she did tell you that, did she?"

"Why, if you are so sure of it without my admitting it, why do you ask again?"

"I suppose because I wanted to make doubly sure."

"Well, then, assurance is doubly sure. I admit she did."

"And you listened to her, George?" said Katherine, reproachfully.

"Listened? Why, of course I did. I couldn't help myself. She said it before I knew what she was going to say. She didn't give me the chance that your man had in that story you were speaking of. I said something that irritated her and she out with it at once as if it had been a crime on your part. I did not look on it in that light, and don't now. Anyhow, you are not going back to the ribbon counter."

"No," answered the young lady, with a sigh, looking dreamily out into the hazy distance. "No, I am not."

"At least, not that side of the counter," said George.

She looked at him for a moment, as if she did not understand him; then she laughed lightly.

"Now," said Morris, "I have done most of the confession on this confession of yours. Supposing I make a confession, and ask you to tell me what she told you."

"Well, she told me that you were a very fascinating young man," answered Katherine, with a sigh.

"Really. And did after-acquaintance corroborate that statement?"

"I never had occasion to tell her she was mistaken."

"What else did she say? Didn't mention anything about my prospects or financial standing in any way?"

"No; we did not touch on that subject."

"Come, now, you cannot evade the question. What else did she say to you about me?"

"I don't know that it is quite right to tell you, but I suppose I may. She said that you were engaged to her."

"Had been."

"No, were."

"Oh, that's it. She did not tell you she was on her wedding tour?"

"No, she did not."

"And didn't you speak to her about her father being on board?"

Katherine laughed her low, enjoyable laugh.

"Yes," she said, "I did, and I did not think till this moment of how flustered she looked. But she recovered her lost ground with a great deal of dexterity."

"By George, I should like to have heard that! I am avenged!"

"Well, so is she," was the answer.

"How is that?"

"You are engaged to me, are you not?"

Before George could make any suitable reply to this bit of humbug, one of the officers of the ship stopped before them.

"Well," he said, "I am afraid we shall not see Liverpool to-night."

"Really. Why?" asked George.

"This haze is settling down into a fog. It will be as thick as pea-soup before an hour. I expect there will be a good deal of grumbling among the passengers."

As he walked on, George said to Katherine, "There are two passengers who won't grumble any, will they, my dear?"

"I know one who won't," she answered.

The fog grew thicker and thicker; the vessel slowed down, and finally stopped, sounding every now and then its mournful, timber-shaking whistle.

Eighth Day

On the afternoon of the eighth day George Morris and Katherine Earle stood together on the deck of the tender, looking back at the huge steamship which they had just left.

"When we return," he said, "I think we shall choose this ship."

"Return?" she answered, looking at him.

"Why, certainly; we are going back, are we not?"

"Dear me," she replied, "I had not thought of that. You see, when I left America I did not intend to go back."

"Did you not? I thought you were only over here for the trip."

"Oh no. I told you I came on business, not on pleasure."

"And did you intend to stay over here?"

"Certainly."

"Why, that's strange; I never thought of that."

"It is strange, too," said Katherine, "that I never thought of going back."

"And—and," said the young man, "won't you go?"

She pressed his arm, and stood motionless.

"Where thou goest, I will go. Thy people shall be my people."

"That's a quotation, I suppose?" said George.

"It is," answered Katherine.

"Well, you see, as I told you, I am not very well read up on the books of the day."

"I don't know whether you would call that one of the books of the day or not," said Katherine; "it is from the Bible."

"Oh," answered the other. "I believe, Kate, you will spend the rest of your life laughing at me."

"Oh no," said the young lady, "I always thought I was fitted for missionary life. Now, look what a chance I have."

"You have taken a big contract, I admit."

They had very little trouble with their luggage. It is true that the English officials looked rather searchingly in Katherine's trunk for dynamite, but, their fears being allayed in that direction, the trunks were soon chalked and on the back of a stout porter, who transferred them to the top of a cab.

"I tell you what it is," said George, "it takes an American Custom-house official to make the average American feel ashamed of his country."

"Why, I did not think there was anything over there that could make you feel ashamed of your country. You are such a thorough-going American."

"Well, the Customs officials in New York have a knack of making a person feel that he belongs to no place on earth."

They drove to the big Liverpool hotel which is usually frequented by Americans who land in that city, and George spent the afternoon in attending to business in Liverpool, which he said he did not expect to have to look after when he left America, but which he desired very much to get some information about.

Katherine innocently asked if she could be of any assistance to him, and he replied that she might later on, but not at the present state of proceedings.

In the evening they went to a theatre together, and took a long route back to the hotel.

"It isn't a very pretty city," said Miss Earle.

"Oh, I think you are mistaken," replied her lover. "To me it is the most beautiful city in the world."

"Do you really mean that?" she said, looking at him with surprise.

"Yes, I do. It is the first city through which I have walked with the lady

210

who is to be my wife."

"Oh, indeed," remarked the lady who was to be his wife, "and have you never walked with—"

"Now, see here," said Morris, "that subject is barred out. We left all those allusions on the steamer. I say I am walking now with the lady who is to be my wife. I think that statement of the case is perfectly correct, is it not?"

"I believe it is rather more accurate than the average statement of the average American."

"Now, Katherine," he said, "do you know what information I have been looking up since I have been in Liverpool?"

"I haven't the slightest idea," she said. "Property?"

"No, not property."

"Looking after your baggage, probably?"

"Well, I think you have got it this time. I was looking after my baggage. I was trying to find out how and when we could get married."

"Oh!"

"Yes, oh! Does that shock you? I find they have some idiotic arrangement by which a person has to live here three months before he can be married, although I was given some hope that, by paying for it, a person could get a special licence. If that is the case, I am going to have a special licence to-morrow."

"Indeed?"

"Yes, indeed. Then we can be married at the hotel."

"And don't you think, George, that I might have something to say about that?"

"Oh, certainly! I intended to talk with you about it. Of course I am talking with you now on that subject. You admitted the possibility of our getting married. I believe I had better get you to put it down in writing, or have you say it before witnesses, or something of that sort."

"Well, I shouldn't like to be married in a hotel."

"In a church, then? I suppose I can make arrangements that will include a church. A parson will marry us. That parson, if he is the right sort, will have a church. It stands to reason, therefore, that if we give him the contract he will give us the use of his church, quid pro quo, you know."

"Don't talk flippantly, please. I think it better to wait until to-morrow, George, before you do anything rash. I want to see something of the country. I want us to take a little journey together to-morrow, and then, out in the country, not in this grimy, sooty city, we will make arrangements for our marriage."

"All right, my dear. Where do you intend to go?"

"While you have been wasting your time in getting information relating to matrimony, I have been examining time-tables. Where I want to go is two or three hours' ride from here. We can take one of the morning trains, and when we get to the place I will allow you to hire a conveyance, and we will have a real country drive. Will you go with me?"

"Will I? You better believe I will. But you see, Katherine, I want to get married as soon as possible. Then we can take a little trip on the Continent before it is time for us to go back to America. You have never been on the Continent, have you?"

"Never."

"Well, I am very glad of that. I shall be your guide, philosopher, and friend, and, added to that, your husband."

"Very well, we will arrange all that on our little excursion to-morrow."

Ninth Day

Spring in England—and one of those perfect spring days in which all rural England looks like a garden. The landscape was especially beautiful to American eyes, after the more rugged views of Transatlantic scenery. The hedges were closely clipped, the fields of the deepest green, and the hills far away were blue and hazy in the distance.

"There is no getting over the fact," said Morris, "that this is the prettiest country in the whole world."

During most of the journey Katherine Earle sat back in her corner of the first-class compartment, and gazed silently out of the flying windows. She seemed too deeply impressed with the beauty of the scene to care for conversation even with the man she was to marry. At last they stopped at a pretty little rural station, with the name of the place done in flowers of vivid colour that stood out against the brown of the earth around, them and the green turf which formed the sloping bank.

"Now," said George, as they stood on the platform, "whither away? Which direction?"

"I want to see," said she, "a real, genuine, old English country home."

"A castle?"

"No, not a castle."

"Oh, I know what you want. Something like Haddon Hall, or that sort of thing. An old manor house. Well, wait a minute, and I'll talk to the station master, and find out all there is about this part of the country."

And before she could stop him, he had gone to make his inquiry of that official. Shortly after he came back with a list of places that were worth seeing, which he named.

"Holmwood House," she repeated. "Let us see that. How far is it?"

George again made inquiries, and found that it was about eight miles away. The station-master assured him that the road thither was one of the prettiest drives in the whole country.

"Now, what kind of a conveyance will you have? There are four-wheeled cabs, and there is even a hansom to be had. Will you have two horses or one, and will you have a coachman?"

"None of these," she said, "if you can get something you can drive yourself—I suppose you are a driver?"

"Oh, I have driven a buggy."

"Well, get some sort of conveyance that we can both sit in while you drive."

"But don't you think we will get lost?"

"We can inquire the way," she said, "and if we do get lost, it won't matter. I want to have a long talk with you before we reach the place."

They crossed the railway by a bridge over the line, and descended into a valley along which the road wound.

The outfit which George had secured was a neat little cart made of wood in the natural colour and varnished, and a trim little pony, which looked ridiculously small for two grown people, and yet was, as George afterwards said, "as tough as a pine knot."

The pony trotted merrily along, and needed no urging. George doubtless was a good driver, but whatever talents he had in that line were not brought into play. The pony was a treasure that had apparently no bad qualities. For a long time the two in the cart rode along the smooth highway silently, until at last Morris broke out with—

"Oh, see here! This is not according to contract. You said you wanted a long talk, and now you are complacently saying nothing."

"I do not know exactly how to begin."

"Is it so serious as all that?"

"It is not serious exactly—it is merely, as it were, a continuation of the confession."

"I thought we were through with that long ago. Are there any more horrible revelations?"

She looked at him with something like reproach in her eyes.

"If you are going to talk flippantly, I think I will postpone what I have to say until another time."

"My dear Kate, give a man a chance. He can't reform in a moment. I never had my flippancy checked before. Now then, I am serious again. What appalling—I mean—you see how difficult it is, Katherine—I mean, what serious subject shall we discuss?"

"Some other time."

"No—now. I insist on it. Otherwise I will know I am unforgiven."

"There is nothing to forgive. I merely wanted to tell you something more than you know about my own history."

"I know more now than that man in the story."

"He did not object to the knowledge, you know. He objected to receiving it from a third person. Now I am not a third person, am I?"

"Indeed, you are not. You are first person singular—at present—the first person to me at least. There, I am afraid I have dropped into flippancy again."

"That is not flippancy. That is very nice." The interval shall be unreported.

At last Katherine said quietly, "My mother came from this part of England."

"Ah! That is why you wanted to come here."

"That is why I wanted to come here. She was her father's only daughter, and, strange to say, he was very fond of her, and proud of her."

"Why strange?"

"Strange from his action for years after. She married against his will. He never forgave her. My father did not seem to have the knack of getting along in the world, and he moved to America in the hope of bettering his condition. He did not better it. My father died ten years ago, a prematurely broken down man, and my mother and I struggled along as best we could until she died two years ago. My grandfather returned her letter unopened when mother wrote to him ten years ago, although the letter had a black border around it. When I think of her I find it hard to forgive him, so I suppose some of his nature has been transmitted to me."

"Find it hard? Katherine, if you were not an angel you would find it impossible."

"Well, there is nothing more to tell, or at least, not much. I thought you should know this. I intended to tell you that last day on shipboard, but it seemed to me that here was where it should be told—among the hills and valleys that she saw when she was my age."

"Katherine, my dear, do not think about it any more than you can help. It will only uselessly depress you. Here is a man coming. Let us find out now whether we have lost our way or not."

They had.

Even after that they managed to get up some wrong lanes and byways, and took several wrong turnings; but by means of inquiry from every one they met, they succeeded at last in reaching the place they were in search of.

There was an old and grey porter's lodge, and an old and grey gateway, with two tall, moss-grown stone pillars, and an iron gate between them. On the top of the pillars were crumbled stone shields, seemingly held in place by a lion on each pillar.

"Is this Holmwood House?" asked Morris of the old and grey man who came out of the porter's lodge.

"Yes, sir, it be," replied the man.

"Are visitors permitted to see the house and the grounds?"

"No, they be'ant," was the answer. "Visitors were allowed on Saturdays in the old Squire's time, but since he died they tell me the estate is in the courts, and we have orders from the London lawyers to let nobody in."

"I can make it worth your while," said George, feeling in his vest pocket; "this lady would like to see the house."

216

The old man shook his head, even although George showed him a gold piece between his finger and thumb. Morris was astonished at this, for he had the mistaken belief which all Americans have, that a tip in Europe, if it is only large enough, will accomplish anything.

"I think perhaps I can get permission," said Katherine, "if you will let me talk a while to the old man."

"All right. Go ahead," said George. "I believe you could wheedle anybody into doing what he shouldn't do."

"Now, after saying that, I shall not allow you to listen. I shall step down and talk with him a moment and you can drive on for a little distance, and come back."

"Oh, that's all right," said George, "I know how it is. You don't want to give away the secret of your power. Be careful, now, in stepping down. This is not an American buggy," but before he had finished the warning, Katherine had jumped lightly on the gravel, and stood waiting for him to drive on. When he came back he found the iron gates open.

"I shall not get in again," she said. "You may leave the pony with this man, George, he will take care of it. We can walk up the avenue to the house."

After a short walk under the spreading old oaks they came in sight of the house, which was of red brick and of the Elizabethan style of architecture.

"I am rather disappointed with that," said George, "I always thought old English homesteads were of stone."

"Well, this one at least is of brick, and I imagine you will find a great many of them are of the same material."

They met with further opposition from the housekeeper who came to the door which the servant had opened after the bell was rung.

She would allow nobody in the house, she said. As for Giles, if he allowed people on the grounds that was his own look-out, but she had been forbidden by the lawyers to allow anybody in the house, and she had let nobody in, and she wasn't going to let anybody in.

"Shall I offer her a tip?" asked George, in a whisper.

"No, don't do that."

"You can't wheedle her like you did the old man, you know. A woman may do a great deal with a man, but when she meets another woman she meets her match. You women know each other, you know."

Meanwhile the housekeeper, who had been about to shut the door, seemed to pause and regard the young lady with a good deal of curiosity. Her attention had before that time been taken up with the gentleman.

"Well, I shall walk to the end of the terrace, and give you a chance to try your wiles. But I am ready to bet ten dollars that you don't succeed."

"I'll take you," answered the young lady.

"Yes, you said you would that night on the steamer."

"Oh, that's a very good way of getting out of a hopeless bet."

"I am ready to make the bet all right enough, but I know you haven't a ten-dollar bill about you."

"Well, that is very true, for I have changed all my money to English currency; but I am willing to bet its equivalent."

Morris walked to the end of the terrace. When he got back he found that the door of the house was as wide open as the gates of the park had been.

"There is something uncanny about all this," he said. "I am just beginning to see that you have a most dangerous power of fascination. I could understand it with old Giles, but I must admit that I thought the stern housekeeper would—"

"My dear George," interrupted Katherine, "almost anything can be accomplished with people, if you only go about it the right way."

"Now, what is there to be seen in this house?"

"All that there is to be seen about any old English house. I thought, perhaps, you might be interested in it."

"Oh, I am. But I mean, isn't there any notable things? For instance, I was in Haddon Hall once, and they showed me the back stairway where a fair lady had eloped with her lover. Have they anything of that kind to show here?"

Miss Earle was silent for a few moments. "Yes," she said, "I am afraid they have."

"Afraid? Why, that is perfectly delightful. Did the young lady of the house elope with her lover?"

"Oh, don't talk in that way, George," she said. "Please don't."

"Well, I won't, if you say so. I admit those little episodes generally turn out badly. Still you must acknowledge that they add a great interest to an old house of the Elizabethan age like this?"

Miss Earle was silent. They had, by this time, gone up the polished stairway, which was dimly lighted by a large window of stained glass.

"Here we are in the portrait hall," said Miss Earle. "There is a picture here that I have never seen, although I have heard of it, and I want to see it. Where is it?" she asked, turning to the housekeeper, who had been following them up the stairs.

"This way, my lady," answered the housekeeper, as she brought them before a painting completely concealed by a dark covering of cloth.

"Why is it covered in that way? To keep the dust from it?"

The housekeeper hesitated for a moment; then she said—

"The old Squire, my lady, put that on when she left, and it has never been taken off since."

"Then take it off at once," demanded Katherine Earle, in a tone that astonished Morris.

The housekeeper, who was too dignified to take down the covering herself, went to find the servant, but Miss Earle, with a gesture of impatience, grasped the cloth and tore it from its place, revealing the full-length portrait of a young lady.

Morris looked at the portrait in astonishment, and then at the girl by his side.

"Why, Katherine," he cried, "it is your picture!"

The young lady was standing with her hands tightly clenched and her lips quivering with nervous excitement. There were tears in her eyes, and she did not answer her lover for a moment; then she said—

"No, it is not my picture. This is a portrait of my mother."

Mrs. Tremain

"And Woman, wit a flaming torch

Sings heedless, in a powder—

Her careless smiles they warp and scorch

Man's heart, as fire the pine

Cuts keener than the thrust of lance

Her glance"

The trouble about this story is that it really has no ending. Taking an ocean voyage is something like picking up an interesting novel, and reading a chapter in the middle of it. The passenger on a big steamer gets glimpses of other people's lives, but he doesn't know what the beginning was, nor what the ending will be.

The last time I saw Mrs. Tremain she was looking over her shoulder and smiling at Glendenning as she walked up the gangway plank at Liverpool, hanging affectionately on the arm of her husband. I said to myself at the time, "You silly little handsome idiot, Lord only knows what trouble you will cause before flirting has lost its charm for you." Personally I would like to have shoved Glendenning off the gangway plank into the dark Mersey; but that would have been against the laws of the country on which we were then landing.

Mrs. Tremain was a woman whom other women did not like, and whom men did. Glendenning was a man that the average man detested, but he was a great favourite with the ladies.

I shall never forget the sensation Mrs. Tremain caused when she first entered the saloon of our steamer. I wish I were able to describe accurately just how she was dressed; for her dress, of course, had a great deal to do with her appearance, notwithstanding the fact that she was one of the loveliest women

I ever saw in my life. But it would require a woman to describe her dress with accuracy, and I am afraid any woman who was on board the steamer that trip would decline to help me. Women were in the habit of sniffing when Mrs. Tremain's name was mentioned. Much can be expressed by a woman's sniff. All that I can say about Mrs. Tremain's dress is that it was of some dark material, brightly shot with threads of gold, and that she had looped in some way over her shoulders and around her waist a very startlingly coloured silken scarf, while over her hair was thrown a black lace arrangement that reached down nearly to her feet, giving her a half-Spanish appearance. A military-looking gentleman, at least twice her age, was walking beside her. He was as grave and sober as she appeared light and frivolous, and she walked by his side with a peculiar elastic step, that seemed hardly to touch the carpet, laughing and talking to him just as if fifty pair of eyes were not riveted upon her as the pair entered. Everybody thought her a Spanish woman; but, as it turned out afterward, she was of Spanish-Mexican-American origin, and whatever beauty there is in those three nationalities seemed to be blended in some subtle, perfectly indescribable way in the face and figure of Mrs. Tremain.

The grave military-looking gentleman at her side was Captain Tremain, her husband, although in reality he was old enough to be her father. He was a captain in the United States army, and had been stationed at some fort near the Mexican border where he met the young girl whom he made his wife. She had seen absolutely nothing of the world, and they were now on their wedding trip to Europe, the first holiday he had taken for many a year.

In an incredibly short space of time Mrs. Tremain was the acknowledged belle of the ship. She could not have been more than nineteen or twenty years of age, yet she was as perfectly at her ease, and as thoroughly a lady as if she had been accustomed to palaces and castles for years. It was astonishing to see how naturally she took to it. She had lived all her life in a rough village in the wilds of the South-West, yet she had the bearing of a duchess or a queen.

The second day out she walked the deck with the captain, which, as everybody knows, is a very great honour. She always had a crowd of men around her, and apparently did not care the snap of her pretty fingers whether a woman on board spoke to her or not. Her husband was one of those slow-going, sterling men whom you meet now and again, with no nonsense about him, and with a perfect trust in his young wife. He was delighted to see her enjoying her voyage so well, and proud of the universal court that was paid to her. It was quite evident to everybody on board but himself that Mrs. Tremain was a born coquette, and the way she could use those dark, languishing, Spanish-Mexican eyes of hers was a lesson to flirts all the world over. It didn't, apparently, so much matter as long as her smiles were distributed pretty evenly over the whole masculine portion of the ship. But by-and-by things began to simmer down until the smiles were concentrated on the most utterly objectionable man on board—Glendenning. She walked the deck with him, she sat in cozy corners of the saloon with him, when there were not many people there, and at night they placed their chairs in a little corner of the deck where the electric light did not shine. One by one the other admirers dropped off, and left her almost entirely to Glendenning.

Of all those of us who were deserted by Mrs. Tremain none took it so hard as young Howard of Brooklyn. I liked Howard, for he was so palpably and irretrievably young, through no fault of his own, and so thoroughly ashamed of it. He wished to be considered a man of the world, and he had grave opinions on great questions, and his opinions were ever so much more settled and firm than those of us older people.

Young Howard confided a good deal in me, and even went so far one time as to ask if I thought he appeared very young, and if I would believe he was really as old as he stated.

I told him frankly I had taken him to be a very much older man than that, and the only thing about him I didn't like was a certain cynicism and knowledge of the world which didn't look well in a man who ought to be thinking about the serious things of life. After this young Howard confided in me even more than before. He said that he didn't care for Mrs. Tremain in that sort of way at all. She was simply an innocent child, with no knowledge of the world whatever, such as he and I possessed. Her husband—and in this I quite agreed with him—had two bad qualities: in the first place he was too easy going at the present, and in the second place he was one of those quiet men who would do something terrible if once he were aroused.

One day, as young Howard and I walked the deck together, he burst out with this extraordinary sentiment—

"All women," he said, "are canting hypocrites."

"When a man says that," I answered, "he means some particular woman. What woman have you in your eye, Howard?"

"No, I mean all women. All the women on board this boat, for instance."

"Except one, of course," I said.

"Yes," he answered, "except one. Look at the generality of women," he cried bitterly; "especially those who are what they call philanthropic and good. They will fuss and mourn over some drunken wretch who cannot be reclaimed, and would be no use if he could, and they will spend their time and sympathy over some creature bedraggled in the slums, whose only hope can be death, and that as soon as possible, yet not one of them will lift a finger to save a fellow creature from going over the brink of ruin. They will turn their noses in the air when a word from them would do some good, and then they will spend their time fussing and weeping over somebody that nothing on earth can help."

"Now, Howard," I said, "that's your cynicism which I've so often deplored. Come down to plain language, and tell me what you mean?"

"Look at the women on board this steamer," he cried indignantly. "There's pretty little Mrs. Tremain, who seems to have become fascinated by that scoundrel Glendenning. Any person can see what kind of a man he is—any one but an innocent child, such as Mrs. Tremain is. Now, no man can help. What she needs is some good kindly woman to take her by the hand and give her a word of warning. Is there a woman on board of this steamer who will do it? Not one. They see as plainly as any one else how things are drifting; but it takes a man who has murdered his wife to get sympathy and flowers from the modern so-called lady."

"Didn't you ever hear of the man, Howard, who made a large sum of money, I forget at the moment exactly how much, by minding his own business?"

"Oh yes, it's all very well to talk like that; but I would like to pitch Glendenning overboard."

"I admit that it would be a desirable thing to do, but if anybody is to do it, it is Captain Tremain and not you. Are you a married man, Howard?"

"No," answered Howard, evidently very much flattered by the question.

"Well, you see, a person never can tell on board ship; but, if you happen to be, it seems to me that you wouldn't care for any outsider to interfere in a matter such as we are discussing. At any rate Mrs. Tremain is a married woman, and I can't see what interest you should have in her. Take my advice and leave her alone, and if you want to start a reforming crusade among women, try to convert the rest of the ladies of the ship to be more charitable and speak the proper word in time."

"You may sneer as much as you like," answered young Howard, "but I will tell you what I am going to do. Two is company, and three is none; I'm going to make the third, as far as Mrs. Tremain and Glendenning are concerned."

"Supposing she objects to that?"

"Very likely she will; I don't care. The voyage lasts only a few days longer, and I am going to make the third party at any tête-à-tête."

"Dangerous business, Howard; first thing, you know, Glendenning will be wanting to throw you overboard."

"I would like to see him try it," said the young fellow, clenching his fist.

And young Howard was as good as his word. It was very interesting to an onlooker to see the way the different parties took it. Mrs. Tremain seemed to be partly amused with the boy, and think it all rather good fun. Glendenning scowled somewhat, and tried to be silent; but, finding that made no particular difference, began to make allusions to the extreme youth of young Howard, and seemed to try to provoke him, which laudable intention, to young Howard's great credit, did not succeed.

One evening I came down the forward narrow staircase, that leads to the long corridor running from the saloon, and met, under the electric light at the foot, Mrs. Tremain, young Howard, and Glendenning. They were evidently about to ascend the stairway; but, seeing me come down, they paused, and I stopped for a moment to have a chat with them, and see how things were going on.

Glendenning said, addressing me, "Don't you think it's time for children to be in bed?"

"If you mean me," I answered, "I am just on my way there."

Mrs. Tremain and young Howard laughed, and Glendenning after that ignored both Howard and myself.

He said to Mrs. Tremain, "I never noticed you wearing that ring before. It is a very strange ornament."

"Yes," answered Mrs. Tremain, turning it round and round. "This is a Mexican charmed ring. There is a secret about it, see if you can find it out." And with that she pulled off the ring, and handed it to Glendenning.

"You ought to give it to him as a keepsake," said young Howard, aggressively. "The ring, I notice, is a couple of snakes twisted together."

"Little boys," said Mrs. Tremain, laughing, "shouldn't make remarks like that. They lead to trouble."

Young Howard flushed angrily as Mrs. Tremain said this. He did not seem to mind it when Glendenning accused him of his youth, but he didn't like it coming from her.

Meanwhile Glendenning was examining the ring, and suddenly it came apart in his hand. The coils of the snake were still linked together, but instead of composing one solid ring they could now be spread several inches apart like the links of a golden chain. Mrs. Tremain turned pale, and gave a little shriek, as she saw this.

"Put it together again," she cried; "put it together quickly."

"What is the matter?" said Glendenning, looking up at her. She was standing two or three steps above him; Glendenning was at the bottom of the stair; young Howard stood on the same step as Mrs. Tremain, and I was a step or two above them.

"Put it together," cried Mrs. Tremain again. "I am trying to," said Glendenning, "is there a spring somewhere?"

"Oh, I cannot tell you," she answered, nervously clasping and unclasping her hands; "but if you do not put it together without help, that means very great ill-luck for both you and me."

"Does it?" said Glendenning, looking up at her with a peculiar glance, quite ignoring our presence.

"Yes, it does," she said; "try your best to put that ring together as you found it." It was quite evident that Mrs. Tremain had all the superstition of Mexico.

Glendenning fumbled with the ring one way and another, and finally said, "I cannot put it together."

"Let me try," said young Howard.

"No, no, that will do no good." Saying which Mrs. Tremain snatched the links from Glendenning, slipped them into one ring again, put it on her finger, and dashed quickly up the stairs without saying a word of good night to any of us.

Glendenning was about to proceed up the stair after her, when young Howard very ostentatiously placed himself directly in his path. Glendenning seemed to hesitate for a moment, then thought better of it, turned on his heel and walked down the passage towards the saloon.

"Look here, Howard," I said, "you are going to get yourself into trouble. There's sure to be a fuss on board this steamer before we reach Liverpool."

"I wouldn't be at all surprised," answered young Howard.

227

"Well, do you think it will be quite fair to Mrs. Tremain?"

"Oh, I shan't bring her name into the matter."

"The trouble will be to keep her name out. It may not be in your power to do that. A person who interferes in other people's affairs must do so with tact and caution."

Young Howard looked up at me with a trace of resentment in his face. "Aren't you interfering now?" he said.

"You are quite right, I am. Good night." And I went up the stairway. Howard shouted after me, but I did not see him again that night.

Next day we were nearing Queenstown, and, as I had letters to write, I saw nothing of young Howard till the evening. I found him unreasonably contrite for what he had said to me the night before; and when I told him he had merely spoken the truth, and was quite justified in doing so, he seemed more miserable than ever.

"Come," he said, "let us have a walk on the deck."

It was between nine and ten o'clock; and when we got out on the deck, I said to him, "Without wishing to interfere any further—"

"Now, don't say that," he cried; "it is cruel."

"Well, I merely wanted to know where your two charges are."

"I don't know," he answered, in a husky whisper; "they are not in the usual corner to-night, and I don't know where they are."

"She is probably with her husband," I suggested.

"No, he is down in the saloon reading."

As young Howard was somewhat prone to get emphatic when he began to talk upon this subject, and as there was always a danger of other people overhearing what he said, I drew him away to a more secluded part of the ship. On this particular boat there was a wheelhouse aft unused, and generally filled up with old steamer chairs. A narrow passage led around this at the curving stern, seldom used by promenaders because of certain obstructions which, in the dark, were apt to trip a person up. Chains or something went from this wheelhouse to the sides of the ship, and, being covered up by boxes of plank, made this part of the deck hard to travel on in the dark. As we went around this narrow passage young Howard was the first to stop. He clutched my arm, but said nothing. There in the dark was the faint outline of two persons, with their backs towards us, leaning over the stern of the ship. The vibration at this part of the boat, from the throbbing of the screw, made it impossible for them to hear our approach. They doubtless thought they were completely in the dark; but they were deluded in that idea, because the turmoil of the water left a brilliant phosphorescent belt far in the rear of the ship, and against this bright, faintly yellow luminous track their forms were distinctly outlined. It needed no second glance to see that the two were Glendenning and Mrs. Tremain. Her head rested on his shoulder, and his arm was around her waist.

"Let us get back," I said in a whisper; and, somewhat to my surprise, young Howard turned back with me. I felt his hand trembling on my arm, but he said nothing. Before we could say a word to each other a sadden and unexpected complication arose. We met Captain Tremain, with a shawl on his arm, coming towards us.

"Good evening, captain," I said; "have a turn on the deck with us?"

"No, thanks," he replied, "I am looking for my wife. I want to give her this shawl to put over her shoulders. She is not accustomed to such chilly weather as we are now running into, and I am afraid she may take cold."

All this time young Howard stood looking at him with a startled expression in his eyes, and his lower jaw dropped. I was afraid Captain Tremain would see him, and wonder what was the matter with the boy. I tried to bring him to himself by stamping my heel—not too gently—on his toes, but he turned his face in the semi-darkness toward me without changing its expression. The one idea that had taken possession of my mind was that Captain Tremain must not be allowed to go further aft than he was, and I tried by looks and nudges to tell young Howard to go back and give her warning, but the boy seemed to be completely dazed with the unexpected horror of the situation. To have this calm, stern, unsuspecting man come suddenly upon what we had seen at the stern of the boat was simply appalling to think of. He certainly would have killed Glendenning where he stood, and very likely Mrs. Tremain as well. As Captain Tremain essayed to pass us I collected my wits as well as I could, and said—

"Oh, by the way, captain, I wanted to speak to you about Mexico. Do you—do you—think that it is a good—er—place for investment?"

"Well," said Captain Tremain, pausing, "I am not so sure about that. You see, their Government is so very unstable. The country itself is rich enough in mineral wealth, if that is what you mean." All the while Howard stood there with his mouth agape, and I felt like shoving my fist into it.

"Here, Howard," I said, "I want to speak to Captain Tremain for a moment. Take this shawl and find Mrs. Tremain, and give it to her." Saying this, I took the shawl from the captain's arm and threw it at young Howard. He appeared then to realise, for the first time, what was expected of him, and, giving me a grateful look, disappeared toward the stern.

"What I wanted more particularly to know about Mexico," I said to the captain, who made no objection to this move, "was whether there would be any more—well, likely to have trouble—whether we would have trouble with them in a military way, you know—that's more in your line."

"Oh, I think not," said the captain. "Of course, on the boundary where we were, there was always more or less trouble with border ruffians, sometimes on one side of the line and sometimes on the other. There is a possibility always that complications may arise from that sort of thing. Our officers might go over into the Mexican territory and seize a desperado there, or they might come over into ours. Still, I don't think anything will happen to bring on a war such as we had once or twice with Mexico."

At this moment I was appalled to hear Glendenning's voice ring out above the noise of the vibration of the vessel.

"What do you mean by that, you scoundrel," he said.

230

"Hallo," exclaimed the captain, "there seems to be a row back there. I wonder what it is?"

"Oh, nothing serious, I imagine. Probably some steerage passengers have come on the cabin deck. I heard them having a row with some one to-day on that score. Let's walk away from it."

The captain took my arm, and we strolled along the deck while he gave me a great deal of valuable information about Mexico and the state of things along the border line, which I regret to say I cannot remember a word of. The impressions of a man who has been on the spot are always worth hearing, but my ears were strained to catch a repetition of the angry cry I had heard, or the continuation of the quarrel which it certainly seemed to be the beginning of. As we came up the deck again we met young Howard with the shawl still on his arm and Mrs. Tremain walking beside him. She was laughing in a somewhat hysterical manner, and his face was as pale as ashes with a drawn look about the corners of his lips, but the captain's eyes were only on his wife.

"Why don't you put on the shawl, my dear?" he said to her affectionately. "The shawl?" she answered. Then, seeing it on young Howard's arm, she laughed, and said, "He never offered it to me."

Young Howard made haste to place the shawl on her shoulders, which she arranged around herself in a very coquettish and charming way. Then she took her husband's arm.

"Good night," she said to me; "good night, and thanks, Mr. Howard."

"Good night," said the captain; "I will tell you more about that mine to-morrow."

We watched them disappear towards the companion-way. I drew young Howard towards the side of the boat.

"What happened?" I asked eagerly. "Did you have trouble?"

"Very nearly, I made a slip of the tongue. I called her Mrs. Glendenning."

"You called her what?"

"I said, 'Mrs. Glendenning, your husband is looking for you.' I had come right up behind them, and they hadn't heard me, and of course both were very much startled. Glendenning turned round and shouted, 'What do you mean by that, you scoundrel?' and caught me by the throat. She instantly sprang between us, pushing him toward the stern of the boat, and me against the wheelhouse. "'Hush, hush,' she whispered; 'you mean, Mr. Howard, that my husband is there, do you not?'

"'Yes,' I answered, 'and he will be here in a moment unless you come with me.' With that she said 'Good night, Mr. Glendenning,' and took my arm, and he, like a thief, slunk away round the other side of the wheelhouse. I was very much agitated. I suppose I acted like a fool when we met the captain, didn't I?"

"You did," I answered; "go on."

"Well, Mrs. Tremain saw that, and she laughed at me, although I could see she was rather disturbed herself."

Some time that night we touched at Queenstown, and next evening we were in Liverpool. When the inevitable explosion came, I have no means of knowing, and this, as I have said before, is a story without a conclusion.

Mrs. Tremain the next day was as bright and jolly as ever, and the last time I saw her, she was smiling over her shoulder at Glendenning, and not paying the slightest attention to either her husband on whose arm she hung, or to young Howard, who was hovering near.

Share and Share Alike

"The quick must haste to vengeance taste,

For time is on his head;

But he can wait at the door of fate,

Though the stay be long and the hour be late—

The dead."

Melville Hardlock stood in the centre of the room with his feet wide apart and his hands in his trousers pockets, a characteristic attitude of his. He gave a quick glance at the door, and saw with relief that the key was in the lock, and that the bolt prevented anybody coming in unexpectedly. Then he gazed once more at the body of his friend, which lay in such a helpless-looking attitude upon the floor. He looked at the body with a feeling of mild curiosity, and wondered what there was about the lines of the figure on the floor that so certainly betokened death rather than sleep, even though the face was turned away from him. He thought, perhaps, it might be the hand with its back to the floor and its palm towards the ceiling; there was a certain look of hopelessness about that. He resolved to investigate the subject some time when he had leisure. Then his thoughts turned towards the subject of murder. It was so easy to kill, he felt no pride in having been able to accomplish that much. But it was not everybody who could escape the consequences of his crime. It required an acute brain to plan after events so that shrewd detectives would be baffled. There was a complacent conceit about Melville Hardlock, which was as much a part of him as his intense selfishness, and this conceit led him to believe that the future path he had outlined for himself would not be followed by justice.

With a sigh Melville suddenly seemed to realise that while there was no necessity for undue haste, yet it was not wise to be too leisurely in some things, so he took his hands from his pockets and drew to the middle of the floor a large Saratoga trunk. He threw the heavy lid open, and in doing so showed that the trunk was empty. Picking up the body of his friend, which he was surprised to note was so heavy and troublesome to handle, he with some difficulty doubled it up so that it slipped into the trunk. He piled on top of it some old coats, vests, newspapers, and other miscellaneous articles until the space above the body was filled. Then he pressed down the lid and locked it, fastening the catches at each end. Two stout straps were now placed around the trunk and firmly buckled after he had drawn them as tight as possible. Finally he damped the gum side of a paper label, and when he had pasted it on the end of the trunk, it showed the words in red letters, "S.S. Platonic, cabin, wanted." This done, Melville threw open the window to allow the fumes of chloroform to dissipate themselves in the outside air. He placed a closed, packed and labelled portmanteau beside the trunk, and a valise beside that again, which, with a couple of handbags, made up his luggage. Then he unlocked the door, threw back the bolt, and, having turned the key again from the outside, strode down the thickly-carpeted stairs of the hotel into the large pillared and marble-floored vestibule where the clerk's office was. Strolling up to the counter behind which stood the clerk of the hotel, he shoved his key across to that functionary, who placed it in the pigeon-hole marked by the number of his room.

"Did my friend leave for the West last night, do you know?"

"Yes," answered the clerk, "he paid his bill and left. Haven't you seen him since?"

"No," replied Hardlock.

"Well, he'll be disappointed about that, because he told me he expected to see you before he left, and would call up at your room later. I suppose he didn't have time. By the way, he said you were going back to England to-morrow. Is that so?"

"Yes, I sail on the Platonic. I suppose I can have my luggage sent to the steamer from here without further trouble?"

"Oh, certainly," answered the clerk; "how many pieces are there? It will be fifty cents each."

234

"Very well; just put that down in my bill with the rest of the expenses, and let me have it to-night. I will settle when I come in. Five pieces of luggage altogether."

"Very good. You'll have breakfast to-morrow, I suppose?"

"Yes, the boat does not leave till nine o'clock."

"Very well; better call you about seven, Mr. Hardlock. Will you have a carriage?"

"No, I shall walk down to the boat. You will be sure, of course, to have my things there in time."

"Oh, no fear of that. They will be on the steamer by half-past eight."

"Thank you."

As Mr. Hardlock walked down to the boat next morning he thought he had done rather a clever thing in sending his trunk in the ordinary way to the steamer. "Most people," he said to himself, "would have made the mistake of being too careful about it. It goes along in the ordinary course of business. If anything should go wrong it will seem incredible that a sane man would send such a package in an ordinary express waggon to be dumped about, as they do dump luggage about in New York."

He stood by the gangway on the steamer watching the trunks, valises, and portmanteaus come on board.

"Stop!" he cried to the man, "that is not to go down in the hold; I want it. Don't you see it's marked 'wanted?'"

"It is very large, sir," said the man; "it will fill up a state-room by itself."

"I have the captain's room," was the answer.

So the man flung the trunk down on the deck with a crash that made even the cool Mr. Hardlock shudder.

"Did you say you had the captain's room, sir?" asked the steward standing near.

"Yes."

"Then I am your bedroom steward," was the answer; "I will see that the trunk is put in all right."

The first day out was rainy but not rough; the second day was fair and the sea smooth. The second night Hardlock remained in the smoking-room until the last man had left. Then, when the lights were extinguished, he went out on the upper deck, where his room was, and walked up and down smoking his cigar. There was another man also walking the deck, and the red glow of his cigar, dim and bright alternately, shone in the darkness like a glow-worm.

Hardlock wished that he would turn in, whoever he was. Finally the man flung his cigar overboard and went down the stairway. Hartlock had now the dark deck to himself. He pushed open the door of his room and turned out the electric light. It was only a few steps from his door to the rail of the vessel high above the water. Dimly on the bridge he saw the shadowy figure of an officer walking back and forth. Hardlock looked over the side at the phosphorescent glitter of the water which made the black ocean seem blacker still. The sharp ring of the bell betokening midnight made Melville start as if a hand had touched him, and the quick beating of his heart took some moments to subside. "I've been smoking too much to-day," he said to himself. Then looking quickly up and down the deck, he walked on tip toe to his room, took the trunk by its stout leather handle and pulled it over the ledge in the doorway. There were small wheels at the bottom of the trunk, but although they made the pulling of it easy, they seemed to creak with appalling loudness. He realised the fearful weight of the trunk as he lifted the end of it up on the rail. He balanced it there for a moment, and glanced sharply around him, but there was nothing to alarm him. In spite of his natural coolness, he felt a strange, haunting dread of some undefinable disaster, a dread which had been completely absent from him at the time he committed the murder. He shoved off the trunk before he had quite intended to do so, and the next instant he nearly bit through his tongue to suppress a groan of agony. There passed half a dozen moments of supreme pain and fear before he realised what had happened. His wrist had caught in the strap handle of the trunk, and his shoulder was dislocated. His right arm was stretched taut and helpless, like a rope holding up the frightful and ever-increasing weight that hung between him and the sea. His breast was pressed against the rail and his left hand gripped the iron stanchion to keep himself from going over. He felt that his feet were slipping, and he set his teeth and gripped the iron with a grasp that was itself like iron. He hoped the trunk would slip from his useless wrist, but it rested against the side of the vessel, and the longer it hung the more it pressed the hard strap handle into his nerveless flesh. He had realised from the first that he dare not cry for help, and his breath came hard through his clenched teeth as the weight grew heavier and heavier. Then, with his eyes strained by the fearful pressure, and perhaps dazzled by the glittering phosphorescence running so swiftly by the side of the steamer far below, he seemed to see from out the trunk something in the form and semblance of his dead friend quivering like summer heat below him. Sometimes it was the shimmering phosphorescence, then again it was the wraith hovering over the trunk. Hardlock, in spite of his agony, wondered which it really was; but he wondered no longer when it spoke to him.

"Old Friend," it said, "you remember our compact when we left England. It was to be share and share alike, my boy—share and share alike. I have had my share. Come!"

Then on the still night air came the belated cry for help, but it was after the foot had slipped and the hand had been wrenched from the iron stanchion.

An International Row

"A simple child

That lightly draws its breath,

And feels its life in every limb,

What should it know of—kicking up a row

(*Note.*—Only the last four words of the above poem are claimed as original.)

"Then America declared war on England."—*History of 1812*

Lady, not feeling particularly well, reclining in a steamer chair, covered up with rags. Little girl beside her, who wants to know. Gentleman in an adjoining steamer chair. The little girl begins to speak.

"And do you have to pay to go in, mamma?"

"Yes, dear."

"How much do you have to pay? As much as at a theatre?"

"Oh, you need not pay anything particular—no set sum, you know. You pay just what you can afford."

"Then it's like a collection at church, mamma?"

"Yes, dear."

"And does the captain get the money, mamma?"

"No, dear; the money goes to the poor orphans, I think."

"Where are the orphans, mamma?"

"I don't know, dear, I think they are in Liverpool."

"Whose orphans are they, mamma?"

"They are the orphans of sailors, dear."

"What kind of sailors, mamma?"

"British sailors, darling."

"Aren't there any sailors in America, mamma?"

"Oh yes, dear, lots of them."

"And do they have any orphans?"

"Yes, dear, I suppose there are orphans there too."

"And don't they get any of the money, mamma?"

"I am sure I do not know, dear. By the way, Mr. Daveling, how is that? Do they give any of the money to American orphans?"

"I believe not, madam. Subscriptions at concerts given on board British steamers are of course donated entirely to the Seamen's Hospital or Orphanage of Liverpool."

"Well, that doesn't seem to be quite fair, does it? A great deal of the money is subscribed by Americans."

"Yes, madam, that is perfectly true."

"I should think that ten Americans cross on these lines for every one Englishman."

"I am sure I do not know, madam, what the proportion is. The Americans are great travellers, so are the English too, for that matter."

"Yes; but I saw in one of the papers that this year alone over a hundred thousand persons had taken their passage from New York to England. It seems to me, that as all of them contribute to the receipts of the concerts, some sort of a division should be made."

"Oh, I have no doubt if the case were presented to the captain, he would be quite willing to have part of the proceeds at least go to some American seamen's charity."

"I think that would be only fair."

Two young ladies, arm in arm, approach, and ask Mrs. Pengo how she is feeling to-day.

Mrs. Pengo replies that she doesn't suppose she will feel any better as long as this rolling of the ship continues.

They claim, standing there, endeavouring to keep as perpendicular as possible, that the rolling is something simply awful.

Then the lady says to them, "Do you know, girls, that all the money subscribed at the concerts goes to England?"

"Why, no; I thought it went to some charity."

"Oh, it does go to a charity. It goes to the Liverpool Seamen's Hospital."

"Well, isn't that all right?"

"Yes, it's all right enough; but, as Sadie was just suggesting now, it doesn't seem quite fair, when there are orphans of sailors belonging to America, and as long as such large sums are subscribed by Americans, that the money should not be divided and part of it at least given to an American charity."

"Why, that seems perfectly fair, doesn't it, Mr. Daveling?"

"Yes, it is perfectly fair. I was just suggesting that perhaps if the state of things was presented to the captain, he would doubtless give a portion at least of the proceeds to an American Seamen's Home—if such an institution exists."

"Then," remarked the other girl, "I propose we form a committee, and interview the captain. I think that if Americans subscribe the bulk of the money, which they certainly do, they should have a voice in the disposal of it."

This was agreed to on all hands, and so began one of the biggest rows that ever occurred on board an Atlantic liner. Possibly, if the captain had had any tact, and if he had not been so thoroughly impressed with his own tremendous importance, what happened later on would not have happened.

The lady in the steamer chair took little part in the matter, in fact it was not at that time assumed to be of any importance whatever; but the two young American girls were enthusiastic, and they spoke to several of the passengers about it, both American and English. The English passengers all recognised the justice of the proposed plan, so a committee of five young ladies, and one young gentleman as spokesman, waited upon the captain. The young ladies at first had asked the doctor of the ship to be the spokesman; but when the doctor heard what the proposal was, he looked somewhat alarmed, and stroked his moustache thoughtfully.

"I don't know about that," he said; "it is a little unusual. The money has always gone to the Liverpool Seamen's Hospital, and—well, you see, we are a conservative people. We do a thing in one way for a number of years, and then keep on doing it because we have always done it in that way."

"Yes," burst out one of the young ladies, "that is no reason why an unjust thing should be perpetuated. Merely because a wrong has been done is no reason why it should be done again."

"True," said the doctor, "true," for he did not wish to fall out with the young lady, who was very pretty; "but, you see, in England we think a great deal of precedent."

And so the result of it all was that the doctor demurred at going to see the captain in relation to the matter. He said it wouldn't be the thing, as he was an official, and that it would be better to get one of the passengers.

I was not present at the interview, and of course know only what was told me by those who were there. It seems that the captain was highly offended at being approached on such a subject at all. A captain of an ocean liner, as I have endeavoured to show, is a very great personage indeed. And sometimes I imagine the passengers are not fully aware of this fact, or at least they do not show it as plainly as they ought to. Anyhow, the committee thought the captain had been exceedingly gruff with them, as well as just a trifle impolite. He told them that the money from the concerts had always gone to the Liverpool Seamen's Hospital, and always would while he was commanding a ship. He seemed to infer that the permission given them to hold a concert on board the ship was a very great concession, and that people should be thankful for the privilege of contributing to such a worthy object.

So, beginning with the little girl who wanted to know, and ending with the captain who commanded the ship, the conflagration was started.

Such is British deference to authority that, as soon as the captain's decision was known, those who had hitherto shown an open mind on the subject, and even those who had expressed themselves as favouring the dividing of the money, claimed that the captain's dictum had settled the matter. Then it was that every passenger had to declare himself. "Those who are not with us," said the young women, "are against us." The ship was almost immediately divided into two camps. It was determined to form a committee of Americans to take the money received from the second concert; for it was soon resolved to hold two concerts, one for the American Seamen's Orphans' Home and the other for that at Liverpool.

One comical thing about the row was, that nobody on board knew whether an American Seamen's Orphans' Home existed or not. When this problem was placed before the committee of young people, they pooh-poohed the matter. They said it didn't make any difference at all; if there was no Seamen's Hospital in America, it was quite time there should be one; and so they proposed that the money should be given to the future hospital, if it did not already exist.

When everything was prepared for the second concert there came a bolt from the blue. It was rumoured round the ship that the captain had refused his permission for the second concert to be held. The American men, who had up to date looked with a certain amused indifference on the efforts of the ladies, now rallied and held a meeting in the smoking-room. Every one felt that a crisis had come, and that the time to let loose the dogs of war— sea-dogs in this instance—had arrived. A committee was appointed to wait upon the captain next day. The following morning the excitement was at its highest pitch. It was not safe for an American to be seen conversing with an

Englishman, or vice versâ

Rumour had it at first—in fact all sorts of wild rumours were flying around the whole forenoon—that the captain refused to see the delegation of gentlemen who had requested audience with him. This rumour, however, turned out to be incorrect. He received the delegation in his room with one or two of the officers standing beside him. The spokesman said—

"Captain, we are informed that you have concluded not to grant permission to the Americans to hold a concert in aid of the American Seamen's Orphans' Home. We wish to know if this is true?"

"You have been correctly informed," replied the captain.

"We are sorry to hear that," answered the spokesman. "Perhaps you will not object to tell us on what grounds you have refused your permission?"

"Gentlemen," said the captain, "I have received you in my room because you requested an interview. I may say, however, that I am not in the habit of giving reasons for anything I do, to the passengers who honour this ship with their company."

"Then," said the spokesman, endeavouring to keep calm, but succeeding only indifferently, "it is but right that we should tell you that we regard such a proceeding on your part as a high handed outrage; that we will appeal against your decision to the owners of this steamship, and that, unless an apology is tendered, we will never cross on this line again, and we will advise all our compatriots never to patronise a line where such injustice is allowed."

"Might I ask you," said the captain very suavely, "of what injustice you complain?"

"It seems to us," said the spokesman, "that it is a very unjust thing to allow one class of passengers to hold a concert, and to refuse permission to another class to do the same thing."

"If that is all you complain of," said the captain, "I quite agree with you. I think that would be an exceedingly unjust proceeding."

"Is not that what you are about to do?"

"Not that I am aware of."

"You have prohibited the American concert?"

"Certainly. But I have prohibited the English concert as well."

The American delegates looked rather blankly at each other, and then the spokesman smiled. "Oh, well," he said, "if you have prohibited both of them, I don't see that we have anything to grumble at."

"Neither do I," said the captain.

The delegation then withdrew; and the passengers had the unusual pleasure of making one ocean voyage without having to attend the generally inevitable amateur concert.

A Ladies Man

"Jest w'en we guess we've covered the trail

So's no one can't foller, w'y then we fail

W'en we feel safe hid. Nemesis, the cuss,

Waltzes up with nary a warnin' nor fuss.

Grins quiet like, and says, 'How d'y do,

So glad we've met, I'm a-lookin' fer you'"

I do not wish to particularise any of the steamers on which the incidents given in this book occurred, so the boat of which I now write I shall call The Tub. This does not sound very flattering to the steamer, but I must say The Tub was a comfortable old boat, as everybody will testify who has ever taken a voyage in her. I know a very rich man who can well afford to take the best room in the best steamer if he wants to, but his preference always is for a slow boat like The Tub. He says that if you are not in a hurry, a slow boat is preferable to one of the new fast liners, because you have more individuality there, you get more attention, the officers are flattered by your preference for their ship, and you are not merely one of a great mob of passengers as in a crowded fast liner. The officers on a popular big and swift boat are prone to be a trifle snobbish. This is especially the case on the particular liner which for the moment stands at the top—a steamer that has broken the record, and is considered the best boat in the Atlantic service for the time being. If you get a word from the captain of such a boat you may consider yourself a peculiarly honoured individual, and even the purser is apt to answer you very shortly, and make you feel you are but a worm of the dust, even though you have paid a very large price for your state-room. On The Tub there was nothing of this. The officers were genial good fellows who admitted their boat was not the fastest on the Atlantic, although at one time she had been; but if The Tub never broke the record, on the other hand, she never broke a shaft, and so things were evened up. She wallowed her way across the Atlantic in a leisurely manner, and there was no feverish anxiety among the passengers when they reached Queenstown, to find whether the rival boat had got in ahead of us or not.

Everybody on board The Tub knew that any vessel which started from New York the same day would reach Queenstown before us. In fact, a good smart sailing vessel, with a fair wind, might have made it lively for us in an ocean race. The Tub was a broad slow boat, whose great speciality was freight, and her very broadness, which kept her from being a racer, even if her engines had had the power, made her particularly comfortable in a storm. She rolled but little; and as the state-rooms were large and airy, every passenger on board The Tub was sure of a reasonably pleasant voyage.

It was always amusing to hear the reasons each of the passengers gave for being on board The Tub. A fast and splendid liner of an opposition company left New York the next day, and many of our passengers explained to me they had come to New York with the intention of going by that boat, but they found all the rooms taken, that is, all the desirable rooms. Of course they might have had a room down on the third deck; but they were accustomed in travelling to have the best rooms, and if they couldn't be had, why it didn't much matter what was given them, so that was the reason they took passage on The Tub. Others were on the boat because they remembered the time when she was one of the fastest on the ocean, and they didn't like changing ships. Others again were particular friends of the captain, and he would have been annoyed if they had taken any other steamer. Everybody had some particularly valid reason for choosing The Tub, that is, every reason except economy, for it was well known that The Tub was one of the cheapest boats crossing the ocean. For my own part I crossed on her, because the purser was a particular friend of mine, and knew how to amalgamate fluids and different solid substances in a manner that produced a very palatable refreshment. He has himself deserted The Tub long ago, and is now purser on one of the new boats of the same line.

When the gong rang for the first meal on hoard The Tub after leaving New York, we filed down from the smoking-room to the great saloon to take our places at the table. There were never enough passengers on board

246

The Tub to cause a great rush for places at the table; but on this particular occasion, when we reached the foot of the stairway, two or three of us stood for a moment both appalled and entranced. Sitting at the captain's right hand was a somewhat sour and unattractive elderly woman, who was talking to that smiling and urbane official. Down the long table from where she sat, in the next fifteen seats were fifteen young and pretty girls, most of them looking smilingly and expectantly toward the stairway down which we were descending. The elderly woman paused for a moment in her conversation with the captain, glanced along the line of beauty, said sharply, 'Girls!' and instantly every face was turned demurely toward the plate that was in front of it, and then we, who had hesitated for a moment on the stairway, at once made a break, not for our seats at the table, but for the purser.

"It's all right, gentlemen," said that charming man, before we could speak; "it's all right. I've arranged your places down the table on the opposite side. You don't need to say a word, and those of you who want to change from the small tables to the large one, will find your names on the long table as well as at the small tables, where you have already chosen your places. So, you see, I knew just how you wished things arranged; but," he continued, lowering his voice, "boys, there's a dragon in charge. I know her. She has crossed with us two or three times. She wanted me to arrange it so that fifteen ladies should sit opposite her fifteen girls; but, of course, we couldn't do that, because there aren't fifteen other ladies on board, and there had to be one or two ladies placed next the girls at the foot of the table, so that no girl should have a young man sitting beside her. I have done the best I could, gentlemen, and, if you want the seats rearranged, I think we can manage it for you. Individual preferences may crop up, you know." And the purser smiled gently, for he had crossed the ocean very, very often.

We all took our places, sternly scrutinised by the lady, whom the purser had flatteringly termed the "dragon." She evidently didn't think very much of us as a crowd, and I am sure in my own heart I cannot blame her. We were principally students going over to German colleges on the cheap, some commercial travellers, and a crowd generally who could not afford to take a better boat, although we had all just missed the fast liner that had left a few days before, or had for some reason not succeeded in securing a berth on the fast boat, which was to leave the day after.

If any of the fifteen young ladies were aware of our presence, they did not show it by glancing toward us. They seemed to confine their conversation to whispers among themselves, and now and then a little suppressed giggle arose from one part of the line or the other, upon which the "dragon" looked along the row, and said severely, "Girls!" whereupon everything was quiet again, although some independent young lady generally broke the silence by another giggle just at the time the stillness was becoming most impressive.

After dinner, in the smoking-room, there was a great deal of discussion about the fifteen pretty girls and about the "dragon." As the officers on board The Tub were gentlemen whom an ordinary person might speak to, a delegation of one was deputed to go to the purser's room and find out all that could be learned in relation to the young and lovely passengers.

The purser said that the dragon's name was Mrs. Scrivener-Yapling, with a hyphen. The hyphen was a very important part of the name, and Mrs. Scrivener-Yapling always insisted upon it. Any one who ignored that hyphen speedily fell from the good graces of Mrs. Scrivener-Yapling. I regret to say, however, in spite of the hyphen, the lady was very generally known as the "dragon" during that voyage. The purser told us further, that Mrs. Scrivener-Yapling was in the habit of coming over once a year with a party of girls whom she trotted around Europe. The idea was that they learnt a great deal of geography, a good deal of French and German, and received in a general way a polish which Europe is supposed to give.

The circular which Mrs. Scrivener-Yapling issued was shown to me once by one of the girls, and it represented that all travelling was first-class, that nothing but the very best accommodations on steamers and in hotels were provided, and on account of Mrs. S. Y.'s intimate knowledge of Europe, and the different languages spoken there, she managed the excursion in a way which any one else would find impossible to emulate, and the advantages accruing from such a trip could not be obtained in any other manner without a very much larger expenditure of money. The girls had the advantage of motherly care during all the time they were abroad, and as the party was strictly limited in number, and the greatest care taken to select members only from the very best families in America, Mrs. Scrivener-Yapling was certain that all her patrons would realise that this was an opportunity of a lifetime, etc., etc.

Even if The Tub were not the finest boat on the Atlantic, she certainly belonged to one of the best lines, and as the circular mentioned the line and not the particular vessel on which the excursion was to go, the whole thing had a very high-class appearance.

The first morning out, shortly after, breakfast, the "dragon" and her girls appeared on deck. The girls walked two and two together, and kept their eyes pretty much on the planks beneath them. The fifteenth girl walked with the "dragon," and thus the eight pairs paced slowly up and down the deck under the "dragon's" eye. When this morning promenade was over the young ladies were marshalled into the ladies' saloon, where no masculine foot was allowed to tread. Shortly before lunch an indignation meeting was held in the smoking-room. Stewart Montague, a commercial traveller from Milwaukee, said that he had crossed the ocean many times, but had never seen such a state of things before. This young ladies' seminary business (he alluded to the two and two walk along the deck) ought not to be permitted on any well regulated ship. Here were a number of young ladies, ranging in age from eighteen upwards, and there lay ahead of us a long and possibly dreary voyage, yet the "dragon" evidently expected that not one of the young ladies was to be allowed to speak to one of the young gentlemen on board, much less walk the deck with him. Now, for his part, said Stewart Montague, he was going to take off his hat the next morning to the young lady who sat opposite him at the dinner-table and boldly ask her to walk the deck with him. If the "dragon" interfered, he proposed that we all mutiny, seize the vessel, put the captain in irons, imprison the "dragon" in the hold, and then take to pirating on the high seas. One of the others pointed out to him an objection to this plan, claiming that The Tub could not overtake anything but a sailing-vessel, while even that was doubtful. Montague explained that the mutiny was only to be resorted to as a last desperate chance. He believed the officers of the boat would give us every assistance possible, and so it was only in case of everything else failing that we should seize the ship.

In a moment of temporary aberration I suggested that the "dragon" might not be, after all, such an objectionable person as she appeared, and that perhaps she could be won over by kindness. Instantly a motion was put, and carried unanimously, appointing me a committee to try the effect of kindness on the "dragon." It was further resolved that the meeting should be adjourned, and I should report progress at the next conclave.

I respectfully declined this mission. I said it was none of my affair. I didn't wish to talk to any of the fifteen girls, or even walk the deck with them. I was perfectly satisfied as I was. I saw no reason why I should sacrifice myself for the good of others. I suggested that the name of Stewart Montague be substituted for mine, and that he should face the "dragon" and report progress.

Mr. Montague said it had been my suggestion, not his, that the "dragon" might be overcome by kindness. He did not believe she could, but he was quite willing to suspend hostilities until my plan had been tried and the result reported to the meeting. It was only when they brought in a motion to expel me from the smoking-room that I succumbed to the pressure. The voyage was just beginning, and what is a voyage to a smoker who dare not set foot in the smoking-room?

I do not care to dwell on the painful interview I had with the "dragon." I put my foot in it at the very first by pretending that I thought she came from New York, whereas she had really come from Boston. To take a New York person for a Bostonian is flattery, but to reverse the order of things, especially with a woman of the uncertain temper of Mrs. Scrivener-Yapling, was really a deadly insult, and I fear this helped to shipwreck my mission, although I presume it would have been shipwrecked in any case. Mrs. Scrivener-Yapling gave me to understand that if there was one thing more than another she excelled in it was the reading of character. She knew at a glance whether a man could be trusted or not; most men were not, I gathered from her conversation. It seems she had taken a great many voyages across the Atlantic, and never in the whole course of her experience had she seen such an objectionable body of young men as on this present occasion. She accused me of being a married man, and I surmised that there were other iniquities of which she strongly suspected me.

The mission was not a success, and I reported at the adjourned meeting accordingly.

Mr. Stewart Montague gave it as his opinion that the mission was hopeless from the first, and in this I quite agreed with him. He said he would try his plan at dinner, but what it was he refused to state. We asked if he would report on the success or failure, and he answered that we would all see whether it was a success or failure for ourselves. So there was a good deal of interest centring around the meal, an interest not altogether called forth by the pangs of hunger.

Dinner had hardly commenced when Mr. Stewart Montague leaned over the table and said, in quite an audible voice, to the young lady opposite him, "I understand you have never been over the ocean before?"

The young lady looked just a trifle frightened, blushed very prettily, and answered in a low voice that she had not.

Then he said, "I envy you the first impressions you will have of Europe. It is a charming country. Where do you go after leaving England?"

"We are going across to Paris first," she replied, still in a low voice.

Most of us, however, were looking at the "dragon." That lady sat bolt upright in her chair as if she could not believe her ears. Then she said, in an acid voice, "Miss Fleming."

"Yes, Mrs. Scrivener-Yapling," answered that young lady.

"Will you oblige me by coming here for a moment?"

Miss Fleming slowly revolved in her circular chair, then rose and walked up to the head of the table.

"Miss Strong," said the "dragon" calmly, to the young lady who sat beside her, "will you oblige me by taking Miss Fleming's place at the centre of the table?"

Miss Strong rose and took Miss Fleming's place.

"Sit down beside me, please?" said the "dragon" to Miss Fleming; and that unfortunate young woman, now as red as a rose, sat down beside the "dragon."

Stewart Montague bit his lip. The rest of us said nothing, and appeared not to notice what had occurred. Conversation went on among ourselves. The incident seemed ended; but, when the fish was brought, and placed before Miss Fleming, she did not touch it. Her eyes were still upon the table. Then, apparently unable to struggle any longer with her emotions, she rose gracefully, and, bowing to the captain, said, "Excuse me, please." She walked down the long saloon with a firm step, and disappeared. The "dragon" tried to resume conversation with the captain as if nothing had happened; but that official answered only in monosyllables, and a gloom seemed to have settled down upon the dinner party.

Very soon the captain rose and excused himself. There was something to attend to on deck, he said, and he left us.

As soon as we had reassembled in the smoking-room, and the steward had brought in our cups of black coffee, Stewart Montague arose and said, "Gentlemen, I know just what you are going to say to me. It was brutal. Of course I didn't think the 'dragon' would do such a thing. My plan was a complete failure. I expected that conversation would take place across the table all along the line, if I broke the ice."

Whatever opinions were held, none found expression, and that evening in the smoking-room was as gloomy as the hour at the dinner-table.

Towards the shank of the evening a gentleman, who had never been in the smoking-room before, entered very quietly. We recognised him as the man who sat to the left of the captain opposite the "dragon." He was a man of middle age and of somewhat severe aspect. He spoke with deliberation when he did speak, and evidently, weighed his words. All we knew of him was that the chair beside his at meal-times had been empty since the voyage began, and it was said that his wife took her meals in her state-room. She had appeared once on deck with him, very closely veiled, and hung upon his arm in a way that showed she was not standing the voyage very well, pleasant as it had been.

"Gentlemen," began the man suavely, "I would like to say a few words to you if I were certain that my remarks would be taken in the spirit in which they are given, and that you would not think me intrusive or impertinent."

"Go ahead," said Montague, gloomily, who evidently felt a premonition of coming trouble.

The serious individual waited until the steward had left the room, then he closed the door. "Gentlemen," he continued, "I will not recur to the painful incident which happened at the dinner-table to-night further than by asking you, as honourable men, to think of Mrs. Scrivener-Yapling's position of great responsibility. She stands in the place of a mother to a number of young ladies who, for the first time in their lives, have left their homes."

"Lord pity them," said somebody, who was sitting in the corner.

The gentleman paid no attention to the remark.

"Now what I wish to ask of you is that you will not make Mrs. Scrivener-Yapling's position any harder by futile endeavours to form the acquaintance of the young ladies."

At this point Stewart Montague broke out. "Who the devil are you, sir, and who gave you the right to interfere?"

"As to who I am," said the gentleman, quietly, "my name is Kensington, and—"

"West or South?" asked the man in the corner.

At this there was a titter of laughter.

"My name is Kensington," repeated the gentleman, "and I have been asked by Mrs. Scrivener-Yapling to interfere, which I do very reluctantly.

As I said at the beginning, I hope you will not think my interference is impertinent. I only do so at the earnest request of the lady I have mentioned, because I am a family man myself, and I understand and sympathise with the lady in the responsibility which she has assumed."

"It seems to me," said the man in the corner, "that if the 'dragon' has assumed responsibilities and they have not been thrust upon her, which I understand they have not, then she must take the responsibility of the responsibilities which she has assumed. Do I make myself clear?"

"Gentlemen," said Mr. Kensington, "it is very painful for me to speak with you upon this subject. I feel that what I have so clumsily expressed may not be correctly understood; but I appeal to your honour as gentlemen, and I am sure I will not appeal in vain when I ask you not to make further effort towards the acquaintance of the young ladies, because all that you can succeed in doing will be to render their voyage unpleasant to themselves, and interrupt, if not seriously endanger, the good feeling which I understand has always existed between Mrs. Scrivener-Yapling and her protégées."

"All right," said the man in the corner. "Have a drink, Mr. Kensington?"

"Thank you, I never drink," answered Mr. Kensington.

"Have a smoke, then?"

"I do not smoke either, thank you all the same for your offer. I hope, gentlemen, you will forgive my intrusion on you this evening. Good night."

"Impudent puppy," said Stewart Montague, as he closed the door behind him.

But in this we did not agree with him, not even the man in the corner.

"He is perfectly right," said that individual, "and I believe that we ought to be ashamed of ourselves. It will only make trouble, and I for one am going to give up the hunt."

So, from that time forward, the smoking-room collectively made no effort towards the acquaintance of the young ladies. The ladies' seminary walk, as it was called, took place every morning punctually, and sometimes Mr. Kensington accompanied the walkers. Nevertheless, individual friendships, in spite of everything that either Mr. Kensington or the "dragon" could do, sprang up between some of the young men and some of the girls, but the "dragon" had an invaluable ally in Mr. Kensington. The moment any of the young ladies began walking with any of the young gentlemen on deck, or the moment they seated themselves in steamer chairs together, the urbane, always polite Mr. Kensington appeared on the scene and said, "Miss So-and-So, Mrs. Scrivener-Yapling would like to speak with you."

Then the young lady would go with Mr. Kensington, while the young gentleman was apt to use strong language and gnash his teeth.

Mr. Kensington seemed lynx-eyed. There was no escaping him. Many in the smoking-room no doubt would have liked to have picked a flaw in his character if they could. One even spoke of the old chestnut about a man who had no small vices being certain to have some very large ones; but even the speakers themselves did not believe this, and any one could see at a glance that Mr. Kensington was a man of sterling character. Some hinted that his wife was the victim of his cruelty, and kept her state-room only because she knew that he was so fond of the "dragon's" company, and possibly that of some of the young ladies as well. But this grotesque sentiment did not pass current even in the smoking-room. Nevertheless, although he was evidently so good a man, he was certainly the most unpopular individual on board The Tub. The hatred that Stewart Montague felt for him ever since that episode in the smoking-room was almost grotesque.

Montague had somehow managed to get a contrite note of apology and distress to Miss Fleming, and several times the alert Mr. Kensington had caught them together, and asked Miss Fleming with the utmost respect to come down and see Mrs. Scrivener-Yapling.

All in all the "dragon" did not have a very easy time of it. She fussed around like any other old hen who had in charge a brood of ducks.

Once I thought there was going to be a row between Montague and Kensington. He met that gentleman in a secluded part of the deck, and,

255

going up to him, said—

"You old wife deserter, why can't you attend to your own affairs?"

Kensington turned deadly pale at this insult, and his fists clinched—

"What do you mean?" he said huskily.

"I mean what I say. Why don't you take your own wife walking on the deck, and leave the young ladies alone. It's none of your business with whom they walk."

Kensington seemed about to reply; but he thought better of it, turned on his heel, and left Montague standing there.

The old Tub worried her way across the ocean, and reached the bar at Liverpool just in time to be too late to cross it that night. Word was passed along that a tender would come out from Liverpool for us, which was not a very cheering prospect, as we would have two hours' sail at least in what was practically an open boat.

Finally the tender came alongside, and the baggage was dumped down upon it. All of us gathered together ready to leave The Tub. Mr. Kensington, with his closely-veiled wife hanging on his arm, was receiving the thanks and congratulations of the "dragon." The fifteen girls were all around her. Before any one started down the sloping gangway plank, however, two policemen, accompanied by a woman, hurried up on board The Tub.

"Now, madam," said the policeman, "is he here?"

We saw that trouble was coming, and everybody looked at everybody else.

"Is he here?" cried the woman excitedly; "there he stands, the villain. Oh, you villain, you scoundrel, you mean rascal, to leave me, as you thought, penniless in New York, and desert your own wife and family for that—that creature!" We all looked at Kensington, and his face was greenish-pale. The heavily veiled woman shrunk behind him and the policeman tried to make the true wife keep quiet.

"Is your name Braughton?"

Kensington did not answer. His eyes were riveted on his wife. "In the name of God," he cried aghast, "how did you come here?"

"How did I come here," she shrieked. "Oh, you thought you slipped away nicely, didn't you? But you forgot that the Clipper left the next day, and I've been here two days waiting for you. You little thought when you deserted me and my children in New York that we would be here to confront you at Liverpool."

"Come, come." said the policeman, "there's no use of this. I am afraid you will have to come with us, sir."

They took him in charge, and the irate wife then turned like a tigress on the heavily veiled woman who was with him.

"No wonder you are ashamed to show your face," she cried.

"Come, come," said the policeman, "come, come." And they managed to induce her to say no more.

"Madam," said young Montague to the speechless 'dragon,' "I want to ask your permission to allow me to carry Miss Fleming's hand- baggage ashore."

"How dare you speak to me, sir?" she answered.

"Because," he said, in a low voice, "I thought perhaps you wouldn't like an account of this affair to go to the Boston newspapers. I'm a newspaper man, you see," he added, with unblushing mendacity. Then, turning to Miss Fleming, he said, "Won't you allow me to carry this for you?"

Miss Fleming surrendered the natty little handbag she had with her, and smiled. The "dragon" made no objection.

A Society For The Reformation Of Poker Players.

"O Unseen Hand that ever makes and deals us,

And plays our game!

That now obscures and then to light reveals us,

Serves blanks of fame

How vain our shuffling, bluff and weak pretending!

Tis Thou alone can name the final ending"

The seductive game of poker is one that I do not understand. I do not care to understand it, because it cannot be played without the putting up of a good deal of the coin of the realm, and although I have nothing to say against betting, my own theory of conduct in the matter is this, that I want no man's money which I do not earn, and I do not want any man to get my money unless he earns it. So it happens, in the matter of cards, I content myself with euchre and other games which do not require the wagering of money.

On board the Atlantic steamers there is always more or less gambling. I have heard it said that men make trips to and fro merely for the purpose of fleecing their fellow-passengers; but, except in one instance, I never had any experience with this sort of thing.

Our little society for the reformation of poker players, or to speak more correctly, for the reformation of one particular poker player, was formed one bright starlight night, latitude such a number, and longitude something else, as four of us sat on a seat at the extreme rear end of the great steamer. We four, with one other, sat at a small table in the saloon. One of the small tables on a Transatlantic steamer is very pleasant if you have a nice crowd with you. A seat at a small table compares with a seat at the large table as living in a village compares with living in a city. You have some individuality at the short table; you are merely one of a crowd at the long table. Our small table was not quite full. I had the honour of sitting at the head of it, and on each side of me were two young fellows, making five altogether. We all rather prided ourselves on the fact that there were no ladies at our little table.

The young Englishman who sat at my right hand at the corner of the table was going out to America to learn farming. I could, myself, have taught him a good deal about it, but I refrained from throwing cold water on his enthusiastic ideas about American agriculture. His notion was that it was an occupation mostly made up of hunting and fishing, and having a good time generally. The profits, he thought, were large and easily acquired. He had guns with him, and beautiful fishing-rods, and things of that sort. He even had a vague idea that he might be able to introduce fox-hunting in the rural district to which he was going. He understood, and regretted the fact, that we in the United States were rather behind-hand in the matter of fox-hunting. He had a good deal of money with him, I understood, and he had already paid a hundred pounds to a firm in England that had agreed to place him on a farm in America. Of course, now that the money had been paid, there was no use in telling the young man he had been a fool. He would find that out soon enough when he got to America. Henry Storm was his name, and a milder mannered man with a more unsuitable name could hardly be found. The first two or three days out he was the life of our party. We all liked him, in fact, nobody could help liking him; but, as the voyage progressed, he grew more and more melancholy, and, what was really serious, took little food, which is not natural in an Englishman. I thought somebody had been telling him what a fool he had been to pay away his hundred pounds before leaving England, but young Smith of Rochester, who sat at my left, told me what the trouble was one day as we walked the deck. "Do you know," he began, "that Henry Storm is being robbed?"

"Being robbed?" I answered; "you mean he has been robbed."

"Well, has been, and is being, too. The thing is going on yet. He is playing altogether too much poker in the smoking-room, and has lost a pile of money—more, I imagine, than he can well afford."

"That's what's the trouble with him, is it? Well, he ought to know better than to play for bigger stakes than he can afford to lose."

"Oh, it's easy to say that; but he's in the hands of a swindler, of a professional gambler. You see that man?" He lowered his voice as he spoke, and I looked in the direction of his glance. By this time we knew, in a way, everybody on board the ship. The particular man Smith pointed out was a fellow I had noticed a good deal, who was very quiet and gentlemanly, interfering with nobody, and talking with few. I had spoken to him once, but he had answered rather shortly, and, apparently to his relief, and certainly to my own, our acquaintance ceased where it began. He had jet black beard and hair, both rather closely clipped; and he wore a fore and aft cap, which never improves a man's appearance very much.

"That man," continued Smith, as he passed us, "was practically under arrest for gambling on the steamer in which I came over. It seems that he is a regular professional gambler, who does nothing but go across the ocean and back again, fleecing young fellows like Storm."

"Does he cheat?" I asked.

"He doesn't need to. He plays poker. An old hand, and a cool one, has no occasion to cheat at that game to get a young one's money away from him."

"Then why doesn't some one warn young Storm?"

"Well, that's just what I wanted to speak to you about. I think it ought to be done. I think we should call a meeting of our table, somewhere out here in the quiet, and have a talk over it, and make up our mind what is to be done. It's a delicate matter, you know, and I am afraid we are a little late as it is. I do believe young Storm has lost nearly all his money to that fellow."

"Can't he be made to disgorge?"

"How? The money has been won fairly enough, as that sort of thing goes. Other fellows have played with them. It isn't as if he had been caught cheating—he hasn't, and won't be. He doesn't cheat—he doesn't need to, as I said before. Now that gambler pretends he is a commercial traveller from Buffalo. I know Buffalo down to the ground, so I took him aside yesterday and said plumply to him, 'What firm in Buffalo do you represent?' He answered shortly that his business was his own affair. I said, 'Certainly it is, and you are quite right in keeping it dark. When I was coming over to Europe, I saw a man in your line of business who looked very much like you, practically put under arrest by the purser for gambling. You were travelling for a St. Louis house then.'"

"What did he say to that?"

"Nothing; he just gave me one of those sly, sinister looks of his, turned on his heel, and left me."

The result of this conversation was the inauguration of the Society for the Reforming of a Poker Player. It was agreed between us that if young Storm had lost all his money we would subscribe enough as a loan to take care of him until he got a remittance from home. Of course we knew that any young fellow who goes out to America to begin farming, does not, as a general rule, leave people in England exceedingly well off, and probably this fact, more than any other, accounted for the remorse visible on Storm's countenance. We knew quite well that the offering of money to him would be a very delicate matter, but it was agreed that Smith should take this in hand if we saw the offer was necessary. Then I, as the man who sat at the head of the table, was selected to speak to young Storm, and, if possible, get him to abandon poker. I knew this was a somewhat impudent piece of business on my part, and so I took that evening to determine how best to perform the task set for me. I resolved to walk the deck with him in the morning, and have a frank talk over the matter.

When the morning came, I took young Storm's arm and walked two or three turns up and down the deck, but all the while I could not get up courage enough to speak with him in relation to gambling. When he left me, I again thought over the matter. I concluded to go into the smoking-room myself, sit down beside him, see him lose some money and use that fact as a test for my coming discourse on the evils of gambling. After luncheon I strolled into the smoking-room, and there sat this dark-faced man with his half-closed eyes opposite young Storm, while two others made up the four-handed game of poker.

Storm's face was very pale, and his lips seemed dry, for he moistened them every now and then as the game went on. He was sitting on the sofa, and I sat down beside him, paying no heed to the dark gambler's look of annoyance. However, the alleged Buffalo man said nothing, for he was not a person who did much talking. Storm paid no attention to me as I sat down beside him. The gambler had just dealt. It was very interesting to see the way he looked at his hand. He allowed merely the edges of the cards to show over each other, and then closed up his hand and seemed to know just what he had. When young Storm looked at his hand he gave a sort of gasp, and for the first time cast his eyes upon me. I had seen his hand, but did not know whether it was a good one or not. I imagined it was not very good, because all the cards were of a low denomination. Threes or fours I think, but four of the cards had a like number of spots. There was some money in the centre of the table. Storm pushed a half-crown in front of him, and the next man did the same. The gambler put down a half-sovereign, and the man at his left, after a moment's hesitation, shoved out an equal amount from the pile of gold in front of him.

Young Storm pushed out a sovereign.

"I'm out," said the man whose next bet it was, throwing down his cards.

The gambler raised it a sovereign, and the man at his left dropped out. It now rested between Storm and the gambler. Storm increased the bet a sovereign. The gambler then put on a five-pound note.

Storm said to me huskily, "Have you any money?"

"Yes," I answered him.

"Lend me five pounds if you can."

Now, the object of my being there was to stop gambling, not to encourage it. I was the president pro tem, of the Society for the Reformation of Poker Players, yet I dived into my pocket, pulled out my purse under the table and slipped a five-pound note into his hand. He put that on the table as if he had just taken it from his own pocket.

"I call you," he said.

"What have you got?" asked the gambler.

"Four fours," said Storm, putting down his hand.

The gambler closed up his and threw the cards over to the man who was to deal. Storm paused a moment and then pulled towards him the money in the centre of the table and handed me my five-pound note.

When the cards were next dealt, Storm seemed to have rather an ordinary hand, so apparently had all the rest, and there was not much money in the pile. But, poor as Storm's hand was, the rest appeared to be poorer, and he raked in the cash. This went on for two or three deals, and finding that, as Storm was winning all the time, although not heavily, I was not getting an object lesson against gambling, I made a move to go.

"Stay where you are," whispered Storm to me, pinching my knee with his hand so hard that I almost cried out.

Then it came to the gambler's turn to deal again. All the time he deftly shuffled the cards he watched the players with that furtive glance of his from out his half-shut eyes.

Storm's hand was a remarkable one, after he had drawn two cards, but I did not know whether it had any special value or not. The other players drew three cards each, and the gambler took one.

"How much money have you got?" whispered Storm to me.

"I don't know," I said, "perhaps a hundred pounds."

"Be prepared to lend me every penny of it," he whispered.

I said nothing; but I never knew the president of a society for the suppression of gambling to be in such a predicament.

Storm bet a sovereign. The player to his left threw down his hand. The gambler pushed out two sovereigns. The other player went out.

Storm said, "I see your bet, and raise you another sovereign." The gambler, without saying a word, shoved forward some more gold.

"Get your money ready," whispered Storm to I did not quite like his tone, but I made allowance for the excitement under which he was evidently labouring.

He threw on a five-pound note. The gambler put down another five-pound note, and then, as if it were the slightest thing possible, put a ten-pound note on top of that, which made the side players gasp. Storm had won sufficient to cover the bet and raise it. After that I had to feed in to him five-pound notes, keeping count of their number on my fingers as I did so. The first to begin to hesitate about putting money forward was the gambler. He shot a glance now and again from under his eyebrows at the young man opposite. Finally, when my last five-pound note had been thrown on the pile, the gambler spoke for the first time.

"I call you," he said.

"Put down another five-pound note," cried the young man.

"I have called you," said the gambler.

Henry Storm half rose from his seat in his excitement. "Put down another five-pound note, if you dare."

"That isn't poker," said the gambler. "I have called you. What have you got?"

"Put down another five-pound note, and I'll put a ten-pound note on top of it."

"I say that isn't poker. You have been called. What have you got?"

"I'll bet you twenty pounds against your five-pound note, if you dare put it down."

By this time Storm was standing up, quivering with excitement, his cards tightly clenched in his hand. The gambler sat opposite him calm and imperturbable.

"What have you got?" said Storm.

"I called you," said the gambler, "show your hand."

264

"Yes; but when I called you, you asked me what I had, and I told you. What have you got?"

"I am not afraid to show my hand," said the gambler, and he put down on the table four aces.

"There's the king of hearts," said Storm, putting it down on the table. "There's the queen of hearts, there's the knave of hearts, there's the ten of hearts. Now," he cried, waving his other card in the air, "can you tell me what this card is?"

"I am sure I don't know," answered the gambler, quietly, "probably the nine of hearts."

"It is the nine of hearts," shouted Storm, placing it down beside the others.

The gambler quietly picked up the cards, and handed them to the man who was to deal. Storm's hands were trembling with excitement as he pulled the pile of bank notes and gold towards him. He counted out what I had given him, and passed it to me under the table. The rest he thrust into his pocket.

"Come," I said, "it is time to go. Don't strain your luck."

"Another five pounds," he whispered; "sit where you are."

"Nonsense," I said, "another five pounds will certainly mean that you lose, everything you have won. Come away, I want to talk with you."

"Another five pounds, I have sworn it."

"Very well, I shall not stay here any longer."

"No, no," he cried eagerly; "sit where you are, sit where you are."

There was a grim thin smile on the lips of the gambler as this whispered conversation took place.

When the next hand was dealt around and Storm looked at his cards, he gave another gasp of delight. I thought that a poker player should not be so free with his emotions; but of course I said nothing. When it came his time to bet, he planked down a five-pound note on the table. The other two, as was usual, put down their cards. They were evidently very timorous players. The gambler hesitated for a second, then he put a ten-pound note on Storm's five-pounds. Storm at once saw him, and raised him ten. The gambler hesitated longer this time, but at last he said, "I shall not bet. What have you got?"

"Do you call me?" asked Storm. "Put up your money if you do."

"No, I do not call you."

Storm laughed and threw his cards face up on the table. "I have nothing," he said, "I have bluffed you for once."

"It is very often done," answered the gambler, quietly, as Storm drew in his pile of money, stuffing it again in his coat pocket. "Your deal, Storm."

"No, sir," said the young man, rising up; "I'll never touch a poker hand again. I have got my own money back and five or ten pounds over. I know when I've had enough."

Although it was Storm's deal, the gambler had the pack of cards in his hand idly shuffling them to and fro.

"I have often heard," he said slowly without raising his eyes, "that when one fool sits down beside another fool at poker, the player has the luck of two fools—but I never believed it before."

266

The Man Who was Not on the Passenger List.

"The well-sworn Lie, franked to the world with all

The circumstance of proof,

Cringes abashed, and sneaks along the wall

At the first sight of Truth."

The Gibrontus of the Hot Cross Bun Line was at one time the best ship of that justly celebrated fleet. All steamships have, of course, their turn at the head of the fleet until a better boat is built, but the Gibrontus is even now a reasonably fast and popular boat. An accident happened on board the Gibrontus some years ago which was of small importance to the general public, but of some moment to Richard Keeling—for it killed him. The poor man got only a line or two in the papers when the steamer arrived at New York, and then they spelled his name wrong. It had happened something like this: Keeling was wandering around very late at night, when he should have been in his bunk, and he stepped on a dark place that he thought was solid. As it happened, there was nothing between him and the bottom of the hold but space. They buried Keeling at sea, and the officers knew absolutely nothing about the matter when inquisitive passengers, hearing rumours, questioned them. This state of things very often exists both on sea and land, as far as officials are concerned. Mrs. Keeling, who had been left in England while her husband went to America to make his fortune, and tumbled down a hole instead, felt aggrieved at the company. The company said that Keeling had no business to be nosing around dark places on the deck at that time of night, and doubtless their contention was just. Mrs. Keeling, on the other hand, held that a steamer had no right to have such mantraps open at any time, night or day, without having them properly guarded, and in that she was also probably correct. The company was very sorry, of course, that the thing had occurred; but they refused to pay for Keeling unless compelled to do so by the law of the land, and there matters stood. No one can tell what the law of the land will do when it is put in motion, although many people thought that if Mrs. Keeling had brought a suit against the Hot Cross Bun Company she would have won it. But Mrs. Keeling was a poor woman, and you have to put a penny in the slot when you want the figures of justice to work, so the unfortunate creature signed something which the lawyer of the company had written out, and accepted the few pounds which Keeling had paid for Room 18 on the Gibrontus. It would seem that this ought to have settled the matter, for the lawyer told Mrs. Keeling he thought the company acted very generously in refunding the passage money; but it didn't settle the matter. Within a year from that time, the company voluntarily paid Mrs. Keeling £2100 for her husband. Now that the occurrence is called to your mind, you will perhaps remember the editorial one of the leading London dailies had on the extraordinary circumstance, in which it was very ably shown that the old saying about corporations having no souls to be condemned or bodies to be kicked did not apply in these days of commercial honour and integrity. It was a very touching editorial, and it caused tears to be shed on the Stock Exchange, the members having had no idea, before reading it, that they were so noble and generous.

How, then, was it that the Hot Cross Bun Company did this commendable act when their lawyer took such pains to clear them of all legal liability? The purser of the Gibrontus, who is now old and superannuated, could probably tell you if he liked.

When the negotiations with Mrs. Keeling had been brought to a satisfactory conclusion by the lawyer of the company, and when that gentleman was rubbing his hands over his easy victory, the good ship Gibrontus was steaming out of the Mersey on her way to New York. The stewards in the grand saloon were busy getting things in order for dinner, when a wan and gaunt passenger spoke to one of them.

"Where have you placed me at table?" he asked.

"What name, sir?" asked the steward.

"Keeling."

The steward looked along the main tables, up one side and down the other, reading the cards, but nowhere did he find the name he was in search of. Then he looked at the small tables, but also without success.

"How do you spell it, sir?" he asked the patient passenger.

"K-double-e-l-i-n-g."

"Thank you, sir."

Then he looked up and down the four rows of names on the passenger list he held in his hand, but finally shook his head.

"I can't find your name on the passenger list," he said. "I'll speak to the purser, sir."

"I wish you would," replied the passenger in a listless way, as if he had not much interest in the matter. The passenger, whose name was not on the list, waited until the steward returned. "Would you mind stepping into the purser's room for a moment, sir? I'll show you the way, sir."

When the passenger was shown into the purser's room that official said to him, in the urbane manner of pursers—

"Might I look at your ticket, sir?"

The passenger pulled a long pocket-book from the inside of his coat, opened it, and handed the purser the document it contained. The purser scrutinized it sharply, and then referred to a list he had on the desk before him.

"This is very strange," he said at last. "I never knew such a thing to occur before, although, of course, it is always possible. The people on shore have in some unaccountable manner left your name out of my list. I am sorry you have been put to any inconvenience, sir."

"There has been no inconvenience so far," said the passenger, "and I trust there will be none. You find the ticket regular, I presume?"

"Quite so—quite so," replied the purser. Then, to the waiting steward, "Give Mr. Keeling any place he prefers at the table which is not already taken.

You have Room 18."

"That was what I bought at Liverpool."

"Well, I see you have the room to yourself, and I hope you will find it comfortable. Have you ever crossed with us before, sir? I seem to recollect your face."

"I have never been in America."

"Ah! I see so many faces, of course, that I sometimes fancy I know a man when I don't. Well, I hope you will have a pleasant voyage, sir."

"Thank you."

No. 18 was not a popular passenger. People seemed instinctively to shrink from him, although it must be admitted that he made no advances. All went well until the Gibrontus was about half-way over. One forenoon the chief officer entered the captain's room with a pale face, and, shutting the door after him, said—

"I am very sorry to have to report, sir, that one of the passengers has fallen into the hold."

"Good heavens!" cried the captain. "Is he hurt?"

"He is killed, sir."

The captain stared aghast at his subordinate.

"How did it happen? I gave the strictest orders those places were on no account to be left unguarded."

Although the company had held to Mrs. Keeling that the captain was not to blame, their talk with that gentleman was of an entirely different tone.

"That is the strange part of it, sir. The hatch has not been opened this voyage, sir, and was securely bolted down."

"Nonsense! Nobody will believe such a story! Some one has been careless! Ask the purser to come here, please."

When the purser saw the body, he recollected, and came as near fainting as a purser can.

They dropped Keeling overboard in the night, and the whole affair was managed so quietly that nobody suspected anything, and, what is the most incredible thing in this story, the New York papers did not have a word about it. What the Liverpool office said about the matter nobody knows, but it must have stirred up something like a breeze in that strictly business locality. It is likely they pooh-poohed the whole affair, for, strange to say, when the purser tried to corroborate the story with the dead man's ticket the document was nowhere to be found.

The Gibrontus started out on her next voyage from Liverpool with all her colours flying, but some of her officers had a vague feeling of unrest within them which reminded them of the time they first sailed on the heaving seas. The purser was seated in his room, busy, as pursers always are at the beginning of a voyage, when there was a rap at the door.

"Come in!" shouted the important official, and there entered unto him a stranger, who said—"Are you the purser?"

"Yes, sir. What can I do for you?"

"I have room No. 18."

"What!" cried the purser, with a gasp, almost jumping from his chair. Then he looked at the robust man before him, and sank back with a sigh of relief. It was not Keeling.

"I have room No. 18," continued the passenger, "and the arrangement I made with your people in Liverpool was that I was to have the room to myself. I do a great deal of shipping over your—"

"Yes, my dear sir," said the purser, after having looked rapidly over his list, "you have No. 18 to yourself."

"So I told the man who is unpacking his luggage there; but he showed me his ticket, and it was issued before mine. I can't quite understand why your people should—"

"What kind of a looking man is he?"

"A thin, unhealthy, cadaverous man, who doesn't look as if he would last till the voyage ends. I don't want him for a room mate, if I have to have one. I think you ought—"

"I will, sir. I will make it all right. I suppose, if it should happen that a mistake has been made, and he has the prior claim to the room, you would not mind taking No. 24—it is a larger and better room."

"That will suit me exactly."

So the purser locked his door and went down to No. 18.

"Well?" he said to its occupant.

"Well," answered Mr. Keeling, looking up at him with his cold and fishy eyes.

"You're here again, are you?"

"I'm here again, and I will be here again. And again and again, and again and again."

"Now, what the—" Then the purser hesitated a moment, and thought perhaps he had better not swear, with that icy, clammy gaze fixed upon him. "What object have you in all this?"

"Object? The very simple one of making your company live up to its contract. From Liverpool to New York, my ticket reads. I paid for being landed in the United States, not for being dumped overboard in mid-ocean. Do you think you can take me over? You have had two tries at it and have not succeeded. Yours is a big and powerful company too."

"If you know we can't do it, then why do you—?" The purser hesitated.

"Pester you with my presence?" suggested Mr. Keeling. "Because I want you to do justice. Two thousand pounds is the price, and I will raise it one hundred pounds every trip." This time the New York papers got hold of the incident, but not of its peculiar features. They spoke of the extraordinary carelessness of the officers in allowing practically the same accident to occur twice on the same boat. When the Gibrontus reached Liverpool all the officers, from the captain down, sent in their resignations. Most of the sailors did not take the trouble to resign, but cut for it. The managing director was annoyed at the newspaper comments, but laughed at the rest of the story. He was invited to come over and interview Keeling for his own satisfaction, most of the officers promising to remain on the ship if he did so. He took Room 18 himself. What happened I do not know, for the purser refused to sail again on the Gibrontus, and was given another ship.

But this much is certain. When the managing director got back, the company generously paid Mrs. Keeling £2100.

The Terrible Experience of Plodkins

"Which—life or death? Tis a gambler's chance!

Yet, unconcerned, we spin and dance,

On the brittle thread of circumstance."

I understand that Plodkins is in the habit of referring sceptical listeners to me, and telling them that I will substantiate every word of his story. Now this is hardly fair of Plodkins. I can certainly corroborate part of what he says, and I can bear witness to the condition in which I found him after his ordeal was over. So I have thought it best, in order to set myself right with the public, to put down exactly what occurred. If I were asked whether or not I believe Plodkins' story myself, I would have to answer that sometimes I believe it, and sometimes I do not. Of course Plodkins will be offended when he reads this, but there are other things that I have to say about him which will perhaps enrage him still more; still they are the truth. For instance, Plodkins can hardly deny, and yet probably he will deny, that he was one of the most talented drinkers in America. I venture to say that every time he set foot in Liverpool coming East, or in New York going West, he was just on the verge of delirium tremens, because, being necessarily idle during the voyage, he did little else but drink and smoke. I never knew a man who could take so much liquor and show such small results. The fact was, that in the morning Plodkins was never at his best, because he was nearer sober then than at any other part of the day; but, after dinner, a more entertaining, genial, generous, kind-hearted man than Hiram Plodkins could not be found anywhere.

I want to speak of Plodkins' story with the calm, dispassionate manner of a judge, rather than with the partisanship of a favourable witness; and although my allusion to Plodkins' habits of intoxication may seem to him defamatory in character, and unnecessary, yet I mention them only to show that something terrible must have occurred in the bath-room to make him stop short. The extraordinary thing is, from that day to this Plodkins has not touched a drop of intoxicating liquor, which fact in itself strikes me as more wonderful than the story he tells.

Plodkins was a frequent crosser on the Atlantic steamers. He was connected with commercial houses on both sides of the ocean; selling in America for an English house, and buying in England for an American establishment. I presume it was his experiences in selling goods that led to his terrible habits of drinking. I understood from him that out West, if you are selling goods you have to do a great deal of treating, and every time you treat another man to a glass of wine, or a whiskey cocktail, you have, of course, to drink with him. But this has nothing to do with Plodkins' story.

On an Atlantic liner, when there is a large list of passengers, especially of English passengers, it is difficult to get a convenient hour in the morning at which to take a bath. This being the case, the purser usually takes down the names of applicants and assigns each a particular hour. Your hour may be, say seven o'clock in the morning. The next man comes on at half-past seven, and the third man at eight, and so on. The bedroom steward raps at your door when the proper time arrives, and informs you that the bath is ready. You wrap a dressing-gown or a cloak around you, and go along the silent corridors to the bath-room, coming back, generally before your half hour is up, like a giant refreshed.

Plodkins' bath hour was seven o'clock in the morning. Mine was half-past seven. On the particular morning in question the steward did not call me, and I thought he had forgotten, so I passed along the dark corridor and tried the bath-room door. I found it unbolted, and as everything was quiet inside, I entered. I thought nobody was there, so I shoved the bolt in the door, and went over to see if the water had been turned on. The light was a little dim even at that time of the morning, and I must say I was horror-stricken to see, lying in the bottom of the bath-tub, with his eyes fixed on the ceiling, Plodkins. I am quite willing to admit that I was never so startled in my life. I thought at first Plodkins was dead, notwithstanding his open eyes staring at the ceiling; but he murmured, in a sort of husky far-away whisper, "Thank God," and then closed his eyes.

"What's the matter, Plodkins?" I said. "Are you ill? What's the matter

275

with you? Shall I call for help?"

There was a feeble negative motion of the head. Then he said, in a whisper, "Is the door bolted?"

"Yes," I answered.

After another moment's pause, I said—

"Shall I ring, and get you some whiskey or brandy?"

Again he shook his head.

"Help me to get up," he said feebly.

He was very much shaken, and I had some trouble in getting him on his feet, and seating him on the one chair in the room.

"You had better come to my state-room," I said; "it is nearer than yours. What has happened to you?"

He replied, "I will go in a moment. Wait a minute." And I waited.

"Now," he continued, when he had apparently pulled himself together a bit, "just turn on the electric light, will you?"

I reached up to the peg of the electric light and turned it on. A shudder passed over Plodkins' frame, but he said nothing. He seemed puzzled, and once more I asked him to let me take him to my stateroom, but he shook his head.

"Turn on the water." I did so.

"Turn out the electric light." I did that also.

"Now," he added, "put your hand in the water and turn on the electric light."

I was convinced Plodkins had become insane, but I recollected I was there alone with him, shaky as he was, in a room with a bolted door, so I put my fingers in the water and attempted to turn on the electric light. I got a shock that was very much greater than that which I received when I saw

276

Plodkins lying at the bottom of the bath-tub. I gave a yell and a groan, and staggered backwards. Then Plodkins laughed a feeble laugh.

"Now," he said, "I will go with you to your state-room."

The laugh seemed to have braced up Plodkins like a glass of liquor would have done, and when we got to my state-room he was able to tell me what had happened. As a sort of preface to his remarks, I would like to say a word or two about that bath-tub. It was similar to bath-tubs on board other steamers; a great and very deep receptacle of solid marble. There were different nickel-plated taps for letting in hot or cold water, or fresh water or salt water as was desired; and the escape-pipe instead of being at the end, as it is in most bath-tubs, was in the centre. It was the custom of the bath-room steward to fill it about half full of water at whatever temperature you desired. Then, placing a couple of towels on the rack, he would go and call the man whose hour it was to bathe.

Plodkins said, "When I went in there everything appeared as usual, except that the morning was very dark. I stood in the bath-tub, the water coming nearly to my knees, and reached up to turn on the electric light. The moment I touched the brass key I received a shock that simply paralyzed me. I think liquor has something to do with the awful effect the electricity had upon me, because I had taken too much the night before, and was feeling very shaky indeed; but the result was that I simply fell full length in the bath-tub just as you found me. I was unable to move anything except my fingers and toes. I did not appear to be hurt in the least, and my senses, instead of being dulled by the shock, seemed to be preternaturally sharp, and I realized in a moment that if this inability to move remained with me for five minutes I was a dead man—dead, not from the shock, but by drowning. I gazed up through that clear green water, and I could see the ripples on the surface slowly subsiding after my plunge into the tub. It reminded me of looking into an aquarium. You know how you see up through the water to the surface with the bubbles rising to the top. I knew that nobody would come in for at least half an hour, and even then I couldn't remember whether I had bolted the door or not. Sometimes I bolt it, and sometimes I don't. I didn't this morning, as it happens. All the time I felt that strength was slowly returning to me, for I continually worked my fingers and toes, and now feeling seemed to be coming up to my wrists and arms. Then I remembered that the vent was in the middle of the bath-tub; so, wriggling my fingers around, I got hold of the ring, and pulled up the plug. In the dense silence that was around me, I could not tell whether the water was running out or not; but gazing up towards the ceiling I thought I saw the surface gradually sinking down and down and down. Of course it couldn't have been more than a few seconds, but it seemed to be years and years and years. I knew that if once I let my breath go I would be drowned, merely by the spasmodic action of my lungs trying to recover air. I felt as if I should burst. It was a match against time, with life or death as the stake. At first, as I said, my senses were abnormally sharp, but, by and by, I began to notice that they were wavering. I thought the glassy surface of the water, which I could see above me, was in reality a great sheet of crystal that somebody was pressing down upon me, and I began to think that the moment it reached my face I would smother. I tried to struggle, but was held with a grip of steel. Finally, this slab of crystal came down to my nose, and seemed to split apart. I could hold on no longer, and with a mighty expiration blew the water up towards the ceiling, and drew in a frightful smothering breath of salt water, that I blew in turn upwards, and the next breath I took in had some air with the water. I felt the water tickling the corners of my mouth, and receding slower and slower down my face and neck. Then I think I must have become insensible until just before you entered the room. Of course there is something wrong with the electric fittings, and there is a leak of electricity; but I think liquor is at the bottom of all this. I don't believe it would have affected me like this if I had not been soaked in whiskey."

"If I were you," I said, "I would leave whiskey alone."

"I intend to," he answered solemnly, "and baths too."

A Case Of Fever

"O, underneath the blood red sun,

No bloodier deed was ever done!

Nor fiercer retribution sought

The hand that first red ruin wrought."

This is the doctor's story—

The doctors on board the Atlantic liners are usually young men. They are good-looking and entertaining as well, and generally they can play the violin or some other instrument that is of great use at the inevitable concert which takes place about the middle of the Atlantic. They are urbane, polite young men, and they chat pleasantly and nicely to the ladies on board. I believe that the doctor on the Transatlantic steamer has to be there on account of the steerage passengers. Of course the doctor goes to the steerage; but I imagine, as a general thing, he does not spend any more time there than the rules of the service compel him to. The ladies, at least, would be unanimous in saying that the doctor is one of the most charming officials on board the ship.

This doctor, who tells the story I am about to relate, was not like the usual Atlantic physician. He was older than the average, and, to judge by his somewhat haggard, rugged face, had seen hard times and rough usage in different parts of the world. Why he came to settle down on an Atlantic steamer—a berth which is a starting-point rather than a terminus—I have no means of knowing. He never told us; but there he was, and one night, as he smoked his pipe with us in the smoking-room, we closed the door, and compelled him to tell us a story.

As a preliminary, he took out of his inside pocket a book, from which he selected a slip of creased paper, which had been there so long that it was rather the worse for wear, and had to be tenderly handled.

"As a beginning," said the doctor, "I will read you what this slip of paper says. It is an extract from one of the United States Government Reports in the Indian department, and it relates to a case of fever, which caused the death of the celebrated Indian chief Wolf Tusk.

"I am not sure that I am doing quite right in telling this story. There may be some risk for myself in relating it, and I don't know exactly what the United States Government might have in store for me if the truth came to be known. In fact, I am not able to say whether I acted rightly or wrongly in the matter I have to tell you about. You shall be the best judges of that. There is no question but Wolf Tusk was an old monster, and there is no question either that the men who dealt with him had been grievously—but, then, there is no use in my giving you too many preliminaries; each one will say for himself whether he would have acted as I did or not. I will make my excuses at the end of the story." Then he read the slip of paper. I have not a copy of it, and have to quote from memory. It was the report of the physician who saw Wolf Tusk die, and it went on to say that about nine o'clock in the morning a heavy and unusual fever set in on that chief. He had been wounded in the battle of the day before, when he was captured, and the fever attacked all parts of his body. Although the doctor had made every effort in his power to relieve the Indian, nothing could stop the ravages of the fever. At four o'clock in the afternoon, having been in great pain, and, during the latter part, delirious, he died, and was buried near the spot where he had taken ill. This was signed by the doctor.

"What I have read you," said the physician, folding up the paper again, and placing it in his pocket-book, "is strictly and accurately true, otherwise, of course, I would not have so reported to the Government. Wolf Tusk was the chief of a band of irreconcilables, who were now in one part of the West and now in another, giving a great deal of trouble to the authorities. Wolf Tusk and his band had splendid horses, and they never attacked a force that outnumbered their own. In fact, they never attacked anything where the chances were not twenty to one in their favour, but that, of course, is Indian warfare; and in this, Wolf Tusk was no different from his fellows.

"On one occasion Wolf Tusk and his band swooped down on a settlement where they knew that all the defenders were away, and no one but women and children were left to meet them. Here one of the most atrocious massacres of the West took place. Every woman and child in the settlement was killed under circumstances of inconceivable brutality. The buildings, such as they were, were burnt down, and, when the men returned, they found nothing but heaps of smouldering ruin.

"Wolf Tusk and his band, knowing there would be trouble about this, had made for the broken ground where they could so well defend themselves. The alarm, however, was speedily given, and a company of cavalry from the nearest fort started in hot pursuit.

"I was the physician who accompanied the troops. The men whose families had been massacred, and who were all mounted on swift horses, begged permission to go with the soldiers, and that permission was granted, because it was known that their leader would take them after Wolf Tusk on his own account, and it was thought better to have every one engaged in the pursuit under the direct command of the chief officer.

"He divided his troop into three parts, one following slowly after Wolf Tusk, and the other two taking roundabout ways to head off the savages from the broken ground and foothills from which no number of United States troops could have dislodged them. These flanking parties were partly successful. They did not succeed in heading off the Indians entirely, but one succeeded in changing their course, and throwing the Indians unexpectedly into the way of the other flanking party, when a sharp battle took place, and, during its progress, we in the rear came up. When the Indians saw our reinforcing party come towards them each man broke away for himself and made for the wilderness. Wolf Tusk, who had been wounded, and had his horse shot under him, did not succeed in escaping. The two flanking parties now having reunited with the main body, it was decided to keep the Indians on the run for a day or two at least, and so a question arose as to the disposal of the wounded chief. He could not be taken with the fighting party; there were no soldiers to spare to take him back, and so the leader of the settlers said that as they had had enough of war, they would convey him to the fort. Why the commander allowed this to be done, I do not know. He must have realized the feelings of the settlers towards the man who massacred their wives and children. However, the request of the settlers was acceded to, and I was ordered back also, as I had been slightly wounded. You can see the mark here on my cheek, nothing serious; but the commander thought I had better get back into the fort, as he was certain there would be no more need of my services. The Indians were on the run, and would make no further stand.

"It was about three days' march from where the engagement had taken place to the fort. Wolf Tusk was given one of the captured Indian horses. I attended to the wound in his leg, and he was strapped on the horse, so that there could be no possibility of his escaping.

"We camped the first night in a little belt of timber that bordered a small stream, now nearly dry. In the morning I was somewhat rudely awakened, and found myself tied hand and foot, with two or three of the settlers standing over me. They helped me to my feet, then half carried and half led me to a tree, where they tied me securely to the trunk.

"'What are you going to do? What is the meaning of this?' I said to them in astonishment.

"'Nothing,' was the answer of the leader; 'that is, nothing, if you will sign a certain medical report which is to go to the Government. You will see, from where you are, everything that is going to happen, and we expect you to report truthfully; but we will take the liberty of writing the report for you.'

"Then I noticed that Wolf Tusk was tied to a tree in a manner similar to myself, and around him had been collected a quantity of firewood. This firewood, was not piled up to his feet, but formed a circle at some distance from him, so that the Indian would be slowly roasted.

"There is no use in my describing what took place. When I tell you that they lit the fire at nine o'clock, and that it was not until four in the afternoon that Wolf Tusk died, you will understand the peculiar horror of it.

"'Now,' said the leader to me when everything was over,' here is the report I have written out,' and he read to me the report which I have read to you.

"'This dead villain has murdered our wives and our children. If I could have made his torture last for two weeks I would have done so. You have made every effort to save him by trying to break loose, and you have not succeeded. We are not going to harm you, even though you refuse to sign this report. You cannot bring him to life again, thank God, and all you can do is to put more trouble on the heads of men who have already, through red devils like this, had more trouble than they can well stand and keep sane. Will you sign the report?'

"I said I would, and I did."

How The Captain Got His Steamer Out

"On his own perticular well-wrought row,

That he's straddled for ages—

Learnt its lay and its gages—

His style may seem queer, but permit him to know,

The likeliest, sprightliest, manner to hoe."

"There is nothing more certain than that some day we may have to record a terrible disaster directly traceable to ocean racing.

"The vivid account which one of our reporters gives in another column of how the captain of the Arrowic went blundering across the bar yesterday in one of the densest fogs of the season is very interesting reading. Of course the account does not pretend to be anything more than imaginary, for, until the Arrowic reaches Queenstown, if she ever does under her present captain, no one can tell how much of luck was mixed with the recklessness which took this steamer out into the Atlantic in the midst of the thickest fog we have had this year. All that can be known at present is, that, when the fog lifted, the splendid steamer Dartonia was lying at anchor in the bay, having missed the tide, while the Arrowic was nowhere to be seen. If the fog was too thick for the Dartonia to cross the bar, how, then, did the captain of the Arrowic get his boat out? The captain of the Arrowic should be taught to remember that there are other things to be thought of beside the defeating of a rival steamer. He should be made to understand that he has under his charge a steamer worth a million and a half of dollars, and a cargo probably nearly as valuable. Still, he might have lost his ship and cargo, and we would have had no word to say. That concerns the steamship company and the owners of the cargo; but he had also in his care nearly a thousand human lives, and these he should not be allowed to juggle with in order to beat all the rival steamers in the world."

The above editorial is taken from the columns of the New York Daily

Mentor. The substance of it had been cabled across to London and it made pleasant reading for the captain of the Arrowic at Queenstown. The captain didn't say anything about it; he was not a talkative man. Probably he explained to his chief, if the captain of an ocean liner can possibly have a chief, how he got his vessel out of New York harbour in a fog; but, if he did, the explanation was never made public, and so here's an account of it published for the first time, and it may give a pointer to the captain of the rival liner Dartonia. I may say, however, that the purser was not as silent as the captain. He was very indignant at what he called the outrage of the New York paper, and said a great many unjustifiable things about newspaper men. He knew I was a newspaper man myself, and probably that is the reason he launched his maledictions against the fraternity at my head.

"Just listen to that wretched penny-a-liner," he said, rapping savagely on the paper with the back of his hand.

I intimated mildly that they paid more than a penny a line for newspaper work in New York, but he said that wasn't the point. In fact the purser was too angry to argue calmly. He was angry the whole way from Queenstown to Liverpool.

"Here," he said, "is some young fellow, who probably never saw the inside of a ship in his life, and yet he thinks he can tell the captain of a great ocean liner what should be done and what shouldn't. Just think of the cheek of it."

"I don't see any cheek in it," I said, as soothingly as possible. "You don't mean to pretend to argue, at this time of day that a newspaper man does not know how to conduct every other business as well as his own."

But the purser did make that very contention, although of course he must be excused, for, as I said, he was not in a good temper.

"Newspaper men," he continued, "act as if they did know everything. They pretend in their papers that every man thinks he knows how to run a newspaper or a hotel. But look at their own case. See the advice they give to statesmen. See how they would govern Germany, or England, or any other

285

country under the sun. Does a big bank get into trouble, the newspaper man at once informs the financiers how they should have conducted their business. Is there a great railway smash-up, the newspaper man shows exactly how it could have been avoided if he had had the management of the railway. Is there a big strike, the newspaper man steps in. He tells both sides what they should do. If every man thinks he can run a hotel, or a newspaper—and I am sure most men could run a newspaper as well as the newspapers are conducted now—the conceit of the ordinary man is nothing to the conceit of the newspaper man. He not only thinks he can run a newspaper and a hotel, but every other business under the sun."

"And how do you know he can't," I asked.

But the purser would not listen to reason. He contended that a captain who had crossed the ocean hundreds of times and for years and years had worked his way up, had just as big a sense of responsibility for his passengers and his ship and his cargo as any newspaper man in New York could have, and this palpably absurd contention he maintained all the way to Liverpool.

When a great ocean racer is making ready to put out to sea, there can hardly be imagined a more bustling scene than that which presents itself on the deck and on the wharf. There is the rush of passengers, the banging about of luggage, the hurrying to and fro on the decks, the roar of escaping steam, the working of immense steam cranes hoisting and lowering great bales of merchandise and luggage from the wharf to the hold, and here and there in quiet corners, away from the rush, are tearful people bidding good-bye to one another.

The Arrowic and the Dartonia left on the same day and within the same hour, from wharfs that were almost adjoining each other. We on board the Arrowic could see the same bustle and stir on board the Dartonia that we ourselves were in the midst of.

The Dartonia was timed to leave about half an hour ahead of us, and we heard the frantic ringing of her last bell warning everybody to get on shore who were not going to cross the ocean. Then the great steamer backed slowly out from her wharf.

Of course all of us who were going on the Arrowic were warm champions of that ship as the crack ocean racer; but, as the Dartonia moved backwards with slow stately majesty, all her colours flying, and her decks black with passengers crowding to the rail and gazing towards us, we could not deny that she was a splendid vessel, and "even the ranks of Tuscany could scarce forbear a cheer." Once out in the stream her twin screws enabled her to turn around almost without the help of tugs, and just as our last bell was ringing she moved off down the bay. Then we backed slowly out in the same fashion, and, although we had not the advantage of seeing ourselves, we saw a great sight on the wharf, which was covered with people, ringing with cheers, and white with the flutter of handkerchiefs.

As we headed down stream the day began to get rather thick. It had been gloomy all morning, and by the time we reached the Statue of Liberty it was so foggy that one could hardly see three boats' length ahead or behind. All eyes were strained to catch a glimpse of the Dartonia, but nothing of her was visible. Shortly after, the fog came down in earnest and blotted out everything. There was a strong wind blowing, and the vapour, which was cold and piercing, swept the deck with dripping moisture. Then we came to a standstill. The ship's bell was rung continually forward and somebody was whanging on the gong towards the stern. Everybody knew that, if this sort of thing lasted long, we would not get over the bar that tide, and consequently everybody felt annoyed, for this delay would lengthen the trip, and people, as a general thing, do not take passage on an ocean racer with the idea of getting in a day late. Suddenly the fog lifted clear from shore to shore. Then we saw something that was not calculated to put our minds at ease. A big three-masted vessel, with full sail, dashed past us only a very few yards behind the stern of the mammoth steamer.

"Look at that blundering idiot," said the purser to me, "rushing full speed over crowded New York Bay in a fog as thick as pea-soup. A captain who would do a thing like that ought to be hanged."

Before the fog settled down again we saw the Dartonia with her anchor chain out a few hundred yards to our left, and, farther on, one of the big German steamers, also at anchor.

287

In the short time that the fog was lifted our own vessel made some progress towards the bar. Then the thickness came down again. A nautical passenger, who had crossed many times, came aft to where I was standing, and said—

"Do you notice what the captain is trying to do?"

"Well," I answered, "I don't see how anybody can do anything in weather like this."

"There is a strong wind blowing," continued the nautical passenger, "and the fog is liable to lift for a few minutes at a time. If it lifts often enough our captain is going to get us over the bar. It will be rather a sharp bit of work if he succeeds. You notice that the Dartonia has thrown out her anchor. She is evidently going to wait where she is until the fog clears away entirely."

So with that we two went forward to see what was being done. The captain stood on the bridge and beside him the pilot, but the fog was now so thick we could hardly see them, although we stood close by, on the piece of deck in front of the wheelhouse. The almost incessant clanging of the bell was kept up, and in the pauses we heard answering bells from different points in the thick fog. Then, for a second time, and with equal suddenness, the fog lifted ahead of us. Behind we could not see either the Dartonia or the German steamer. Our own boat, however, went full speed ahead and kept up the pace till the fog shut down again. The captain now, in pacing the bridge, had his chronometer in his hand, and those of us who were at the front frequently looked at our watches, for of course the nautical passenger knew just how late it was possible for us to cross the bar.

"I am afraid," said the passenger, "he is not going to succeed." But, as he said this, the fog lifted for the third time, and again the mammoth steamer forged ahead.

"If this clearance will only last for ten minutes," said the nautical passenger, "we are all right." But the fog, as if it had heard him, closed down on us again damper and thicker than ever.

"We are just at the bar," said the nautical passenger, "and if this doesn't clear up pretty soon the vessel will have to go back."

The captain kept his eyes fixed on the chronometer in his hand. The pilot tried to peer ahead, but everything was a thick white blank.

"Ten minutes more and it is too late," said the nautical passenger.

There was a sudden rift in the fog that gave a moment's hope, but it closed down again. A minute afterwards, with a suddenness that was strange, the whole blue ocean lay before us. Then full steam ahead. The fog still was thick behind us in New York Bay. We saw it far ahead coming in from the ocean. All at once the captain closed his chronometer with a snap. We were over the bar and into the Atlantic, and that is how the captain got the Arrowic out of New York Bay.

My Stowaway

"Ye can play yer jokes on Nature,

An' play 'em slick,

She'll grin a grin, but, landsakes, friend,

Look out fer the kick!"

One night about eleven o'clock I stood at the stern of that fine Atlantic steamship, the City of Venice, which was ploughing its way through the darkness towards America. I leaned on the rounded bulwark and enjoyed a smoke as I gazed on the luminous trail the wheel was making in the quiet sea. Some one touched me on the shoulder, saying, "Beg pardon, sir;" and, on straightening up, I saw in the dim light a man whom at first I took to be one of the steerage passengers. I thought he wanted to get past me, for the room was rather restricted in the passage between the aft wheelhouse and the stern, and I moved aside. The man looked hurriedly to one side and then the other and, approaching, said in a whisper, "I'm starving, sir!"

"Why don't you go and get something to eat, then? Don't they give you plenty forward?"

"I suppose they do, sir; but I'm a stowaway. I got on at Liverpool. What little I took with me is gone, and for two days I've had nothing."

"Come with me. I'll take you to the steward, he'll fix you all right."

"Oh, no, no, no," he cried, trembling with excitement. "If you speak to any of the officers or crew I'm lost. I assure you, sir, I'm an honest man, I am indeed, sir. It's the old story—nothing but starvation at home, so my only chance seemed to be to get this way to America. If I'm caught I shall get dreadful usage and will be taken back and put in jail."

"Oh, you're mistaken. The officers are all courteous gentlemen."

"Yes, to you cabin passengers they are. But to a stowaway—that's a different matter. If you can't help me, sir, please don't inform on me."

"How can I help you but by speaking to the captain or purser?"

"Get me a morsel to eat."

"Where were you hid?"

"Right here, sir, in this place," and he put his hand on the square deck-edifice beside us. This seemed to be a spare wheel-house, used if anything went wrong with the one in front. It had a door on each side and there were windows all round it. At present it was piled full of cane folding steamer chairs and other odds and ends.

"I crawl in between the chairs and the wall and get under that piece of tarpaulin."

"Well, you're sure of being caught, for the first fine day all these chairs will be taken out and the deck steward can't miss you."

The man sighed as I said this and admitted the chances were much against him. Then, starting up, he cried, "Poverty is the great crime. If I had stolen some one else's money I would have been able to take cabin passage instead of—"

"If you weren't caught."

"Well, if I were caught, what then? I would be well fed and taken care of."

"Oh, they'd take care of you."

"The waste food in this great ship would feed a hundred hungry wretches like me. Does my presence keep the steamer back a moment of time? No. Well, who is harmed by my trying to better myself in a new world? No one. I am begging for a crust from the lavish plenty, all because I am struggling to be honest. It is only when I become a thief that I am out of danger of starvation—caught or free."

"There, there; now, don't speak so loud or you'll have some one here.

You hang round and I'll bring you some provender. What would you like to have? Poached eggs on toast, roast turkey, or—"

The wretch sank down at my feet as I said this, and, recognising the cruelty of it, I hurried down into the saloon and hunted up a steward who had not yet turned in. "Steward," I said, "can you get me a few sandwiches or anything to eat at this late hour?"

"Yessir, certainly, sir; beef or 'am, sir?"

"Both, and a cup of coffee, please."

"Well, sir, I'm afraid there's no coffee, sir; but I could make you a pot of tea in a moment, sir."

"All right, and bring them to my room, please?"

"Yessir."

In a very short time there was that faint steward rap at the state-room door and a most appetising tray-load was respectfully placed at my service.

When the waiter had gone I hurried up the companion-way with much the air of a man who is stealing fowls, and I found my stowaway just in the position I had left him.

"Now, pitch in," I said. "I'll stand guard forward here, and, if you hear me cough, strike for cover. I'll explain the tray matter if it's found."

He simply said, "Thank you, sir," and I went forward. When I came back the tray had been swept clean and the teapot emptied. My stowaway was making for his den when I said, "How about to-morrow?"

He answered, "This'll do me for a couple of days."

"Nonsense. I'll have a square meal for you here in the corner of this wheel-house, so that you can get at it without trouble. I'll leave it about this time to-morrow night."

"You won't tell any one, any one at all, sir?"

"No. At least, I'll think over the matter, and if I see a way out I'll let you know."

"God bless you, sir."

I turned the incident over in my mind a good deal that night, and I almost made a resolution to take Cupples into my confidence. Roger Cupples, a lawyer of San Francisco, sat next me at table, and with the freedom of wild Westerners we were already well acquainted, although only a few days out. Then I thought of putting a supposititious case to the captain—he was a thorough gentleman—and if he spoke generously about the supposititious case I would spring the real one on him. The stowaway had impressed me by his language as being a man worth doing something for.

Nest day I was glad to see that it was rainy. There would be no demand for ship chairs that day. I felt that real sunshiny weather would certainly unearth, or unchair, my stowaway. I met Cupples on deck, and we walked a few rounds together.

At last, Cupples, who had been telling me some stories of court trials in San Francisco, said, "Let's sit down and wrap up. This deck's too wet to walk on."

"All the seats are damp," I said.

"I'll get out my steamer chair. Steward," he cried to the deck steward who was shoving a mop back and forth, "get me my chair. There's a tag on it, 'Berth 96.'"

"No, no," I cried hastily; "let's go into the cabin. It's raining."

"Only a drizzle. Won't hurt you at sea, you know."

By this time the deck steward was hauling down chairs trying to find No. 96, which I felt sure would be near the bottom. I could not control my anxiety as the steward got nearer and nearer the tarpaulin. At last I cried—

"Steward, never mind that chair; take the first two that come handy."

Cupples looked astonished, and, as we sat down, I said—

"I have something to tell you, and I trust you will say nothing about it to any one else. There's a man under those chairs."

The look that came into the lawyer's face showed that he thought me demented; but, when I told him the whole story, the judicial expression came on, and he said, shaking his head—

"That's bad business."

"I know it."

"Yes, but it's worse than you have any idea of. I presume that you don't know what section 4738 of the Revised Statutes says?"

"No; I don't."

"Well, it is to the effect that any person or persons, who wilfully or with malice aforethought or otherwise, shall aid, abet, succor or cherish, either directly or indirectly or by implication, any person who feloniously or secretly conceals himself on any vessel, barge, brig, schooner, bark, clipper, steamship or other craft touching at or coming within the jurisdiction of these United States, the said person's purpose being the defrauding of the revenue of, or the escaping any or all of the just legal dues exacted by such vessel, barge, etc., the person so aiding or abetting, shall in the eye of the law be considered as accomplice before, during and after the illegal act, and shall in such case be subject to the penalties accruing thereunto, to wit—a fine of not more than five thousand dollars, or imprisonment of not more than two years—or both at the option of the judge before whom the party so accused is convicted."

"Great heavens! is that really so?"

"Well, it isn't word for word, but that is the purport. Of course, if I had my books here, I—why, you've doubtless heard of the case of the Pacific Steamship Company versus Cumberland. I was retained on behalf of the company. Now all Cumberland did was to allow the man—he was sent up for two years—to carry his valise on board, but we proved the intent. Like a fool, he boasted of it, but the steamer brought back the man, and Cumberland got off with four thousand dollars and costs. Never got out of that scrape less than ten thousand dollars. Then again, the steamship Peruvian versus McNish;

that is even more to the—"

"See here, Cupples. Come with me to-night and see the man. If you heard him talk you would see the inhumanity—"

"Tush. I'm not fool enough to mix up in such a matter, and look here, you'll have to work it pretty slick if you get yourself out. The man will be caught as sure as fate; then knowingly or through fright he'll incriminate you."

"What would you do if you were in my place?"

"My dear sir, don't put it that way. It's a reflection on both my judgment and my legal knowledge. I couldn't be in such a scrape. But, as a lawyer—minus the fee—I'll tell you what you should do. You should give the man up before witnesses—before witnesses. I'll be one of them myself. Get as many of the cabin passengers as you like out here, to-day, and let the officers search. If he charges you with what the law terms support, deny it, and call attention to the fact that you have given information. By the way, I would give written information and keep a copy."

"I gave the man my word not to inform on him and so I can't do it to-day, but I'll tell him of it to-night."

"And have him commit suicide or give himself up first and incriminate you? Nonsense. Just release yourself from your promise. That's all. He'll trust you."

"Yes, poor wretch, I'm afraid he will."

About ten o'clock that night I resolved to make another appeal to Roger Cupples to at least stand off and hear the man talk. Cupples' state-room, No. 96, was in the forward part of the steamer, down a long passage and off a short side passage. Mine was aft the cabin. The door of 96 was partly open, and inside an astonishing sight met my gaze.

There stood my stowaway.

He was evidently admiring himself in the glass, and with a brush was touching up his face with dark paint here and there. When he put on a woe-begone look he was the stowaway; when he chuckled to himself he was Roger Cupples, Esq.

The moment the thing dawned on me I quietly withdrew and went up the forward companion way. Soon Cupples came cautiously up and seeing the way clear scudded along in the darkness and hid in the aft wheelhouse. I saw the whole thing now. It was a scheme to get me to make a fool of myself some fine day before the rest of the passengers and have a standing joke on me. I walked forward. The first officer was on duty.

"I have reason to believe," I said, "that there is a stowaway in the aft wheelhouse."

Quicker than it takes me to tell it a detachment of sailors were sent aft under the guidance of the third mate. I went through the saloon and smoking room, and said to the gentlemen who were playing cards and reading—"There's a row upstairs of some kind."

We were all on deck before the crew had surrounded the wheelhouse. There was a rattle of steamer folded chairs, a pounce by the third mate, and out came the unfortunate Cupples, dragged by the collar.

"Hold on; let go. This is a mistake."

"You can't both hold on and let go," said Stalker, of Indiana.

"Come out o' this," cried the mate, jerking him forward.

With a wrench the stowaway tore himself free and made a dash for the companion way. A couple of sailors instantly tripped him up.

"Let go of me; I'm a cabin passenger," cried Cupples.

"Bless me!" I cried in astonishment. "This isn't you, Cupples? Why, I acted on your own advice and that of Revised Statutes, No. what ever-they-were."

"Well, act on my advice again," cried the infuriated Cupples, "and go to—the hold."

296

However, he was better in humour the next day, and stood treat all round. We found, subsequently, that Cupples was a New York actor, and at the entertainment given for the benefit of the sailors' orphans, a few nights after, he recited a piece in costume that just melted the ladies. It was voted a wonderfully touching performance, and he called it "The Stowaway."

The Purser's Story

"O Mother-nature, kind in touch and tone.

Act as we may, thou clearest to thine own"

I don't know that I should tell this story.

When the purser related it to me I know it was his intention to write it out for a magazine. In fact he had written it, and I understand that a noted American magazine had offered to publish it, but I have watched that magazine for over three years and I have not yet seen the purser's story in it. I am sorry that I did not write the story at the time; then perhaps I should have caught the exquisite peculiarities of the purser's way of telling it. I find myself gradually forgetting the story and I write it now in case I shall forget it, and then be harassed all through after life by the remembrance of the forgetting.

There is no position more painful and tormenting than the consciousness of having had something worth the telling, which, in spite of all mental effort, just eludes the memory. It hovers nebulously beyond the outstretched finger-ends of recollection, and, like the fish that gets off the hook, becomes more and more important as the years fade.

Perhaps, when you read this story, you will say there is nothing in it after all. Well, that will be my fault, then, and I can only regret I did not write down the story when it was told to me, for as I sat in the purser's room that day it seemed to me I had never heard anything more graphic.

The purser's room was well forward on the Atlantic steamship. From one of the little red-curtained windows you could look down to where the steerage passengers were gathered on the deck. When the bow of the great vessel plunged down into the big Atlantic waves, the smother of foam that shot upwards would be borne along with the wind, and spatter like rain against the purser's window. Something about this intermittent patter on the pane reminded the purser of the story, and so he told it to me.

There were a great many steerage passengers coming on at Queenstown, he said, and there was quite a hurry getting them aboard. Two officers stood at each side of the gangway and took the tickets as the people crowded forward. They generally had their tickets in their hands and there was usually no trouble. I stood there and watched them coming aboard. Suddenly there was a fuss and a jam. "What is it?" I asked the officer.

"Two girls, sir, say they have lost their tickets."

I took the girls aside and the stream of humanity poured in. One was about fourteen and the other, perhaps, eight years old. The little one had a firm grip of the elder's hand and she was crying. The larger girl looked me straight in the eye as I questioned her.

"Where's your tickets?"

"We lost thim, sur."

"Where?"

"I dunno, sur."

"Do you think you have them about you or in your luggage?"

"We've no luggage, sur."

"Is this your sister?"

"She is, sur."

"Are your parents aboard?"

"They are not, sur."

"Are you all alone?"

"We are, sur."

"You can't go without your tickets."

The younger one began to cry the more, and the elder answered, "Mabbe we can foind thim, sur."

299

They were bright-looking, intelligent children, and the larger girl gave me such quick, straightforward answers, and it seemed so impossible that children so young should attempt to cross the ocean without tickets that I concluded to let them come, and resolved to get at the truth on the way over.

Next day I told the deck steward to bring the children to my room.

They came in just as I saw them the day before, the elder with a tight grip on the hand of the younger, whose eyes I never caught sight of. She kept them resolutely on the floor, while the other looked straight at me with her big, blue eyes.

"Well, have you found your tickets?"

"No, sur."

"What is your name?"

"Bridget, sur."

"Bridget what?"

"Bridget Mulligan, sur."

"Where did you live?"

"In Kildormey, sur."

"Where did you get your tickets?"

"From Mr. O'Grady, sur."

Now, I knew Kildormey as well as I know this ship, and I knew O'Grady was our agent there. I would have given a good deal at that moment for a few words with him. But I knew of no Mulligans in Kildormey, although, of course, there might be. I was born myself only a few miles from the place. Now, thinks I to myself, if these two children can baffle a purser who has been twenty years on the Atlantic when they say they came from his own town almost, by the powers they deserve their passage over the ocean. I had often seen grown people try to cheat their way across, and I may say none of them succeeded on my ships.

300

"Where's your father and mother?"

"Both dead, sur."

"Who was your father?"

"He was a pinshoner, sur."

"Where did he draw his pension?"

"I donno, sur."

"Where did you get the money to buy your tickets?"

"The neighbors, sur, and Mr. O'Grady helped, sur."

"What neighbours? Name them."

She unhesitatingly named a number, many of whom I knew; and as that had frequently been done before, I saw no reason to doubt the girl's word.

"Now," I said, "I want to speak with your sister. You may go."

The little one held on to her sister's hand and cried bitterly.

When the other was gone, I drew the child towards me and questioned her, but could not get a word in reply.

For the next day or two I was bothered somewhat by a big Irishman named O'Donnell, who was a fire-brand among the steerage passengers. He would harangue them at all hours on the wrongs of Ireland, and the desirability of blowing England out of the water; and as we had many English and German passengers, as well as many peaceable Irishmen, who complained of the constant ructions O'Donnell was kicking up, I was forced to ask him to keep quiet. He became very abusive one day and tried to strike me. I had him locked up until he came to his senses.

While I was in my room, after this little excitement, Mrs. O'Donnell came to me and pleaded for her rascally husband. I had noticed her before. She was a poor, weak, broken-hearted woman whom her husband made a slave of, and I have no doubt beat her when he had the chance. She was

301

evidently mortally afraid of him, and a look from him seemed enough to take the life out of her. He was a worse tyrant, in his own small way, than England had ever been.

"Well, Mrs. O'Donnell," I said, "I'll let your husband go, but he will have to keep a civil tongue in his head and keep his hands off people. I've seen men, for less, put in irons during a voyage and handed over to the authorities when they landed. And now I want you to do me a favour. There are two children on board without tickets. I don't believe they ever had tickets, and I want to find out. You're a kind-hearted woman, Mrs. O'Donnell, and perhaps the children will answer you." I had the two called in, and they came hand in hand as usual. The elder looked at me as if she couldn't take her eyes off my face.

"Look at this woman," I said to her; "she wants to speak to you. Ask her some questions about herself," I whispered to Mrs. O'Donnell.

"Acushla," said Mrs. O'Donnell with infinite tenderness, taking the disengaged hand of the elder girl. "Tell me, darlint, where yees are from."

I suppose I had spoken rather harshly to them before, although I had not intended to do so, but however that may be, at the first words of kindness from the lips of their countrywoman both girls broke down and cried as if their hearts would break. The poor woman drew them towards her, and, stroking the fair hair of the elder girl, tried to comfort her while the tears streamed down her own cheeks. "Hush, acushla; hush, darlints, shure the gentlemin's not goin' to be hard wid two poor childher going to a strange country."

Of course it would never do to admit that the company could carry emigrants free through sympathy, and I must have appeared rather hard-hearted when I told Mrs. O'Donnell that I would have to take them back with me to Cork. I sent the children away, and then arranged with Mrs. O'Donnell to see after them during the voyage, to which she agreed if her husband would let her. I could get nothing from the girl except that she had lost her ticket; and when we sighted New York, I took them through the steerage and asked the passengers if any one would assume charge of the children and pay their passage. No one would do so.

"Then," I said, "these children will go back with me to Cork; and if I find they never bought tickets, they will have to go to jail."

There were groans and hisses at that, and I gave the children in charge of the cabin stewardess, with orders to see that they did not leave the ship. I was at last convinced that they had no friends among the steerage passengers. I intended to take them ashore myself before we sailed; and I knew of good friends in New York who would see to the little waifs, although I did not propose that any of the emigrants should know that an old bachelor purser was fool enough to pay for the passage of a couple of unknown Irish children.

We landed our cabin passengers, and the tender came alongside to take the steerage passengers to Castle Garden. I got the stewardess to bring out the children, and the two stood and watched every one get aboard the tender.

Just as the tender moved away, there was a wild shriek among the crowded passengers, and Mrs. O'Donnell flung her arms above her head and cried in the most heart-rending tone I ever heard—"Oh, my babies, my babies."

"Kape quiet, ye divil," hissed O'Donnell, grasping her by the arm. The terrible ten days' strain had been broken at last, and the poor woman sank in a heap at his feet.

"Bring back that boat," I shouted, and the tender came back.

"Come aboard here, O'Donnell."

"I'll not!" he yelled, shaking his fist at me.

"Bring that man aboard."

They soon brought him back, and I gave his wife over to the care of the stewardess. She speedily rallied, and hugged and kissed her children as if she would never part with them.

"So, O'Donnell, these are your children?"

"Yis, they are; an' I'd have ye know I'm in a frae country, bedad, and I dare ye to lay a finger on me."

"Don't dare too much," I said, "or I'll show you what can be done in a free country. Now, if I let the children go, will you send their passage money to the company when you get it?"

"I will," he answered, although I knew he lied.

"Well," I said, "for Mrs. O'Donnell's sake, I'll let them go; and I must congratulate any free country that gets a citizen like you."

Of course I never heard from O'Donnell again.

Miss McMillan

"Come hop, come skip, fair children all,

Old Father Time is in the hall.

He'll take you on his knee, and stroke

Your golden hair to silver bright,

Your rosy cheeks to wrinkles white"

In the saloon of the fine Transatlantic liner the Climatus, two long tables extend from the piano at one end to the bookcase at the other end of the ample dining-room.

On each side of this main saloon are four small tables intended to accommodate six or seven persons. At one of these tables sat a pleasant party of four ladies and three gentlemen. Three ladies were from Detroit, and one from Kent, in England. At the head of the table sat Mr. Blair, the frosts of many American winters in his hair and beard, while the lines of care in his ragged, cheerful Scottish face told of a life of business crowned with generous success.

Mr. Waters, a younger merchant, had all the alert vivacity of the pushing American. He had the distinguished honour of sitting opposite me at the small table. Blair and Waters occupied the same room, No. 27. The one had crossed the Atlantic more than fifty times, the other nearly thirty. Those figures show the relative proportion of their business experience.

The presence of Mr. Blair gave to our table a sort of patriarchal dignity that we all appreciated. If a louder burst of laughter than usual came from where we sat and the other passengers looked inquiringly our way the sedate and self-possessed face of Mr. Blair kept us in countenance, and we, who had given way to undue levity, felt ourselves enshrouded by an atmosphere of genial seriousness. This prevented our table from getting the reputation of being funny or frivolous.

Some remark that Blair made brought forth the following extraordinary statement from Waters, who told it with the air of a man exposing the pretensions of a whited sepulchre.

"Now, before this voyage goes any further," he began, "I have a serious duty to perform which I can shirk no longer, unpleasant though it be. Mr. Blair and myself occupy the same state-room. Into that state-room has been sent a most lovely basket of flowers. It is not an ordinary basket of flowers, I assure you, ladies. There is a beautiful floral arch over a bed of colour, and I believe there is some tender sentiment connected with the display;—Bon Voyage, Auf Wiedersehen, or some such motto marked out in red buds. Now those flowers are not for me. I think, therefore, that Mr. Blair owes it to this company, which has so unanimously placed him at the head of the table, to explain how it comes that an elderly gentleman gets such a handsome floral tribute sent him from some unknown person in New York."

We all looked at Mr. Blair, who gazed with imperturbability at Waters.

"If you had all crossed with Waters as often as I have you would know that he is subject to attacks like that. He means well, but occasionally he gives way in the deplorable manner you have just witnessed. Now all there is of it consists in this—a basket of flowers has been sent (no doubt by mistake) to our state-room. There is nothing but a card on it which says 'Room 27.' Steward," he cried, "would you go to room 27, bring that basket of flowers, and set it on this table. We may as well all have the benefit of them."

The steward soon returned with a large and lovely basket of flowers, which he set on the table, shoving the caster and other things aside to make room for it.

We all admired it very much, and the handsome young lady on my left asked Mr. Blair's permission to take one of the roses for her own. "Now, mind you," said Blair, "I cannot grant a flower from the basket, for you see it is as much the property of Waters as of myself, for all of his virtuous indignation. It was sent to the room, and he is one of the occupants. The flowers have evidently been misdirected."

The lady referred to took it upon herself to purloin the flower she wanted.

As she did so a card came in view with the words written in a masculine hand—

To Miss McMillan, With the loving regards of Edwin J—

"Miss McMillan!" cried the lady; "I wonder if she is on board? I'd give anything to know."

"We'll have a glance at the passenger list," said Waters.

Down among the M's on the long list of cabin passengers appeared the name "Miss McMillan."

"Now," said I, "it seems to me that the duty devolves on both Blair and Waters to spare no pains in delicately returning those flowers to their proper owner. I think that both have been very remiss in not doing so long ago. They should apologise publicly to the young lady for having deprived her of the offering for a day and a half, and then I think they owe an apology to this table for the mere pretence that any sane person in New York or elsewhere would go to the trouble of sending either of them a single flower."

"There will be no apology from me," said Waters. "If I do not receive the thanks of Miss McMillan, it will be because good deeds are rarely recognised in this world. I think it must be evident, even to the limited intelligence of my journalistic friend across the table, that Mr. Blair intended to keep those flowers in his state-room, and—of course I make no direct charges—the concealment of that card certainly looks bad. It may have been concealed by the sender of the flowers, but to me it looks bad."

"Of course," said Blair dryly, "to you it looks bad. To the pure, etc."

"Now," said the sentimental lady on my left, "while you gentlemen are wasting the time in useless talk the lady is without her roses. There is one thing that you all seem to miss. It is not the mere value of the bouquet. There is a subtle perfume about an offering like this more delicate than that which Nature gave the flowers—"

"Hear, hear," broke in Waters.

"I told you," said Blair aside, "the kind of fellow Waters is. He thinks

307

nothing of interrupting a lady."

"Order, both of you!" I cried, rapping on the table; "the lady from England has the floor."

"What I was going to say—"

"When Waters interrupted you."

"When Mr. Waters interrupted me I was going to say that there seems to me a romantic tinge to this incident that you old married men cannot be expected to appreciate."

I looked with surprise at Waters, while he sank back in his seat with the resigned air of a man in the hands of his enemies. We had both been carefully concealing the fact that we were married men, and the blunt announcement of the lady was a painful shock. Waters gave a side nod at Blair, as much as to say, "He's given it away." I looked reproachfully at my old friend at the head of the table, but he seemed to be absorbed in what our sentimental lady was saying.

"It is this," she continued. "Here is a young lady. Her lover sends her a basket. There may be some hidden meaning that she alone will understand in the very flowers chosen, or in the arrangement of them. The flowers, let us suppose, never reach their destination. The message is unspoken, or, rather, spoken, but unheard. The young lady grieves at the apparent neglect, and then, in her pride, resents it. She does not write, and he knows not why. The mistake may be discovered too late, and all because a basket of flowers has been missent."

"Now, Blair," said Waters, "if anything can make you do the square thing surely that appeal will."

"I shall not so far forget what is due to myself and to the dignity of this table as to reply to our erratic friend. Here is what I propose to do—first catch our hare. Steward, can you find out for me at what table and at what seat Miss McMillan is?"

While the steward was gone on his errand Mr. Blair proceeded.

"I will become acquainted with her. McMillan is a good Scotch name and Blair is another. On that as a basis I think we can speedily form an acquaintance. I shall then in a casual manner ask her if she knows a young man by the name of Edwin J., and I shall tell you what effect the mention of the name has on her."

"Now, as part owner in the flowers up to date, I protest against that. I insist that Miss McMillan be brought to this table, and that we all hear exactly what is said to her," put in Mr. Waters.

Nevertheless we agreed that Mr. Blair's proposal was a good one and the majority sanctioned it.

Meanwhile our sentimental lady had been looking among the crowd for the unconscious Miss McMillan.

"I think I have found her," she whispered to me. "Do you see that handsome girl at the captain's table. Really the handsomest girl on board."

"I thought that distinction rested with our own table."

"Now, please pay attention. Do you see how pensive she is, with her cheek resting on her hand? I am sure she is thinking of Edwin."

"I wouldn't bet on that," I replied. "There is considerable motion just now, and indications of a storm. The pensiveness may have other causes."

Here the steward returned and reported that Miss McMillan had not yet appeared at table, but had her meals taken to her room by the stewardess.

Blair called to the good-natured, portly stewardess of the Climatus, who at that moment was passing through the saloon.

"Is Miss McMillan ill?" he asked.

"No, not ill," replied Mrs. Kay; "but she seems very much depressed at leaving home, and she has not left her room since we started."

"There!" said our sentimental lady, triumphantly.

"I would like very much to see her," said Mr. Blair; "I have some good news for her."

"I will ask her to come out. It will do her good," said the stewardess, as she went away.

In a few moments she appeared, and, following her, came an old woman, with white hair, and her eyes concealed by a pair of spectacles.

"Miss McMillan," said the stewardess, "this is Mr. Blair, who wanted to speak to you."

Although Mr. Blair was, as we all were, astonished to see our mythical young lady changed into a real old woman, he did not lose his equanimity, nor did his kindly face show any surprise, but he evidently forgot the part he had intended to play.

"You will pardon me for troubling you, Miss McMillan," he said, "but this basket of flowers was evidently intended for you, and was sent to my room by mistake."

Miss McMillan did not look at the flowers, but gazed long at the card with the writing on it, and as she did so one tear and then another stole down the wrinkled face from behind the glasses.

"There is no mistake, is there?" asked Mr. Blair. "You know the writer."

"There is no mistake—no mistake," replied Miss McMillan in a low voice, "he is a very dear and kind friend." Then, as if unable to trust herself further, she took the flowers and hurriedly said, "Thank you," and left us.

"There," I said to the lady on my left, "your romance turns out to be nothing after all."

"No, sir," she cried with emphasis; "the romance is there, and very much more of a romance than if Miss McMillan was a young and silly girl of twenty."

Perhaps she was right.

About Author

Robert Barr (16 September 1849 – 21 October 1912) was a Scottish-Canadian short story writer and novelist.

Early years in Canada

Robert Barr was born in Barony, Lanark, Scotland to Robert Barr and Jane Watson. In 1854, he emigrated with his parents to Upper Canada at the age of four years old. His family settled on a farm near the village of Muirkirk. Barr assisted his father with his job as a carpenter, and developed a sound work ethic. Robert Barr then worked as a steel smelter for a number of years before he was educated at Toronto Normal School in 1873 to train as a teacher.

After graduating Toronto Normal School, Barr became a teacher, and eventually headmaster/principal of the Central School of Windsor, Ontario in 1874. While Barr worked as head master of the Central School of Windsor, Ontario, he began to contribute short stories—often based on personal experiences, and recorded his work. On August 1876, when he was 27, Robert Barr married Ontario-born Eva Bennett, who was 21. According to the 1891 England Census, the couple appears to have had three children, Laura, William, and Andrew.

In 1876, Barr quit his teaching position to become a staff member of publication, and later on became the news editor for the Detroit Free Press. Barr wrote for this newspaper under the pseudonym, "Luke Sharp." The idea for this pseudonym was inspired during his morning commute to work when Barr saw a sign that read "Luke Sharp, Undertaker." In 1881, Barr left Canada to return to England in order to start a new weekly version of "The Detroit Free Press Magazine."

London years

In 1881 Barr decided to "vamoose the ranch", as he called the process of immigration in search of literary fame outside of Canada, and relocated to London to continue to write/establish the weekly English edition of the Detroit Free Press. During the 1890s, he broadened his literary works, and started writing novels from the popular crime genre. In 1892 he founded the magazine The Idler, choosing Jerome K. Jerome as his collaborator (wanting, as Jerome said, "a popular name"). He retired from its co-editorship in 1895.

In London of the 1890s Barr became a more prolific author—publishing a book a year—and was familiar with many of the best-selling authors of his day, including :Arnold Bennett, Horatio Gilbert Parker, Joseph Conrad, Bret Harte, Rudyard Kipling, H. Rider Haggard, H. G. Wells, and George Robert Gissing. Barr was well-spoken, well-cultured due to travel, and considered a "socializer."

Because most of Barr's literary output was of the crime genre, his works were highly in vogue. As Sherlock Holmes stories were becoming well-known, Barr wrote and published in the Idler the first Holmes parody, "The Adventures of "Sherlaw Kombs" (1892), a spoof that was continued a decade later in another Barr story, "The Adventure of the Second Swag" (1904). Despite those jibes at the growing Holmes phenomenon, Barr remained on very good terms with its creator Arthur Conan Doyle. In Memories and Adventures, a serial memoir published 1923–24, Doyle described him as "a volcanic Anglo—or rather Scot-American, with a violent manner, a wealth of strong adjectives, and one of the kindest natures underneath it all".

In 1904, Robert Barr completed an unfinished novel for Methuen & Co. by the recently deceased American author Stephen Crane entitled The O'Ruddy, a romance.Despite his reservations at taking on the project, Barr reluctantly finished the last eight chapters due to his longstanding friendship with Crane and his common-law wife, Cora, the war correspondent and bordello owner.

Death

The 1911 census places Robert Barr, "a writer of fiction," at Hillhead, Woldingham, Surrey, a small village southeast of London, living with his wife, Eva, their son William, and two female servants. At this home, the author died from heart disease on 21 October 1912.

Writing Style

Barr's volumes of short stories were often written with an ironic twist in the story with a witty, appealing narrator telling the story. Barr's other works also include numerous fiction and non-fiction contributions to periodicals. A few of his mystery stories and stories of the supernatural were put in anthologies, and a few novels have been republished. His writings have also attracted scholarly attention. His narrative personae also featured moral and editorial interpolations within their tales. Barr's achievements were recognized by an honorary degree from the University of Michigan in 1900.

His protagonists were journalists, princes, detectives, deserving commercial and social climbers, financiers, the new woman of bright wit and aggressive accomplishment, and lords. Often, his characters were stereotypical and romanticized.

Barr wrote fiction in an episode-like format. He developed this style when working as an editor for the newspaper Detroit Press. Barr developed his skill with the anecdote and vignette; often only the central character serves to link the nearly self-contained chapters of the novels. (Source: Wikipedia)

NOTABLE WORKS

In a Steamer Chair and Other Stories (Thirteen short stories by one of the most famous writers in his day -1892)

"The Face And The Mask" (1894) consists of twenty-four delightful short stories.

In the Midst of Alarms (1894, 1900, 1912), a story of the attempted Fenian invasion of Canada in 1866.

From Whose Bourne (1896) Novel in which the main character, William Brenton, searches for truth to set his wife free.

One Day's Courtship (1896)

Revenge! (Collection of 20 short stories, Alfred Hitchcock-like style, thriller with a surprise ending)

The Strong Arm

A Woman Intervenes (1896), a story of love, finance, and American journalism.

Tekla: A Romance of Love and War (1898)

Jennie Baxter, Journalist (1899)

The Unchanging East (1900)

The Victors (1901)

A Prince of Good Fellows (1902)

Over The Border: A Romance (1903)

The O'Ruddy, A Romance, with Stephen Crane (1903)

A Chicago Princess (1904)

The Speculations of John Steele (1905)

The Tempestuous Petticoat (1905–12)

A Rock in the Baltic (1906)

The Triumphs of Eugène Valmont (1906)

The Measure of the Rule (1907)

Stranleigh's Millions (1909)

The Sword Maker (Medieval action/adventure novel, genre: Historical Fiction-1910)

The Palace of Logs (1912)

"The Ambassadors Pigeons" (1899)

"And the Rigor of the Game" (1892)

"Converted" (1896)

"Count Conrad's Courtship" (1896)

"The Count's Apology" (1896)

"A Deal on Change " (1896)

"The Exposure of Lord Stanford" (1896)

"Gentlemen: The King!"

"The Hour-Glass" (1899)

"An invitation" (1892)

" A Ladies Man"

"The Long Ladder" (1899)

"Mrs. Tremain" (1892)

" Transformation" (1896)

"The Understudy" (1896)

" The Vengeance of the Dead" (1896)

"The Bromley Gibbert's Story" (1896)

" Out of Thun" (1896)

"The Shadow of Greenback" (1896)

"Flight of the Red Dog" (fiction)

"Lord Stranleigh Abroad" (1913)

"One Day's Courtship and the Herald's of Fame" (1896)

"Cardillac"

"Dr. Barr's Tales"

"The Triumphs of Eugene Valmont"